TITLES

Peter Evans

BALLANTINE BOOKS • NEW YORK

The characters, names, companies and incidents in this novel, except for incidental references to public figures, are all imaginary and do not refer to or portray any actual persons or companies.

Library of Congress Catalog Card Number: 78–4204

ISBN 0–345–25957–2

Manufactured in the United States of America

First Edition: September 1978

Paperback format
First Edition: September 1979

For Pamela

Book One

1

In London a girl was sitting at the foot of a brass bed. She was smoking a cigarette and staring out of the window at the treetops in Eaton Square. She was naked except for panties. A man lay in the bed, beneath the rumpled sheet, sleeping on his back.

In a little while it would be light enough to tell the time by the small clock that ticked faintly on the man's side of the big bed.

It was a large room. This was the girl's third visit but already she knew its shape, its contents and colors; she knew what clothes were in the closets and what some of the letters said that were tied in pink ribbon at the bottom of the handkerchief drawer.

It isn't enough to love and be loved, she decided. With love, one had to dictate the strategy. The woman who doesn't understand that will lose everything in the end.

She tapped the ash into her cupped hand. She got off the bed and went to the window. The window was open about six inches. She bent down and blew the ash into the night air. She stood by the window for a while, finishing her cigarette. She inhaled deeply. The smoke came out of her mouth in a deep sigh.

She threw the cigarette out of the window and returned to the bed.

The man turned in his sleep with a small contented groan. The girl smiled down at him and touched his ankle, which poked out from beneath the chocolate-brown sheet. It was almost like touching a woman's skin. His face was luminous beneath his tousled blond hair.

If only his constituents could see him now, she thought. She stood up again.

"Don't go."

"I thought you were asleep," she said.

"I am."

"I have to go soon."

"Not yet."

"Darling, I must."

"What time is it?"

"I don't know. It'll soon be light."

The man rolled over and reached for the clock.

"Don't turn on the light," she said.

The man stared at the small face of the clock for a few moments, moving it backward and forward before his eyes.

"It's only five-fifteen."

"My hair's still damp at the back," she said, touching the back of her neck.

"I'm not surprised."

"I must change the sheets," she said.

"I'll do it later."

"*You?*"

"I'm not as hopeless as you think. Come and let me hold you."

"No."

"Why not?"

"You know why not."

"You didn't mean it."

"I meant it."

"Come here," he said.

"Darling, it's no good."

"I want you. Feel me."

"No. What time does she get back?"

"About lunchtime. She's leaving Charminster around ten."

"With the children?"

"Yes."

"Good."

"Why do you say *good* like that?"

"You'll be pleased to see them, won't you?"

"The kids? I suppose so."

"Well then, good."

"I adore you."

"And when the kids are around she doesn't get you all to herself."

The man sat up in the bed and sniffed the air.

"Have you been smoking?"

"Don't worry. I threw the evidence out of the window. She won't find a thing."

"I wasn't thinking of that. I simply ask—"

"You don't have to lie to me."

"Come here, woman."

"No."

"We can talk better together."

"I have nothing to say."

"I want to hold you."

"This is getting very monotonous. Do you know that? Just accept it. It's over. Lovers no more."

"*Why?*"

"Jesus. Don't you *ever* listen?"

"I love you."

"And I love you. But I can't go on being this much in love with somebody and—I can't live on the outside looking in. We've been over it a dozen times. I don't want you to leave your wife and children. I don't expect it. I understand all that. Your life is tangled enough."

"What can I do? What do you *want* me to do?"

"Nothing. I don't expect you to do a thing."

"If we could give it a little time—"

"Time for what? For her to find out? She's already discovered that somebody's been using her lousy toothbrush!"

"You left it wet."

"What should I have done? Dried it in front of the fire? Gone over the fucking bristles with my hair dryer?"

They both giggled.

"Oh Christ, darling," he said.

She returned to the bed and let him take her in his arms.

"The trouble is, my sweet, your morality is all about discretion and my morality's about—"

"About what?"

"I don't know. Something else. Whatever makes me feel good, I suppose."

He kissed her naked breast.

"That?"

"It'd never work. You and me. Imagine the scandal! The headlines."

"Don't be silly."

"In love you're too much the man, not enough the politician."

"Only you know that."

"Don't you believe it. It shows. Believe me, darling. It shows."

"You know what I'm thinking?" he said. He propped himself up on one elbow and looked down at her.

"Tell me."

"*You* want out. It's *you*."

"Because I love you. Because we hurt each other too much. One of us has to be sensible."

"I've never made you cry."

"Only young girls cry with their eyes," she said quietly.

She held him close, with the passion of despair.

After a little while she said, "If this got out—to the press. The son of one of the most famous Englishmen in history, a government minister, the proud father of three rapid-fire children—and my lover!"

"We must accept the absurdities of fame as well as its advantages," he said.

"You're thirty-four years old. What would you do? Politics is your life."

"I'd have you."

"You see what I mean? You're not being realistic."

"This isn't the time to be having this conversation."

"When is the time? It wasn't in Ireland. It wasn't in Paris. It wasn't last night. It isn't this morning. The division bell's gone, my love. It's time to vote. I'm voting to end it now."

"What about me?"

"You've got Serena. You've got your great family name. The kids, a future in the House. To tell you the truth, I'm not worried about you one little bit."

"And you?"

"Oh, I'll rub along."

"Be serious."

"Is this the time?"

"Yes."

"I'm being serious. I'll get by. I don't *need* the shade of a family tree. I don't *need* the warmth of a coat of arms."

"Neither do I."

"Oh yes you do, my love."

It was light in the room now. The man got out of bed, went to a closet and took out a terry-cloth robe. He put it on.

"Do you want to bathe?" he said.

"I'll bathe at home. It's safer. I don't want Serena complaining about strange blond hair in the plughole."

"Very well."

"You really must get yourself organized. Your next mistress. Make sure she has Serena's color hair, uses the same scent. It'll make life a whole lot easier for everybody. Get a lady who doesn't smoke."

He sat down on the bed.

"Would you like some coffee?"

"No thanks."

"I feel terrible."

"I'm sorry. I was being mean. I do love you and it is for the best."

"Kiss me."

She kissed him gently on the lips. It could have been the first kiss, or the last.

"There's no other way?"

"There are girls that men talk about and there are girls that men don't talk about."

She got off the bed and slipped on her dress.

"I've had a lot of lovers," the girl said. "Nobody gossips, not many people even suspect. My reputation's in good nick."

"Then why, for Christ's sake—"

"*You* can't risk it."

"Why *me* all the time?"

"You're too afflicted by family honor, by respectability."

"That's bloody unfair," he said.

"Life's unfair."

She put on her stockings and shoes. She sat in front of the dressing-table mirror and patted her cheeks and pushed her fingers through her hair. She stared hard at her own reflection as if at a stranger one half remembers from a long time ago, from another place.

She put the pack of cigarettes and a lighter into her evening purse.

She looked around the room.

"Serena is a lucky woman," she said. "I hope she appreciates what she's got." She picked up a blue silk coat from the back of an armchair.

"I don't know what to say," the man said in a flat voice.

He sat on the bed, not moving. He had a distinguished pale boyish look, as if he'd come from a long line of hemophiliacs.

"Just say good-bye."

"All right."

"Say it."

"Good-bye."

"I want you to mean it."

"I mean it," the man said.

"I'll lock my windows just in case," the girl said. She smiled at him but his face stayed serious and pale. She wanted to hold him. She wanted to kiss him.

"Don't forget the sheets," she said.

She went out of the room and slowly walked down the three flights of stairs.

She was on the first-floor landing when she heard the man begin to open all the windows in the bedroom.

There would be no smoke when Serena returned.

The girl closed the street door quietly behind her.

She crossed Eaton Square. She walked quickly. There was nobody about. Sloane Street was deserted. The signals went through their changes slowly, like bored performers working to an empty house. In the distance, in one of the small cobbled mews, she could hear a milkman making his deliveries. The sound of bottles carried on the morning air. A cart horse stomped and snorted a couple of times, trying to wake itself up.

The girl turned into Hans Place. She saw nobody at all.

Nobody saw Georgina Game crying.

2

"I urge you to return to the island as soon as possible." David Cornelius spoke in a low, guarded voice. He was a priest with a lawyer's mind. He could have made it as a politician, too. All the way. He didn't trust telephones. He even suspected some of the things he heard in the confessional. "It would look better if you were here . . . at the end," he said, adding almost as an afterthought, "Your Highness." Sometimes protocol was better than sermons.

Philippe looked at his watch. It was not quite four-thirty in the morning. He had been asleep for less than an hour. Violet shadows lingered in the corners of the bedroom like pieces of unconsumed night. He closed his eyes, trying to think. The air was soft and still and spiced with good smells from the night almost gone, from the warm June day that was just beginning.

"I will come," Philippe said quietly. Father Cornelius was not a man who telephoned people at such an hour without very good reason.

"You still have the plane?" the priest asked. "In Paris?"

"Yes," Philippe said. He replaced the receiver slowly without saying good-bye.

"All things come to him who knows how to wait," Philippe said softly. It was almost a sigh. He smiled down at the girl sleeping by his side. Her small serious face was almost childlike against the black satin pillow. Philippe sat absolutely still. The girl did not stir. He did not wish to wake her. The news he had just received was better than passion.

His father was dying.

At last. Thy kingdom come, Philippe thought. Thy will be done.

It cannot be more than a question of days, perhaps even hours. Father Cornelius was emphatic about that.

It was a familiar promise, of course. A promise that had thrilled and disappointed Philippe for many years. Only now he knew the promise was to be fulfilled: he had a profound sensibility to great things.

He stroked the girl's soft blond hair, and dreamed. For the first time in his life Philippe was conscious of his happiness: not the anticipation of happiness, nor the memory of it, but happiness here and now. He was convinced he deserved it.

He slipped out of bed and went naked to his dressing room. He moved like an athlete, up on his toes, a middleweight in the early rounds. He hummed the tune "Goodnight, Irene." It was the latest song rage from America. He closed the door carefully behind him and switched on the sixteen bare light bulbs that surrounded his dressing-table mirror. It gave the large Victorian room a theatrical appearance. He noticed the soft warm jasmine smell of the girl's scent on his body. *Joy* seemed to be the scent all the girls were wearing that year. He pushed his face close to the ablaze mirror and ran his fingers through his hair: it was still as black as a raven's wing, thanks to Raoul Richelieu, but it wasn't young hair any more and that was beginning to show. He smiled ruefully at his reflection. His face would soon be old enough to be ravaged by sleep.

The thought did not disturb him too much. Philippe had an almost thuggish sensuality. He knew it was more lethal than charm, which he was not without. He understood why women pursued him with their attentions. He was forty years old, six-feet-one in height. He was lean and still genuinely taut. He had the aura of someone without friends: he looked like a man who knew how to be cruel. His eyes were pale and extraordinarily blue: his great-great grandmother had been the natural daughter of Frederick William III, the King of Prussia. Princess Marie-Thérèse Louise had brought Hanoverian determination to the family's Gallic aplomb. He had the proper assurance of a true prince. Some women thought him like a Medici in appearance. Some women called him a bastard and still fell for his *soigné* smile. Philippe belonged to that class of men who are expected merely to play at passion and keep beyond the aggrandizement of love.

Philippe was also a gambler. He believed that no seat is luckier than the seat just occupied by a dead man. It was a good enough reason for being in St. Saladin as quickly as possible.

He slipped on an ankle-length white toweling bathrobe and dialed Captain Casenave's number in Mortefontaine.

Casenave answered on the fourth ring, his voice thick with sleep.

"Have the plane ready to depart at nine o'clock. I am returning to St. Saladin," Philippe said. Brusqueness was not rudeness with him but a fashion of speech.

When he had replaced the receiver, Edouard Casenave swore. He looked at the small Cartier alarm clock on his bedside table. It was four-fifty. He reached for his address book. He prayed that his crew and the mechanics were all in their proper places, in their right beds.

He had a headache.

He wished he had a woman to make him coffee.

3

The Hereditary Prince André Antonin Philippe, Marquis of Murat, member of the Supreme Cross of the Order of Croissy, winner of the Croix de Guerre and Médaille Militaire, sat impassively in one of the six brown chamois-leather armchairs in his private airliner. He had waited a very long time for this moment. Yet not a hint of feeling now showed on his suntanned face.

Trained in the art of reserve, Philippe considered any public display of emotion to be weak and vulgar. Only those who knew him well might have sensed the imprisoned smile.

On the flight deck of the Airspeed Ambassador, *Royal Hunter II,* Captain Casenave finished his third cup of American-blend black coffee. It had been an uneventful flight and only second stewardess Mlle. Elizabeth Ledoux had failed to make it. She was not a particularly pretty girl, nor very compliant. Captain Casenave had no doubt in his mind that the Prince would dismiss her.

Casenave had been cleared at 19,000 feet by Le Bourget air traffic control, which took him below most of the cumulus. He had tried to make the flight more interesting for himself by ignoring the radio beams; he had plotted a visual course crossing Mâcon, St. Étienne, and down as far as Avignon before swinging left. He enjoyed flying by the seat of his pants. He had escaped to England in 1940 in a Farman F222 and was one of the five French pilots who took part in the Battle of Britain. He was still at heart a wet-beam man, an old-fashioned iron-beam skywinder: there wasn't a river or railroad in Western Europe he couldn't tag at 20,000 feet. Instrument flying was no flying at all.

The winds had been just about everything the boys in the meteorological bureau had said they would be and Casenave had arrived more or less in the right place, one minute forty-five seconds ahead of his E.T.A. He called the St. Saladin tower and was authorized to begin his descent to 4,000 feet at 1,000 feet per minute. He eased back the throttles. Twenty tons of technological hedonism began the long gentle drop to earth.

Captain Casenave switched on the *No Smoking* sign, although he knew the Prince did not smoke; he switched on the seat-belt sign, although he knew the Prince had been securely strapped in from the moment he stepped aboard the plane at Le Bourget. Not to have gone through the safety procedures would have incurred the displeasure of the Prince. It is by being meticulous about small rituals and courtesies that men like Captain

Edouard Casenave keep their jobs with men like Prince Philippe.

The slow, curving Lucky Horseshoe beach, fringed with olive trees and sheltered from the winds and the *mistral* by mountains, gave way to the precipitous limestone cliffs. The little island well deserved its nickname the Fief of Baghdad, Casenave thought.

The cabin of *Royal Hunter II* was originally designed to carry forty-seven passengers. Now it was an almost exact replica of the rosewood study in the Prince's Paris apartment on the Île St.-Louis. The nineteenth-century hand-knotted carpet, the Sheraton writing table, the signed and dated Corot landscape gave flying a curious, almost languid air of carriage-day charm.

At this moment, Philippe was unaware of his immediate surroundings. He stared through the small Plexiglas porthole at the domain that would soon be his. Chiffons of scud, like discarded veils, floated by outside. The eyes of the Prince remained expressionless, the color of old denim left too long in the sun.

The mesmeric pitch of the twin engines changed perceptibly from tenor to a deeper, more measured note of anticipation, like the prelude to a Verdi *finale*. The wingstrips glinted abruptly in the noon sunlight.

Philippe could see the shadow of his plane, a dark traversing crucifix, speeding like a speculative blessing over the terraces of fine houses smothered in climbing vetches, crossing cool arcaded squares and narrow ancient saffron streets and low villas. He could trace the Sacred Ravine of Eagles, a deep gorge surrounded by tall eucalyptus trees. Filled with an aqueous turquoise light, its steep slopes were scarred with igneous red rocks and caves which once sheltered ambuscades, brigands, and the partisans who plagued the army of Charles V in 1536.

To the east was the village where reclusive potters made jars in the same way the Romans did. Their ancestors, forced laborers from Genoa, had settled in that remote spot more than four hundred years ago. *Figon,* a Genoese patois, was still the language they spoke among themselves.

Philippe knew the history of his land better than any

man. He knew his people. "The lineage of my humblest
peasant is equal to the royal blood of Windsor," he had
once boasted to an English prince. It did not occur to
Philippe that the Englishman might not be pleased by
such a claim.

Captain Casenave was ordered into a holding pattern
at 4,000 feet. Saladin control was having its usual trouble deciding which runway to allocate to *Royal Hunter
II*. There were two runways at Saladin's Dauphin Airport. "Decisions, decisions," Casenave said under his
breath. He was becoming aware of his tiredness. At
least Dauphin's meditative controllers would soon be
put out of their misery as far as the Prince's aircraft was
concerned. The British had already announced plans to
inaugurate the world's first Comet jet service, between
London and Johannesburg. It would begin a new era in
air travel. Dauphin, built on a 2,005-feet-high plateau,
was not large enough to take the big jets that would be
developed during the next decade. The longest of the
two ungrooved runways was an east-west strip 4,150
feet long and notorious for its tricky crosswinds. There
was no room for expansion on Dauphin's present site.
Two years from now, Captain Casenave would be putting down at Toulon. He knew the Prince would not be
able to resist the new toy.

Casenave continued to circle. I'm becoming cynical,
he thought. And then he thought about that.

The Prince did not find it at all uncomfortable to be
kept waiting in a place where everything he saw was his,
or very soon would be, and where everything that happened concerned him. How very different he was from
his father, Philippe thought. His father had never made
much of the pleasures of ruling. Tactics, manipulation,
the strategies of statesmanship, such things always appeared to exhaust Prince Maximilien. Even the satisfaction of giving orders, of being obeyed and making people jump, had long ceased to be anything but a harping
gratification to the old man.

Philippe had never understood his father. It was a
failure that separated the two men more conclusively
than even their mutual distrust. Philippe understood his
people but not his own father who ruled them. It puz-

zled him, at least whenever he thought about it. It was not the sort of conundrum that Philippe thought about very often.

Captain Casenave was finally ordered to runway one. He turned *Royal Hunter II* left out of its containing ring and prepared for the final approach. As he always did, Casenave took his line from the third of the five famous domes of the St. Saladin casino. The mosque-like domes glistened like giant gilded onions baking in the early-summer heat. Philippe called the casino his onion factory that made cabbage—and princes. It was one of his rare jokes. Philippe was usually never more serious than when he was making a joke.

Philippe sighed, but not sadly. He felt almost care-free, in fact. Fate has probably saved more ships than compasses, he thought, remembering the island's strange and venturesome history. Philippe now had several million very good reasons to be grateful to great-great grandfather Tullio for his timely onion shed. And to great-great grandmother Princess Marie-Thérèse Louise for her timeless wiles.

Royal Hunter II touched down with a ponderous, almost sutured sense of gravity.

4

The telephone had an impatient, determined sound. The sound that telephones always seem to acquire after about six rings.

Isak Girod found it with her left hand and answered it without opening her eyes.

"Yes?" Her voice had that flat dry croak of early-morning speech.

"Mlle. Girod?" The voice sounded solicitous and uncertain, as if it habitually reached wrong numbers.

"Yes."

"Mlle. Girod, this is Josephine . . . Josephine at M. Richelieu?"

"Hello Josephine at M. Richelieu."

Isak placed her hand over the mouthpiece and cleared her throat. Josephine was the little red-haired girl who had been the manicurist and was now Richelieu's receptionist. She had a posh new probationary Rive Gauche accent, but Isak remembered her. Isak was the sort of woman who remembered other women's vulnerabilities.

"Mlle. Girod! It is twelve-thirty! Your appointment with M. Richelieu was for noon!"

Isak opened her eyes. The bright sunlight suffused the curtained room with the bronzed glow she remembered from early-autumn evenings in Chamonix. She lay still.

She instinctively knew that Philippe had left the house.

She closed her eyes again.

"My appointment?"

"With M. Richelieu. You had a twelve o'clock appointment with M. Richelieu himself." Josephine sounded petulant, but it may merely have been panic. Richelieu was a martinet, a stickler for promptness no matter how distinguished or fashionable the client may be. It was part of the Richelieu style. Rich women are spoiled women and spoiled women long to be bossed, even humiliated a little.

His real name was Raoul Frot. At twenty-nine, he was probably the world's most exclusive hairdresser. "I make a point of avoiding women with no money," he had once told Isak. "It makes life less tiresome." He had introduced Isak to Philippe at a party at his penthouse in the Bois. His parties were famous. He looked like a tennis star but his renowned ability to summon up tears, emotional breakdowns and even high fevers at will ended his military call-up after three weeks' soldiering at a barracks near Marseille.

"I'm simply devastated to have missed Ho's massacre of Caobang," he told *Paris-Presse* in an interview that many of his friends thought went too far even for Raoul Richelieu. He framed his discharge papers bearing the legend *inapte à servir*; the gilt frame hung in Richelieu's hunting lodge near St.-Germaine-en-Laye above a desk that once belonged to his hero Napoleon.

Raoul Richelieu impressed the hell out of girls like Josephine.

"M. Richelieu was going to do the cut today personally. You have *forgotten?*" Josephine could no longer keep the sense of horror out of her new voice.

"You didn't get my message? My dear, my secretary telephoned the salon yesterday evening before six o'clock," Isak lied calmly. "We had to cancel the appointment."

"Oh." Josephine's voice was suddenly very small and very fragile. "M. Richelieu doesn't seem to have been told." She sounds like Shirley Temple going down with the Good Ship Lollipop, Isak thought without any sense of guilt at all.

She said, "I cannot possibly do anything about it now. I'm in the middle of a meeting with a producer from London. I'm sorry you didn't get my message. Give M. Richelieu my personal regards . . . and my commiseration, of course." Raoul's tyranny never bothered Isak. Screw him.

She put down the telephone. It is all right to lie when the truth is so boring.

"Philippe!"

She called his name almost involuntarily. She knew there would be no answer. The house felt different when he was away. His presence brought the house alive, infected it with a sense of purpose.

People didn't understand when Isak Girod told them that Philippe was capable of that kind of magic. People didn't understand Philippe at all.

Isak and Philippe had been lovers for three years. They had made love the first night they met at Richelieu's party. Philippe was not her first man but he had taught her almost everything she knew, in and out of bed. His games were her games now. His tastes were her tastes. "No woman ever became wanton all at

once," he once said to her. "But when she is determined
. . . she gets there soon enough."

Yet the passion that kept them together was not exactly love, and not exactly hate either. Philippe avoided
the insipid obligations of love; he resisted the self-
intimidation of hatred. They remained devoted to each
other even while pursuing the most vivid and complicated affairs with others.

Philippe encouraged her infidelities and her confes-
sions. No man had ever understood Isak so well. Her
willingness and her wildness took flight in fantasies
fueled by Philippe himself. In the beginning Isak's elaborate inventions were enough. But the men in her inventions were real men, men they both knew, authentic
men who became by degrees a threat then a challenge
and finally an indispensable need.

"Yes, do it. Go with him. Really. I won't be angry."

"I want to, you know that?" Isak warned him.

"Of course."

"Yes?"

"Yes. But you must always tell me."

"Oh yes, Philippe. Everything. I want to tell you everything he does to me."

"When?"

"There is a saying. It is better to begin this evening
than not at all."

And so the game began.

Suffering, cumulative and addictive, was at the very
soul of their relationship. Philippe wanted Isak soiled
and whorish and always graphic; he sometimes felt that
he needed to push her to the very limits of sexual degra-
dation. With whores Philippe felt safe: with a whore he
could almost dream of love.

Isak saw in his needs absolution for her own desires.
Their affinity was complete. It was defiling, delicious. It
was dangerous.

"Tell me, Isak," he would say.

"And then?"

"And then?"

"And then?"

"Tell me."

Sometimes Philippe wept. Isak held him, smiling, the

scent of debauchery still on her. Conspired infidelity is the most intimate secret a man and a woman can share, she thought. Isak's unfaithfulness had become their umbilical cord. The understanding between them was perfect. Raoul Richelieu's instinct for casting was uncanny, it was immaculate. Richelieu was an evil genius; today Rasputin would have been a hairdresser.

Isak pulled back the black satin sheet that covered her nakedness. A fine gold chain around her waist glistened dully against the Mediterranean sheen. She had that transparent topaz tan that looks so good on twenty-three-year-old skins. She loved her own body. She sometimes wondered whether she had a soul at all: the lusts and greeds, the pleasures and cravings of her flesh determined her destiny.

She rolled slowly onto her back. Her left hand, palm up, lay on her open mouth; she stared at the high encrusted ceiling. The fingers of her right hand moved down her body, almost floating across the humid silky skin.

She thought about Philippe.

She never thought about the others when she was alone.

Her fingers were now Philippe's fingers. Self-love was his love. She felt him move inside her. Her eyes opened wider, like gaping wounds. Her mouth shaped his name, a silent scream, a splinter of silence torn from her throat. Then she moaned, just once, a hurt wild lonely animal sound.

She lay very still.

She ached.

After a while her breathing became regular, a little moist, languorous. The room smelled of her. A single damp strand of hair fell across her forehead. It was like a flaw in a piece of porcelain.

5

He woke with a startled snort. The book on his lap fell to the floor. There was a dribble of froth in one corner of his mouth. What had awakened him was a polite but persistent tapping on his study door.

"Cornelius? David, dear chap, are you at home? May I come in? Cornelius?"

Father Cornelius looked at his watch. It took him a little time to focus. It was six forty-five. He was dressed. At first he couldn't work it out. Was it six forty-five in the evening? How long had he been in the chair? There was a bad taste in his mouth. His body felt heavy and sluggish and the muscles in his neck ached. Surely he had dozed off for only a moment or two.

The polite tapping continued.

"David?"

Cornelius remembered slowly. He had been reading some Maupassant. He had dipped into the book after speaking to Philippe in Paris.

Then he recalled the dream.

The recurring dream about his childhood in St. Louis, Missouri.

He had been walking by the river with his mother. The bank had caved in. His mother was swept away. Her face was always indissolubly blended with his own. He threw bluebells into the river.

His mother always wore the same dress in the dream. It was the dress she wore the day he graduated from St. Louis University and took her to lunch in that little Italian café behind Union Station. The day he told her he was going to join the Church.

"David?"

"Yes, yes, do come in," Cornelius said. He stood up

20

gently. He picked up the book from the carpet and dropped it onto his chair.

Alwyn Brand, Prince Maximilien's aide-de-camp, slid around the door as if determined to enter the room through as narrow a gap as possible. His smooth cheeks were slightly flushed. He wore a heavy woollen dressing gown, almost khaki in color, over strangely schoolboyish blue-and-white-striped pajamas. His white veiny feet were encased in carpet slippers piped with yellow imitation fur. The peculiarities of the English climate created many strange and durable habits.

"Good morning, Alwyn. Are you on your way to bed, or just getting up?"

Brand ignored the question. He said, "David, I've been *hammering* at your door for ten minutes. Max is conscious. He is asking for you."

Brand spoke with a prissy Balliol accent that might just as easily have belonged to a woman; it never bothered him when telephone operators called him Miss.

Cornelius walked across to the large window at the end of the room and drew the curtains. The shutters had not been closed. The sea was dark vinyl blue. It was going to be another very warm day. Below, a woman was walking alone on the wet hard part of the beach. The tide was going out. Cornelius jabbed the window open with his forefinger and the sound of the sea floated into the room, faint, cajoling. Cornelius felt dank, as if he had been sitting in a train all night. He needed a shave. He wiped a thin shine of sweat from his forehead.

Brand came further into the room and switched off the table lamp. Its glow had turned to a pale buff color in the brilliant blue light streaming through the window. He picked up an empty glass from the table and inspected it like a careful hostess checking for smears before a dinner party.

Cornelius had removed only his shoes before falling asleep but he couldn't remember doing so or where he had put them. He stood very still, hands on hips, his eyes searching the room.

Brand lifted the glass close to his long, slightly hooked nose and sniffed audibly. He replaced the glass on the table and made a disapproving face that non-drinkers can't help making when confronted with serious alcohol. He restrained himself with great difficulty from saying something droll and disparaging.

"Glenfiddich. Twelve years old," Cornelius said. "And not at all medicinal."

Brand still said nothing. A bleak reproving smile balanced on his wire-thin lips.

Cornelius continued to look for his shoes. He liked Alwyn Brand. The Englishman had a brilliant mind and his effeminate manner didn't bother Cornelius, usually. Brand was also a Biblical papyrologist of considerable repute. The two men argued endlessly about theology and, for some reason that neither really understood, economics. Brand argued pedantically and frequently lost his temper in a petulant fashion; Cornelius was a debater, expedient and cool. Cornelius never relaxed his vigilance, even in banter.

At this moment he was anxious to avoid conversation of any kind with the hovering Englishman. He felt a small hangover coming on.

"I thought you Jesuits drank only Vat 69?" Brand said with gentle malice.

"Jesus was a bit of a rebel too, Alwyn," Cornelius grunted. He was on his knees, feeling beneath the low armchair.

"His immoderate dissidence led to His death," Brand said. "Although, of course, there is still doubt whether He was primarily crucified for religious or political reasons."

Cornelius recovered his left shoe.

"I'll grant you the authorities weren't too pleased with Him," Cornelius said. "Didn't He liken them to a bunch of vipers?" He sat down and put on his shoe.

Brand walked to the window and sniffed the air in much the same way he had sniffed the Glenfiddich. He seemed to be just as disapproving. He closed the window a few inches.

He said, "Had Jesus shown a little more moderation He could have saved himself and His unfortunate friends—not to mention the authorities—a great deal of unpleasantness."

Cornelius was on his knees again, sweeping his hand beneath the chair in his search for the other shoe.

"It's over there, beneath the bureau," Brand said.

"Thank you," Cornelius said politely, getting to his feet rather stiffly. He retrieved the shoe and returned to the armchair.

"He could have avoided a great deal of trouble all round," Brand said.

He was watching Cornelius closely now.

"Well, I guess that's how it goes, Alwyn old sport," Cornelius said. He noticed himself slipping into the mocking English colonial vernacular he used when Brand was getting on his nerves. "The glorious liberty of the children of God and all that." He pulled his lace tight and made a bow he would have to loosen later.

Brand said nothing. Cornelius fell into the silence as if it were a well-laid trap. "Anyway, dear chap, I think of myself in far more humbler terms. I'm just a simple shepherd at heart," he said. He regretted the phrase at once. He knew the way Brand's mind worked. Cornelius was like a *Times* crossword addict who knew the compiler's weaknesses, and all his tricks.

"Did you know that the use of 'good' in 'I am the good shepherd' is the Greek *kalos* and not *agathos*?" Brand said at once. "It alters the meaning considerably. From 'morally good' to simply 'skillful.' Not the same kettle of fish at all."

"Then let us say that my merit doesn't survive translation," Cornelius said. He was now wide awake. On his guard. This was no casual theological chitchat. Brand was telling him to be careful. But careful of what? Careful of whom?

The old armchair surrounded Cornelius like a worn boxing glove. He pulled the book from under his thigh and put it on the small oak table by his side. He didn't attempt to rise.

He wanted Brand to continue talking. He hoped the Englishman would say something that would at least point him in the right direction.

But it seemed that Brand had said everything he had to say on the subject. He was fresh out of parables.

"You'd better cut along," Brand said, standing over him. "Time isn't exactly on Max's side."

Cornelius stood up. He collected a prayer book and his rosary from the bureau. "Yes," he said quietly. "Thank you for waking me."

He left the tall Englishman standing in the middle of the room. In his pajamas and dressing gown, Brand looked like a child who has just awakened in the middle of the night in a strange room and is about to burst into tears.

6

Lionel Hammond was a tall lean man with a professorial air. Young movie actresses, especially the serious ones, often found him sexy, in a Lincolnesque sort of way. He had the wary look of a man who kept his mind permanently on a safety chain.

It was true that Lionel Hammond preferred introspection to conversation. But at this precise moment, his thoughts fell somewhat short of profundity. He was thinking about moving to smaller, less expensive premises in Shepherd's Market; he was thinking about cutting down his smoking; he was thinking about Georgina Game.

He was also thinking about the deep scratch someone had carved in the door of his new Rolls-Royce. The insurance company had written it off as "envy damage." That kind of thing happened a lot these days. He'd just have to learn to live with it, the claims adjuster said with a smile that inflicted its own particular kind of envy damage.

Actually, what Lionel Hammond was really doing was trying very hard *not* to think about Warren Masters.

A week ago Lionel Hammond had ceased to be the most successful independent agent in London. A week ago his client Warren Masters had ceased to be the biggest British movie actor in the business.

For three years in a row, despite the apathy of the critics, Masters had topped the Motion Picture Exhibitors' Poll of European Box-Office Champions. He had been enshrined in the Motion Picture Hall of Fame. His first two Hollywood movies—he played Sir Walter Raleigh in one, and a Russian spy in the other—put him in the world's top ten. "An old ham sandwiched between Martin and Lewis and Gary Cooper," Masters said. His last picture had earned him an Oscar nomination. His portrayal of a cockney gigolo pawing his way to the top was the best thing he'd ever done.

Then, at age forty-two (or thirty-six, according to his official biography), Masters got stoned three weeks into an Anglo-French picture in a town called Ras Kaboudia in Tunisia. He fell into a deep slumber with a hashish joint in his mouth and a beautiful Arab boy between his thighs.

The juxtaposition was fatal.

The blaze took several hours to bring under control.

Warren Masters was given the leading obituary in the London *Times*. It referred to his "authentic masculinity" and "vivid sensual gusto." He was lamented as "an original artist with style and humor and extravagant tastes."

The importance of Warren Masters, the *Times* concluded, had increased greatly in recent years. He had become a legendary star in the eyes of the cinema public and especially in the eyes of the immediate postwar generation. Only in death was his sense of timing so miscalculated.

Hammond stood in the middle of his large office, listening to the rain. There was a pale expression on his face that could have been worry, plain weariness, or the first installment on a bleak smile.

From the next room came the faint sound of his secretary typing in her steady fifty-words-a-minute way. She was answering the letters of condolence, mostly from fans, mostly forwarded from newspapers, movie magazines, and the various studios Warren had worked for. Studios never replied to fan mail for dead actors. Probably for much the same reason the trade papers didn't waste space on actors' obituaries.

Dead actors don't take ads.

Dead actors don't make movies.

Hammond had decided to acknowledge every letter personally.

He fixed a red-tipped Marlboro into a short ivory holder and placed it in his mouth. He dropped the pack on to his desk. The Philip Morris signature scrawled across the pack looked like every actor's autograph he'd ever seen. More a proclamation than a signature. Actors.

He patted his jacket pocket for his lighter.

The lighter—four ounces of eighteen-carat Cartier craftsmanship—was designed to look like a carriage bolt. He pressed the nut and a fine blue flame rose from the middle of the hexagonal head.

Hammond inhaled slowly. After a few moments he turned and walked a few paces to a corner of the room where a dozen ten-by-eight photographs of Georgina Game lay spread out on the carpet like a spilled deck of playing cards.

Hammond stared down at them, wishing he had remembered to tell Robin Villiers to give them a matte finish. Georgina had a thing about glossies.

It didn't matter now. The damage had been done. Villiers had tried to get her to show more cleavage. She wouldn't and the anger—a sense of affront and reproach—was there in her face in every shot. It had been a strained session. Villiers, a small middle-aged homosexual who'd made his name photographing Somerset Maugham and Noël Coward before the war, had been reduced to tears.

Hammond wondered what Georgina Game's autograph looked like. Only that was something else she wouldn't do. Sign autographs.

The agent stared down at the faces on the floor. They stared right back at him. A kaleidoscope of withering insolence. Georgina Game was something else again.

Hammond played with the lighter in his hand as if it

were one solid-gold worry bead. His manicured thumb-nail glided through the engraving along the side of the bolt like a blind man following a familiar passage in braille. The engraving, a facsimile of Warren Masters' handwriting, said: *To Frankenstein from his grateful Monster.*

Hammond now had his mind firmly fixed on Georgina Game. She was going to need very special handling. A new approach.

It was easier said than done.

Georgina Game was intelligent, beautiful, independent—Daddy was Harry Ogilvy who was rebuilding half of London. She was a cool lady. Sometimes, Hammond suspected, it was an effort for her not to be downright disdainful.

But, and nobody ever tried to deny it, Georgina Game was one hell of a sexy lady.

Hammond pushed the photographs around the floor with the pointed toe of his shiny black brogue.

The more Hammond looked at them the more he recognized the fact that Villiers had somehow caught the face of a woman who, unlike most actors, had outgrown the childhood tricks of escape through fantasy and lies. The directness, the strength and boldness and sensuality of Georgina Game—it was all there in those pictures.

He picked up the nearest print and studied it for a long moment. Her eyes were her best feature. They were wide-set and almost black. Light tawny flecks glistened in them like shreds of gold. In the black-and-white prints they looked incandescent.

Hammond took the photograph to the window and held it to the light, almost at arm's length. Her nose was as small and perfect as most noses are ever going to be without a scalpel. There were hollows in her cheeks you could store grain in. Her hair had the pale natural glow of a Lent lily.

It was all there. Even in a set of pictures taken by a pansy who didn't understand her at all.

Hammond took the picture and dropped it onto the floor with the others.

She was difficult, of course. She could be bloody impossible at times—but she knew exactly what she wanted. That kind of drive has a fuel, a *furor*, all its own.

Georgina Game wanted stardom, on her terms, not so much for the glory and the gravy, but as some people want to climb mountains and swim across great seas— for the challenge and the sweet wind-sown smell of success.

"I do not care to live my life in a fishbowl, Mr. Hammond, nor do I care to live outside . . . outside ordinary time and space the way Warren Masters lives," she told him the first time they met.

Hammond was amused by her solemn dispatching tone. She sounded like the new duchess telling the old butler how things have to be done around here from now on. It didn't occur to her that *she* was auditioning for *him*.

"I intend to do this thing well, Mr. Hammond. I don't intend being just another starlet. I'm not the kind of actress who can become whatever the studios want her to become. For better or worse, I'm Georgina Ogilvy."

This was before she took her American mother's maiden name because there was already another actress named Georgina Ogilvy registered with Equity. Hammond was pleased about that. Georgina Ogilvy didn't have a marquee feel.

Georgina Game. That had enough *electrics* running through it to light up Broadway, London, and half of Paris.

"I'm not a sweater girl, Mr. Hammond. I'm not whistle bait. I'm not a Loomis Dean layout in *Life* magazine. I'm me. And I'm the best kind of me there is."

To Hammond's ear she had the sort of American accent he liked best—the sort most Americans think is English. Probably Bryn Mawr and Boston, he decided. But he was wrong about Bryn Mawr.

When she had reached the end of her instructions Hammond said quietly, "Do you always wear white gloves, Miss Ogilvy?" He'd never been to lunch with an actress in white gloves before.

"I'm just particular where I leave my dabs," she said.

Her voice, at that moment, had the pure sound of distilled sex. That was when Lionel Hammond decided he would represent her after all.

Hammond slowly tapped out the last half-inch of his Marlboro into an old brass ashtray from Boodle's. How the ashtray found its way into his office was one of those mysteries. It just appeared one morning on the windowsill. He wasn't a member of the club. He'd never even been a guest there.

He found it difficult to concentrate this morning. He began to reach for another cigarette but changed his mind halfway to the desk. He was smoking far too much.

He stood in the middle of the room, bouncing his gold lighter in the palm of his hand, as if trying to guess its weight. Georgina would never be the sort of star who distributes goodies from Cartier's. Like most born-rich girls, Georgina knew how to use money without actually parting with it. There was a definite knack to that.

"One usually gets a far better service by promises than by presents," she said.

Georgina Game was another kind of monster. But at least she was a damn sight more discreet than Warren Masters had been.

"These attempts to relate one's private life to one's work—bullshit, Lionel, absolute bullshit," Georgina said coolly when he'd tried to fix up an interview with Louella Parsons. "It's nobody's business what I wear to bed or whom, if anyone, I choose to entertain between my sheets."

She hated interviews. "The fact is," she said, "a woman can't win. When people start talking about an actor it's recognition. He's made it. When an actress gets talked about, it's usually a conviction."

Georgina Game was definitely another kind of monster. But she had never promised to be anything else. *I'm me.* She'd been blunt enough about where she stood. *I'm the best kind of me there is.*

Lionel Hammond couldn't argue with that. The trouble was, the best kind of Georgina Game simply wasn't selling. There was no mystery why that was. It was a combination of things. A combination of Georgina Game's obstinacy, Georgina Game's perversity, and Georgina Game's principles. She had everything going for her except a willingness to play ball with the system.

She was a good actress. The London Film Critics Circle called her performance in *The Glass Chrysalis* "the outstanding debut of the year."

Hammond believed in her.

An actress is not necessarily a star because her name is above the title of her pictures or because the critics like her. In a true star, he believed, a spiritual force is at work. A star has a mercurial soul that is all its own. The real star must be created and driven by . . . an *idea*. It was hard to put into words, but that was how he felt about Georgina Game. Why else would he put up with her? It wasn't for the money he made out of her.

Hammond sighed. He sensed there was a most dangerous conjunction of stars in the skies hanging over his head.

He lit another cigarette.

The drizzling rain had stopped. Berkeley Square looked miserable. Men in pale poplin raincoats and girls in transparent plastic raincoats hurried along, dodging the summer showers. The traffic moved slowly.

He missed Warren. He really should think about organizing a memorial service soon.

7

The walk from Cornelius' rectory in the west wing of the palace to Prince Maximilien's chambers took nearly five minutes. Cornelius breathed deeply through his nose noisily, like a fighter. He must have gone through more than half a bottle of whisky since supper. At this rate Maximilien would outlive him yet.

The corridors, lined with Hamons and Fromentins, a couple of Monets, an inferior Signac, and a doubtful Corot, seemed endless. People who sneered at the smallness of St. Saladin had never been obliged to walk through these corridors at seven o'clock in the morning. Hiking through Carrara marble halls was not Father Cornelius' idea of exercise.

He stopped and bent down to loosen his lace.

The old Prince lay very still. His cancer-bleached face seemed to be part of the pillow on which he lay. It reminded Cornelius of a battlefield long after the war had moved on. The trenches and the craters were still there, shallow indentations that would soon be covered by pastures of peace. Only the agonies of long ago lingered like a grieving grayness in the air about him.

Maximilien seemed incapable of movement; his almost fleshless arms lay outside the covers as if already sepulchrally fixed alongside his body. His deterioration in the few hours Cornelius had been away was startlingly visible. The bed and the whole room seemed to have grown massively around him. The smell of medicine, the smell of desolate loneliness, saturated the room.

The nurse stood up and went over to Cornelius. She was a small Italian woman with a round solemn face and dark, almost black rings beneath her eyes. Her skinny white-stockinged legs were planted in heavy white shoes that seemed to be several sizes too large for her. Cornelius thought of Minnie Mouse.

"His Highness has morphia now. The doctor say you can have five minutes, yes?" She spoke in a normal conversational voice. Cornelius noticed that professionals never used that hushed tone ordinary people used in the presence of the dying. Nursing was a hard business.

"Thank you, sister," he said, picking up the same companionable tone without realizing it.

"I will be just outside the door if you need me, yes?" she said in her chatty voice. She made a note on a yellow-colored chart pinned to a clipboard. She read over what she'd written, tapping her untidy teeth gently with a thin black ball-point pen. She replaced the clipboard on a small table loaded with medicines, kidney-

shaped basins, syringes, mysterious stainless-steel in-
struments, and sharp-looking scissors. She casually
covered the clipboard with a folded handtowel and
dropped the pen into the breast pocket of her white
tunic-dress.

"No more than five minutes, please, Father," she
said.

"Five minutes."

"Please." She smiled and unsmiled quickly, almost
surreptitiously, as if she were ashamed of being caught
in the act.

She went outside and turned to face the priest.

"Five minutes," she said again, holding up five
splayed fingers by the side of her small round face. She
pulled the heavy door toward her with both hands. It
closed silently, without even a click.

Did closing doors disturb the dying? Cornelius wondered.

"David? Is that you?" The voice seemed to come
from a long way off, thin and metallic, like a sound
traveling down a railroad track.

"I was sleeping," the priest said. He moved closer to
the bed. "We didn't expect you to awaken so early."

"No," the Prince answered.

"I'm sorry, Your Highness. I wanted to be here when
you woke," Cornelius said gently. He sat in the high-
backed chair by the bed, where the nurse had been sitting. He could feel the heat of her on the velvet seat. He
felt uneasy. It wasn't how a priest was supposed to feel
at all, especially not now.

The room was too neat. Its personality had been
scrubbed away. Its character, its history, all the ghosts
had fled. It was no worse than a hotel room, Cornelius
told himself. The room of a man in transit, of a traveler,
a bird of passage. A pilgrim.

He knew he was only kidding himself.

It was as if a sickness had sapped the room, sucked it
dry, bone dry. Another part of his mind was concentrating, guiltily, on something else. He was trying to figure
out whether his career in St. Saladin was all used up.
He thought about the dangers of risking too little in the
beginning, hoping for too much later . . . but, then, the

risk ratio in any man's life is a very personal calculation. The pure mathematics of the soul. He had written that once in a theological thesis at St. Louis U. He distrusted Stosch's policies. The man disquieted him. Cornelius could wheel and deal with the best of them but he also knew that more and more St. Saladin was being governed by influence, by license and sufferance, and not by law. He didn't want to become another Stosch puppet. With Maximilien dead and Philippe—

"I had a nightmare," the Prince said.

"A nightmare?"

"It's cruel of God to leave a dying man alone with his imagination in the night."

"Dreams—"

"A fertile imagination, it's the last thing a man in my position wants," the Prince said. His clawlike hand plucked feebly at the cover.

"My father killed himself."

"Killed himself, Your Highness?"

"He stopped taking the pills that were keeping him alive. Did I never tell you that?"

"No, I don't believe you ever did."

Maximilien's father had come to him in a dream that night. He had sat by the side of his bed with a vividness that was still undissolved.

"My father was here," the Prince said. "He didn't speak, but he was here, in this room, in that chair. He sat and looked at me, nodding, understanding."

Cornelius said nothing. It must have been parents' visiting night, he thought. The thought disturbed him.

"When I was a child my father threatened to swallow a silver spoon. He told me he wanted to die with a silver spoon in his mouth. But in the end he simply stopped taking the pills."

"That was very wrong of him," Cornelius said. He was not certain how much of what the Prince said could be put down to the rambling of a drugged mind. "God doesn't approve of such impertinence."

"My father had contempt for all outside opinion."

The Prince tried to smile, but he was already stretched beyond his limits. "Like me," he added. His eyes had a strange muculent light.

"How can I answer such sacrilege?" Cornelius said. He tried to speak in a half-chiding, half-amused voice but the balance wasn't right and it didn't sound at all the way he wanted it to.

"Religion is just a lot of ransom notes," the Prince said.

"But you paid?"

"The threat between the lines."

"That's not—"

"My money was never really on your Man, priest."

"Faith in the death and resurrection of Jesus Christ—"

"All bets are off," the Prince said.

"Your Highness, the greatest—"

"I shall miss my titles—in the commonness of the grave."

"All men are royal in the Kingdom of Heaven," Cornelius said too automatically for his own comfort.

"All corpses are common, David."

"No."

"The buried are the true bourgeoisie."

"You're wrong. The dead are—"

"Dead. Mutton. Bianca understood that. That's why it was so easy for her to do it, to leave me."

For the first time in his adult life, David Cornelius felt on the verge of panic. His mind was full of disordered impulses. His head ached. He didn't know how to cope with this clever dying man, filled with drugs and memories and no illusions. In spite of his efforts to stop it, the thought of his mother drowning where the Mississippi and Missouri meet kept intruding in his mind.

"She was such a whore, Bianca, a little *nymph du pavé*. She died on her back, with her legs open, the mother of my son—"

"The Kingdom of God is within us," Cornelius said. He was anxious to get the dying man's mind on a more reverent track, certainly something less secular than the earthy Bianca.

"The sins of many men were within her."

"Sir—"

"Her dress allowance alone was enough to endow a small mission." The old man smiled. It was a very small smile, more a stain in his eyes than a smile, really. But it was enough to release the tension and Cornelius was grateful for that. Later the priest wondered how the dying man's mind had worked. The Prince had never mentioned Bianca to him before, never mentioned her name, let alone her morals. "Did you reach my son?" the Prince asked suddenly. His voice had changed. It was weaker, yet more urgent.

"Yes. He's returning. I talked to him early this morning in Paris."

The old man closed his eyes for another long moment, as if pausing, painfully, for breath. When he opened his eyes again he began to speak in an almost absentminded sort of way. "There are places in the world where the winter's dead can't be buried until the spring. The earth's too hard to break," he said.

"In Canada—" Cornelius said.

"Those poor souls in their thin cotton shrouds—your Man doesn't care, David. He's so unkind . . . leaving only the dreams."

"He *does* care," Cornelius said.

"At least I gave him half a lifetime of liberty," the Prince said.

"Half a lifetime?" Cornelius had lost the thread.

"Philippe—" the Prince said. A small quiver of animation went through his body. "I was never free."

He was silent for a long time after that. He seemed to have slipped into a coma, yet he had an unsettled look. Cornelius felt his hand. It was very cold. It was like touching a piece of iced meat.

After a long time the Prince opened his eyes for the last time.

"David?" His voice was barely audible. The priest had to bend his head down very close to the gray, barely moving lips. "You must . . ."

"Your Highness? I can't—"

"Stosch."

"You want to speak to Stosch?"

The dying man's eyes widened. He prized the words out of himself at great cost. "Stosch—taken too . . ."

He was slipping downhill fast.

"Strength."

"Yes," the priest said, not understanding. "Strength."

"Tell Philippe—from strength."

"Yes."

"I was wrong."

"You must rest now, Your Highness."

"Tell him—"

"Philippe will be here soon," the priest said. "Rest."

The gray lips moved once more. The priest lowered his head until he could feel their cold outline touching his ear, and the terrible chill of dying breath.

"A brand—of treachery."

The silence that followed was final.

"God bless you," Cornelius said in a voice he knew the Prince could no longer hear. "God bless."

The old man wasn't dead but a dimension had slipped away: the material world had ceased to exist and the spiritual world had yet to come. The priest administered Extreme Unction and said the prayers for the dying soul.

Did he imagine the growing stagnant smell of chemical disintegration as the old man's life turned not to dust, and not to ashes, but to effluvium and lymph? Dust was only the convenience food of death, he thought. Dust was the pablum the church marketed for those who could not stomach the real thing. The asylum of life was so unsafe; he hoped that death was only a temporary humiliation.

His mother's dress was green paisley silk. Sometimes, in the dream, she wore a chiffon face veil. She had been a very beautiful woman.

The nurse came into the room quietly. She went over to the bed and felt for the Prince's pulse.

"I think you should leave now, Father," she said.

"Yes," he said obediently like a child.

The plastic oxygen tent had been folded back over the bed like sheets of cellophane. Maximilien looked as white and fragile as an orchid waiting to be packed into a cellophane box.

"Please," the nurse said, smiling her zipper smile.

He closed the door silently behind him, without a click, using both hands.

8

The aircraft taxied toward the group of men who stood about a hundred yards from the single-story white stucco arrivals building. It was also the departures building. It had been built by the Germans during the war. The flowers and fresh paint and a faked Braque mural didn't hide its bleak Nazi Renaissance look. A neon sign over the main door welcomed you in English to St. Saladin. The *in* in Saladin had fused.

Philippe looked beyond the pale reflection of his own face to the men who had come to meet him.

Paul Duclos stood close to Roberto Cheroffini. They were the two most senior ministers in the cabinet. His father's oldest and closest friends.

There was the tall rangy figure of Alwyn Brand, his father's aide-de-camp and who knew what else besides.

Next to Brand was Leon Kun, a small, wary, white-mouse-colored man from the Finance Ministry.

On Kun's immediate left was Hans Dieter Stosch.

Stosch was the man Philippe gave most of his attention to. Slim and blond with a tight, good-looking face without charm, Dieter Stosch was Controller of the St. Saladin Statistical Digest, the document known in the profession of gambling—when it was known at all—as the SS Memorandum. With its overtones of espionage and power, the SS Memorandum had always fascinated Philippe. Its importance to the tiny state was immeasurable. Although St. Saladin did not compare to, say, Hong Kong or Beirut or Zurich as a trading post of information, it had the best private intelligence system in the world. The SS Memorandum had been useful to Washington, Whitehall, and Bonn as well as to the Sûreté Nationale's secret police unit in Paris. Dieter

Stosch was the youngest Controller since René Chalot founded the Statistical Bureau in 1871. He was also by far the most brilliant.

Except for Dieter Stosch, the men stood in that awkward self-conscious way that reminded Philippe of politicians having their pictures taken for posterity before some conference to prevent a war, or to start one.

Stosch had the look of a man who didn't confer with anybody about anything.

He looked like a man who had been teethed on an iron abacus.

The men wore pale, mostly sand-colored suits. Nobody, except Father Cornelius, who stood apart from the others, wore black. The flagpole on the arrivals building was flagless.

Philippe guessed his father was hanging on.

A red and white jeep towing a flight of steps with *Dauphin International* painted on the sides in blue dayglo paint started to move toward the aircraft.

The driver wore brilliant white overalls and very dark sunglasses. He sat ramrod straight behind the wheel of the jeep, looking directly ahead, thin as a flute. Philippe wondered why security men were always so obvious. This one parked the jeep a few yards from a second group of men who stood almost huddled together despite the heat and the space.

They looked different from the St. Saladin men. They were more relaxed, a lot less formal. A couple had removed their jackets. One man, the oldest-looking, wore creased blue serge trousers. He squatted on the ground, rummaging in a deep rexine case from which he eventually removed a heavy Graflex camera. The man standing next to him tapped the shabby case with the toe of his brown suede shoe and said something that made the others in the group laugh. The old man straightened up and wiped the top of his pink bald head with the heel of his hand. He seemed unprepared for the heat. He didn't join in the laughter. He looked like the kind of man who rolled up his trousers at the seaside. The man in the suede shoes patted the photographer's arm in a gesture of atonement.

They were a fairly representative group of the world's press.

The press had always treated Philippe with courtesy, and sometimes with affection too, although affection was not an emotion he sought even from his closest friends.

His gambling, his women, his follies—his *destiny*—it was easy enough to understand the sort of appeal the Hereditary Prince André Antonin Philippe held for the newspapers of the world.

"There is Aly Khan, Rubirosa, and me," Philippe once said to a lady columnist from Chicago. "What will you people fill your rags with when we're gone?"

"You are indestructible," she had answered.

He was good copy and he knew it.

He would see that the photographers got the pictures they had come to get. But he would remain silent. No quotes. No statements.

He wanted the world to admire his dignified grief.

He had rehearsed a smile full of pain and purpose.

It was taking Captain Casenave much too long to park the plane, thanks to a fussy ground marshaller.

"What's with this guy?" he asked the tower irritably.

"He is studying for a degree in applied pedantics," the bored voice came back in Casenave's earphones. Casenave grinned good-naturedly but he wouldn't be sorry when they stopped using Dauphin. They were a bunch of amateurs.

The marshaller was finally satisfied with the lineup. He signaled approval with white table-tennis bats held above his head in a wide-apart V sign.

"And you, my friend," Casenave said aloud.

He cut the engines and switched off the seat-belt sign in a single movement of his left hand. They had been assing about for almost nine minutes.

Catharine Gaillard put down the newspaper cross-word puzzle she'd been working on for most of the flight, snapped open her safety belt, and went to collect Philippe's jacket from the wardrobe. She was returning with it before the propellers had stopped rolling and the chocks were on.

Philippe admired her soft unbrassiered movement as

she came toward him, smiling. Her breasts moved with
a gentle, almost sea-like swell beneath the thin gray silk
blouse. You knew you were looking at a woman when
you looked at a woman like Catharine Gaillard. Too
many women these days wore more harness than a dray
horse.

Catharine Gaillard was aware of his frank gaze. Her
nipples stood out. She returned his look. She had the
eyes of a woman accustomed to admiration. It was a
look that got right through to Philippe. Women should
be brazen.

"I do hope you enjoyed the flight, Your Highness,"
Catharine said.

She smiled close to his face. She used little makeup.
Her teeth were very white and evenly set. Her breath
smelled of chlorophyll and coffee.

"Thank you," Philippe said. He stood up and allowed
her to help him on with his jacket.

She must have been five feet nine or ten, he estimated. A perfect height for a woman. She was not exactly beautiful but she had that provocative ambiguity
that is so malleable to fantasy: Catharine Gaillard could
be anything he chose.

The door of the forward cabin slid open. Bright
blinding sunlight tore into the plane like a flash flood,
drenching everything with a wave of hot humid Mediterranean air. Outside, the steps were locked against the
plane door amid a bustle of co-ordinated activity.

Philippe fastened the middle button of his single-
breasted jacket. He had chosen his suit carefully that
morning. The slim red ribbon of the Legion of Honor
looked best against a dark-gray background. Blue was
too obvious. He adjusted his cuffs and discreetly
checked his fly with a casual downward sweep of his
right hand. Catharine noted the movement: Philippe reminded her of an actor standing in the wings, waiting
for his cue.

Satisfied and composed, knowing his lines and every
gesture, Philippe made his way toward his own private
stage.

He paused at the top of the mobile stairway.

It looked, as he had meant it to look, like an emotional hesitation, a sudden piquant qualm.

The photographers jostled each other at the foot of the ramp, anxious to capture this first moment of his historic homecoming.

Philippe contrived to look sad, burdened, determined. He half-lifted his left hand in a small salute, his palm with its deep multiple fate lines facing the cameras. (The New York *Daily Mirror* would later blow up and publish on its front page one of these pictures of Philippe's palm with a sensational prediction by the English clairvoyant Waldo Bragg.)

The sky was so blue it hurt Philippe's eyes. He blinked hard several times. He knew exactly the impression he was creating. Audacity may have created kings, but it was playacting that sustained princes.

He did not find it a difficult role to perform at all.

He was almost enjoying himself.

He became conscious of Father Cornelius' measuring stare as he descended the steps. At the bottom he solemnly shook hands with Duclos and Brand. He turned to Roberto Cheroffini and pressed his shoulders between his hands, a cabalistic grip, and kissed his cheeks with affection.

The cameras clattered like easing rifle bolts. It made a good picture.

Cheroffini had been in charge of his early education before Philippe went to Charterhouse in England.

Philippe noticed that the photographers did not take a single picture when he shook the hand of Leon Kun from the Finance Ministry.

"I'm Kun," the little finance official said.

"I know who you are, or you wouldn't be here," Philippe told him quietly.

The photographers couldn't get enough shots of his meeting with Dieter Stosch.

They had done their homework.

Philippe shook the controller's hand firmly but briefly. Their eyes met determinedly. Stosch's eyes were the color of tool steel. Philippe had deliberately not invited him to Dauphin. Nevertheless, Philippe was careful to give him a small candid smile of gratitude. It was always an advantage to let others think they have duped you.

The Prince turned and walked swiftly toward Father Cornelius, who was waiting beside a black Mercedes. There were no handshakes between the two men. The priest nodded his head as he opened the door of the limousine. No words were spoken. Philippe lowered his head and climbed in and slid across the black leather seat to the opposite corner in one smooth movement. Cornelius followed him almost at once. The chauffeur closed the door behind them. The whole business took seconds.

Philippe's sudden exit surprised the press men. They came running across the apron as the car pulled away, sending a flutter of strolling gulls a few feet into the air.

The photographers took pictures of the departing car as it gathered speed.

The gulls returned to earth.

The press men gathered in a group.

"So, tell me the news?" Philippe said, turning toward the priest.

"He had a very bad night. I have administered Extreme Unction. I felt you should be here."

"Yes. Thank you," Philippe answered.

"He rallied at about seven-thirty this morning. A small rally. We had a conversation. For a few minutes he was quite lucid. I told him you were on your way."

"I haven't seen my father for three years," Philippe said. "When I think of him now I think of him as he was when I was a child. I think of him in his uniform. He was a handsome man, but too weak."

"Felix Blundell has been here since Tuesday but he's returning to London tonight. He says there's nothing more he can do that the local doctors can't do just as well at this stage."

"Did he get his knighthood, Blundell?"

"Next time apparently," Cornelius said, remembering Philippe's fascination with such things.

"Ah," said the Prince. "Next time."

The two men lapsed into silence. The car gathered speed as it moved through the airport's manicured gardens. Sprinklers languidly twisted sprays like pearled lassos over stiff-bladed lawns. The car moved onto the access road and merged with the motorway traffic gathering speed. The longest stretch of the motorway formed the giant causeway connection to the mainland, at La Tour Fondue, and was another legacy of the German occupation. The chauffeur stopped accelerating at 55 miles per hour and kept the needle steady. The priest pressed a button by his left hand and the partition between them and the driver closed with the sound of scissored silk.

"Something's happening but I don't know what," Cornelius said quietly, staring straight ahead. It was a sentence that seemed to be part of another, much longer conversation. And in a way it was.

"Who's with me?" Philippe half turned in his seat and looked hard at Cornelius.

The priest's grizzled slum-saint face gave a peculiar intensity to his green eyes, which were the color of crème de menthe frappé.

"Duclos and Cheroffini are hard to fathom." Cornelius had a thoughtful expression. "They're ambitious guys."

"God's chicken! They're seventy years old," Philippe said in a quiet incredulous voice. "How can you be seventy years old and ambitious?"

"Perhaps when you get to be—" Cornelius began.

"Cheroffini, maybe. Duclos—we'll see. Where does the Englishman stand?"

"Alwyn Brand?"

"Alwyn Brand," Philippe said. His voice had no expression.

"A floating voter. A pragmatist. We can get him." There was a long silence.

"So, you, maybe Cheroffini, Alwyn Brand." Philippe said at last. "Stosch's got the heads of departments, I presume?"

"Kun, of course."

"Kun." Philippe smiled his search-and-destroy smile. "The sergeant! I wouldn't trust him to make change at Prisunic. The others? The Analysis Directorate? What about Records? The Intelligence and Surveillance people? The desk lady?"

The desk lady. Philippe knew the jargon well. He knew a great deal more about the Bureau than Cornelius thought possible. "St. Saladin's just another company town. They're all nice to the boss," the priest said softly.

"Who the hell was for my father? What could he have been thinking of?"

The priest shrugged, his face impassive, his hands tucked in his armpits. "Stosch runs the casino. The casino pays the wages, determines the economy," he said.

"An economy based on the whims of gamblers and whores," Philippe said dismissively. "What's that? Clickola prosperity. You don't run that. You reap it."

"Maybe so, but he's accountable to no parliament, to no public opinion, no shareholders. It's a strong hand. He has the means of paying his personal spies, his informers. Your father couldn't move against him without somebody warning him beforehand. He has made himself feared—and that sure beats respect."

"I've been away too long," Philippe said.

The limousine sped quietly along the highway. They traveled through hills and woods that changed color, unfolded, altered texture by the minute: now khaki, now glistening green, now wind-tousled and sultry and scarred. A tiny kingdom the color of dried blood and prinked with minuscule brush strokes. A small land exhausted and bludgeoned and buried by time. A wondrous land. Philippe's land.

Philippe watched the priest. He wondered how old the American was: he thought fifty, although the white, almost shaggy hair made him look older than that.

"Hans Dieter Stosch," Cornelius said slowly. He was aware of Philippe's gaze. "He was born with teeth and stubble."

"An ogre?" Philippe said. He was smiling cynically, watching the priest all the time. Cornelius was very still, laboriously staring ahead, like a man sitting for his portrait.

"A martinet. He's an intelligent man. Never underestimate him. An intelligent man who knows how to use intelligent men. He has . . . control. A great calm."

"Maybe this control, this calm—maybe it's just . . . insensibility?" Philippe said.

"And his silence is what? Ignorance? I don't think so."

"Men have drowned in the shallows—looking for the unplumbed depths of a schlemiel."

"Stosch is no schlemiel, Your Highness."

"You speak with the authority of a man of God, of course."

"Of course," Cornelius said, staring ahead.

"What else?"

"When it comes down to the wire—he doesn't buy his way out," Cornelius said.

"Then?"

"He is a violent man. Controlled violence—the deterrent philosophy."

Philippe smiled and thought for a moment and then he said, "Violence is a detail of state, a corporate gambit. We must all do disagreeable things sometimes."

"You approve?"

"Violence is as statutory with governments today as it is with the *milieu*."

"The *milieu*?"

"The *pègre*—the underworld."

"The mob," the priest muttered.

"If I'm going to walk through the valley of the shadow of death, Father Cornelius, I've got to be *numero uno*."

"What you mean is—"

"What I say."

"If that—"

"If that means being the meanest son of a bitch in the valley, so be it."

Cornelius gave a grin. He felt curiously at home with Philippe's unexpected American phrases. He'd almost forgotten that the Prince had been attached to American units for most of the war. He'd been with the U.S. 1st Division for the invasions of Sicily and Italy.

"You can bleach my soul later," Philippe said.

"It's one interpretation of Psalm 23."

"It's the only realistic one."

The priest lifted his white eyebrows but didn't argue

the point. Instead he said quietly, "Cut off your enemy's testicles, he'll still be your enemy. Even sopranos scratch."

"Who's talking about cutting off a man's balls?" Philippe said without smiling. "Princes are privileged to kill."

It was hard to tell when Philippe was being serious. Cornelius said carefully, "Compromise is sometimes—"

"I don't want Dieter Stosch pressing the juice of his inheritance in my valley," Philippe said abruptly. He sounded on edge for the first time.

Cornelius continued to look ahead, into the middle distance of no-man's-land. It was safer out there, he thought.

"I was surprised to see Stosch at Dauphin," he said, after a suitable silence.

"J'embrasse mon rival, mais c'est pour l'etouffer," Philippe said quietly. The calm was back in his voice.

"Je ne sais pas," Cornelius said. "I'm still struggling with *la plume de ma tante.*"

"I embrace my rival, but I do so to choke him. One of De Gaulle's favorite sayings. He stole it from Racine. Racine probably stole it from a lavatory wall."

"Obviously lavatory walls aren't what they used to be."

"Oh?" It was Philippe's turn to press up an eyebrow.

"I like to see what's on the menu," Cornelius said. "Even when I'm not allowed to order."

Philippe grinned. The remark seemed to relax him. "You've done a good job, Cornelius. Thank you."

"Thank your father. It was his idea to get an American in. The Italians couldn't squawk. Even the French couldn't think of anything to bellyache about. Cornelius Compromise, that's me." He turned and looked at Philippe quickly. "At least I keep their heads down."

He was a little heavier than Philippe remembered him, his hair whiter and longer. He had the sort of craggy dependable face that is often a rallying point in a tavern brawl. It was a face that would pass muster in a cathedral or a cathouse. David Cornelius was an historical throwback: priest-politician. He didn't miss a thing. Recommended by Cardinal Spellman, he had been St.

Saladin's court prelate for eleven years. Philippe could buy the consciences of twenty ordinary priests; he wanted this man's mind, a mind precisely suited to a life at court.

"I was thanking you for what you've done for me, keeping me in touch," Philippe said. "I know it wasn't always easy—walking that tightrope. So . . . thank you."

"This morning," Cornelius said, changing the subject with the abruptness of the embarrassed, "your father seemed to be altering his mind about something. He said he was wrong."

"You cannot imagine how that interests me now," Philippe said drily. He had a look of amusement mingled with genuine interest. Cornelius went on as if the Prince had not said a word.

"He said he was wrong and to tell you—'*from strength.*'"

"'From strength'?"

"That was all he said." Cornelius shook his head. "It was near the end of his . . . rally. He was well-nigh incoherent. He mentioned Stosch's name."

"What did he say about Stosch? Tell me. *Exactly.*"

"Just his name." The priest frowned, trying to remember. "Then something about treachery. 'A kind of treachery, a sort of treachery.'"

Philippe's face showed everything and nothing, like a Rorschach spillover. "I was away too long," he said again. He sounded oddly detached, as if recalling an expensive lesson.

"You're back now," Cornelius said. "The politics begin."

"We have no politics in St. Saladin. Just power. You either have the power—or you have zero. You call it a shutout, I believe."

"A shutout," Cornelius said. He suddenly felt homesick. How ridiculous for a man to be homesick, he thought. It wasn't the old familiar phrase that triggered it; it nearly always happened after he'd dreamed about his mother. "No train ever passes through St. Louis." She used to recite the legend to impress on him the pointlessness of ever leaving that important city. But he'd watched the beautiful locomotive engines in their traps, shining and feline, straining to get out, to scorch across the land—the Diplomat, the Colorado Eagle, the Rebel, the Knickerbocker. He always knew he would leave on one of them one day.

"It's a hard thing to be a prince. But that's what I am," Philippe said after a long silence. "I'm a prince. That's my trade. I intend to practice it."

Cornelius had no doubts. Philippe *was* a prince. He lived in a world where there were no options, no alternatives. He'd been born into the prince business. It was like belonging to a tribe. Or a religion.

The car hit a dog on the road.

"Go on," Phillipe ordered the driver, who was beginning to slow down.

Like all good killers, Philippe never looked back.

The car moved swiftly through the low-lying plains where a bloody battle recorded by Tacitus was fought in A.D. 67. Within fifteen minutes they were on the outskirts of the town.

St. Saladin was arranged like a vast and beautiful amphitheater on slopes of startling steepness. It was a walled town. The wall had crumbled in many places now and so had the old watchtowers that had been built every few hundred yards or so, but the two great gates remained. They entered through the west gate.

The driver dropped down to little more than ten miles an hour. He began to twist and turn through sagging patternless streets made for ambush and built for barricades. Streets designed as trenches against artillery, mysterious unpaved thoroughfares, death traps for the cavalry.

The Germans came in 1940 with their tank landing ships. St. Saladin fell inside forty minutes.

Not a shot was fired.

Philippe and Father Cornelius entered the Royal Palace at twenty-seven minutes past two o'clock.

Fragments of white plaster stuck to Prince Maximilien's blueing lips; plaster caked his hairline like calcified dandruff.

The maskmaker had come and gone.

The old Prince had a painless sculpted look.

He had been dead for little more than an hour.

Philippe kissed his father's forehead with more a sense of protocol than reverence, or love. As he did so he remembered kneeling down and kissing the marble floor of the palace when he was seven years old because his father had said that Carrara was the temperature and the texture of death.

But his father was wrong.

The dead were colder and harder than that.

9

"Mr. Strauss on two, Mr. Hammond." A woman of about forty-five poked her head around the door. She looked like the kind of woman who smells of lemon slivers and Earl Grey tea.

"Thank you, Molly," Hammond said. He stepped behind his old-fashioned partners' desk and sat down in the tall wing chair.

"Biron. Good morning to you. We're lunching today?" Hammond gave a small bored smile to the chandelier, admiring its fanciful drops and pinnacles of fleurs-de-lis. "Good show," he said after a while. A bored smile had atrophied on his face. He surveyed his oak-paneled room. A brass-inlaid bookcase filled with leather-bound volumes covered the wall facing his desk. A set of hand-tinted Old London engravings hung on the wall between the tall narrow windows behind him. It was a beautiful office. He would hate having to give it up. Warren said you could lose a golf ball in the rough of the carpet. A brown Chesterfield couch, four armchairs, and a zebra-wood games table still left the room with a spacious feeling.

"It's a sickness of the world," Hammond said after a few minutes. "Maybe the Chancellor will double the

Production Fund in the autumn budget." He held the telephone a few inches from his ear as Strauss said something in a voice that was much too loud. It was extraordinary how the slightest trace of a foreign accent was exaggerated on the telephone.

After a few more moments, Hammond said, almost abruptly, "Shall we say twelve forty-five at the Caprice, then? Fine. See you then, my friend."

He replaced the receiver and looked at his half-smoked cigarette with narrowed eyes. It was the sort of look that would sit perfectly beneath a judge's black cap. He stubbed the cigarette out with one twist and buzzed the intercom.

"Book a table at the Caprice for one o'clock, will you, Molly dear?" He spoke with his mouth close to the prewar machine on the corner of his desk.

"Two?"

"Yes."

"Shall I order the car?"

"I think not. The walk will do me good."

Molly Longman was one of those excellent English secretaries who spend weekends in the country with old unseen friends. "An old maid not unmade," Warren had said accurately. Hammond had been there. A one-night stand in Brussels. It had been a good night for both of them. But neither he nor Miss Longman had ever mentioned it since. Sometimes Hammond wondered whether he'd imagined the whole business. But he hadn't. He didn't have that sort of imagination. And there was still the smallest deepest whitest scar on his left shoulder that a forensic specialist could no doubt match up with a molar somewhere in Molly's mouth. That mouth butter wouldn't melt in.

At twelve-twenty, she came back with a red leather portfolio filled with the letters she had typed that morning to Masters' bereaved fans.

"It's still raining," she reminded Hammond in a voice starched with Rodean respectability. She stood by his side and watched him sign each short letter with his small monkish signature.

Hammond hesitated, his fountain pen poised over the last letter, and considered the sky. He had no idea what he expected to see up there. He'd read somewhere that most Englishmen could predict the weather because the government had withheld meteorological forecasts for security reasons in the war. He wasn't one of them. He only knew that when it rained a lot of movies went over budget and everybody seemed surprised. Apparently none of those English weathercocks worked in the movie business.

"I should think it'll clear up in ten minutes or so," he said, for no reason. He finished his signature, blotted it carefully, and handed the portfolio back to Molly Longman.

"Anyway I want to walk. I don't get nearly enough exercise," he said in his mild colorless voice. He had eliminated every trace of class, history, even feeling from that voice. It was a voice softened with a kind of interrogator's anodyne, a voice without prejudice or passion, a voice which contained neither credulity nor trust. In the twelve years she had worked for him, only once had Molly Longman heard it contain any feeling, any warmth, any real . . . passion. Just that once. It was as if he had revealed a terrible weakness within himself, a secret failing. It was a secret they shared but never talked about. But Molly Longman thought about it. She thought about it a lot.

When she had gone, Hammond stood up and began to pace around the office in slow wide circles, his hands clasped behind his back. It was natural that the death of an old friend should set him musing about his own life. He was fifty-six now, fifty-seven in August. He felt fit. He had kept his weight down to one-seventy, although it crept up to one-seventy-three some evenings after a good dinner. He was relatively abstemious, although he smoked too much. He had never been under a surgeon's knife in his life. But, apart from the cosmetic surgery on his nose and around the eyes, neither had Warren Masters.

There was a time when Lionel Hammond believed that a man who was able to check the willful forces of instinct within himself was able to determine his own fate. It had been a naive presumption. He recognized that now. And he recognized what life had done to him to change his mind.

You can't annul fate as if it were a bad contract or a lousy marriage. A man doesn't die because he is sick or too old, or because he drives his car too fast or boards the wrong plane . . . or even because he falls asleep with a cigarette burning between his lips. A man dies because he has been born. Birth was man's first lousy contract.

"What's the name of that church they call the actors' church, Molly?" He spoke into the big box on his desk. "The one in Covent Garden."

"St. Paul's," Molly's voice crackled with alarming static.

"I want to talk with the vicar after lunch. We must arrange some sort of memorial service."

Molly Longman made a note.

"What was he, Molly? A Protestant?"

"I've really no idea. Would you like me to find out?"

"It's not that important. Let's talk to the vicar. Find out what the form is about these things."

Lionel Hammond left his office at twelve-forty. It was a good ten-minute walk to Arlington Street. He was in no particular hurry to meet Biron Strauss. The rain had stopped. He crossed the square and strolled at a leisurely pace along Berkeley Street toward the Ritz.

The sun was surprisingly warm when it broke through the billowy white-fringed clouds, and strong enough to create those illusory puddles of water on the drying pavements. Somewhere at the back of his mind Hammond recalled Masters' saying that he was an atheist. Hammond wondered whether a memorial service would be appropriate after all.

He was already eight minutes late when he turned into Piccadilly. He didn't walk any faster. As he waited for the traffic signals to change at the corner of Dover Street, he saw Biron Strauss on the other side of Piccadilly turning into St. James'. The agent turned away from the curb and studied a window filled with tartan cloth. He didn't want to be seen actually arriving at the Caprice with Strauss.

Biron Strauss had turned up in London in 1948 and

almost at once put together a low-budget thriller in partnership with the late Lew Bannenberg. The couple became known as the B-hivers.

Strauss was carefully reticent as to his ancestry. His German accent had been unmistakable before Marie Kordermann, the voice coach, helped him develop a mid-Atlantic sound. "He says he is a Jew but I don't believe him," Lew Bannenberg said. "He's a Jew like Jolson's a jigaboo."

A Biron Strauss picture seldom sold in the markets outside Britain and the Commonwealth. But he prepared his budgets with a scalpel and never failed to turn a fat personal profit. To give his pictures what he called "global clout," he always cast an aging Hollywood "name" in the lead. "The nostalgia mileage left in those Hollywood retreads is amazing," he said in a trade-paper interview. He was sued for libel and disappeared for a year, owing several thousand pounds around town to restaurants, process laboratories, cutting studios, and to his tailor.

During his absence several pictures were made in Ireland by a producer named S. T. Rauss.

Strauss had been back in circulation for about a year. His debts settled, his pictures carried his own name again—that is, the name he came to London with in 1948.

"It was sad news about Warren," Strauss said when the two men were seated at a large round table on the far right at the wrong end of the room. Hammond didn't mind. Agents got seated according to the status of their guests. It was a fate they shared with journalists and publicity people. They were now in a part of the restaurant where the waiters watched over the diners with more an air of surveillance than service. The table had been laid for four. A waiter removed the surplus cutlery.

"He was a lovely man. He always wanted to do a picture for me, you know." Biron Strauss spoke with the studied care of a man not using his own language. "He always said to me, 'Biron, my darling'—you know how he always called everybody darling and dear heart, man or woman it didn't matter—'you come up with the

right script, Biron, and I'll do it for you for nothing. I
owe you.' He loved me. I loved him. I knew him . . . I
knew him when, as the saying goes."

"I didn't know that," Hammond said.

"Sure. He came to me—he still had his army haircut.
Like a convict he looked. He came up to the office I
had in those days. In Berwick Street. His discharge papers were still wet, I swear to you."

The timing of Strauss's story was all wrong. Warren
Masters had been discharged from the navy, not the
army, in 1945, at least three years before the producer
turned up in London. Hammond didn't bother to point
out the discrepancy. Movie reminiscences would be dull
stuff without the contradictions, and without the incom-
patibilities of historical coloring.

"I can see him now, God rest his soul. Standing in
front of my desk. 'I want to be an actor, Mr. Strauss. I
want to be a star.' Right away I see he has it. He's like a
guy with six pair of balls, like a bunch of grapes. I tell
him go to the provinces, get into a good rep company,
learn the trade of acting, learn the business, then come
talk to me. I give him a straight steer. He never forgot
that. Never."

"I didn't realize Warren had worked in the provinces," Hammond said in his mild, deceptive voice.

"He didn't. The way it turned out, Bob Rabin at
RKO put him in that piece of shit they shot in Yugosla-
via to use up all that blocked dinar. They should have
left it blocked. A piece of shit."

"That piece of shit that grossed $17 million?" said
Hammond.

"He never forgot my advice," Strauss said.

He ordered Dutch smoked eel and Boeuf Strogonoff.
"Did you go to the funeral, Lionel?" he asked when the
agent had given his order to the waiter.

"There was a private service. There wasn't much of
Caesar to bury."

"There is nothing certain in this world. If anything is
subject to the whims of chance it is life. A little too
much cold, or heat, not to mention all the other things
that can happen, and we move from existence to eternity."

"Warren died from too much heat," Hammond said. "Nothing is privileged against fate, Lionel. Not money, not youth, not even talent."

Strauss smelled of cologne. His sulphur-colored tan came from a lamp and looked like makeup in artificial light and jaundice in the open. His hair had been dyed mahogany brown, except for the temples which had been left untouched. The gray was meant to give him a distinguished air. It merely emphasized the bluff. In his blue silk-shantung suit and built-up shoes, Strauss reminded Hammond of a male impersonator. One capable of killing with her bare hands.

The smoked eel arrived. Hammond skipped the first course. The evening before he had weighed one-seventy-two. The wine steward offered Hammond the list. "We'll have a bottle of the Lafite. That all right with you, Biron? The Lafite? You're having Strogonoff, yes?"

"The Lafite is fine," Strauss said. He bent his head close to the eel and didn't look up until it was all gone. It didn't take two minutes. He pushed the plate away with his thumb. His fingernails were manicured and varnished, a vanity which drew unnecessary attention to the corkscrew deformation of the index finger on his right hand.

"Did you see the Easter returns for *The Amsterdam Job*?"

"No," Hammond said. He tried to remember something about the picture.

"Fantastic. I've made seventeen pictures now, Lionel. And not one turkey. Okay, all right, clambakes, program pictures. But the worst I've done is break even. Not bad. Aren't you supposed to get as many turkeys with the little ones—seventy percent. Am I right or am I right?"

"If you get hurt with a big one you really catch your nuts in the mangle."

"Seventeen," Strauss said. He exuded an astonishing air of confidence in his pictures and in his own judgment. His wallet always contained trade press reports giving the receipts of his latest production. It was raw energy and a certain amount of pure larceny that made Biron Strauss successful.

"I got Pat O'Brody over for that one," Strauss said. He slid a *Kine Weekly* review across the table beneath the flat palm of his hand, like a spy passing secrets.

"Pat Brody," corrected Hammond quietly.

"In all those old Warner pictures," said Strauss. "Cagney, Bogart, Raft and O'Brody. He still means something. The kids today, they love him. He's an occult figure."

"He's what?"

"An occult figure. The British Film Institute, they even want him to lecture. Art and the Chicago Mowing Machine. He's an occult figure."

"A cult figure," Hammond said, working it out.

"The kids, they love him."

"He has a great face," Hammond said. "One of the great gangster faces."

"He's a nuclear scientist in *The Amsterdam Job*."

"That was very imaginative of you, Biron." Hammond's voice conveyed nothing but the words he spoke.

"He's a bit unsteady on his pins now. We couldn't shoot him moving too much. It gave us problems in the last chase sequence. The critics loved that chase. Around the Whispering Gallery. You know—in St. Paul's?"

Hammond wondered where cult figures ended and geriatrics began.

"He looks older when he moves," Strauss said. He carefully folded the *Kine* review and returned it to his wallet. He slipped the wallet into his inside breast pocket. "Next time like as not I'll just release the stills." He grinned. "Art and the fucking Chicago Mowing Machine. Who are these guys kidding?" They sat in silence for a while.

Hammond looked around the restaurant. The place was full. He knew at least a dozen faces, apart from the famous faces that everybody knew. He wished he'd bought into the place when he had the chance. It was too late now.

"Now, Lionel, I want to tell you . . . My next one is going to be my big one. I've been threatening you with

it for a long time. Now I've got it together. A great
story, the money, a great director—"

"Who is?" Hammond knew how to cut to the heart of
bullshit.

"Renato Alighieri."

"That's not bad, Biron."

"Only the best thing to come out of Italy since Sil-
vana Mangano."

"Alighieri's very good," Hammond admitted. *"Via
Death* has grossed $4 million. He brought it in for un-
der $170,000."

"He's still wet behind the ears. He gave them
change." Strauss almost sneered.

A waiter arrived with the Strogonoff followed by a
waiter with a medium filet steak for Hammond. The
wine steward opened the Lafite. He poured a taste into
Hammond's glass. Hammond went through the sipping-
smelling routine and nodded his approval. Strauss
waited impatiently for the activity around them to melt
away.

"Alighieri is working over the script in Rome. With
Emil Siegelman," Strauss said as softly and as casually
as he could when all the waiters had gone.

"The man who wrote *Danger East*?" A careful ear
might have detected the very faintest hint of surprise in
Lionel Hammond's voice.

"Lionel, this *is Danger East.*"

"How on earth did you get your hands on that, Biron? Every major studio in the business has been—"

Strauss tapped the side of his nose with the crooked
index finger. "Let us say I've made a very interesting
deal with Mr. Siegelman." Strauss sighed. "I've made
the break, Lionel."

"Just mind your balls," Hammond said. His voice
was impassive, but his eyes were no longer bored.

"We go in the autumn in Spain with two weeks of
interiors at Elstree." Strauss sipped his wine and replaced the glass on the table without comment. He patted his full wet lips slowly with the rose-colored napkin,
which he held to his mouth with both hands. It was an
effeminate gesture, like a woman blotting fresh lipstick.
He furled the napkin and laid it alongside his plate.

"Now, Lionel," he said. "I'm looking for the girl. You've read the book. Of course you have. Everybody has. A modern face, but classy. Sexy, cool, somebody who—"

"You should get your man first. You can't get the girl in focus until you've got your Jem Farrar. Warren would have been perfect. The accent might have been a problem. But if you go with somebody like—"

"Montgomery Clift," Strauss said. He failed to stop a small smirk buckling his mouth.

"You've got Clift?"

"If I want him. He's keen as mustard. But I don't know. I hear that he can be trouble. A little difficulty with the . . ." Strauss rocked an imaginary glass close to his mouth. "Maybe I'll shoot for a couple of unknowns. With Alighieri maybe that's best."

"Well," said Hammond. He could have meant anything.

Biron Strauss seemed lost in some remote idea. At last he bent his new-colored head toward the agent. "This girl you have? Georgina Gam—"

"Game."

"It could do things for a girl like that," Strauss said. "You could use a new biggie on your books."

Hammond ignored the gibe. "We'd have to see a script," he said.

"I'm not showing anyone anything until the boys have got it right. The script we have now is good but it's too . . . workmanlike."

Hammond looked at him with a carefully blank face. "We'll have to see something on paper, Biron."

"What's her price these days, by the way?"

"Fifteen thousand," Hammond said without missing a beat.

"I heard less than that," Strauss said. "A lot less. What did Carol Reed pay for that bit she did for him?"

"She's moving up all the time. A year from now you won't be able to talk to me about Georgina Game for less than thirty thousand pounds. Carol paid what was right eight months ago. Ask him to show you her café scene with Warren. He says she's the best thing since Viv Leigh."

Hammond's diffidence enabled him to trade in superlatives with plausible humility.

"I'd probably pay the fifteen," Strauss said. "But let's get one thing straight. I want total commitment. Postproduction publicity, interviews, personal appearances. All the bullshit. I don't want an absent star when I come to sell the product."

"How's the Strogonoff?" Hammond asked politely.

"I'm told her ego isn't always in the right place. Is that right, Lionel?" Strauss persisted.

"She isn't mad about personal publicity, if that's what you mean."

"She'll just have to get mad. I don't aim to buy a hundred twenty pounds of smoke." Biron Strauss was serious. He finally had his hands on the big one. He had fought off the pack. He had come through from nowhere—literally from nowhere. He had hustled and cheated and lied but he had never been afraid, he had never been scared off by the noise and the clamor of the battle. Lionel Hammond admired him for that. Strauss's pursuit of recognition had an air of revenge for some deep personal injury. It wasn't pleasant but Hammond had seen it before in other men and he understood it now.

"This one's the big tilt, Lionel, the headline event."

"What's the budget?"

"I'll bring it in at a million-two," Strauss said.

"Dollars?"

"Dollars. Forty-three shooting days."

"Color?"

"Eastman."

"It sounds all there, Biron."

"It's all there. I can't afford mistakes at this stage of the game. You know what I mean?"

"Of course."

"I know this book. I've read it in English, I've read it in German, in French. Even the goddam author hasn't done that. It's got everything, whatever language. It's as global as greed. And the girl's part . . . Let me tell you, Lionel, it's better than you are."

Hammond smiled at the idea.

"So, anyway," Strauss said. "You say ten thousand pounds for the girl."

"Fifteen," said Hammond.

"Don't overdrive the green, my friend."

"It's still fifteen."

Strauss sighed heavily, the sigh of a misunderstood benefactor. "You're a hard man, Hammond," he said. "But if I go with Monty Clift, and if he approves of your girl—you've got yourself a deal."

He offered Hammond his hand.

"Biron, we've got no deal," Hammond said, ignoring the hand. "We've got nothing until we see a script."

"Jesus Christ, Lionel. Your girl should be paying *me* fifteen grand to be in the picture."

It was a line that could have been banter or bluster or simply a producer's gambit, but Hammond sensed it covered something more than irritability: Biron Strauss had malice in his voice.

Strauss recognized it too. He said quickly, smiling: "I'm a good guy. I'll still pay you the money."

"Have you got a starting date?"

"Probably September fifteenth, no later than the thirtieth."

"I'll talk to Georgina," Hammond said. He made a note. He made a note of everything.

10

"He's got Alighieri. He's getting out a script with Siegelman in Rome now. He's ready to pay fifteen thousand."

"It's still a Biron Strauss picture, Lionel," Georgina Game said quietly. She wondered just how serious her agent was. The unrevealing blandness of his recitation annoyed her. He could be too donnish, too bloody bookish sometimes. It was so exhausting trying to figure out what he really felt about anything. She said, "Once a Biron Strauss always a Biron Strauss, that's what I say."

"Forget Strauss for a moment. Put him out of your mind. We are talking about an Alighieri picture. A book by one of the best American writers since—since Mailer. We're talking about Monty Clift."

"Mr. Clift is lovelier than the moon," Georgina said.

"Trans-Investments is putting up seventy percent of the money," Hammond said. "Film Finance are in for ten. It's a safe operation. Moneywise it's as safe as houses."

There was a long silence before Georgina Game said anything.

"Last year we turned down . . . how many pictures? Seven? We were being selective. We were being careful. Now, suddenly, we are talking about involving ourselves with this . . . fifth-rate person. I don't believe this is happening to me, Lionel."

"It's basically an attractive offer," Hammond said. "Let's wait for the script before closing the door."

"*You* wait for the script if you want to, Lionel. As far as I'm concerned the door was never open, not even the tiniest crack."

Georgina replaced the telephone with a languid arc of her naked arm.

She said, "Darling, do that again. Yes, there!"

Richard Antrobus slipped his finger expertly between her lips, teasing the spot as she turned on her side toward him. "Give us this day our diurnal coitus," he said.

"You're a wicked man. You know far too much about ladies." She picked up the rhythm of his small gentle circling movements with two fingers on his mouth. "You make me feel as horny as hell. And you have a very mean mouth."

"I used to have a generous mouth but I gave most of it away," he said. He slowly licked her circling fingers.

"You have a childish sense of humor. Has anyone ever told you that?"

Antrobus curled two fingers inside her, behind the pubic bone, and urged her toward him with just enough roughness to both thrill and threaten her. She moaned and pushed herself toward him. "Oh unendurable apocalyptic pleasure. I adore a man who knows how to be mean in bed."

Richard Antrobus kissed her wide glistening forehead like an evangelist blessing a pious child. "What was that little drama all about?" His fingers stayed gently hooked inside her, caressing now but poised to hurt. His sense of control over her, the almost menacing contiguity of his embrace, thrilled Georgina in quite an extraordinary way.

She said, "My agent has found me a lovely picture . . . but. A big but."

"A big but what?" He flexed his fingers, prompting, a careful torturer increasing an electric charge. Georgina made a sound somewhere between exhortation and protest.

"But—the producer is an absolute louse. Bye-bye lovely picture. Life is too short." Her voice sounded small and broken. They lay very close, very still, facing each other in the wide bed, caught in each other's sudorous warmth. The room was becoming indistinct with early dusk. She lifted the side of her face onto his chest, half turning her body onto his. His hair was very damp and had curled into ringlets. She could hear his heart pumping like a muffled drum-beat through his firm unaccentuated pectoral muscle. He had a lean sexy body with a chic cover of flesh, thin as Job paper. Richard Antrobus reminded her of the Canova sculpture of Perseus. A body forged by passion. "I'd have to be crazy to even think about it," she said.

"Are you going to be a great big movie star, Miss Game?"

"Why? Are you a star fucker, Mr. Antrobus?"

"Yes. Are you going to be a great big movie star?"

"Of course," Georgina Game said seriously.

"And do you always get what you want?"

"I guess," she said.

"And what do you want exactly?"

"More," she said.

The crescentic grip of his two fingers inside her slowly intensified . . . threatening, promising. "Oh yes

. . . *more.*" The final word was swallowed in his mouth as their teeth touched. She took hold of his wrist and tried to force the rhythm.

"Shhh," he said.

He turned her onto her back. He watched her face all the time with a kind of hungry assurance. Kneeling above her, he ran his hand slowly between her legs from her knees to the top of her thighs.

"Now open," he said gently.

She spread her legs. He stared shamelessly down at her. "You have the most amazingly beautiful body," he said.

He knew it sounded trite, but he always said it. When he really meant it—and he truly meant it now—the words sounded inadequate, and cheap. He was touched by a sense of sadness at the thought that his love talk had ceased to have validity. He had forgotten how to be sincere, how to be spontaneous in bed. He had never been sincere and spontaneous when he was not in bed, of course. Nobody ever is. But there was a time, in bed . . . Now all the compliments he paid, all the promises he made, all the soft endearments—they were just words he had learned too well and trotted out too often. *I used to have a generous mouth but I gave most of it away.* When had he first said that to a girl? There must have been a time when it was said spontaneously, when he had thought it amusing too.

"I want you to look at me," Georgina told him. She lifted her left foot level with her right knee and let her steepled leg topple outward. Her luminous blond hair became the apex of a voluptuous triangle. "Now," she reached for him, "I want you *now.*"

He slid into her quickly up to the hilt. She gasped as their pubic bones hit hard against each other, butting, forcing, each refusing to submit. Georgina came first, muffling her scream, the back of her fist rammed into her mouth. Antrobus felt huge inside her. After a little while she whispered, "Let me." Her muscular contractions, strong and pulsing, grew around him. "Don't move," she said. "Don't move." His breath smelled of the red wine they had drunk at lunch. "Be still," she whispered. *"Be still."* Her vaginal muscles entwined him in the rhythm she wanted. She knew she was in charge now.

The turnabout was so sudden that Antrobus could not believe what had happened. He sounded like a wounded animal when he came. Georgina held him very tight. She patted his head, murmuring sounds of solace, calming sounds. She was grinning. It was beautiful. She had won.

After a little while she lit a cigarette and said, "You certainly do know how to screw a lady, Mr. Antrobus."

"You," he said. "It was *you*. That must have registered four point nine on the Richter scale."

"You're a giant gizmo performer. A herculean fuck."

"Gizmo? There's no such word."

"I've just made it up for you," Georgina said. "Gizmo. I like it. It's you."

"I always thought you were a distinguished virgin."

"You prefer virtuous women?"

"Yes . . . but I like to sleep with the other kind."

"Typical!"

"I'm pleased you're the other kind."

"I'll say this for you, Antrobus. You are the only man I know who's managed to become dissolute without losing his energy."

"I'm eternally searching for eternal fidelity."

"Tell me. Did you think you would get me into the sack so quickly?"

"Did I have a Game plan, you mean?"

"Be serious."

"I was under the impression you had got *me* into bed. This *is* your apartment?"

"*Did* you?"

"I always play better away from home."

"*Did* you?"

"Well . . . four hours is very good, but it isn't quite the record," Antrobus said.

"Good." Georgina twisted out her half-smoked cigarette in an ashtray she held in her lap. She sat cross-legged at the top of the bed, naked to the waist, the sheet carelessly covering her loins. "I would hate to be thought of as some sort of record," she said. "Records are so vulnerable these days."

"But memories are forever," Antrobus said.

"So long as you remember to write them down," Georgina said. She put the ashtray on the small table by the side of the bed.

"I never do, alas. Write them down," Antrobus said. He trickled his finger down her naked spine, vertebra by vertebra. "When I ran away with the divine Caroline I thought about it. But it seemed so cold-blooded. It's a pity because you really do forget so much."

Georgina sat very still, smiling at him. Her breasts were not large but set high and wide apart on her thorax. Perfect breasts should live at enmity with each other, his father had once told him. The right breast should look to the right and the left to the left. This was the first time in his life that Antrobus had seen truly perfect breasts. There was not the smallest trace of a fold beneath them. They were the same shape when she was lying down as when she was upright. He deliberately passed the back of his hand across the erect nipples. He felt, as he often felt after making love, a small sense of affection, a little amused.

"You have the most beautiful Grecian back."

Georgina said, "Tell me something about yourself."

"Such as?"

"Anything," she said. "Everything. Warts and all."

"What can I say?" he said with as much negligence as he could feign. "I'm a frightful snob. I'm more often broke than not. I belong to one of the first families in England . . . and am therefore quite treacherous. I've dabbled in most things—adultery, attempted suicide, art . . . the three A's."

Richard Antrobus listened to himself talking, listened to his familiar jokes and phrases polished with use, judging the impression he was making, cutting a few words here, adding a sentence or two someplace else. It was a scene he had played so often before. An amalgam of guile, truth, masquerade, insinuation, lies, and genuine self-revelation. Even his smile was calculated. His waiter's smile, Caroline had called it, a smile he used on flag-day collectors, cuckolded husbands and creditors alike. It was a slanting, almost shy smile. A smile he could use to charm or to freeze, with the merest adjustment of his eyes. On his passport he'd described his eyes as gunmetal gray. And his occupation: explorer.

"You should write a book," Georgina said. "You might very well be the last English gentleman left alive."

A distant lingering roll of thunder sounded outside; Georgina switched on a bedside lamp. Antrobus lay on his back, his hands tucked behind his head. He knew he looked good. He worked out at the gym every day, a fact that he never included in his *curriculum vitae*.

"I was asked to write my story for a Sunday newspaper, actually. I must say I was tempted. I was strapped to the ceiling at the time and they were offering eight thousand quid. Provided I dished all the dirt. Couldn't bring myself to do it in the end."

"I thought I *had* read your story somewhere," Georgina said.

"That was Caroline's version. They offered her *twenty* thousand. Ironic, isn't it? Money goes to money, as the saying goes. She had no qualms at all about spilling the beans."

"Good for her. Discretion is so false," Georgina said. She seldom practiced what she preached.

"She made me sound like such a shit."

"Aren't you?"

"Perhaps."

"Well then."

"Before you consider other people you must consider yourself. Before giving you have to acquire. The simple economic determinism of survival," he said. He smiled in case it sounded too unpleasant.

"What is she like? She looks very pretty in her photographs."

"Caroline Wylie?" he said, using her maiden name. "She's your average run-of-the-mill eloping white spoiled-rotten heiress. I was mad about her."

"She was quite a catch," Georgina said.

"Catching an heiress in London isn't difficult. The difficult part is to fall in love with her in spite of her boodle. Unfortunately, I managed that rather too well." There was nothing in his tone to suggest that he believed it. It was simply something he always said, a part of his patter: it gave him an aura of romantic tragedy which women seemed to like.

Georgina was still sitting in her straight-backed way. She looked down at Antrobus with a half-smile on her face. Men hated love affairs with happy endings, so why should she feel sorry for him? But, she thought, he is rather lovely. She ran her fingers through his dark brown hair; it was now almost dry after his passionate exertions.

"Was she good in bed?" she asked. Women always want to know that the moment they have a man in common.

"Not at first, but then she was a child. She was just sixteen when we legged it off to Mexico. I was twenty-six—a dirty old man, according to the popular press."

"How long did it last? The actual marriage?"

"Three years and a couple of months. It shouldn't have survived that long. The scandal kept it going in a funny sort of way. It became a sort of defiance thing, staying together. We were hopelessly incompatible."

"You became quite notorious. I knew exactly who you were the moment you walked into the room—"

"The playboy who married Caroline Wylie for her bread."

"The dirty old man who married Caroline Wylie for her bread."

"Fuck you."

"Yes please," Georgina said in a theatrical purring voice.

Antrobus kept his hands behind his head, staring at the ceiling. He was momentarily happy, and smugly tired. He was trying to remember exactly where he was—beyond the fact that he was in Georgina Game's large accommodating bed. She had driven him from the lunch party at Liz Huntington's new flat in Fulham. She had driven stylishly and fast in a small red Italian job, pushing the gears through racing changes, heel-and-toeing like a rally veteran. He'd been quite squiffy. He hadn't paid much attention to the route she weaved through the back streets, avoiding entirely the Fulham Road and Kings Road. He'd been fascinated by her bare feet. She had amazingly high insteps, he suddenly remembered. Slowly the rest of the journey began to fall into shape. He'd told her that he desired to suck her big toe and she had gone into a long and involved story (at least it seemed involved to him) about a scene in an Erich von Stroheim picture concerning a statue, a large toe, and a frustrated wife.

"People used to throw bread rolls at him in restaurants," Antrobus said.

"At whom?" Georgina asked.

"At Erich von Stroheim. The man you love to hate."

He must have been very sloshed. He smiled foolishly. At least he'd remembered the conversation: sometimes he couldn't remember what the hell he'd said. With the antennae of a drinking man he continued to feel out the situation in which he now found himself. He remembered coming into a mansion block close to Hans Place, just behind Harrods. It may have been Hans Street, or perhaps Hans Crescent. Somehow, at this stage, it seemed impolite to inquire.

The room was sparsely furnished, very cool. The bleached floor was covered by a couple of large raccoon rugs. The walls and the curtains were pale beige. The headboard was a huge old castle door lacquered white. One wall contained several Audubon prints and a framed butterfly collection in mother-of-pearl. His clothes were draped over a small paisley-covered sofa. There was a refectory table with a record player, some glossy magazines, a pre-Columbian head. A brass lamp, a small clock that had stopped at three-forty, a crystal ashtray, a packet of American cigarettes, a gold Asprey lighter and several recent novels cluttered the table on Georgina's side of the bed.

"Are you leaving, going to lie there all evening, or taking me to dinner?" Georgina said. There was a suspicion of irritability in her voice. Antrobus wasn't at all hungry; he had a slight hangover forming behind his right eye.

"Dinner, why not?"

"Then we could come back here. For a little nightcap."

"You are insatiable, woman."

"It's just your lucky day, Richard Antrobus. What's your astrological sign?"

Antrobus pretended to have to think about it. "Pisces," he said with an air of doubt. The deliberate vagueness enabled him to be precise about his actual birthday. He counted his birthday cards with as much pride today as he did in the nursery. They stayed on his mantelpiece for weeks, dusted daily like trophies; cards from beautiful ladies were especially prized.

"March the first—St. David's Day," he said.

He found it was as well to give them something to associate it with. St. David's Day was not in itself memorable like the first day of grouse shooting or the opening of the partridge season . . . but it was all there was.

"That is Pisces, isn't it? March the first?"

Georgina nodded solemnly.

"I might have known," she said. "Charming, secretive, sarcastic. Extravagant. Probably living on credit. Pisces the fish. You could have a small drink problem, too."

"I never touch small drinks," he said, using his father's pompous voice.

"Exactly. You're also a dreamer. You'll never be rich unless you inherit it—or marry it, of course."

"I've tried that, as you've so charmingly pointed out. I married millions."

Georgina slipped off the bed and retrieved her Pucci dress from the sofa.

"When I was a small girl it was my ambition to spend a million pounds in a single year. It's still a rather tempting idea," she said.

"You couldn't do it. It's just one of those things that can't be done," Antrobus said, watching her closely as she stood absolutely naked, her eyes searching the room for something.

"*I* could do it."

She picked up a hanger from beneath the table and slipped it into the silk dress. "Your trousers are going to be terribly creased," she said. She hung her dress on the back of the door. "You are an amazingly typical Pisces. Let me see your feet. I'll bet you've got tiny feet." She pulled back the sheet that covered Antrobus. "There! Size seven probably. Such pretty little feet."

"You really believe in that rubbish, don't you?"

"It isn't rubbish."

"Rubbish."

"Renoir, Chopin, Handel . . . they were all Pisces. Are you at all artistic, Mr. Antrobus?"

"I paint the toenails on my pretty feet all the time," he said.

He was angry. Disappointed that she didn't know he really was a very accomplished sculptor. Before the business with Caroline, he'd been one of the most promising protégés of his stepfather, Sir Wilfred Antrobus.

"You have to make up your mind. You can either be the best sculptor in all of England—or a kept prick," Sir Wilfred warned him when the affair was blowing up.

"I can be both," Antrobus answered too lightly.

"Then I shall never speak to you again," the old man said. And he never had. It hurt Antrobus more than anything else that had ever happened to him in his life.

Georgina picked up her lemon-colored panties from the sofa and left the room. Antrobus heard a bath being run. When she returned, she wore a pale-blue man's bathrobe. It was loosely tied at the waist and revealed her nakedness in a way that began to arouse him all over again.

"You're doing that on purpose," he said.

"No I'm not. We're going out to dinner," she said. She removed the lemon panties from a pocket in the large robe and adjusted them on her head as a mop cap.

"You look very silly," he said.

"One of the problems with Pisces men is that they never spot the main chance," she said.

"You were accusing me of opportunism a few moments ago," Antrobus pointed out.

"A few Pisces make good con men," she said. "But strictly smalltime. Nothing grand, nothing glorious, nothing really imaginative."

"Well, Miss Game, I reckon that just about sums me up in your eyes. . . ." Antrobus was smiling but he suspected it was the truth.

"Not entirely, lover," she said grinning, going toward the bed.

Afterward Antrobus said, "Shall I see you again? After tonight?"

"I don't know," she told him. "I'll have to think about it."

Georgina Game hated losers. Losers frightened her. And Richard Antrobus was the worst kind of loser of all. Because in his heart he knew what he was, and how it would end.

11

The light was fading into a June twilight the color of old parchment. Dieter Stosch sat behind a large antique desk in his office above the *salles privées* of the Princess Royale Gaming Casino. A bank of telephones connected him to the "uncles" controlling security on the casino floor. There were direct lines to the Analysis Directorate, Intelligence and Surveillance Services, Finance Control, and the Records Bureau. Steel bars covered the tall windows overlooking the courtyard. A pair of Brussels verdure hunting tapestries covered the side walls. The office was part of a large suite that had belonged to Princess Bianca. It was where she had entertained her lovers, and where she died in 1939 in a suicide pact with a handsome young banker named Hieronymous Blucher. The morbid history of the suit never worried Stosch. A photograph of the Princess stood on the marquetry table. Next to the picture were porcelain figures of Ottavio and Pantalone.

The presence in his room of Bianca's photograph, with that fixed *désolé* smile photographs of the distant dead always seem to acquire, puzzled Stosch's aides. But Dieter Stosch was not a man who invited questions.

Now, in the twilight, Stosch was studying the picture of Bianca with particular care.

Philippe's mother. It showed. It showed in the eyes. The straight aristocratic nose. It showed in the strong sensual mouth. To see a face inherited, passed along the line feature by feature—it was remarkable. That photograph told Stosch a great deal about the man he would now have to . . . deal with. His trip to the airport that afternoon had been well worthwhile. It confirmed many things in Stosch's mind. The Prince was vain but he had an insolent courage that men of his kind considered an obligation. It was a singleness of style that often faltered into fanaticism, a weakness of old family pride. Still, Philippe also had egotism and egotism was putty in the hands of men like Dieter Stosch. But egotism without ethics—that was volatile, unpredictable. It was not amenable to reason.

Stosch frowned. The expression in his eyes was grave and concerned. He returned the photograph of Bianca to the marquetry table and went back to his desk. He sat down slowly and placed his hands together, as if in prayer, on a slim red folder. He would have to tread carefully. He knew that. It was not that he hated Philippe. No. Stosch did not pursue private vendettas. Hating never concerned him. He would no more bear a grudge against a man than bear malice against a used-up tube of toothpaste. Men were simply machines of his resolve. They were bought and judged according to their usefulness. When they were no longer useful they were . . . discarded. Unfortunately, Philippe could not be discarded. He was a threat, but he was also vital to Stosch's plans.

The first faint sounds of the evening's gambling, the steady hum of multilingual conversation, the plainsong of the croupiers—the hubbub of greed—drifted up into the room. People playing hunches. People playing systems—Paroli, Labouchére, Breadwinner, Martingale, the Chaser: Stosch knew them all, and more. People calculating. People praying. People plunging. The winners, and the losers.

It wasn't a good sound. "Maggots in the millen-

nium," Maximilien had called it. "Rats gnawing at cas-
tles in the air."

Stosch got up and closed the window and went back
to his desk and sat down again with the red folder before him. Silence seemed to grow around him. He
opened a side drawer in his desk and took a tablet from
a jar. He slipped the tablet into his mouth and closed
the drawer slowly, pushing steadily with his thumb. He
had lost too much time today. What with Philippe's ar-
rival . . . and Maximilien's death. He studied the name
on the front of the red folder for a very long time, as if
it were a cipher to be broken, a set of hieroglyphics to
be interpreted.

Antrobus: Richard, Charles, Edward.

Stosch stared at the name with a thoughtful expression on his face. The name Antrobus. It rang a bell, a
small bell, at the back of his mind. He opened the
folder and extracted the first foolscap folio. He read it
slowly:

> Antrobus. No aliases. Occupation: sculptor. Also
> worked as property developer and investment bro-
> ker. Current address: 17 Bruton Terrace, Belgra-
> via, London. Rented on three-year lease at fifteen
> hundred pounds per annum.

Stosch impatiently flipped over a few pages as if he
had reached a dull passage in a novel. He picked up one
of the telephones. "Leon Kun," he said quietly.

The prissy voice of the Finance Controller came on
the line almost at once. "Kun speaking," he said in German. His voice fitted his face exactly. Kun was bald
and obsessively clean-shaven. He sometimes shaved
three times a day. He was very pale. His eyes were the
bright and blank eyes of a man who could have been
raised in a vicarage or brought up in the midst of evil.

"Leon. There is only one entry in Red Wolf this
month. Can this be correct?" Stosch spoke sharply in
perfect French.

"There were originally three, Dieter," Kun answered,
slipping into French, flushing slightly at the implied re-

buke. "Count Metaxos died in Lisbon. Three days
ago."

"Died? How so?"

"A self-inflicted wound. A .32 through the right temple. Our people are satisfied nobody else was involved.
There was of course a Priority Alpha investigation. The
full report is being prepared for you now. He had two
other evident debts. The hotel bill for . . . in dollars,
two thousand sixty and eighty-five cents American. He
was also overdrawn at the Tottenham Court Road
branch of Martin's Bank, London. That amounts to . . .
in sterling, seventeen thousand pounds and fourteen
shillings."

Had he been asked, Kun could have given the exact
dimensions of the hole in the dead man's temple, the
number of bone splinters removed from the carpets and
wall of the hotel room.

Kun was a man of ledgers: his whole life could be
written in the arithmetical language of balance sheets,
exchange rates, inventories, and schedules. He was a
specialist. He knew things that everybody else was ignorant of. He was ignorant of things that everybody else
accepted as common knowledge.

"You said there was a third entry?" Stosch said.

"That was Figdor Harsant. He evened up the Cannes
Alert yesterday. A $117,000 check drawn on the Mos-
cow Narodny Bank. Made payable to the casino."

"So citizen Antrobus is our only runner. Good. Very
good. Exceptional for June."

"Antrobus had a Red Wolf raised in Nice last September. He evened up in December," Kun said.

"Now he's back again. So soon."

"Five months," Kun said.

"Very well. That is all. Thank you, Leon."

Stosch put down the telephone and continued to read
slowly the file on Richard Antrobus. Occasionally he
stopped to check a point with the Analysis Directorate
or to ask Records to clarify a fact here, an item there.

A Red Wolf Alert was given top priority in the St.
Saladin Statistical Digest. Dieter Stosch gave it all his
personal attention. Ninety-seven casinos and gambling
organizations around the world, including illegal opera-

tions in Japan, Venezuela, and Uruguay, had their money on Stosch. It cost $125,000 a year to get the sealed, hand-delivered (often via some obliging diplomatic bag) monthly copy of the SS Memorandum. Under Stosch's direction the Memorandum had become the single most powerful document in the gambling industry. Its pages detailed the precise movements, current methods, and the profits and losses of the world's leading amateur and professional high rollers. Losing and winning streaks were recorded and analyzed. Unusual shifts in fortunes were noted, and often predicted. The Memorandum contained technical and psychological examinations of the newest systems being operated in Europe, North and South America, the Middle East and Asia. Stosch had personally anticipated the threat of infrared dark glasses enabling players to read premarked cards. It saved casinos millions. With a vocabulary as colorfully daedalian as *Variety's* showbiz jargon, the Memorandum tracked the migration of "subway dealers," "dildocks," "grifters," "skinners," and "barons." It established credit for unknowns and froze the accounts of the illustrious. People were banned, welcomed, feared, and favored by casinos in every corner of the earth because of half a dozen lines and a stolen photograph in a publication they never knew existed.

A Red Wolf Alert was automatically raised on all players with debts exceeding $50,000. On May 30 in Deauville, Richard Antrobus dropped $51,400 in five hours and forty minutes. Known personally to the directors of the casino, he had been given ten weeks to square it away. Interest would be charged at twelve and one half percent per month.

The Red Wolf file on Antrobus was thorough. An almost perfect example of a Memorandum profile, down to the name of his gunmaker (William Evans of St. James's Street, London) and the age of his Bristol motor car (two years old).

Richard Antrobus belonged to that English class that assumed the best people never worked. He was thirty-four years old (six years older than the age usually printed in the English press), five feet ten inches tall with straight brown hair and gray eyes. No visible scars. Left-handed. He had not been circumcised. It was strange how very few Englishmen of his sort were.

Stosch read slowly, assimilating dates and figures and sums of money, passport and account numbers, measurements and statistics. He studied the copies of Antrobus' birth certificate and marriage lines. Stosch had a way of putting old pieces of information together and coming up with new answers, fresh facts. Kun called it the Stosch Dimension.

Antrobus had been married briefly to Caroline Wylie, a copper heiress. Her estimated fortune on January 31 was $47 million. They had been divorced in Durango, Mexico. There were more dates and details and names. Her lovers, his lovers. There were no children.

Stosch yawned and switched on the reading lamp. He turned a page. Antrobus, he read, was a member of Whistlers.

Stosch smiled.

It was amazing how much you could tell about an Englishman from his club.

You could guess an American's income almost to the thousand by the way he cut his steak and an Italian's by the way he cut his fingernails. You could describe what kind of house and family a German had by the shoes he wore. You could learn many things about a Frenchman by the state of his teeth.

But once you knew an Englishman's club you had the very measurements of his soul.

He read on, frowning.

Richard Antrobus was the kind of gambler casinos didn't like. He habitually doubled up when he was on a winning streak. He had the knack of quitting at the peak of his luck and not returning until the following season. If at all.

Stosch opened the second drawer of his desk and lifted his feet onto the edge. His shoes were slim, black, and had real silk laces. They had been made for him in baby crocodile leather by a bootmaker in the rue St.-Honoré.

Hans Dieter Stosch could have told you a lot about the kind of man who bought such footwear.

Captain Dieter Stosch, a special services officer attached to Field Marshal von Runstedt's Third Panzer Division, came to St. Saladin as a conqueror in the first week of October 1941.

He was born in Coburg, in western Germany. His family originally came from Bavaria, where his grandfather had been a mathematician of repute. As a child, Stosch was withdrawn but obstinate. By the time he started school, at the age of five, he was able to read and write and cope with the homework set for his twelve-year-old brother Manfred. Stosch had also inherited his grandfather's mathematical brilliance.

In 1937, Stosch received his law degree and doctor of jurisprudence degree from the University of Munich. He was twenty-two years old. Shortly after his graduation, his father died in an automobile accident and Stosch took over the family's law office in Coburg. His courtroom manner earned him a nickname: the Prussian Advocate.

In December 1940 he was commissioned in the Wehrmacht, and six months later fought in the spearhead of the invasion of Russia. Wounded in the legs and abdomen shortly after crossing the Dnieper River, he was awarded the Iron Cross First Class.

St. Saladin, occupied jointly by the Germans and Italians since July 1940, was a recuperative posting.

In the midst of war, the island was still prismatic with pleasure. The hotels and cafés bulged with high-class whores, officers, collaborators, rich refugees, wheeler-dealers of every kind and every race. The black market flourished. People went to parties, gave dinners, made love and, of course, gambled.

In December 1941, Captain Stosch was transferred to General von Brauchitsch's Headquarters Staff and appointed to the new post of St. Saladin Liaison Officer. He felt like a military impostor after the rigors of the Russian campaign. This wasn't his idea of war. He protested the appointment. "Practice your charm, my dear Captain," General von Brauchitsch told him, laughing a thin dry laugh. He refused to rescind the order.

Stosch would never return to active service. His right leg had been shattered by a mortar shell that exploded beneath his car on the outskirts of Kiev. The driver, a former janitor at the University of Westphalia, was blown to bits. Shrapnel severed the carotid and sub-clavian arteries of Colonel von Frick, who sat beside Stosch in the back of the car. The colonel drowned in his own blood. Smothered in gobbets of human debris, Stosch was found fully conscious picking out pieces of blood-soaked upholstery and metal from his wounds. Always after that, on the bad days, a steady consumption of paracodeine tablets would be necessary to dull the intense pain that gnawed through his legs and spread into the pit of his stomach.

Stosch had been in his new office in the Hotel Prince Tullio only a few hours when the telephone rang and Paul Duclos introduced himself in excellent German and invited him to dinner at the palace the following evening.

"There is something you wish to discuss?" Stosch asked.

"I had hoped we could make our first meeting a social occasion, Captain," Duclos said affably.

"Very well. The hour?"

"Eight o'clock in my suite?"

"That is possible," Stosch said. He stared at the blank pages of his diary.

"With your permission, Captain, I shall ask Roberto Cheroffini to join us," Duclos said. His voice stopped exactly where charm ends and oiliness begins. "Count Cheroffini is minister responsible for foreign affairs. A very good friend of Prince Maximilien."

"You have my permission," Stosch said in the stiff correct tone he'd used with clients in Coburg.

"Until tomorrow evening, Captain."

Stosch put down the ornate Victorian telephone. He took a tablet from the box of paracodeines he kept in his desk. He chewed it thoughtfully. He couldn't imag-ine what they would have to talk about. He was puzzled by the role he was expected to play in St. Saladin. It was as if he were representing a client whose guilt was absolute.

The St. Saladin courtiers, in dinner jackets, were waiting for him in Duclos' drawing room. It was a large high-ceilinged room decorated in muted pastel green and lit with a crystal chandelier. The chandelier made the agreeable sound of ice being stirred in a tumbler as an occasional breeze came through the French windows, which had been left ajar despite the lateness of the year.

The room had the elegant, slightly faded look of an old luxury hotel suite. A Gobelin tapestry hung on one wall. But Stosch was astonished to see in a carved ebony cabinet a complete set of porcelain comedy figures. They were probably from the Nymphenburg factory and almost certainly modeled by the great ceramic artist Bustelli. Even the Bavarian National Museum in Munich didn't possess a complete set. These were the finest creations of the German baroque period Stosch had ever seen.

It was impossible to tell by as much as a flicker of an eyelash that porcelain figures were his passion. His face gave nothing away. It was a lawyer's trick learned from criminals. Stosch's own modest collection, inherited from his father, was limited to a fairly fine Ottavio, and a Pantalone that had been spoiled by some poor coloring at the end of the nineteenth century.

"Some whisky before dinner, Captain?" Paul Duclos said. He had already taken a glass in his hand. "It isn't black market. It comes straight from the palace cellars. Acquired quite properly in more tranquil times."

"Thank you, a small amount," Stosch said with careful courtesy. He stood not quite at attention.

Duclos raised the glass and a bottle of Sterling Old Lowland Scotch level with his face and poured with a steady hand. He reminded Stosch of an ancient apothecary measuring out a precious elixir drop by drop.

Duclos was a man of unguessable age. He was probably of less than average height but his dapper style made him appear diminutive. He had a narrow straw-colored face with the eyes of a playful snake. He wore rings on his fingers and had a curious habit of wriggling with effeminate self-esteem every time he finished whatever he had to say.

"You were on the Russian front, I understand from General von Brauchitsch," Cheroffini said.

"Yes."

"Herr Hitler seems to think that the Red Army is done for," Cheroffini said.

"The Führer has assured the German people that the enemy in the East has been struck down and will never rise again," Stosch said, quoting Hitler's recent broadcast almost word for word. It was best to be simply reportorial in such matters. He indicated neither agreement nor disbelief.

"But the war continues in the East, surely?" said Duclos, lifting his left eyebrow in an actory arch as he handed Stosch his whisky.

"Small pockets of resistance are inevitable in such a vast terrain," Stosch said. "The Führer says the epitaph is already written."

"Soldiers fill the graves and politicians call it victory," Duclos said with an indulgent chuckle.

"And others get rich on the pennies stolen from the eyes of dead men," Stosch said.

The quietness of his voice was extraordinary.

Duclos and Cheroffini exchanged quick glances. The two men had a limpet sense of partnership.

Count Cheroffini was a man of fifty or so, with the twilight good looks of an aging gigolo.

Duclos was the first to speak, *"Touché,* Captain." He patted the German's arm. The hard well-muscled tension in Stosch's bicep warned him to proceed carefully. "Let me tell you something. St. Saladin's very existence is built on the sands of chance. We are washed by the oceans of greed. We know it. We accept it. We are a dynasty shaped by amity and avarice, a little venality . . ."

Stosch watched Duclos' face closely as the politican made his pitch. The three men continued to converse in German. Stosch gave no indication that he was equally versed in French. It gave him an edge. He was a man who liked to have an edge.

"Like Herr Hitler's, our business depends on a kind of thraldom. . . ." Duclos began a sly smile of sanctioned duplicity but it failed against Stosch's icy detachment. The smile remained half-finished.

Stosch sipped his Scotch. It really was very good. Duclos had handed it to him straight, with no offer of soda or anything else. It was that sort of Scotch.

"Wouldn't you say, Captain, that it is reasonable to use any expedient to insure one's future prosperity?" Duclos performed his curious seismic squirm. "The only sound principle is to have no principle at all perhaps," he added and wriggled again.

Stosch shrugged. "We all do what we have to," he said softly. He had no particular expression on his face or in his voice. Nothing provokes people more than indifference.

"And in the West? The English seem to be maintaining their ability to muddle through. How long can they last, do you think?"

"It is difficult to estimate a survival sustained by accident and luck," Stosch answered.

"All the same, it's hard not to admire the courage of a people who refuse to accept defeat," Duclos said. His tone was meant to convey more exasperation than sympathy.

"It is wiser to admire the strength and design and purpose that makes defeat inconceivable from the start," the German said. Stosch treated the war with a professional seriousness, a pride with which only cricket is treated by the English, and only money by the French.

Cheroffini was now regarding Duclos with a hint of anxiety in his eyes, willing him to change the subject quickly. Duclos altered course almost imperceptibly.

"Unlike the Fatherland, Captain, we cannot hope to distinguish ourselves in the expensive business of war," he said. "So we prepare ourselves for . . ." He hesitated as if searching for a suitably modest enterprise in which to plunge St. Saladin. "Let us say we prepare ourselves for the pageantries of peace." He finished with an apologetic shrug.

Stosch permitted himself a small smile. He was taking mental notes on the technique of Duclos—a politician, he suspected, who would not necessarily balk at sacrificing his country to an insensate greed. Or was that merely what he was supposed to think?

"I hate the drudgery, the *palaver* of war," Duclos went on with a self-deprecating smile. "I want to bear the palm, I suppose, without getting all that dust up my nostrils."

To Duclos, sycophancy was no dishonor. "My dear Cherry," he'd once told Cheroffini, "I aspire to the depths of diplomacy. The highest art of duplicity known to man." It was not the whole truth but it was a truth, Cheroffini supposed. He was content to let Duclos run with the ball. He enjoyed watching the subtle struggle that was going on between these two men: the struggle between bullshit and bluntness. The contest was more equal than he would have thought possible. The outcome unpredictable.

The Count crossed the room and poured himself a second small Scotch. It gave him the opportunity to study the German from another angle. Their investigations in Coburg and Munich suggested he was the man they needed. Stosch was tough and Teutonic, but he was not a member of the Nazi party. That might be a very important consideration one day. He had a suspicion of companionship, the mark of the natural loner: a bird of prey is never gregarious. Cheroffini felt that suspicion was a kind of contentment within the tall hard young German. He seemed to be almost nursing his sense of aloneness. Aloneness was his strength. He used it like a weapon.

Cheroffini rejoined the conversation. "May I freshen your drink before we go in to dinner, Captain?"

"Thank you, no," Stosch said.

The dining room was candlelit and intimate.

"In peacetime this suite belongs to Prince Philippe." Duclos smiled as if reading the German's mind. "His Royal Highness specializes in dinners *à deux*."

"The Prince is with De Gaulle in London," Cheroffini said.

"Ah. One of the so-called Free French," Stosch said. His smile was bleak.

"He was in London when war was declared. Had he

been in Berlin . . ." Duclos turned the palm of his hand over slowly. "The luck of the draw."

"It is unfortunate that the armistice terms state that French nationals caught fighting against the Fatherland will be immediately shot," Stosch said.

He still had the same bleak smile.

The two courtiers exchanged their quick mind-frisking glances.

It was Cheroffini who spoke.

"May I remind you, Captain, that St. Saladin is a neutral sovereign state? His Royal Highness is not a French national." He spoke slowly, in a calm reasonable tone.

"Isn't that rather like Caernarvon claiming immunity for the Prince of Wales?" Stosch said. His smile was still there. It was still bleak.

"Is that a legal opinion, Captain Stosch? Or military absolutism?" Cheroffini asked. He looked at the German steadily.

"It is a fact," Stosch said. "War transcends moral judgment." His smile was impregnable. "In war there is only the law of tyranny and triumph."

The two courtiers looked at the young German with searching eyes. Neither spoke. Neither felt like debating the point. Cheroffini rubbed his chin. Duclos watched him.

The three men sat in tall-backed chairs. The back of Duclos' chair came nearly twelve inches above his head. It gave him a boiled-down look. Even his movements looked small.

Stosch accepted the lull in the conversation without concern. His silence came easily.

Duclos had chosen a simple summery Moselle to go with the Sole Walewska. The slatey German wine was chosen in Stosch's honor, a Bernkasteler Green Label. "We have been dealing with the House of Deinhard since 1812," Duclos said, noticing the German's interest in the label and anxious to end the silence.

"I hope that our relationship will be as durable and as . . . satisfactory, Captain Stosch," Duclos said. He had the smile of a superior gangster. He lifted his glass. "To our future friendship and the immutable friendship of our peoples." He spoke in the formalized tone that politicians use to hide the fact they are trafficking in dangerous bromides.

"To all our futures," Count Cheroffini intoned. The candlelight softened the lines in his face. But the lines had added character as well as age to his handsome features and now he looked like a waxworks figure, a figure without a past. His eyes, in the shadows, showed no sign of occupancy at all. Of the two, Cheroffini was the more interesting—almost certainly the most dangerous. Stosch had *Fingerspitzengefuhl*—a sixth sense—about such men. Cheroffini sat very straight in the high-backed chair, smiling gently, slowly swirling the pale Moselle in his glass. He barely sipped the wine.

"You are not married, Captain?" he asked when the coffee had been poured.

"No."

"A fiancée, perhaps?"

"No."

Cheroffini sighed. "You are a fortunate man," he said. "I myself speak as the victim of several marriages. Marriages in which passion, money, plunder, and politics have all played a part—and, as you see, taken their toll."

Stosch nodded solemnly. It sounded like a speech the Count had used before. He'd heard many similar speeches in his chambers, and in the courtroom, usually from men obliged to make a little smoke.

"I live with my own defects," Stosch said. "Why should I have to live with those of another?"

Duclos and Cheroffini regarded him with unconvincing admiration. There was another stretched-out silence in the small room before the manservant arrived with several boxes of cigars and placed them on the table by Cheroffini's coffee. Stosch was waiting for the chance to make his move. "And now, gentlemen," he said, looking at his watch and rising to his feet in one movement. "I must return to my billet." He chose the word *billet* carefully for its military ring. The courtiers saw it as a subtle snub, a slur on the Hotel Prince Tullio. They lived in that kind of world: a world where the shades of status and insult were infinite.

"I thank you for dinner, for the excellent German wine, and for your interesting company," Stosch said. He gravely shook hands with the two courtiers. Duclos and Cheroffini were stunned by the suddenness of his departure.

It was a fine cool night. Stosch dismissed his driver. He wanted to walk back to the hotel. He wanted to think. The evening had been carefully stage-managed. But for what purpose? He needed to figure out the characters of the two men so anxious to favor him with their attentions. Once he had worked out their characters, he would have a better chance of discovering their motives. Behind Duclos' cynicism, he sensed a need. And Cheroffini—Cheroffini's reflective calm, his subtle compliments, could have been masking almost anything, from contempt to panic. But why, if they simply wanted to cultivate a friend in the German camp, why didn't they go to work on von Brauchitsch? The general was better placed to help them get whatever it was they wanted. Von Brauchitsch was far more susceptible to flattery. A narcissist with a marketable conscience, the general was obviously their best bet. So why were they bypassing von Brauchitsch for a mere captain? It didn't make sense.

Stosch walked slowly on the uneven cobblestones, his black-gloved hands clasped behind his back. He turned into the rue Antonin. He could hear a jazz band playing an American tune that had been popular in Coburg just before the war.

The stars were very bright. The war seemed remote. A line of Renault taxicabs waited a few yards from the Nine Lives nightclub. The doorman, a giant of a man in a Cossack cloak and hat, had an olive-skinned face that seemed exempt from all intelligent life. He lounged against the wall, yakking with the cabdrivers.

As Stosch approached the club, a group of people emerged talking and laughing in the unnaturally loud voices of people who have spent their lives talking above the sound of music at other people talking above the sound of music. There were three women in evening clothes, a couple of men in dinner jackets, and a German colonel. The doorman sprang into action. He called up the first taxicab in the rank with a great flourish of authority.

"*Zwei*," the officer said in a slurred voice. The tallest of the three women took hold of his hand and pressed her mouth against his ear. She was a couple of inches taller than the officer. Her bright red lipstick made her face seem inhumanly white. Her yellow silk dress was skintight: she could not be wearing anything beneath it.

"*Zwei*," the colonel said again, stumbling a little bit. He pointed to the taxis.

"*Zwei?*" The doorman looked blank.

"*Deux, dos, doppio*," the tall woman said in a hard sober voice. "*Deux*."

"Ah! *Deux*," the doorman said. The process of comprehension worked its way across his face like a fox crossing some vast wasteland.

The colonel grabbed the tall woman in a fumbling embrace. Her hand slipped down between them and felt him as they swayed together in the doorway. The blue light of the Nine Lives sign bathed them in a deathly glow as if their faces had been drained of life. The second woman, a blonde with frizzed hair and a narrow fur stole draped around her bare white shoulders, started to croon to the music coming up from the basement club. "Yes, my heart belongs to . . . da-da, dadada, dadada, dad!" The colonel slipped his hand into the tall woman's yellow dress and squeezed her breast as if testing the ripeness of a melon.

"*Zwei*," he shouted jubilantly.

"*Ja, zwei!*" the tall woman said in a voice quite different from the voice she had used on the doorman. "*Zwei, deux, dos, doppio* . . . mmm."

The third woman, who had been studying her mouth in a compact mirror, averted her eyes in a mime of modesty. The two men stood behind her, grinning. They were elderly men who might have been genuinely embarrassed.

What happened next happened quickly.

The tall woman screamed and leapt apart from the colonel. The front of her dress was splattered with vomit. The colonel stumbled to the curb and dropped heavily to his knees with excretory moans of self-pity.

Stosch crossed the street. He felt ashamed to belong to the same race, to be wearing the same uniform. He did not recognize the colonel.

The tall woman wept in the doorway. One of the elderly men knelt down before her and attempted to clean up her dress with a handkerchief. The vague embarrassed grin hadn't quite faded from his face. The other women and the man looked on. Nobody spoke. There was just the tall woman weeping.

Dieter Stosch remembered the road to Kiev . . . the leaden smell of blood, von Frick's brains covering him like semolina, clogging his nostrils.

He tried to walk faster.

His legs ached terribly.

He felt in his pocket for a tablet.

It was fifteen minutes past midnight when Count Cheroffini and Paul Duclos made their report. Maximilien had spent the evening with his mistress. He had bathed and dressed again. He had performed particularly well. He felt the smugness of a man who understands the tricks but not the art of love.

Maximilien was shorter than he appeared to be in photographs and in the cinema newsreels and his complexion was darker than artists usually painted it. He had recently grown a droopy gray moustache which gave him the look of a distinguished officer of a fashionable regiment. It was the perfect finish for a man who loved uniforms, who coveted decorations and rejoiced in the reviews and ceremonies of St. Saladin's Palace Guard.

It was easy enough to underestimate his political savvy. The fact that he had studied at the Paris School of Economic and Political Science had been removed from his official biography: it was incompatible, he said, with the state's neutral image. He was a cunning stylist. His tinselly public demeanor, the ornamental pride he took in his miniature domain, were calculated to create an aura of affecting harmlessness in a carelessly cruel world.

Educated at the Lycée Condorcet and Princeton,

Count Roberto Cheroffini held the grand title of Lord Privy Seal. His early ministerial duties had consisted largely of the education of Prince Philippe. Now he was Maximilien's legal right hand. He kept inside the rules, but whatever the Prince wanted, the imaginative legalism of Cheroffini's mind would find a way to get. He was an expert at staying a comma ahead of the letter of the law. "Roberto was conceived inside a legal loophole," Maximilien liked to say.

Maximilien's study was small and intimate by palace standards. Part of a much larger room at one time, the ceiling was high, white and gold. White and gold bookshelves lined two walls. The Prince sat beneath a portrait of Princess Marie-Thérèse Louise at the age of seventeen. It was the Prince's favorite ancestral portrait, probably because people remarked how alike they were around the eyes and mouth.

On the wall to his left were a dozen Picasso lithographs, a sequence of interpretations, from naturalistic to abstract, of a couple copulating.

Duclos and Cheroffini settled themselves into armchairs that were part of a semicircle of deep-brown leather chairs facing Maximilien's desk. The desk was discreetly mounted on a six-inch dais to ensure his sublimity. The air of informality didn't hide the uncompromising autocracy of a man who never for a moment forgot that by birth and habit he was a prince. His interest in democracy never exceeded the sympathetic.

"It is the worm of politics that nothing can be done simply and aboveboard," Maximilien opened the conversation with amiable irony. He took a thin black Turkish cigarette from a heavy gold box. The cigarettes were made for him in Paris from an expensive stock of Macedonian leaf. He never offered them around. "It was ever thus, I suppose," he said. His voice was thoughtful. He lit the cigarette with a gold lighter. "And so, gentlemen. What have you to tell me. How was this kraut?"

Duclos spoke first. "An interesting evening. He's pretty much what we expected. Sharper in the flesh, perhaps. His sense of solitariness is . . . vivid."

"He has a brittle quality," Cheroffini said.

"Von Brauchitsch was right," Duclos said. "The captain is without much sense of humor."

The Prince shrugged impatiently. "Too much humor in a man can be fatal. Like liver in a Strasbourg goose. Did he notice the Bustelli collection?"

"Almost at once," Cheroffini said.

"And?"

"Nothing."

"Nothing? That's interesting," the Prince said. "How many men can look upon the passion of their lives—a woman, a yacht, a painting—and say . . . nothing. Tell me—his face. What did his face show?"

Cheroffini was always surprised by Maximilien's questions. "I saw nothing," he admitted. "His face was also silent. Even Harlequin and Lalage, the two most beautiful . . ." He didn't bother to finish the sentence.

"He is inhuman, perhaps," suggested Duclos wryly.

"Because he showed no human greed? No. To be able to distinguish between wants and necessities— that's also the mark of a clever man," the Prince said slowly.

Ash from his cigarette fell onto the desk.

"And a dangerous man," Cheroffini suggested.

The Prince smiled. He seemed almost set at ease by that thought. He leaned forward and blew the ash from his desk.

Cheroffini looked like a man who has boarded a slow train by mistake. He felt tired. It was going to be a long night. There was a sense of pressure in the atmosphere. It would rain soon. He said, "He's not a member of the Nazi party but he's loyal to the Fatherland."

"He has a touching belief in the invincibility of the Führer," Duclos said.

"The Allies will no doubt disabuse him of that belief in time," the Prince said.

"If not?" Cheroffini asked.

"Either way . . ." The Prince made a vague motion in the air with his cigarette. "A German who believes in the Führer without the encumbrance of party membership. Win or lose . . ."

"There are hazards in such a course," Cheroffini said.

"We follow the fashion of dangerous times," the Prince said.

"Stosch has a lawyer's mind, a soldier's experience," Duclos said, catching the drift. He was a man committed to watching which way the wind blows.

There was a small silence. Duclos half-suppressed a sneeze and said, *"Gesundheit!"*

"When the war is over—" Cheroffini began.

"When the war is over, St. Saladin will face its severest challenge," the Prince said. Two small blotches the color of stewed plums appeared in his cheeks.

"May I ask how Your Highness sees Prince Philippe fitting—"

The Prince made a contemptuous sound with his tongue. "Philippe doesn't have it. He'll never be fit to rule anything except an exercise book."

The Count kept the sense of alarm from showing in his face. He said, "Prince Philippe's succession is—"

"My son's succession is predestined—an impulse of nature as certain as my own mortality."

"I don't see, sir—"

"What fascinates the child is the puppet. What matters to the man are the wires. Philippe must be . . . securely wired. Neither you nor Paul will live forever, although you'll both outlive me. Our country needs new blood, new ideas. Ability, vision . . . men capable of regenerating and securing the future."

Duclos touched his nose with a silk handkerchief that smelled faintly of bergamot. When he had finished it was as if he had wiped away every trace of expression from his dry narrow face. He tucked the handkerchief into his sleeve and waited almost motionless.

Cheroffini nodded but said nothing. His silence was accepted as tacit approval by Maximilien.

"I'm sorry, Roberto, to have to say these things to you," the Prince said. "I understand your feelings for Philippe. You always did your best for him. If I appear to be selfish, it is only in the cause of St. Saladin. No effort, no sacrifice is excessive if it furthers the interest of our country." He lingered on the word *sacrifice*. "Philippe must learn to subordinate his ego to the security of St. Saladin."

The Count drew a deep breath. "You envisage Prince Philippe as a figurehead, a symbol, sir. But the constitutional justification for creating—"

"Fatherhood," the Prince interrupted, "is the fundamental justification for Philippe's existence. His historical role is to provide St. Saladin with an heir and a future. Fortunately, we can all rest assured he is capable of that."

The diversion was skillful and complete.

He turned to the silent Duclos. "You hear all the gossip, my dear Paul. How many . . . miscarriages have his women had, do you suppose?"

"His Highness's less than paternal feelings do not spur him to strict accountancy, sir," Duclos answered readily, emerging cautiously from his shell.

The Prince laughed. "I would give a lot to be such a stud again." There was a tone of bantering condescension in his voice.

"Philippe should make no worse a contribution to our history than some fine romance," Duclos said. He could hug the curve of an awkward adjustment better than anyone. Cheroffini sometimes thought that Duclos did not belong to the twentieth century at all. It was as if he had escaped through a black hole in history, he belonged in the eighteenth century, amid the foppish conspiracies of the Dauphin and Mirabeau. "It's said that Philippe's most active hours are spent in bed," Duclos said, looking from Cheroffini to the Prince.

"I'd like to wake up with half the energy Philippe goes to bed with," the Prince said.

It began to rain heavily, the way it was never supposed to rain in St. Saladin, according to the travel brochures.

Duclos stood up and walked softly around the desk to close the French windows behind the Prince.

The sound of rain seemed despairing to Cheroffini. What was being discussed here—and glossed over—was a sellout, a supreme policy of theft. A stratagem that meant Philippe's removal from all power in the state. The compensation was to be an inviolable retirement—in full regalia—of indolence and luxury. To reign but not to rule.

Duclos took a pair of gold-rimmed spectacles from his breast pocket. Removing a silk handkerchief from his sleeve, he began to polish the lenses with a delicate meticulousness. He was almost blind in one eye, his left, but the exigencies of vanity prevented him from wearing his spectacles most of the time and never in the presence of women—and men he didn't like. Cheroffini enjoyed Paul's weaknesses; not for the first time he thought how close tolerance was to skepticism.

"Unlike our Monégasque friends," the Prince was saying, "we are not in a position to relegate our casino to the sector of private enterprise . . . To put it plainly, gentlemen, a prosperous casino is what St. Saladin is all about. And a prosperous casino must have a strong man at the helm. A man with extraordinary qualities. The health of our future demands the health of the casino. The course of the one depends upon the progress of the other. . . ."

They would talk and talk through the night. Maximilien would invite their suggestions, listen to everything they said. Appear to be swayed this way and that way. He would ask questions and appear to ponder. But when all was said and done he would do exactly what he wanted to do. He would also be careful to mention the collective responsibility of cabinet decision.

The rain stopped.

Cheroffini opened the French windows. In the distance the first columns of pale luminous rays were appearing between the trees like clever lighting bringing to life a vast and beautiful stage set. Somewhere a bird was beginning to scratch the silence with a detached legato sound.

The Count took a deep breath. The sweet scent from the encircling lemon groves mingled with the smell of cedar and pine trees. It was a curiously nostalgic aroma but he couldn't think why. It had something to do with childhood.

He followed the discussion in the gray suburbs of his consciousness. Paul Duclos was beginning to repeat himself, to ramble.

The smell, the mingling of pine and cedar, nostalgic and elusive, puzzled Cheroffini. A single bird, too small and too far away for him to recognize, flew across the tops of the trees. The foliage of the trees looked like one big black cloud. The bird was probably a mallard. Cheroffini's grandfather, who was half English, had taught him the old collective nouns for every waterfowl you could think of. A sord of mallards, a dopping of sheldrakes, a covert of coots, a sedge of herons, a desert of lapwing. A walk of snipe. He loved that, it always made him smile. He remembered teaching these old country terms to Philippe when the Hereditary Prince was no more than six years old. He wondered whether he still remembered them. Everything goes so fast, he thought. The happy times slip by so fast. If only one could slow them down. He remembered teaching Philippe how to fish at night by torchlight, by the *fasquié*. How many times had they gone out together with the fishermen to set the nets for *palangies* and *gourbins*? Fifty nights? A hundred nights? "My favorite smell in all the world," young Philippe had told him once, "is the smell of bouillabaisse cooking on the beach over fires of pine logs and fir cones." Was it still? he wondered.

Cheroffini was turning away from the window when it came to him. The mingling of pine and cedar . . . the tang of boxes of freshly sharpened pencils, the smell of the classroom.

It's strange how the net of memory works, he thought. The smallest tiddler is never quite lost.

It was almost daylight.

Cheroffini switched off the lamp on Maximilien's desk.

Duclos looked tired. Cheroffini saw for the first time that there were fine weblike wrinkles in the tissues of his eyelids. The furrows that ran from each side of his straight nose to the outer corners of his lips seemed deeper than usual. Only Duclos' voice defied the weariness in his face. Like a woman, he was indefatigable in the discussion of detail. His voice had a curiously dated quality, a phonograph record of somebody long dead. When Cheroffini closed his eyes it was like listening to the chatter of a familiar ghost.

"History is never the story of rewarded virtue. There

is no compensation for the raped and no residual value in chastity."

"What you're saying, Paul, is . . . fuck 'em all?" the Prince cut in in a dry bored voice.

"Exactly. We must subscribe to the safe harlotry of history," Duclos said.

The Prince rewarded him with a small smile. "The harlotry of history," he said slowly, as if rolling a fine wine in his mouth. "I like that." He looked as fresh as when they had entered the room almost five hours ago. It was sometimes hard to believe that he was more than ten years older than both Duclos and the Count. The three men had reached that age when they felt like contemporaries.

Their most important memories, their most shaping experiences, were mostly shared ones. Their fears and hopes and what was left of their dreams were all much the same now. They told the same stories and it was often difficult to settle who had told a story first or to whom it had really happened. Did the Prince catch Duclos in bed with the English duchess and her sister, or was it Cheroffini who enjoyed their charms? They all remembered the occasion well—but differently. They had reached that time of life when love-making is often on a man's mind but seldom on his agenda. "My fantasies fatigue me now," Duclos had said. "My imagination ripens and my body rots."

The Prince was lighting another cigarette. Cheroffini counted seven black studs in the ashtray on his desk. He tried to pick up the threads of the conversation. He hoped that Maximilien hadn't noticed his abstraction. The fresh air had woken him up considerably.

The talk had turned to Dieter Stosch's legal position after the war. Cheroffini concentrated hard.

"War is never a bad experience for nature's criminals." Duclos was talking. "The end of wars—the hullabaloo, the dust. It favors the escape of the clever ones, the extrication of even the most wicked."

"What are we to presume, then?" Cheroffini asked. He was feeling his way back into the conversation. "That Captain Stosch is culpable? Or merely clever?"

"My dear Cherry, does it matter?" Duclos answered affably. "You miss my point entirely. Culprit, refugee, exile—these are all words, just words."

When Duclos goes, Cheroffini thought, nobody would ever call him Cherry again.

"Six months after it's all over, whichever way it goes, there'll be only winners and losers, victims and victors—"

"Lifers and fugitives?" Cheroffini said.

Behind Maximilien the landscape grew sharper. The trees seemed to be advancing through a mist. A small breeze moved the dark-green damask curtains. The movement reminded Cheroffini of a giant bird flexing its wings before flight. The Prince patted a yawn with three fingers. He looked at his watch as the clock on the mantelpiece began to whir softly before striking five times. He pushed back his chair and stood up, grunting good-humoredly at his stiffness.

Duclos and Cheroffini immediately got to their feet. Duclos rubbed his knees ruefully.

"It's been a long session, gentlemen," the Prince said. "Let's juggle with words no longer. I am well satisfied. I have sufficiently settled my thoughts . . . with your inestimable help." He walked slowly around the big desk and stood close to the two courtiers. He put his arm around Cheroffini's shoulder.

"We want Dieter Stosch. It is agreed. Yes?"

"Agreed," Duclos said.

The Count knew he had no choice. Who'd said that countries are governed either by accident or by one man? Yet Cheroffini knew that he would have to carry his share of responsibility for the decision made that night. And one day he would have to answer to Philippe.

"Good," Maximilien said in a cheerful voice. He moved his smile from Duclos to Cheroffini, where it rested, searching, like a feeble flashlight trying to pick out letters on a neglected road sign. Finally satisfied that he was on the right road, the Prince said, "So! Let us find out the good captain's price. And then, gentlemen . . . we fasten our teeth."

Cheroffini undressed quickly. He put on white silk pajamas and slipped into the large four-poster bed. He was exhausted and pleased the bed was empty. The cold sheets refreshed him for a few mind-cranking seconds. He wondered how long it would take Duclos to realize what Stosch's price would be. And how long after Duclos had worked that one out would he tumble to the fact that Max knew the answer all along?

Cheroffini smiled.

The chill had gone out of the sheets. He pulled the covers over his head to hide the light.

12

Dieter Stosch reached for the telephone closest to him and said quietly, "The Red Wolf is ready now." He replaced the receiver gently, like an adulterer who has made a furtive call in the night. He felt drained. He always felt drained after an RW session. It was not easy trying to pin down people who live by hunches *and* mathematics, people whose creed was chance and superstition, who were forever in and out of luck, in and out of funds.

Even so, it was a satisfying exhaustion. The exhaustion some men feel after winning a clever game of chess and other men feel after laying an experienced woman better than she's ever been laid before.

He wondered what time it was. He never wore a watch. There was no clock in the room. Old René Chalot had shrewdly forbidden clocks in the gaming rooms—"the tick-tock of time is an intolerable intrusion"—and his edict had not only survived a hundred years but had been extended to every room in the old palace building, except those apartments personally occupied by members of the royal family. There had been

a clock in Stosch's room once; it had been removed
along with the body of Princess Bianca in 1939.

Stosch slid the RWA file on the Englishman Domi-
nick Antrobus to one side. He limped slightly as he
crossed the room to the black lacquer Riesener cabinet
which had once contained the underwear of Marie Antoinette at Versailles and now contained nothing more
intoxicating than the finest liquor. He filled a crystal
tumbler with crushed ice from a small black refrigerator
built into the cabinet. He swirled the ice around the
glass a few times, emptied it into a vacuum bucket. He
wiped the glass with a white cambric cloth. He poured a
large Scotch from a square decanter. He worked with
methodical professionalism. Beyond the glow from the
green-shaded reading lamp on his desk, the room reeled
back into deep shadows like the dimly painted back-
grounds of Rembrandt's last years. A mysterious dusk,
immeasurably remote, engulfing and dissolving. There
was a stillness, the extraordinary stillness of an empty
church, about the room. It was always there. That curious mixture of spiritual serenity and sheer spookiness.

Stosch stood where he was, enjoying the Scotch. He
wore gray gabardine trousers and a dark linen jacket
cut in the style of what German officers called a *Lit-
evka*, the traditional Wehrmacht smoking jacket

He rolled the old-fashioned glass between the palms
of his hands as he pulled back his head and stretched to
his full sinewy height. He had a striking appearance.
People looked at him in the street with curiosity, and
sometimes with apprehension. He might have been
forty, or more; he might have been a lot less. He wasn't
the sort of man you put an age to. His hair was cut
close to his head, a wheat field scythed and sun-
bleached. His face was like stoved-in sculpture. His eyes
were sensual and by no means friendly. He smiled seldom. He smiled as if it caused him pain. It was a gun-
barrel kind of smile. It compelled your attention and it
kept you at bay.

Stosch turned slowly. Sipping his drink, he crossed
the room into the Rembrandt shadows to where the
porcelain figures of Ottavio and Pantalone stood on the
marquetry table. He touched a switch. Recessed spots in

the high ceiling illuminated the pieces with two fingers of phosphorescent light, suggesting celestial favor.

He traced the tip of one finger over the cold smooth contours of Ottavio. It had been his father's favorite piece. Stosch preferred the Pantalone, despite its faked and slightly flawed coloring.

It was strange how these two figures, eight inches high, so delicate in appearance, hauled such a heavy cargo of old times. To look at them for more than a moment was to start the remorseless rolling stock of memories.

Stosch lifted his glass in a silent toast. He thought of Lalage, Colombine, Harlequin, Isabella, Donna Martina . . . He remembered the first time he had set eyes on those classic figures so absolved from the laws of time by the genius of Bustelli. Now Maximilien, who had no such exemption from those laws, was dead. Stosch had waited a long time to collect his prize. The finest Bustelli collection in the world. He would have to rearrange the lighting, find a new home for Ottavio and Pantalone.

His reverie was interrupted by a single brisk tap on the door.

"Enter," he said, turning away from the figures.

Genevieve Lacroix came into the room. She was carrying a tray with coffee and a slice of Linzertorte.

"I thought you might be ready for this," she said, "since you missed dinner."

"That was thoughtful of you." He watched her cross the room. She wore a simple black dress. It was the sort of dress that could be made severe or seductive by the merest adjustment of attitude. She was an attractive woman. She had a seasoned unself-conscious look, a style that combined Parisian elegance with Pitman efficiency. She looked like a lady who could hold an intelligent conversation—and her liquor. She was thirty years old. Her skin was flawed by too much sun. Her eyes were her best feature. They were quietly luscious, green like woodland shadows one hour before dark.

"Mlle. Gaillard is waiting to see you," she said in a quiet friendly voice. She placed the tray on his desk and picked up the Red Wolf file.

"I've made a few amendments," Stosch said.

Genevieve Lacroix riffled through the pages.

"So I see," she said. There was no surprise in her voice. No resentment or accusation.

"It must be in the bag for our London people in the morning," Stosch said. "Duclos is meeting with the British Consul at the Tullio at nine-thirty. Be sure he has it by nine."

She glanced at her wristwatch. It was eleven-thirty. She guessed there was at least three hours' work ahead of her.

"Has Mlle. Gaillard been here long?"

"About an hour."

Stosch nodded thoughtfully. "Ask her to come in."

"Alwyn Brand telephoned. He wants to discuss Prince Maximilien's funeral arrangements with you. I've penciled him in for eleven o'clock tomorrow morning."

"Yes," said Stosch. If Genevieve Lacroix had suggested eleven o'clock then eleven o'clock would be exactly right.

"You'd better ask Cornelius, too."

"I've already done so," she said. "Also Duclos and Cheroffini."

Cornelius once called her "the best pair of pants in the Bureau."

Stosch didn't care for the priest's American slang but he couldn't fault his sentiment.

Genevieve Lacroix was a lady with a handful of trigger fingers. She was more than Stosch's personal aide, much more than an internuncio; she understood exactly how St. Saladin politics worked, the subtle internecine jealousies and rivalries, the curly lines of communication through the bureaucratic and social labyrinth. She was the supreme mistress of the Bureau's many delicate skills. Stosch trusted her more than he trusted any man.

There wouldn't be a great deal to discuss with Duclos, Cheroffini, and the others. Like Queen Victoria, Maximilien had left precise instructions concerning the details of his obsequies. He wished to be buried at sea in full military uniform. The route along which his funeral cortege traveled to the quayside—the royal flag-draped casket carried on a gun carriage borrowed from a French army barracks in Nîmes—would be decorated with red, gold, and purple crêpe for twelve hours only.

Gaming was to be suspended for three minutes while the casket was committed to the deep.

"Will there be anything else this evening?" Genevieve Lacroix asked, moving toward the door.

"That'll be all."

"I'll ask Mlle. Gaillard to come in."

Catharine Gaillard's smile was fresh and unstrained. She showed no sign of having been kept waiting so long. She knew Stosch too well to offer her cheek. She shook his hand. Her grip was firm.

"I've kept you waiting," Stosch acknowledged without apologizing. "Will you join me in a coffee? Or something stronger, perhaps?"

"Something stronger, perhaps," she said.

"Of course." He moved across to the liquor cabinet and opened the doors. He waved the back of his hand slowly over the array of bottles.

"A vodka Gibson, thank you."

"Is that what they're drinking in Paris these days?"

"Only among friends."

Stosch took a tall moulded-lip glass and half-filled it with crushed ice and splashed it over with a quarter of an inch of Noilly Prat dry vermouth.

"Among friends? How do you mean?"

"There's so *much* anti-American feeling in Paris now, you just don't believe. Last week *Le Monde* printed a whole editorial complaining about the chewing-gum wrappers on the streets and the dangers of Coca-Cola . . ."

"The dangers of Coca-Cola?"

"The symbol of Uncle Sam. It is only envy, maybe."

"Envy is a sinew of the soul," Stosch said. "You shouldn't dismiss it lightly."

"You heard about the demonstrations against Eisenhower?"

"Only the French would have the perversity to demonstrate against the soldier who liberated France,"

Stosch said. He poured a couple of inches of Stolichnaya vodka into the glass and stirred it gently with a long silver spoon.

Catharine smiled. "Liberation isn't always proof of justice. Parisians still feel occupied in many ways . . . so many American uniforms, so many American government people . . . they are everywhere."

"Isn't that good for the economy? Aren't they free with their money, the Americans?"

Catharine Gaillard shrugged the way only a Frenchwoman can shrug when she has no answer.

"They are too free with Christian names. Even on first acquaintance they call you by your given name. They are very loud, you know, very immature. Too young to be telling half the world—"

"Too young?"

"Next month Paris will be two thousand years old—"

"So half the city drinks dry martinis behind locked doors?"

Catharine laughed. "Americans," she said. "All their values are based on: How much?"

"God is gelter," Stosch said.

"And infinite in His profit?"

"The French know that better than anyone." He poured the Gibson into a martini glass through a silver mesh strainer. Catharine watched him with fascination. He did everything with such precision. He worked with a deliberate, almost mesmeric calm.

"Lemon?"

"Please."

He twisted a piece of lemon over the glass. He dropped the peel into the drink and wiped his fingers.

"There." He handed her the glass. "One vodka Gibson."

She sipped it slowly, studying him over the rim of the glass.

"Mmm. One *very* good vodka Gibson. Even *Le Monde* would have to approve."

"Please." He held out his hand, indicating an armchair.

Catharine sat down. There was the intimate sound of nylon on nylon as one leg crossed the other. The armchair was low. Her charcoal-colored shantung skirt rode several inches up her thigh. It was quite deliberate. Her twelve-denier stockings were barely there at all.

Stosch looked away.

Catharine often wondered about him. He had almost the same kind of repressed animalism that Philippe had—yet there was something about Dieter Stosch that didn't fit. It wasn't that he had no gift for friendship. Nor that he lacked the aristocratic disdain that she found so exciting in the Prince. It wasn't as easy as that. She sometimes felt as if she'd almost completed a large and complicated jigsaw puzzle and *knew* she was going to have just one piece too many; or one piece would be lost. It was muddling. She had heard all the rumors, of course. Stosch was a pederast. He was asexual. He'd been genitally mutilated in the war. She seldom paid much attention to rumor, but it was curious that she didn't know of a single girl who had been to bed with him. What drove him? She'd read somewhere that men are motivated by sex or money or power. Well, if it wasn't sex—

"How was the flight from Paris?"

"Fine. Mlle. Ledoux failed to make the connection."

"The Prince?"

"He behaved like a man coming to mourn. I suspect he felt like a man coming to collect."

Stosch smiled.

He finished his Scotch and poured himself a cup of black coffee. He stirred it slowly.

"What have you got for me?"

Catharine took a long white envelope from her purse.

"My report. Up until two days ago," she said.

"This woman Isak Girod. She interests me. What is your reading of her?" he asked. He placed the envelope on his desk.

"His permanent woman. She has moved into the Île St.-Louis apartment, but she keeps her own place in St.-Germain-des-Prés."

"How serious is this affair, do you think?"

"Difficult to say. She has others."

"Does he know?"

"Perhaps. She is discreet, yet not discreet. The theater, film premières, the best restaurants—the safe out-in-the-open places always. They are usually well-known men, often friends of the Prince."

"She is an actress?"

"Yes."

"Anything else?"

"A *clandé* pro? That occurred to me. But I don't think so. With actresses there are always rumors."

"These relationships—could they be platonic?" Stosch asked.

"As a woman I have to say . . . the sort of men—no, possibly not always platonic. But there are no times, no places. . . ."

He went across to his desk and poured himself another coffee. Catharine followed him with her eyes. He returned and stood in front of her. His hand beneath the saucer held the coffee level with his chest. From where she sat she could not see his face.

Catharine said, "Some kind of understanding?"

"It's always possible. Is it likely?"

"He still has his other women. He has many appetites." She nodded to the envelope on the desk. "It is all there. Some strong stuff." She tried to judge whether he wanted her to go on. Maybe he got his kicks from conversation. She said, "He's into whores. Sometimes the cheaper girls on the avenue Wagram. He likes to haggle." She felt at a disadvantage not being able to see his face. She said, "He is into threesomes . . ."

"Do we have the names?"

"Several names, yes. But only the professionals."

"The Girod woman isn't involved in these games?"

"There is one unidentified woman who *might* be Girod—that's in the report."

"Is he . . . homosexual?"

"It seems unlikely. Although he did go to an English public school."

Stosch nodded. He finished his coffee. He put the cup and saucer back on his desk and picked up the envelope.

"I shall read this tonight—with interest," he said. She recognized the concluding tone in his voice. It was as apparent as if he'd handed her her coat. She finished the Gibson and put the glass on the floor by her chair.

"Tell me, Mlle. Gaillard. How are you enjoying your new career?"

"I wouldn't do it for Air France," she said.

"You're not bored?"

"It's a good deal less . . . *demanding* than being a whore," she said almost cheerfully. It never worried Catharine, owning up to her profession. A lot of the girls in the *clandé* avoided the word whore. Some convinced themselves they weren't in the game at all; they played blindman's buff with their consciences.

Catharine didn't look like a whore and she didn't think like a whore. That was her strength.

"You still have some . . . good friends?" Stosch asked.

"Of course," she said. "A girl can't expect to fly forever."

Stosch nodded.

She was on her way to the door when she noticed the large dictionary.

"Oh, may I look something up very quickly?" she asked. She touched the book on his desk.

Stosch moved his palm slowly upward.

"Of course. You have a sudden thirst for knowledge?"

"A word I didn't know. A crossword I was doing on the plane this morning."

"Are you an addict?"

"You'd be surprised how lonely a girl gets between . . . engagements. Some girls knit. Some get rid of unwanted hair. Others sleep. I did crosswords."

Catharine frowned in concentration as she turned over the thin pages of the big dictionary.

"I have a small pocket dictionary but it isn't in that—ah, here we are. *Interregnum.*"

She read the entry several times. She turned back to the front of the book and checked the key to the pronunciation. She said aloud, "Interregnum." She pronounced it slowly and carefully as if it were a word in a foreign language she had to remember.

She closed the book using both hands and smiled at Stosch.

"I like to discover new words," she said.

"Knowing too many words can be confusing," he said. He rolled his thumb across the middle and index fingers of his right hand. "This is . . . communication."

"Of course—only I happen to love words. Words are . . . words are information. I'm a girl who likes to be informed. I like to know what's going on in the world." She smiled. "I want to be rich as well, of course."

"The richer a person gets the more the words he uses have different meanings," Stosch said.

"I'm not nearly rich enough to know that."

He crossed the room and opened the door for her. They stood very close for a moment. He looked at her intently but said nothing. She could feel his breath on her face.

"Good night, M. Stosch." Catharine held out her hand. His intent gaze made her feel uncomfortable. He took hold of her hand and held it close to his body.

"Dollars, Mlle. Gaillard, are a safer investment than dictionaries."

Catharine laughed and he released her hand.

"I'll remember that," she said.

"Do," Stosch said.

"I shall," she said.

Interregnum—a breach of continuity; an interval; pause; a vacant space. Stosch began to frown until a series of deep vertical furrows ran along the top of his eyebrows like a white picket fence. *Authority or rule exercised during a vacancy of the throne, or a suspension of the usual government. A cessation or suspension of the usual ruling power.*

He closed the dictionary slowly.

His eyes were like embedded bullets, cordite bruised, revealing nothing of value.

13

It had been a satisfactory evening. Richard Antrobus was nearly eight hundred pounds up, most of it taken off Biron Strauss. Not that Strauss was any pigeon at seven-card stud, but the producer's mind had been elsewhere. For the last twenty minutes it had been like taking candy from a baby. Antrobus had visions of cleaning up enough to settle his Deauville marker.

Strauss finally quit after staying to the death with two pair, aces and kings, with Antrobus showing three queens from card five.

"Enough already," Strauss said in a surrendering voice. He lifted his hands level with his shoulders and seemed to be pushing at some heavy invisible door with his soft white palms.

"It's always a pleasure to do business with a gentleman," Antrobus said. He hid his disappointment with a smile.

Strauss paid out in large white five-pound notes which he counted hurriedly between thumb and forefinger like a bad-tempered bank teller.

"I'll buy you a drink," Antrobus said.

"That's very civilized of you," Strauss said, moving his mid-Atlantic accent closer to England and, he hoped, Oxford, in deference to Antrobus.

"So what do you know, Richard?" Strauss said. They had given their orders. The producer found it hard to appear casual. He was not a good loser. They had walked to the Dorchester bar from the game in Curzon Street in a silence you could have built a small mausoleum around.

"Your name came up the other day," Antrobus said.

He frowned as if trying to recall the occasion more precisely.

It pleased Strauss to think that his name had been mentioned—that he had actually been discussed—in the kind of circles in which Richard Antrobus moved. The ill-tempered grief went out of his face almost at once.

"Yes?" he said encouragingly.

"Yes. Where the dickens was it now?" Antrobus pretended to ransack his memory. He was actually thinking about how very good it had been in Georgina Game's bed. He was still thinking about that when the waiter arrived with two large Gordons with ice and lemon. He added a token of tonic and left the splits on the table along with a dish of mixed nuts. "Oh, I know," Antrobus said, reaching for the nuts. "That young actress— the girl in *The Last Sky*."

Strauss's face collapsed with disappointment, as if someone had cut the guy-ropes holding it taut. "That little bitch," he said. His voice had a vehemence that interested Antrobus immediately.

"She spoke very well of you," he said. "What *is* her name?"

"Georgina Game," Strauss said. He took a large gulp of his drink. A slice of lemon went into his mouth. He spat it back into the glass as if it were a yellow slug that had crawled onto his tongue and died.

"Georgina Game," Antrobus said slowly. "Right." His grin subsided into something more sympathetic. "Not your favorite lady, Biron?"

"She's just turned down my next picture." There was a look on his face that Antrobus found both distasteful and comic.

"Plenty more fish in the sea, old boy," Antrobus said. He didn't try very hard to make it sound reassuring.

"The pawnbrokers putting up the money, they got a thing about her. You know her well—milady Game?"

"I sat next to her the other day at one of Lizzie Huntington's luncheon parties," Antrobus said carelessly. "I must say she does have a certain paprika."

"*Danger East*—you read it? That part, your Aunt Edna could ring bells."

Antrobus smiled but it had no connection with humor.

"Great parts make great stars," Strauss said, proving, if nothing else, that he'd read the collected wit and wisdom of Goldwyn, DeMille, and Harry Cohn.

"Why's she against it?"

"Because she's a prune-picker, a *dummkopf*, I don't know."

"Biron, old chum, you thrive on disasters."

Antrobus caught the barman's eye and made small rapid circles over their glasses with his index finger.

"They tell me: get Monty Clift, you got a deal. I get Monty Clift. Then they say: get Georgina Game, she's classy, she's a comer. Okay, I say, no sweat. Jesus Christ! Without that eighteen-carat cow—you can stick a lily in my hand."

There was a small stir as Laurel Powell came into the bar with her agent and a couple of pretty young men. She was five years and a couple of marriages past her Hollywood prime but she still put on a great show. She was doing a picture at Pinewood for half her old price and twice the tantrums. She saw Strauss and stopped by the table. Strauss introduced her to Antrobus. Close up she was hard-faced. She smiled like she didn't trust the stitches.

"Walking death in diamonds," Strauss said when she'd gone.

"Don't you own *Danger East*?" Antrobus didn't want to let it go. He liked to watch Strauss squirm.

"An option. A six-month option. Seven weeks are down the pan already."

The waiter brought another round and a fresh bowl of nuts. The two men said nothing while he added tonic and removed the empties. Strauss's gaze wandered to the telephone at the end of the bar. Producers get anxious if they're not near a telephone.

"After twenty-six weeks I'm in the hole to Siegelman for more than I made my last two pictures for," he said morosely.

"You lose the option?"

"Check."

"I see your problem."

Strauss smiled bravely. "I've had the skids put under me by experts, Richard. I've been screwed, pumped full of shit, and *yentzed* by heavyweights. I'm going to be beaten by this uppity shikse?"

"Siegelman surely knows the fix you're in. Won't he extend the option?"

"For free? Would you? I wouldn't! Mr. Siegelman isn't a guy who concerns himself with ideas of self-sacrifice."

"Couldn't—"

"If I'm not off the ground by October thirty, Mr. Siegelman'll laugh all the way to Chase-Manhattan."

"The rights revert to him?"

"The whole kit and caboodle clean through. The merchandise goes back in the window."

"Why are your people sticking on Georgina Game, for fuck sake?"

"Don't be too naive, my friend."

"I don't—"

"Do you think those pimps and polo players in California haven't already got a lock on the next option? All those Apaches have to do is string me along. October, I'm dealt out. It's a wind-up, Richard."

"Jesus."

"Your Man, not mine."

"It's a rough old business, Biron."

"I'm a counter-puncher since Fanny was a girl's name. I'm not finished. Not yet."

"You've got, what, four months? A hard row to hoe."

"Four months, a lot can happen."

"I wish you luck."

"Biron Strauss is no quitter."

For a moment Antrobus felt almost sorry for him. He made it sound like the world against Biron Strauss. But, then, Strauss probably wasn't telling him the whole story anyway. Just the edited highlights, the bits that made him look like Mr. Clean. Antrobus remembered Georgina Game's contempt for Strauss, the angry way she'd turned down the picture once his name was mentioned. Was that an act?

"Is she in on the wind-up?"

"Who the hell knows?"

"You've tried money, of course?"

"The whole smear."

"There's no justice, Biron."

"Justice I'm not worried about. Justice never tallies with taking care of number one. Survival, the primal elements, that's what it's about."

Strauss sipped his drink and thought for a moment.

"Greed—now that I can understand," he said. "I can deal with greed. Greed is a kind of strength, handled properly. A pragmatic principle. Okay, greed, you know where you are with greed. But this girl—this muff—she gets offered the best bloody part since *Johnny Belinda* and she doesn't want to know."

The telephone rang. The barman took the call. He looked around the bar for a moment but whoever he was looking for wasn't there. He said half a dozen words into the mouthpiece, chuckled briefly, and replaced the receiver. Strauss looked disappointed.

"In screen time, it's not so much," the producer said. "In screen time, Monty Clift's got the picture. But the girl's got ten minutes in the middle, a death scene that'll break your heart. It's an Oscar down cold if she's half as good as she thinks she is."

"It's a marvelous book," Antrobus said, vaguely recalling a review he'd read in a newspaper or magazine somewhere or other. He hadn't read a book in years.

"So, you tell me, what's her game?" Strauss asked.

"I don't know," Antrobus answered shortly. He was becoming bored with the question, tired of listening to Strauss's problems. He had his own problems to worry about. Like finding $51,400 to settle his Deauville marker. The early euphoria he felt about the debt had faded. The Deauville business was no longer another romantic scrape, another Richard Antrobus adventure to be told and retold, exaggerated and embellished in clubs and Mayfair drawing rooms. There was no Caroline Wylie to bail him out this time. He recognized the seriousness of his situation, like a man coming out of an anesthetic, his dream already gone. Pretty soon, he knew himself well enough, his nerves would be stretched to breaking point. The eight hundred quid he had taken off Biron Strauss was a drop in the bucket. He had to stop kidding himself. To live the kind of life he'd grown used to with Caroline a man needed money. Serious money. And he needed it fast.

"Let me tell you something," Strauss said. "Last year—" his eyes searched the clipping he'd extracted from his wallet—"last year . . . here it is. The Screen Actors Guild estimated that seventy-two percent of all featured and supporting roles were written for men." He hit the cutting with his deformed index finger flicked from his thumb.

Antrobus studied the ice in his drink.

"That leaves twenty-eight percent for the women, right?"

"A drop in the bucket," Antrobus said.

"The rate sheet don't lie," Strauss said. "There's Wyman, Gardner, Kerr, who else? They cop everything worth a damn. Georgina Game's never seen a script that hasn't had Kerr's fingerprints all over it. What's left for kids like her?"

"Not a lot."

"Chickenshit," Strauss said. "Chickenshit's what's left." He carefully refolded the *Variety* clipping and replaced it in his wallet. "Girls don't sell movies. This year only two actresses—Grable and Doris Day—in the top ten. Last year, Grable and Esther Williams. The year before, Grable and Bergman. Actresses—you're lucky if you see thirty cents on your dollar." He took a handful of nuts and ate them, quickly, one by one, from his cupped hand. "But whatever—the Apaches still want Georgina Game. I'd like to blot her off the map. You know, there's a producer in Mexico who actually shoots actors who give him too much lip."

An idea had slowly begun to form in Antrobus' mind.

"How much?" he said quietly.

"How much what?" The wired look of a small field animal came into Strauss's eyes. A peanut stopped halfway to his wet mouth. "You mean—take care of her? Get rid of her?"

"Don't be stupid, Biron. How much if I *delivered* her."

"Richard, don't be funny with me now."

"I'm serious, Strauss. Say."

"Never crap a crapper," Strauss said. The peanut went into his mouth.

"I'm serious," said Antrobus. "How much?"

"The usual agent's commission. Ten percent."

"Fifty percent. Cash. And nobody's to know I'm involved."

"You're talking like a guy with a paper asshole, Richard, if I may say so."

"Yes or no?"

"You met her once?"

"Yes."

"Once! Richard, please, I'm not in the mood for your jokes. You are not a sensitive man."

"Fifty percent. Half of whatever you pay her. Cash. And I've never been more serious in my life. I'll get you Georgina Game."

"You expect me to pay her her full fee plus half again for you."

"You've got it."

Strauss called for another round.

"Even supposing I agreed, it would take more than your charm—"

"Strauss, you've got nothing to lose. Without her you might as well kiss the picture good-bye now and you know it."

"I'll give you twenty-five percent up to twenty thousand pounds. Fifteen percent thereafter," Strauss said, but not as if it mattered.

"Strauss, you've just spent the last hour telling me how you're dancing on a hot griddle. Now you're quibbling over—"

"I like to quibble. Quibbling is second nature to me."

"But not to me," Antrobus said.

The drinks arrived. Neither man spoke for several minutes.

It was Strauss who broke the silence.

"You have a quarrelsome vivacity, Richard. But I

suspect the amount is academic. You get me Georgina Game and you can have your fifty percent."

"Up to and over twenty thousand pounds?"

"Up to and over twenty thousand pounds," Strauss said. "All the way."

"It's a deal," Antrobus said and the two men shook hands.

"C.O.D.," Strauss said, signaling for the check and pointing to Richard Antrobus.

14

Dieter Stosch stepped out of the shower, his lean body glistening, his blond hair plastered tight to his skull. Icy rivulets trickled out of his nostrils and ears and mouth and from between his legs. He was making a small noise that was neither a whistle nor a whimper. It was a sound that seemed to convey no pain and no pleasure. It was the pure sound of athletic martyrdom. He took one of the half-dozen black bath towels that hung on wooden pegs outside the shower and began to rub himself dry before a workout mirror that covered the far wall of his private gymnasium.

Scars like dry riverbeds, white as fishbone, were carved into his muscular legs and criss-crossed deep into his abdomen and genitals. Despite the disfiguration, it was a superb body, a body that had been tested to the very limits of its animality, as hard and spare and purposeful as flint.

Finally dry, he poured a fine layer of cold-pressed Egyptian body oil over his scarred stomach. The smell of cinnamon and cloves spiced the air, sharpening the sweet stale smell of sweat that already permeated the room. He massaged the oil into the sinewy bands of recti muscles flexed barely beneath the surface of his skin.

Watching himself closely in the large mirror, Stosch spread the saffron-colored oil across his narrow hips and downward over the iliac crest and into his groins and pelvis and genitals and between his strong legs. His powerful blunt fingers worked the expensive lubricant into the crevices and joints, ligaments and muscles of his body. He worked slowly, with the passionate concentration of a man replenishing energy and restoring lost youth, in silence. It was that special silence of self-absorption that goes into the finest art. His penis had grown large with all the oiled attention, but was not hard.

After fifteen minutes he was finished.

He studied himself once more in the mirror, turning slowly this way and that, like a woman considering a daring new dress with a combination of reproof and pleasure.

Finally, after a brief dismissing nod of satisfaction to his reflection, Stosch removed a black hooded robe from a closet built into the wall behind the sliding workout mirror.

He slipped into the robe gently, easing his arms through the wide sleeves.

He tied the robe loosely around himself, like a prizefighter on his way to the ring.

The robe gave him a severe yet monkish look, a pious purposeful air. He left the gymnasium and walked swiftly, barefoot, to his *petit appartement* above the palace's mirrored and gilded Chambre de Parade in which Maximilien's catafalque, mounted upon a roulette wheel, symbolizing the greatest game of chance of them all, waited.

He went directly to his bedroom. Like many people who are not born to live in palaces, Stosch cherished the intimacy of his rooms. It was a room, his bedroom, that could not have been described as either masculine or feminine, as most bedrooms can be. Tortoiseshell-colored, lit by skylights, it contained a large Italian bed, a refectory table, bookcase, and an old military chest that smelled faintly of camphor and wax. Two tapestried armchairs were arranged on either side of a marble fireplace. Over the fireplace were twelve etchings of the Black Forest by Laurens Janscha. An angular poppy-red Cabistan carpet covered half the wide polished-oak floorboards.

He sat at the refectory table.

Propped between the pieces of an ivory chess set was Catharine Gaillard's report. He took the envelope in one hand and picked up a silver paper knife with the other. He seemed to be in no hurry. He seemed to be lost in thought. Outside, the sea rose and fell away again, like a sleeping monster, breathing deeply, sighing, dreaming; silence, Stosch felt, was the sound of a calm sea at two o'clock in the morning.

He split open the envelope and extracted the report. The product. It had been typed on a portable typewriter, double-spaced with wide margins in which Catharine had added some afterthoughts and observations in a light script written at a speed which slightly compressed the letters and gave them a forward *italic* slope. There were, in fact, two separate sheaves; one was headed *H.R.H.* The second, thinner sheaf was headed *I.G.* Neither Philippe nor Isak Girod was referred to by name throughout the thirty-seven pages.

Stosch sucked in his breath and seemed to hesitate for a moment before rising. He crossed the room and put Debussy's *Sonata in G Minor* on the record player. It was far from Debussy's best work. Written when he was dying, his swan song, it betrayed his fatigue, his defiance, the effort and the terrible toll. Stosch, if he were ever moved at all, was moved by that which was extended to the limits—a racehorse, a painter, a gambler, a dying composer. When they had nothing left, when they had done everything they could and still they tried—that, for Dieter Stosch, was beauty.

The pages on Isak Girod were mostly biographical. Catharine understood that information came before evidence: first the dossier, then the indictment. Nothing was wasted, nothing was unimportant.

Isak Girod was an actress, aged twenty-four. Her father a florist in Chamonix. Her mother left home when Isak was nine years old; she now lived in the small town of Mont-St.-Michel with her lover, a director of a textile business. Catholics, Isak's parents had never divorced. Isak no longer spoke to her mother; there was now a half-brother she'd never seen.

Isak had had a varied education: "Two years Sorbonne; six months as an usherette at the Chaillot Theatre; eleven months in the Folies Bergère," Catharine noted drily. She had played Ophelia ("none too well," according to a margin note) at the Marigny Theatre and understudied Blanche in *A Streetcar Named Desire* at the Théâtre Edouard VII.

During the run of the Tennessee Williams play she met Philippe at a party given by Raoul Richelieu, the hairdresser. The meeting was a setup suggested and paid for by Philippe. She had had several affairs before Philippe came on the scene. Notably a year-long liaison with the singer Yves Segni. Segni blew his own head off with a .44 Magnum in his chalet in Arosa ten days after Isak left him for Philippe. In his will, the singer left Isak the gun, the chalet, and seventy thousand dollars. "She has not relinquished *any* part of her inheritance," Catharine observed in the margin. Five weeks after Yves Segni calamitously messed up the original decor, Isak and Philippe spent a long weekend at the chalet. Catharine made no marginal comment.

Isak had acted less and less since beginning her affair with Philippe; it was not possible to say whether this was because he objected to her career, or because she had not been offered very much in recent months.

There was a lot more stuff. Names and addresses of Isak's friends. The name of her agent, her doctor, where she bought her clothes and shoes, where she banked, the stocks she held.

Stosch came to the end of the report and folded it carefully and returned it to the envelope. It was not a lot but it was a start. When it had been evaluated and checked out against information coming in from all the other sources—he would know all there was to know about Mlle. Isak Girod.

He turned his attention to the report on H.R.H.

It was longer than the Girod product, but it read smoothly. Catharine Gaillard never dealt in emotion,

never went in for rhetoric. Stosch preferred a single verifiable fact to a string of clever inferences. He did not
care for other people's hypotheses, bias, and opinion.
Facts, incidents, information were put down in a skillful efficient narrative style. A lot of what she'd written
was confirmation of what Stosch already knew, but he
didn't mind that.

There was one long quote from a *clandé* whore that
particularly interested him and he read it several times.
It was probably transcribed from a tape recording.

"He has been here three or four times. Once with a
woman he said was his wife but, of course, I know he
has no wife. She could have been another pro—from
another *clandé*, perhaps. No? It does not matter. Anyway, this time he wanted to be beaten while she
watched. All the time she taunted him. She was very
good, very graphic, pitiless. I thrashed him hard. I offered her the whip but she said she was not a flagellant.
She was very aroused though. Afterward we made love,
the girl and me. She was very beautiful. He insisted on
candlelight and she stayed in the shadow. Perhaps she
was famous, or somebody else's wife. I was curious,
naturally—but sometimes it is best not to know, no?
She had made love to many women before me, I can
tell you that."

Stosch slowly folded the report. It was a first-rate
product. Catharine Gaillard knew her business. She was
the cleverest if not the most beautiful of the fifteen
women who worked in the field for the Memorandum.
The girls were prostitutes of the very highest class, including several well-known models, a couple of high-
echelon French actresses, and a titled woman who belonged to one of the oldest families in Rome. They all
lived splendidly immersed in the international life of
sexuality, pleasure—and gossip.

Prostitution at this level was the perfect cover. There
was little hand-holding: each girl was out on her own.
Only when a particular surveillance was required was
she told to cultivate a particular lover, or to penetrate a
certain circle.

Genevieve Lacroix was the go-between. She was

known only as Mlle. Chaire. Inside the Bureau she was called "the desk lady."

The girls were highly paid, even by their own exceptional standards, but did not know by whom, or for what purpose the product was required. Stosch, known as Principal Consumer, worked through Mlle. Chaire. The girls believed they were employed by one or another of the international intelligence agencies. A belief Mlle. Chaire encouraged. Nothing could be traced to St. Saladin. Nothing could be traced to the SS Memorandum. It was a sophisticated network based on a principle stretching back to long before Rahab the harlot betrayed Jericho to Joshua.

Stosch found it extraordinary how quickly men under the influence of illicit passion acquired a mawkish trust in the implausible loyalty of the women they laid.

He smiled bleakly as that thought came to him again. Hadn't he committed the same mistake with Catharine Gaillard? There had been no sexual involvement, but he had allowed her to get too close. She was the only operative who knew how the setup worked. Since being planted on Philippe's staff, she had been permitted to contact Principal Consumer direct and without question.

Her value to the Bureau was proven and incalculable. Her lovers included a chief in the French Ministry of the Interior, a senior English diplomat at the Embassy in Paris, and one of the richest financiers in Europe.

It would be a pity to lose those connections. But when a girl got out of line . . .

He reached for the telephone and dialed three digits. A soft feminine voice answered.

"We have a problem," Stosch spoke slowly, giving the listener time to wake up. "We have to economize."

"The name?"

"Mlle. Catharine Gaillard."

"How very disappointing."

"As soon as possible," Stosch said.

"Naturally."

Stosch replaced the telephone in the cradle. He switched off the light and removed his black robe and went to bed naked.

Such a waste, he thought. But it had to be. He knew it would be quick and clean.

Dieter Stosch had the best "economist" in the game.

15

Georgina Game woke up a few minutes after nine o'clock. She was in her own bedroom, and alone. She hadn't worked for two months and when she didn't work, she became rather oversocial. But she always liked to wake up in her own bed, preferably unaccompanied. She had never been keen on the morning-after routine that one went through with an overnight lover—the *boff de politesse*, the seemly bath, the light breakfast, and the quick getaway. Georgina smiled and stretched herself in a catlike way, drowsily shaking off the slumber still in her body.

She had dined the previous evening at Liz Huntington's. Liz made her laugh; she was good news. A successful model, Liz Huntington knew masses of the right people. She had a busy little brain and her parties were cast with extreme care.

There had been eighteen people at last night's dinner. Liz, in her straight-arm fashion, had highly recommended a German diplomat. She whispered he was going to be the next head of the West German Chancery in London. Unfortunately, Georgina found him mortally unattractive, despite his well-connected gossip. She left early, slipping out after coffee. She was surprised Liz hadn't already been on the telephone complaining, demanding to know why she hadn't paid more attention to the German, after all the trouble she'd gone to getting him there just for her! It would all be said in a wounded tone of personal letdown. Liz's reprimands always ended the same way: Georgina was throwing away her chances. Georgina knew why Liz was popular with other women: she had the knack of showing concern for the love lives of others—and kept her own affairs to herself. She was a great simplifier.

The sound of a key in the front door interrupted Georgina's musing. The door opened and closed again. There was a deep sigh of exertion as the visitor bent down to retrieve the newspapers and the mail.

"Mrs. Harris?"

"Me, Miss Georgina."

"Good morning." Georgina was surprised by the cheerfulness in her own voice. She really must get more early nights.

"It's a lovely morning, for a change."

"Good," Georgina answered.

Mrs. Harris went through to the kitchen. The sound of water filling the kettle, the dull plop of the gas ring, the cheerful clatter of cups and saucers. All the oddly comforting sounds of domesticity. It was the one routine that didn't lead to boredom, Georgina thought.

Another deep sigh as Mrs. Harris sat down and took off her outdoor shoes and put on the moccasins Georgina had brought back from Spain for her last year.

"Do you know anyone who wants a kitten?" Mrs. Harris called from the kitchen.

"No," Georgina said firmly. "How many this time?"

"Five."

"You'll have to do something about that animal of yours," Georgina said.

"She keeps getting raped, dear."

"I thought it was romance."

"Bloody romance."

"Poor puss. How sad."

"At least she gets her share."

Georgina laughed. "She sure as hell does."

"Did you hear that storm in the night?" Mrs. Harris changed the subject.

"A storm? I slept like a log."

"Raining cats and dogs. One cup, is it—?"

"Please." Georgina smiled at Mrs. Harris' worked-at worldliness. She liked to pretend that nothing shocked her.

"We might get a bit of summer now that lot's out of the way."

"What lot?"

"That thunderstorm."

Georgina stretched herself slowly with a small mugient hum of well-being. She raised herself on one elbow and arranged the pillows behind her.

"What's happening in the world today, Mrs. Harris?" she called out. She hoped it would encourage her to bring in the newspapers. Mrs. Harris didn't hear, or didn't want to.

Georgina fell back onto the pillows and waited. She looked down and cupped her naked breasts approvingly. She was surprised to see how hard her nipples were. The discovery made her feel quite sexy. Perhaps she should slip something over her shoulders before Mrs. Harris came in with the tea. But she couldn't be bothered to get out of bed. Mrs. Harris had seen erect nipples before. At least Georgina hoped she had.

Mrs. Harris backed into the room carrying the tea tray, the morning newspapers under her arm. She was a small, slightly overweight woman in her early fifties with wiry ginger hair going gray. She wore a floral-patterned apron over a pale-blue rayon dress. It was the dress she had bought for her niece's wedding at Easter; she always liked to dress "a bit near the mark" when she worked for Miss Game.

"There we are," she said. She put the tray down on Georgina's lap.

Georgina picked up the glass of plain hot water. Hot water, first thing in the morning, was very good for the complexion: it washed and activated the kidneys, Georgina said. She had a beautiful complexion—"like an abalone pearl," a lover had once told her. It was funny how she had remembered the compliment but not the man who'd made it. It was not merely a phrase to flatter. She knew that. She had turned down several soap commercials.

Mrs. Harris took the empty glass and put the newspapers on the bed beside the tray.

"And 'ere's your linens."

"Linen drapers—papers," Georgina said.

"Very good," Mrs. Harris said. She was teaching Georgina cockney rhyming slang. "I don't know why you wastes money on that lot."

"I like to know what's going on in the world," Georgina said. She poured her tea.

"You're morbid," Mrs. Harris said. "Morbid."

"Could be," Georgina said. She added milk from a small silver jug.

"I've got enough worries 'ere without reading what's up in China," Mrs. Harris said. She went out with a kind of beset dignity. A moment later the radio came on. "Mairzy doats and dozy doats and—" The rest was drowned out by the purposeful moan of the Hoover.

Georgina picked up the three letters on her breakfast tray. One was from Claridge's. She opened that first. It was, as she'd guessed, the bill for the lunch she'd had three months ago with an old friend from Sarah Lawrence.

The second letter was from a dress shop in Bond Street inviting her to an autumn preview and offering a twenty percent discount. That was worth looking into, she thought.

The third letter was handwritten and had a local postmark. It was from Richard Antrobus. It was brief, and discreet. He said how very much he'd enjoyed meeting her the other day. He hoped she was well, and what was she doing on the seventeenth? Would she care to go to the Gold Cup at Ascot? He would arrange a hamper from Fortnum and Mason. He would telephone. He sent his best wishes and signed off with his full name.

He had style, she had to admit that. A Fortnum's hamper, indeed.

She skimmed through the *Times*, then the *Daily Express*. Both newspapers carried stories about two Foreign Office diplomats who'd disappeared and were believed to be making for Moscow. Both papers hinted at a first-rate spy scandal. It was nice to be in the know. According to her German dinner companion, the missing diplomats were a couple of homos named Burgess and Maclean. Was it Maclean who'd been head of the American Department? And Burgess a second secretary in the Embassy in Washington? According to Heinie they were both long-term Soviet agents—moles, he'd called them—and not the only ones buried inside the British Foreign Office, either.

Georgina wished she'd paid more attention to the German. She opened the *Daily Express* and turned to Lord Luck.

Aries. Your intuition and commercial acumen will see you through. Don't be afraid to strike a hard bargain. An unexpected invitation.

"Ascot Races here I come, do-dah, do-dah."

"Did you call, Miss Georgina?" Mrs. Harris popped her rusty-gray head around the door, pulling the suddenly silent Hoover behind her.

"I was singing," Georgina said. She had a feigned look of hurt dignity.

"Thought you was 'ollering."

"You could run me a nice bath."

"The dust that collects in that blessed 'all," Mrs. Harris said. She went out to prepare the bath.

Georgina got up and slipped on her pale-blue bathrobe. *Don't be afraid to strike a hard bargain.* That wasn't telling an Aries very much.

"I don't know why you keeps all those cars around the side of that bath." Mrs. Harris came back to tell Georgina her bath was ready. "Keep falling in the water. They're a bloomin' nuisance."

"You can't complain they're dust collectors," Georgina said.

"Little boys' things. Don't know why you don't get rid of 'em."

"My *collection*?" Georgina said, using an astonished Lady Bracknell voice. "Get rid of *my* collection?"

"You'll step on one of them one of these mornings. Break your neck."

The collection had started as a joke. A lover had claimed that all women were divided into Ferrari females and Lagonda ladies. Georgina, he said, was definitely a Lagonda lady. The following day he'd sent her a model of an early Lagonda. She put it on the side of the bath and forgot all about it—until another lover noticed it and sent her a model of his own two-litre Aston-Martin. Somebody else noticed the Lagonda and Aston-Martin and, assuming she had a passion for model cars, contributed a beautiful 1934 Chrysler Airflow with its waterfall grill, built-in wings and headlamps.

And so the collection grew.

There were now nine models on the porcelain grid, from an Alvis to a rare Russian Zis.

It was one way of keeping score.

Did Mrs. H. guess their significance? Probably. Georgina recalled one of her mother's sayings: "Servants never see what we show them, but they'll always see what we hide from them."

She lay and soaked for over an hour. The telephone rang several times but she had told Mrs. Harris to answer it and say that Miss Game was not at home.

She was looking forward to having lunch with her father. She hadn't seen him for a whole month. He'd probably built six small-to-large towns in the meantime. She was proud of her father, but still resented being called an heiress in the newspapers. It made it sound as if her career were a sort of pastime, like horseback riding or attending charity balls.

Harry Ogilvy was born in a coal-mining village in Lanarkshire in Scotland. He was an only child. He was ten weeks old when his father died in a pit fall which killed sixty-seven miners and all but finished off the village. His mother died when he was ten and he was taken in by the sisters of a Catholic convent on the outskirts of Edinburgh.

He was a small, weak-chested, inside-himself boy—never any trouble, they said—whose blond innocent good looks aroused both pity and interest. He had an aureole of private vengeance which the nuns mistook for a kind of piety.

He left the convent at fourteen to work in an estate agent's office in Dundee. Property became his passion. Very soon he proved to be a schemer with a considerable talent for intrigue. By the time he was twenty-three, he owned some two hundred properties in Dundee and Edinburgh and the surrounding countrysides, including a textile machinery factory and a linen mill.

After making his first million pounds, he moved south to London. Within a year he'd earned the nickname Harry Ogre, courted and married an American girl from an intellectually prominent family, and bought the former home of Lord Walswan on Curzon Street.

He had no illusions. He accepted his unpopularity as a fact of life. "At no point of my career could I have acted other than I did," he told the *Financial Times* in a rare interview. Harry Ogilvy had no interest in art, literature, or music. The gentlemanly pursuits of the countryside left him cold. Business—land deals, property speculation, the cut and thrust of takeover battles—was the driving force in his life. To get what he wanted, Harry Ogilvy used money, flattery, abuse, and threats.

Elizabeth Game was the youngest daughter of a Boston lawyer named James Minto Game, who had married a Radcliffe student, Rachel Blackman, from New York. James Minto was narrowly beaten for the governorship of Massachusetts the year Elizabeth graduated from Vassar. She had inherited her mother's lustrous Semitic beauty, was well-connected, and determined to push Harry on a better road.

Ogilvy was not convinced that a social career was open to him in London. "London isn't Boston," he warned his young bride. "Wealth doesn't atone for low origins."

"London isn't a lot of places, Harry," she said.

It was a surprisingly happy and successful marriage. Elizabeth gained a reputation as "the woman who could handle Harry." It was perfectly simple, she explained. Her husband respected people who had the guts to stand up to him. "People who put up with his tyranny and rages are as much to blame as Harry is himself," she said. "All strong men go to extremes if they're not challenged." She made it sound a simple matter.

But despite their social success, and Harry's growing recognition as a public figure, Harry Ogilvy had few real friends.

Elizabeth was returning from a short holiday in Sardinia when their private plane failed to lift off and crashed at one hundred and twenty miles an hour into a clump of pine trees due to be cut down the following day.

The pilot, Elizabeth, and Elizabeth's gynecologist died in the holocaust. Elizabeth was seven and a half months pregnant.

Georgina was ten years old.

"I lost my own mother when I was Georgina's age," Harry said when they brought him the news.

"He made it sound like a self-accusation," his secretary said.

Georgina accepted her mother's death with a sense of relief, with controlled excitement, and with only the smallest sense of loss: the thought of another child in the house had threatened her deeply and now the threat had gone.

She felt for the first time in her life a feeling of uniqueness, and an embroilment with life.

A friend who had gone to see Elizabeth off at the airport, found her wedding ring a little way from the wreckage. She sent it to Harry. Georgina now wore the ring on the middle finger of her right hand. On the inside of the ring was inscribed: *My Eternal Game —H.* Georgina wept when she first read it. The tears absolved her sense of guilt.

Harry grieved for Elizabeth in his fashion, but it was not a public grief. Only those who knew him well sensed the sadness. He became more meditative, a little more unpredictable.

He resolved that he would never marry again, and he never had. There had been several mistresses along the way. "Daddy's *demimondes*," Georgina called them with a precocity that contained neither jealousy nor resentment. She made it a practice from the beginning— and she was not quite twelve years old when Harry first brought a mistress to the house on Curzon Street—to address Harry's women by their first names. She was never reluctant to criticize—their clothes, their makeup, the scent they wore, the way they did their hair.

Not very long after Elizabeth's death, Georgina inherited her reputation as "the only woman who can handle Harry." Harry's women never disputed the claim. "Georgie girl's got Harry wrapped around her little finger," they said. The clever ones tolerated her; the others toadied up to her. She enjoyed her almost sensual power, and the strange harm she could inflict with a look of disapproval, a word of reproach.

As with nearly all first-generation rich men, Harry Ogilvy brought up his daughter like a princess. She learned to ride, ski, and sail. She attended ballet classes, spoke French and Italian, learned to play tennis, backgammon, and chess with champions. By the time she was thirteen, Harry was able to say with justification, "My daughter has all the aloofness of old money."

She had the best of everything. Elizabeth had insisted on an American education and Georgina's name was down for Miss Porter's School in Farmington, Connecticut, the week she was born. But Georgina showed that she had a will of her own. She chose Sarah Lawrence over Vassar, which had been Elizabeth's wish.

The most maturing experience of Georgina's life had been her mother's death, and the second most maturing experience had been losing her virginity to one of her mother's old flames, Charles Tobias Emerson, of Boston. Georgina was six years old before she realized that "of Boston" was not part and parcel of his name, since that was how her mother had always introduced him.

Georgina was returning to London from her last term at Sarah Lawrence. She had arranged to stop over in New York for five days to meet her mother's sister, Aunt Dorothy, who now lived in Williamsburgh, Virginia, and to pose for a *Vogue* magazine layout on the new international beauties.

Aunt Dorothy arrived at the Chambord with Charles Tobias Emerson in tow. He was quietly spoken, had nice hands and a gentle smile. He was fifty-five years old and Georgina knew at once that he was going to be her first lover.

That evening he took her to dinner at the Colony and then dancing at El Morocco. At two o'clock in the morning, Georgina told him she wanted to go home.

"The Plaza, Tom," Emerson told his chauffeur when they had settled back in his long black limousine.

"No, Charles."

"Where then?"

"I don't want to go back to the Plaza tonight. I want you to take me to your apartment. I want you to make love to me the best way you know how."

"Make that Sutton Place," Emerson said to his driver in a matter-of-fact way. There was a total absence of surprise in his voice. That impressed Georgina a lot. He took hold of her hand but said nothing.

He had a confident Princeton charm. But behind his exquisite correctness, Georgina felt the irresistible rottenness of a man who neither pursued nor resisted women.

That night Emerson was to come as close to fright as ever he'd come in his life.

"You're a virgin," he said in an accusatory voice.

"I wish to renounce my childish ways," she said. She spoke in the little-girl tone she'd often used to coax her father into a good humor.

It did nothing to relax Emerson at all.

"You've never slept with a man before?"

"I was afraid of having babies."

"You were—"

"I've done other things."

"What other things?"

"You know." She didn't expect him to make such heavy weather of her innocence.

"Petting?"

She pushed herself closer to him, enjoying his hardness which seemed to be pressed up against the entire length of her belly. It was a threatening feeling. It felt hot, much hotter than the rest of his body. She really shivered with anticipation.

She wondered what her mother would have thought of the picture they made at that moment.

She shivered again, stricken and aroused by the idea.

"What's the matter?"

"Nothing," she said. "Nothing's the matter."

"Petting?" he prompted again.

"Petting and stuff," she said.

"And stuff?"

"I've been," she said, "down on boys."

"Have you now?"

Georgina recognized the relief in his voice and something else that might have been amusement.

"Sure. A lot of girls do it. Girls my age. Girls even younger sometimes." She remembered the catchy phrase Kitty Cutforth kept using all last term. "A little fellatio on the patio," she said.

"That's nice," Emerson said softly, smelling her young hair.

"It never hurt anyone."

"It surely never did," he said.

Georgina had never done such a thing to a boy, or a man, in her life but she wanted to shock Charles Tobias Emerson, of Boston, out of any lingering chivalric reluctance he might have about going through with her seduction.

"I love it," she said in an encouraging voice.

She gently touched him with her fingertips, exploring the soft swollen vein that ran along the side of his hard penis. It feels like a fountain-pen bladder, filled with jello, she thought, smiling. Blueberry jello, probably.

He lifted her head and kissed her gently on her smiling mouth.

"Why are you smiling?" he asked.

"Nothing—I'm happy."

He kissed her lips again, pressing a little harder, and this time she opened her mouth and their tongues touched. She could taste the fresh Ipana not quite smothering the smell of cigar and cognac on his breath. She was sorry he'd cleaned his teeth. It spoiled the masculine taste of his mouth. Could a man be both antiseptic and amorous? she wondered.

"I want you to go down on me," he said. He was above her now, looking down into her face.

"I want you in me first. I want your beautiful thing inside me," she said. "Then I'll take you in my mouth."

She slid her sharp thumbnail into the slit of his penis, as deep as she could, and kept it there. She felt him react, with an intake of breath like a shuddering sigh, but he said nothing. It's like holding a razor to a man's throat, she thought. He had collapsed and lay by her side very still, as if afraid to breathe.

"Should I file my nails?"

"No," he said. "They're just jake."

"Yes?"

"Who taught you that?"

"What?"

"That!"

"Nobody. I believe it must come rather naturally to me. Do you like it?"

"Do I like it!"

"More?"

"That's just perf."

She turned her nail ever so slightly in the slit.

"The turn of the screw," she said.

"Oh Christ," he said quietly several times. "Oh Christ."

"I want you inside me," she said, putting a new ominous sound into her voice. *"Now!"*

"Darling—Georgina, sincerely, sweetheart—"

"I want your experience. Not your sincerity, Mr. Emerson. In matters of grave importance, style, not sincerity, is the vital thing."

"Oh Christ."

"O. Wilde."

"O. Wilde?"

"In matters of grave importance, style, not sincerity, is the vital thing. —Oscar Wilde."

"Jesus," Emerson said in a voice slightly more aggravated than amused.

"I think you'll find you're wrong."

"I can't compete with schoolgirl erudition," Emerson said. He was angry. He could feel the hardness going out of his penis.

Georgina felt it, too.

"Where do you think you're going?" she said, using her nail. It did the trick. She felt him grow again in her hand. He felt enormous.

She became serious.

"I want you inside me. *Please.*"

"Darling, please understand. I do want—"

"Just a minute." There was a different kind of urgency in Georgina's voice. "Where's the bathroom?"

"Through the door, on the left. Are you all right?"

"Don't go away," she said, squeezing him. She threw

back the sheet that covered them and slid off the bed and crossed the room quickly, as if her milky nakedness embarrassed her.

She fell against the door inside the dark room. She put her hand down and felt herself carefully. She was sure she was bleeding, although she wasn't due for at least ten more days. She found the bright bathroom light and checked her fingers. She was just very very wet.

She smiled at her reflection in Emerson's magnifying shaving mirror. "Okay, Mr. Emerson," she said softly. "Coming—ready or not."

She sniffed her fingers. She reached for the gold faucet but it was an automatic bathroom reaction and she changed her mind almost at once. She rather *liked* the way her fingers smelled. "Enough of being the nice guy," she lisped to herself in the mirror. She smiled with her teeth, like Bogart, and stroked the pearled wetness between her thighs. She sniffed at her fingers again, slowly, like a woman with a new scent.

She switched off the light, and returned to Emerson's bedroom. He was propped up on one elbow, waiting for her.

"Ta-daaa!" she said, posing for a moment in the doorway, her arms raised above her head.

He didn't say a word. She moved toward the bed as sinuously and as slowly as she could. Her cunt was on a level with his half-open lips with their sensual curves. "Yes," he said. He opened his mouth, wider, like a gasp, as she continued to move toward him slowly.

She locked herself onto his mouth and grabbed the back of his head, her fingers buried deep in his heavy graying hair.

His tongue, his flexed defiling tongue, went into her.

Her back curved, her blond hair flew about her as she was filled to the brim with sweet sensations.

The room became a brilliant flower garden seen through a filmy haze. The colors melted in a rush of noiseless movement, absorbing one another in a rich bursting bloom in space, vast, illimitable, bounded only by the night sky itself.

Afterward he told her, "You have such softness—and no weaknesses at all."

"It was lovely."

"Did you come well?"

He lay alongside her, bent sideways to the right, and slightly forward, emphasizing the muscly strength of his torso. It was a good body for a man of his age and he knew it.

"I thought I'd died and gone to heaven. Is that coming?"

"It'll do," he said.

"You have a beautiful body."

"How do you feel?"

"About what?"

"About losing your virginity."

"Unburdened."

"Truly?"

"Criss-cross my heart and swear to Bob."

"You don't hate me?"

"You're forgiven," she said, blessing him with the Sign of the Cross. "*Losing* one's virginity—it's such a negative way of looking at it."

She sat up cross-legged, facing him, cupping his penis in both her hands. "Look what I've *found*," she said eagerly. Her face was full of smiling exaggerated wonder. She examined his genitals with intense guileless fascination.

"Do you like it?"

"It's so inoffensive now. It's like a sleeping shrimpy moist mouse."

"It's bad form to tell a man he's shrimpy—even when he is."

"Does it always . . . deflate afterward?"

"For a little while."

"How long is a little while?"

"You'll find out soon enough."

"Yes?"

He felt her warm breath on him, then her teeth, then the melting honey spittle of her tongue as she finally took him wholly into her soft mouth. She felt no anxiety at all. She pulled back, gently, as Emerson grew larger and harder.

"How lovely," he said almost incoherently. A moan

began to grow in his throat and his face reddened and became distorted.

Charles Tobias Emerson made the most of Georgina's absolution during the days and nights that followed and Georgina learned a lot of all there is to learn about sex and passion and appetites and all the interwoven intrigues that two minds and two bodies are capable of. And most of all, she learned the audacities and the art of loving people as they want to be loved.

Georgina arrived a few minutes after one o'clock.

"Mr. Harry Ogilvy's table," she told the headwaiter.

"This way, Miss Game."

He led the way through the quiet, spacious, deceptively full restaurant to a window table on the Davies Street side of Claridge's. Harry Ogilvy stood up and kissed his daughter's cheek. He sat down almost at once. He was some three or four inches shorter than Georgina. Unlike a lot of really successful men of small or only average height, he was uncomfortable in the presence of tall women. (He had once lived with a Balmain model for nearly two years and Georgina had never seen them standing side by side, not even at home.)

"Honeybunch, how are you?"

"Blooming."

"You look blooming. Are you in love?"

"Certainly not. Some people have natural tans. I have this natural randy radiance."

"You shouldn't talk like that to your old father. A glass of champagne?" He nodded to the opened bottle of Krug that stood in the ice bucket by the table.

"That would be lovely."

He reached for the bottle but the wine steward got there first, appearing from nowhere with no sense of hurry at all. He poured the wine into a long-stemmed tulip-shaped glass and retreated into the invisible shadows that waiters of his class seem to carry with them.

"You're resting," Ogilvy asked. "As they say in the trade?"

"As they say in the trade."

"By choice I hope?"

"Of course," Georgina said, smiling gently.

"You don't get bored?"

"I enjoy it. I hate the early mornings when I'm on a picture. I'm like a whore. I can't stay in bed long enough."

"But what do you do with yourself all day?"

"I don't know. The days seem to fly fast enough. There's always something I have to do, somebody I have to see."

"It's all a game," he said. "It will not be long a-playing. Time's the chariot carrying us away." He raised his glass. "May you live all the days of your life, darling."

They drank the toast.

"Wouldn't it be nice if we could bribe the charioteer to drive a little slower . . . take the long way around," she said.

"See that man over there?" He nodded toward a thin sardonic-looking man lunching alone. "He eats here every day. Pots of money. What does he eat? Every day the same thing—green salad and a glass of milk. His stomach—"

"The ironies of fate, my love," Georgina said. "It happens like that in the world." There was no sympathy in her voice. "The poor have large families and kings go childless. A rich man kicks off in his prime, the beanless go on forever."

"I was sorry to read about your friend Warren Masters, by the way."

"It was very sad, wasn't it."

"I thought at one time you and he—"

"Daddy! Do you mind? He was ginger."

"Ginger?"

"Ginger beer. Queer. He was a raving fag, Daddy!"

"I didn't know that."

"AC-DC but mostly DC—very *deecee*." She pronounced it the way the English upper-class pronounce *dicey*.

"I had no idea," her father said.

"You weren't supposed to, were you?"

"He seemed so masculine."

"Men are usually wrong about other men," she said.

"Perhaps."

"No perhaps about it," she said firmly. "I liked Warren. He was such a tremendous snob."

"It's extraordinary how snobbery and sodomy go hand in hand . . . so to speak."

Georgina smiled. "I would never marry an actor. Too dodgy by half."

"Talking of marriage . . . a grandson to spoil . . ."

"Christ Almighty, you're not getting broody on me are you?"

"Lonely," he said.

"Ha!" she scoffed.

He grinned easily. "Well, I'd like to see you settled—"

"*Settled?*"

"You know what I mean."

"I want to make a go of acting first," she said. She studied her nails as if she wished he would change the subject.

"But you have," he said. "Made a go of acting."

"Not yet. I've made a start, that's all. A good start."

"I honestly can't see why you can't marry *and* be a film star," he said. It wasn't the first time he had made the point.

"Fillum stars," she said with a heavy Swedish accent. "Fillum stars have to maintain their mystery. You can't be a married lady and be *mysterious*, dollink."

Harry Ogilvy laughed and touched her hand across the table.

"Perhaps mysterious isn't quite the word I'm looking for," she said. "But actresses have to hold something back. There has to be some . . . enigma. Have you ever heard of a married lady being called *enigmatic*?"

"What about all these extravagantly married actresses in Hollywood I read about?"

"There is usually a maze before the matrimony."

"It sounds a dubious theory to me," he said.

"Somebody once psychoanalyzed Albert Einstein's fame back in the thirties. They discovered that he was popular simply because people didn't know what the hell he was talking about. The *unfathomableness* of his theory was irresistible, you see."

"Surely it's all relativity," he said.

"That's a terrible pun, Daddy."

"That's a terrible theory, Georgina."

Georgina sipped her champagne and glanced around the room. She counted three millionaires, one ex-king, a cabinet minister, and one of the richest women in the world lunching with a young man who might have been a gigolo or her grandson.

"You know," Harry Ogilvy said, "it took me twenty-something years to discover that most women's mysteries are more a matter of corsets than conundrums."

"You don't believe that!"

"The same old whisper beneath the whalebone."

"Whalebone!"

"Negligee, then."

"There are whispers and whispers."

"You've heard one—"

"Piffle."

"True."

"Is that why you won't marry again? You could start another family of your own—instead of hanging around waiting for me to do all the dirty work."

Ogilvy smiled but there was a desolate stillness in his eyes. "There's an old Scots saying—when your first wife dies she makes such a hole in your heart that all the rest slip through."

"I always thought—"

"Let me ask you something," he said quickly. "If you want to be carnival queen, don't you have to ride on the float?"

Georgina thought about that for a few moments.

"Well," she said when she was ready. "A certain kind of stardom is like . . . menace. It's best achieved by ambiguity—a certain elusiveness."

"Go on."

"Somebody said to me once that legends must hide the intimate habits of family life. They must resist the cosy familiar routines that carry ordinary people."

Ogilvy studied his daughter as she talked. She had his blond hair, but those brown-black eyes with tawny flecks in them were her mother's, as was the voice and the way of putting things. She had the same sort of beauty—a delicacy which some wild flowers have and which is not without strength and a certain courage, too.

"Real movie stars are not made of home truths—that's what I'm trying to say. That's what *I* think anyway," she said.

"It's a strange business, your business," Ogilvy said. "It's more complicated than it looks from the outside."

"It's all a lot of shit, really," she said, a little embarrassed. What she'd just said sounded so pompous now she thought about it. "Anyway, Harry Ogilvy—*tycoon*—you're a bigger star than I'll ever be," she said quickly.

"Popular imagination always exaggerates the achievements and the wealth of people like me," he said.

"Not true, not true," she said. "Tell me the secret of your success, Mr. Ogilvy."

He sipped his wine and wiped his mouth with the napkin and straightened himself in his chair.

"Always deal with people with as much honesty as is compatible with self-interest," he said. He was smiling but the smile did not extend above his mouth. Georgina noticed the stillness in his eyes, the lids slanted like those of an eagle scenting prey. For maybe the third time in her life she saw the something in his face which could inflict fear—or at least apprehension—in others. She saw him as a man, another adult, and not merely as her own father. It was an extraordinary sensation.

"If you know how to use a hungry politician he is of far more use to you than a well-fed banker," he said.

The waiter refilled their glasses and withdrew.

"Do you remember bringing me here when I was twelve years old?" Georgina wanted to change the subject, change the expression in his eyes. "It was my birthday. I was very nervous. For some reason I thought you were going to give me a lecture about the facts of life." She looked across the room. "We sat at that table over there—where Marcel Boussac is sitting now."

"I don't recall the particular occasion," Ogilvy said.

"Do you remember what you told me that day?"

"No. What did I tell you?"

"You said that when property and land are soft and

when the market was hungry and tired, I was to buy. And when things got hot and boom was in the air, I was to sock my money away and sit tight. I was twelve years old!"

"That *was* my lecture to you on the facts of life," Ogilvy said. "I hope you took it to heart."

"I remembered every word, didn't I?"

"Good. A girl can possess savvy or she can possess passion in life. She can't have both."

"What's the difference?"

"Savvy calculates, examines, thinks things through. Passion annihilates reality, it's castle-building. A girl with savvy knows that *everything* is possible under the right conditions. If she has only passion—passion's an obsession and obsession makes one blind to everything else. Total eclipse."

"What if a girl has a passion for money?"

"There is a lot of difference between avarice and being aesthetically aware of the advantages of collateral," he said.

"That's a politician's answer," Georgina said.

"That's a rich man's excuse," he said.

"It's so unromantic to be rich."

"But so useful."

When they had ordered, Georgina said: "I like your hair that length." It curled over his collar. He was perspiring, very faintly. The beads of sweat gleamed in his thinning hairline in the sunlight from the window. It had never occurred to Georgina that her father was ever nervous and she missed the telltale signs now. She made two vertical lines on the crisp white tablecloth with the blade of the fish knife that she held in her hand like a pencil. Was it possible, she thought, to love somebody, and not like them? Certainly there had been men she'd fancied sexually and disliked intensely as human beings. Sometimes she was afraid that she felt more an allegiance to her father than a genuine affection. She dismissed the idea with a visible shake of her head, like a small shudder.

"A few weeks ago I looked at my life very carefully, not to say critically," Ogilvy said suddenly. "I stripped myself down, the way one strips down a rogue car, looking for the faults, part by part. It was the sort of self-examination every man probably makes when he gets to my time of life. You suddenly get scared of the dark that might be concealed by the light or something. You start rummaging—salvaging what assets you can from the past."

There was a strange, almost piercing regret in his voice that Georgina had never heard there before, not even when her mother died. It made her feel uncomfortable.

"I know I'm a man of terrible will. I'm a good enemy for any man to have. I know these things." He tried to smile but it was a crippled kind of smile that implored and disturbed at the same time. "Oh I'm not repentant—just a little—the surroundingness of everything sometimes—sometimes I must be like other men."

He stopped talking but it was like an actor drying up on stage, anxious to be prompted, looking for help. Georgina looked into her wine and said nothing. She felt he was on the edge of some painful confession. How could she help? How could she guess at the complicated traceries of this complicated man's guilt?

Her father remained silent for a long moment.

"It's difficult." He spoke slowly. He seemed suddenly drained. "For some time now I've had this compulsion to tell you . . . A little while ago you said that I should marry again. Start a new family."

He held up his hand to stop Georgina from interrupting him.

"Sometimes I've suspected you felt I didn't grieve enough when your mother—"

"I never felt that. Never. I knew. I knew what you were going through. I know you."

"Then it was . . . I don't know. Conscience, maybe."

"Let me make it easier for you, Daddy. When I was fifteen one of your *demimondaines* told me. The baby Mummy was carrying . . . I hated her for telling me. Telling the truth—sometimes that's a horrid thing to do. It's too easy to hurt people with the truth. Sometimes it's enough just to think the truth and let it go at that."

"Love can be gruff, love can be unkind and even ruthless—but it's still love."

"I think I always understood that there was a bond between you and Mummy that was more than ordinary love," Georgina said gently.

"We had a very close friendship. It was that sort of friendship which sometimes happens between a man and a woman who are such opposites they will never really understand each other. That Einstein business is quite right. The undiscoverable can hold people together. We found a peace in the labyrinth of each other."

"That's nice," Georgina said. She smiled. "Yet Mummy always knew how to handle you?"

"I let her think so."

"And now you let me think so?"

He reached across the table and stroked Elizabeth's ring on his daughter's hand.

She said, "I guess all children want their parents to be more innocent than is humanly possible—or advisable."

"I haven't hurt you, have I?"

"Don't be silly."

"Sometimes when a thing is said it explains a great number of other things."

"Do you want to tell me who, whose—?"

"No."

"I *like* you, Harry Ogilvy," she said.

Ogilvy brought out a small-caliber smile from his armory of expressions. "What do you want, daughter?" he asked with a tone of exaggerated caution.

"Nothing."

"Nothing?"

"Honest Injun." She leaned forward and whispered, "The wine steward looks like a rusticated Ruritanian."

After lunch Ogilvy said, "I'd like to see you settle down soon." They were standing in the small marble hall of the hotel, waiting for Harry's car.

"Someday my prince will come," she said, holding his arm with both her hands.

He said, "As long as you're happy. You *are* happy?"

"Oh I am. I am," she said with teasing solemnity.

"You promised to send me some new photographs. The ones who-was-it did?"

"Robin Villiers."

"He's very famous."

"Ginger."

"You surprise me."

"I don't!"

"No."

"They weren't very good. Perhaps one or two aren't bad. I'll get a set from Lionel Hammond for you," she said without enthusiasm.

"Someday my prints will come," he said.

Georgina licked her forefinger and made an imaginary score on an imaginary wall.

16

Catharine Gaillard sat on the balcony in the warm sunshine. It was shortly after nine o'clock in the morning, and real June weather. The sky was of the palest blue. She had slept well and would have slept longer had Edouard Casenave not telephoned at eight o'clock to tell her she had the day off. Her annoyance at being awakened so early had now gone and she was actually pleased with her early start on the day. She sipped her orange juice and read the note she had written:

Boaty darling—
Ville D'Avaray was lovely, lovely. I loved the smells, the old wine, making love with you in a strange hotel with only a stone lion in the courtyard. Let's go back. I'm missing your loveliness madly—so soft and so hard—in all the right and improper places! —C.

She smiled with satisfaction. She addressed the envelope, marked it *Private and Confidential*, and slipped the note inside. She stood the letter against the coffee-pot. She wished she could return to Paris with it. It was perfect flying weather. She leaned back and closed her eyes, not thinking, feeling the warmth of the sun on her face.

The telephone's ringing in the room startled her as if from a deep sleep. Perhaps it was Casenave calling to say the plans had changed and they were returning to Paris after all.

"Hello?"

"Catharine? Catharine Gaillard?"

"Yes." She was surprised when it wasn't Casenave's voice. "Who is this?"

"Can't you guess?"

A single shallow frown appeared between her fine eyebrows.

"I'm sorry I can't. It's too early in the day for guessing games."

"Alwyn Brand."

"Alwyn. Alwyn Brand. How are you?" There was unmistakable delight in her voice.

"You haven't forgotten me?"

"*Dieu, quelle surprise.*"

"A nice surprise I hope?"

"*Bien sûr.*"

"*Heureusement . . .*"

"It's been so long! What are you doing in St. Saladin? So bright and early." Catharine sat down on the bed.

"A little business—and I sincerely hope a little pleasure, too," Brand said.

"How did you know I was here?"

"A little bird told me."

"A little bullfinch, no doubt." She grinned.

"I say, have you had breakfast, my dear?"

"I'm having it now."

"*Alors déjeuner?* Are you free? Do say yes."

"*Par hasard, je suis libre.* Free as the air."

"How lovely. Perhaps we could motor over to St.

Paul. A glass of wine Aux Oliviers and lunch at the Colombe d'Or."

"What could be nicer?"

"Nothing." He hesitated for a moment. "Except perhaps a picnic."

"A picnic! I haven't been on a picnic since I was ten years old. A picnic's a lovely idea. Let's have a picnic!"

"A picnic it is. I'll pick you up at—say eleven-thirty. Is that agreeable to you?"

"Terrific." Catharine laughed.

"Splendid."

"You've made my day."

"Eleven-thirty. Only could you possibly meet me in the main square. The Marie-Thérèse, I think it's called."

"Are you too ashamed to be seen picking me up, Mr. Brand?" There was a wheedling reproach in Catharine's voice, purely professional.

"Not at all, my dear." Brand's voice had an almost governessy English tone. "I assure you it is out of no sense of propriety that I am reluctant to visit your hotel. It's simply these snakes-and-ladders streets. My driving isn't up to all that lively reversing, especially on the wrong side of the road."

Catharine laughed good-humoredly.

"In the main square at eleven-thirty. I look forward, Alwyn."

A picnic! It was a lovely surprise. She looked out of the window toward the pink mountains in the distance. She thought about Brand. He was a strange bird. An alarmingly angular Englishman, he had visited her a dozen times or so when she was in the *clandé*. She couldn't remember now who'd introduced him but his references must have been impeccable. The avenue Foch establishment was the best house in Paris.

She ran a bath.

Brand had never made love to her, he had never even touched her, nor did he ever expect to be touched. He had required her to dress primly, and talk about her life, her adventures and quests. *Quests* was one of his words. Men who wanted nothing but conversation weren't so unusual. Many men who could afford the pleasures of avenue Foch had exhausted the more ordinary pleasures of sex. Alwyn Brand was one of those men. He was a cultured, civilized man, elegant and aloof. His sexual aberrations were part of his charm. He had a genuine shyness, a gentleness Catharine liked, although his tone could move from polite to peremptory in a single sentence. He'd been a regular visitor for about a year and then, suddenly, shortly before she joined the Bureau, he stopped coming to avenue Foch. She slipped into the bath. She tried to picture him in her mind. His face—his face gave nothing away. It reminded her of a tall elegant town house that had been closed down for the summer. She'd always supposed he had something to do with the British Foreign Office. Probably because of some remark he'd made. But what? When she'd mentioned his name to Boaty he'd never heard of him. Of course, Boaty probably would say that, particularly if Brand were in intelligence or one of the security agencies. Brand and Boaty—they both came from the same dry mold of refinement that was so peculiarly English: the sort of Englishmen who turn up for the first day of a Test Match, the last day at Wimbledon . . . and in the middle of the dirtiest deals. The truth was, Catharine couldn't work Brand out at all, and that was unusual for her. She couldn't decide whether he was a hard man in a soft job, or a soft man in a hard job. Even the most secretive marks usually left some clue to their real identity, their real occupations, even when they lied and lied and used stratagem after stratagem. Alwyn Brand had left no clues, no hints. He was a shadow within a shadow. But, for all that, she thought, he was hardly a charismatic enigma. Had he not turned up in St. Saladin that morning, Catharine would probably have never given him another thought in her life. That was the truth of the matter. But he had turned up! And on a very dull day, too.

She climbed out of the bath and dried herself slowly. Perhaps because they had never been intimate, Catharine felt almost shy about seeing Brand again. She decided to wear a peasant skirt, a cream calico blouse, and sandals. She screwed her pretty dark hair back in an elastic band. The blouse had wide short sleeves.

When she lifted her arms to fix her hair she showed the dark hair of her unshaven armpits.

She wore no makeup. She carefully smeared her face with an expensive suntan lotion. She looked about fifteen now. She hadn't done the schoolgirl trick for several years; she was rather pleased at being able to carry it off still, although she told herself she was simply dressing for a day in the country.

She twirled slowly in front of the wardrobe mirror. Her skirt floated up her long bare legs revealing white cotton *fleur-de-lis* panties. That'll do, she preened.

She felt almost drowsy with delight.

A white butterfly floated into the room like a cool scrap of muslin. She watched it for several minutes.

It was still only ten-thirty.

She opened the bureau drawer and took out the dozen pieces of hotel notepaper and one envelope. She went out onto the balcony and wrote a short note to her sister in Marigny. Catharine was a bad correspondent. She didn't keep in touch with her only sister, her only relative in all the world, nearly often enough. She wrote:

> Darling S—Delayed in sunny St. Saladin for a day or so. Your news is in remarkably short supply. So is mine, except that my guppy Erasmus finally checked out—know anyone who needs one empty fishtank with plastic diver and fiberglass rock??? An old beau (English, very, but a bit of a mystery!) has just turned up out of the red, white and blue. We're off on a *pukka* picnic. I'll make an aunt of you yet! *Je t'embrasse.* . . .

> Catharine

She addressed the envelope, as she always did, in block capitals, because her writing was sometimes less than legible. She stood the letter against the coffeepot with her first letter. Two letters in one morning! She was feeling very industrious, very pleased with herself.

Shortly before eleven-thirty, she went downstairs and handed the letters to the manager. He was a slim white-faced young man, no more than thirty, but already going bald.

"Would you mail these for me, please," she smiled. She handed him the letters with her key.

"Of course, Mlle. Gaillard." He put the key into a pigeonhole behind the desk. "Will Mademoiselle be in for lunch today?" He looked at her with large dark empty eyes.

"No—but Captain Casenave will be calling me. Would you tell him—yes, I'd like to have dinner with him this evening." She had been too bad-tempered to give him a straight answer when he'd asked this morning. "Gentlemen never wake ladies up at the crack of dawn and ask them leading questions," she'd said. He said he'd call back—when she was in a better mood.

"Very well, Mlle. Gaillard," the manager said. "Have a pleasant day."

He took a folder from a shelf beneath the desk and removed a sheet of stamps. He tore off a couple and stuck one on each of Catharine's envelopes as he watched her disappear through the revolving door at the foot of the wide marble staircase. When she had gone he slipped the letters into his jacket pocket and hit the pushbell on the desk.

An old man, built like an overweight jockey, with a thin worried face and a gray stubbly moustache, came out from a room behind the reception desk.

"Monsieur?" He had shifty rat-gray eyes, the more attractive of which was made of glass.

"Mind the desk, Abbas," the manager said brusquely. "I have things to take care of."

"Monsieur." There was a lifetime of regret in the old man's voice.

"First—fetch me some note paper."

The old man went back into the room behind the desk. There was a slamming of cupboards. He returned with the paper.

The manager took it and went upstairs, two at a time, without appearing to hurry.

Catharine's room was at the end of the corridor on the second floor, room 27. It was one of the best doubles in the hotel, with a balcony view of the mountains.

He opened the door with his passkey and slipped inside, closing the door softly and dropping the latch behind him in one movement. He stood tensely against the door for a moment. His face was blank. His dark empty eyes swiveled slowly around the room.

Not many people left their hotel rooms so tidy. A pair of high-heeled shoes stood neatly together by the side of the bed. An overnight case sat on the rack. A pair of black panties were on top of the case. A paperback novel, place-marked with a folded Kleenex tissue, lay on the writing table by the window.

He took a breath and crossed the room quickly.

He removed the writing paper from the bureau and replaced it with the sheaf he'd brought with him. He held the original writing paper up to the light and saw the faint impression of the last letter Catharine had written. He grunted with satisfaction.

In the bathroom he tore the writing paper into small pieces and dropped it into the lavatory bowl and pulled the heavy old-fashioned chain.

He took out the letters Catharine had given him to mail and set fire to them with a squat chrome lighter. He held them by the corner until they had almost completely burned. He didn't want to read them. He didn't want to know. The less he knew the better. He dropped the charred burning remains into the bowl and flushed the cistern a second time.

In the bedroom he checked the wastepaper basket. It was empty. He picked up her panties and slowly smelled them. He went back into the bathroom, still holding the silk panties to his nose. A few pieces of charred paper floated in the bowl. He pulled the chain again.

He took Catharine's sponge bag from the small marble table and filled it with her toothpaste, toothbrush, her soap, and various creams and makeup. He included a pair of stockings that she'd left to dry on the shower rail and, finally, the used panties.

He checked the balcony.

Her breakfast things hadn't been cleared away. She'd just had coffee and orange juice. The croissants were untouched, the two tiny jars of marmalade unopened.

Next to the coffeepot on the white wrought-iron table, together with a small tip for the waiter, was a black leather book.

A diary—and he'd almost missed it!

He felt his heart knocking. He opened the small book as if it might explode.

A dictionary!

He grinned with relief and left it where it was.

He wiped a small trickle of sweat, like a tear, from his right eyelid as he walked quickly back to the door of the room. He opened the door slowly, just a few inches, and listened. The sleeping silence of a hotel corridor. A special silence he'd never been able to understand. He slipped out, carrying Catharine's sponge bag close to his chest, half-hidden beneath his black jacket.

He had been in the room less than four minutes.

He pressed for the elevator and waited nervously for it to descend to the second floor. He stepped inside, closed the heavy gates, and pressed the basement button.

In the basement, he opened the furnace and threw in the sponge bag. There was a faint whooshing sound as the nail-polish remover exploded.

He returned to the front desk, wiping his sweaty palms with a clean white handkerchief.

17

"News desk," Richard Antrobus said.

He knew exactly what he had to do: afterward he couldn't remember a single moment when he really had to think about it. The plan arrived in his head, ready-made, booted and spurred and perfect. It was so simple. It was only its simplicity that worried him for a while. Nothing's that simple, he thought, that easy. He looked at it every which way. Six ways from Sunday. It was just beautiful.

"Putting you through now." The male operator spoke in a bored South London accent.

"News desk." This voice was brisk, a voice used to dealing with problems quickly. It was neither friendly nor unfriendly, but a voice poised to swing either way.

"Hello, old boy. It's Richard Antrobus here."

"Hel-*lo*." The voice was surprised out of its stride and neutrality. "The boot *is* on the other foot. What can we do for *you*?"

"I'm trying to get in touch with Waldo Bragg. I've lost his bloody number."

"He's not on the staff." The voice was suddenly guarded.

"I know that," Antrobus said.

"I'm not sure actually whether I've got his new home number—I know he's recently changed it. Perhaps . . ."

Antrobus expected problems. "Let me give you this number. Perhaps you could ask Waldo to call me?"

"That'd be favorite."

"Flaxman 0495."

"Flax oh-four-nina-fife. Right. Got it. Bit worried about our future are we, Richard?"

"Aren't we all?"

"I wouldn't trust that old queen's predictions further than I could throw his crystal balls." The brisk voice had become chatty and confiding. Antrobus recognized the prelude to a bit of free pumping. He really didn't like journalists, he decided.

"That old queen's had rather a long reign on your rag," he said.

"Yeah, well—Bragg sells papers. That's what they tell me. He's the first thing my old lady turns to every morning."

"If you'd give him that number," Antrobus said.

"At night, ice."

"What?"

"Ice at night—and Bragg in the morning. The old lady. Turns to ice at—"

"Oh yes," Antrobus said with a dull polite laugh. He tried to imagine what the man on the other end of the line looked like. He said, "Get Waldo to cross her Uranus with Pluto one morning. See what happens."

"Be better off crossing her hot chocolate with Courvoisier. At least I'd have three stars going for me."

Waldo Bragg rang back within ten minutes.

"Richard Antrobus!" The two words conveyed inquisitive delight and half-belief.

"Waldo. It's nice to hear your voice again."

"Don't say it unless you mean it."

"I mean it."

"Where have you *been*?"

"All over," Antrobus said.

"All over who? Or is it whom?"

"I thought it was about time we got together again," Antrobus said. "You old bum." Bragg loved a little faggoty ragging.

"Absolutely," Bragg said. "True, true."

"I have a thought which might interest you."

"Yes?"

"What are you doing tomorrow?"

"Lunching with you?" Bragg suggested coquettishly.

"Fine fellow," Antrobus said. "Where?"

"Who's in the chair?"

"You're richer than me," Antrobus said without a qualm.

"In that case—somewhere cosy. The Isola Bella in Frith Street?"

"Isola Bella at one o'clock."

"Twelve-thirty. It suddenly fills up at one. The service goes all to pieces."

"Twelve-thirty," Antrobus said.

"I'm longing to see you again," Bragg said in his effeminate voice, silky with solicitation. "I might even wear my new frock!"

At twelve noon the next day, Antrobus took the tube to Tottenham Court Road. He felt oddly elated. He walked rapidly down Charing Cross Road. It was a warm sunny day. The voice of Billy Eckstine crooned from a record store. People seemed content to walk at a more leisurely pace than usual, as if controlled by the slow foxtrot rhythms of the Eckstine song, their city faces held that much higher, soaking up the sunshine while it lasted. For once flaming June was living up to its reputation.

In Foyles, the paperback department was cool and not very busy, and dark after the bright sunshine. An Indian girl in rimless glasses and a sari sat inside a Dickensian cash booth reading something in Hindi that made her frown a lot. Antrobus waited a few moments for his eyes to adjust to the warehouse gloom of the old shop.

The Indian girl looked up for a few seconds, then returned to her book. Her frown deepened.

Antrobus quickly found the *S* shelves at the far end of the department. He ran his eye along the rows and rows of books. Salinger, Schulberg, Scott, Simenon, Stein . . . shit! They didn't have it.

He carefully checked the last books in the *R* section. Then he went through the first books on the *T* shelves. It wasn't there.

He went over to the girl in the cash booth.

"Do you have *Danger East* by Emil Siegelman? There doesn't appear to be a copy on the shelves."

The Indian girl closed her book and pushed it to one side. She didn't bother to mark her place. She opened a well-thumbed catalogue. A tiny ruby shone in the side of her nose like a phosphorescent ladybird.

"*Danger East,*" she said in a soft gentle voice. She could have been talking to herself. "Would that be under Politics or Geography?"

Antrobus assumed she was addressing him.

"No dear. It's a novel. A best seller."

"Oh," she said but there was no surprise in her voice.

She closed the first catalogue and carefully placed it on top of the Hindi book that had had her looking so bothered; she didn't seem like a lady who worried easily. She opened a second catalogue. It took a little time. She was in no hurry.

"Yes, here it is. *Danger East* by Emil Siegelman. Two shillings and sixpence."

"I know that. Do you have it?"

"Under *S* for Siegelman—over there."

"I know where it should be. But it isn't." Antrobus spoke slowly, as if addressing a very small child.

"Then we don't have it." She smiled, as if they had solved the problem.

"Thank you very much," Antrobus said with a smile you could have skated on.

"Have you tried across the street?" she asked. "In the hard-back section?"

They had a copy. It cost eighteen shillings and was the fifth printing. For that money, Antrobus wanted it wrapped and that took a little while. It was ten minutes to one when he cut through Manette Street into Greek Street. Soho was like a small village bustling with office girls in their summer dresses making for Soho Square and St. Anne's churchyard, to eat their sandwiches, to lift their skirts to sunbathe and be ogled. He wanted to linger with them. He loved the smells of Soho. He had to force himself to walk swiftly. He turned right into Bateman Street and then into Frith Street. It only took a few minutes but he was already beginning to feel sticky when he arrived at the restaurant.

"You're late," Waldo Bragg said petulantly. He was sitting at a table by the window.

"I'm sorry, Waldo—but I wanted to buy you a present." He sat down and slid the book across the small table.

Waldo's scowl disappeared at once.

"A present! How lovely! What a nice surprise, Richard."

People at nearby tables looked across at the two men and smiled.

Antrobus wanted to tell him to keep his voice down. Instead he said quickly, "Don't open it now, Waldo."

"Why? Is it . . . something naughty?" Bragg asked in his carrying wicked-queen voice.

"Wait and see," Antrobus said in a low exemplary tone.

"A drinkie-poo?" Bragg said. His voice may have been a shade less bruitish, but not much.

Antrobus could still feel people watching them with knowing smiles.

"Campari soda." He was almost whispering now.

"Two Campari sodas," Bragg said. The waiter placed large hand-written menu cards in front of the two men.

"Si, Signor Waldo, sir. *Subito,* Campari soda, right aways."

"He's from Brindisi," Waldo said, as if that meant something. "A very sweet boy. He has the tiniest feet. Did you see? It's almost a shame to spoil them with shoes."

Antrobus couldn't help smiling. "So how have you been, you old fart?" He knew he would have to listen to Bragg's troubles sooner or later so he might as well get them out of the way now. Bragg's left shoulder pushed forward. His head tilted upward like a gently reined-in mare, his lips pursed.

"I'm still with Bill. But we do irritate each other, beyond bearing sometimes. We had a terrible to-do at Christmas. It was grisly. I thought, this is it, this is the finisher." Bragg had a tone of wifely woe. "I told him to get out, you know."

"But he didn't go?"

"Well, what would he do? What would *I* do? I'm not at my best with my back to the wall, dear." Bragg slipped in the little self-deprecating joke. "It's been thirteen years, you know—Bill and me. It'd be silly to put the kibosh on it now. We have our own rooms—"

"I didn't realize it was so long," Antrobus said. "Thirteen years. It's a long time."

"I know he loves me."

"And you?"

"Wicked as ever. I fall madly in love every five minutes. Celibacy is the shortest distance between two sailors."

"Do you know what you really want, Waldo?"

"Besides the fleet? I don't know. I suppose I have a secret itch to be lonely, lionized, and stinking rich."

"And will you be?"

"I can't predict my own future," Bragg said.

"Does William still look after your money?"

"What's left of it—after the tax people have had their grubby little paws all over it."

The waiter returned with the drinks.

"*Un'* Campari soda for sir," he said. He set the glass down in front of Antrobus. "*E un'* Campari soda for Signor Waldo. So!"

"How perfectly lovely," Bragg cooed. "Nello, you are a genius." He patted the waiter's bottom.

"You want to order now?" the waiter asked.

"Melon. Then the sole. Grilled. On the bone," Antrobus said without hesitation. The solemn rigmarole of ordering in restaurants like this bored him silly.

The waiter scribbled it down on his pad. *"Sì signor,* beautiful, *melone frappé,* very good, the sole, grilled off the bone, is good, *molto buono."* He didn't actually kiss his own fingertips but you could see the idea cross his mind.

"On the bone," Antrobus said.

"Sì, sì. On the bone." He turned to Bragg who was still gently caressing his bottom. "And Signor Waldo? To begin. A few escargots? Moules mariniére?"

Bragg changed his mind about five times, flirting all the while with the good-looking waiter from Brindisi, before he settled for gaspacho, then calf's liver and bacon. Of course, he was absolutely right. It was the perfect choice, a selection of subtle complexity! Nello complimented him as if he had just cracked the Enigma cipher.

Bragg ordered Mateuse rosé, as Antrobus thought he would. It was quite extraordinary how so many queers settled for rosé wine.

Nello went away, reading from his order pad, his lips moving, like a man reading Keats alone in a country garden.

"You're going to have a very interesting offer in October or November, an extraordinary invitation," Bragg said suddenly. A faint look of contemplation came into his face. It was almost exactly the same look of meditative suffering that took El Greco a couple of years to get exactly right on the face of *Christ carrying the Cross.* It was one of Antrobus's favorite paintings in the Prado. He was amused to be reminded of it now by Waldo Bragg. "Something very exciting will come your way around the end of October." Bragg talked slowly, like a man unscrambling a garbled message from another world that only he could hear.

The sudden prediction was one of Bragg's great

ploys—the bolt from the occult that couldn't be contained. His conversations were littered with irresistible bulletins about the future—a change of job, scenery, mistress, fortune, heart, or dentist; trouble with your car, legs, drains, boss. His range of prophecy was infinite.

"You know I don't believe in all that bullshit, Waldo."

"Something to do with the cinema," Bragg went on, undeterred. "I see the letters *S* and *B* or a *P*."

"Baden Powell? Scouting?"

"Take the piss if you want to, my lovely. You'll see."

Bragg never lost his temper when Antrobus teased him about his "gift." He had a dark smudge in the middle of his forehead, a birthmark about the size and color of a nickel. He called it his third eye.

Waldo Bragg was barely five feet six inches tall. He wore expensive clothes with that air of careless defiance that middle-aged men must have to carry off fashions that are much too young for them. He wore a bottle-green and brown blazer-striped Cecil Gee cardigan over a yellow brushed cotton shirt with a pastel yellow tie. From ten yards, and silent, he had an air of butch athleticism. That fit stockiness that reminded a lot of people of Gene Kelly. Any closer than that and the amaryllis and ambiguity hit you and the game was up.

Antrobus leaned forward and sniffed at Waldo's smooth, discreetly rouged cheek.

"Do you like it?" Bragg said.

"What's it called?"

"White Hunter."

"You smell like a sheik's daybed."

"It was very expensive. Bill bought it for me—when we made up."

"Grounds for divorce right there," Antrobus said.

He finished his Campari soda as the melon and gaspacho arrived.

"You mentioned on the telephone that you had an idea . . ." Bragg said when the waiter had gone. There was a subtle shift of sensibility in his voice. He was bored with being teased. He wanted to get on with the business. It was his lunch. He wanted something out of it—and he certainly wasn't going to get Richard's body.

His voice, when he was being serious—and he was always serious about business—lost its pansy poshness. The original cockney came through like cheap stuffing seeping from a gash in a silken sofa.

"How much do you charge for private readings these days, Waldo, by the by?"

"I don't turn teacup tricks anymore," Waldo said.

"No?"

"I've got the daily column, a nice byline. A couple of mags under different monikers. The syndication on top of that. Who needs the other shit?"

"Have you ever thought about how much lolly there is in Hollywood—in the other shit?"

"Hollywood?"

"U.S.A."

"There's a bloke there already. Carroll Righter. He's got that place sewn up tighter than Nello's bum."

"There's always room for one more on top. . . ."

"Cheeky."

"Did you ever hear of a woman in Paris called Lily Bourguiba?"

"No. Should I have?"

"A very macabre story."

Outside an old beggar woman went by, barking at people like an angry dog.

"Back in the twenties. Lily Bourguiba," Antrobus said when the barking woman had gone. "She got started when she was seventeen. Predicted that the mayor of her town was suffering an acute attack of Mercury over Saturn in the Twelfth House of Death and Malaise. It all boded bad for the poor bastard—a most malign conjunction of fearful consequence."

"True, true," Bragg said absently, watching Nello overdoing the customer-relations number with a pretty girl at a nearby table.

"The very night of her prediction—are you listening to me, Waldo?"

"The very night of her prediction—" Bragg said, not taking his eyes from the waiter.

"The mayor's house burnt to the ground. One dead

mayor. Several dead children. And a wife who ended
her days in the booby hatch."

"So?"

"Lily never looked back. The word spread. Far and
wide. Diaghilev, Isadora Duncan, Mistinguett, Susanne
Lenglen—there wasn't a star, a celebrity, there wasn't a
crowned head in Europe that didn't want Lily's dope
sheet."

Antrobus had Bragg's full attention again.

"When she died—she was twenty-nine—Lily was
probably the richest self-made woman in France," Antrobus said.

"I'm not with you."

"Lily Bourguiba started with a single well-advertised
prediction," Antrobus said slowly.

"So?" Bragg lifted one unnaturally black eyebrow.

"Lily's prediction was a cinch."

"How—"

"She started the fire herself."

"How do you know that?"

"She committed suicide. They found her diaries."

"Jesus Christ," said Bragg. "Is *that* your idea?"

"I'm not suggesting you burn down Metro-Goldwyn-
Mayer."

"Oh good. I thought you were being mischievous for
a minute."

"I'm simply pointing out the advantages of making a
prediction you *know* is going to happen."

"A breeze," Bragg said. His eyes looked blank. "A
simple twist of the wrist—"

"I know something only you, Waldo Bragg, *can* make
happen," Antrobus said slowly.

"Look, Richard, let's start this whole conversation
again because I'm very confused. Are you saying—"

"You know Georgina Game?"

"I know *of* her."

"She is—"

"She was a friend of Warren Masters. Warren and I
were *very* close at one time. I warned him, don't take
that picture in Tunisia. I knew something bad would
happen. The first time he'd ever ignored my advice."

"It was a sad business," Antrobus said. He was anx-

ious not to get sidetracked. "Anyway, his friend—
Georgina Game—she's passionate about astrology. I
mean—*passionate*."

"Is she now?"

"There is a certain role that is made for her. But for
one reason or another she just isn't interested."

Antrobus tapped the book that lay wrapped on the
table between them. "This, as they say, is the property."

"Yes?" Waldo Bragg drew the word out slowly, slipping in an *r* sound.

A waiter removed the first lot of plates and cutlery as
Nello arrived with the main course. The two men froze,
waiting for the flurry of activity around them to end.
Nello poured more wine into their glasses. Bragg said
nothing to encourage him to linger; he kept his hands to
himself. Antrobus knew he had him hooked; he also
knew that Bragg was streets ahead of him.

"Now if you were to tell her that this was the one
part she had to accept." Antrobus tapped the book very
slowly with his finger. "The one movie the heavens ordained—a role of immense importance to her whole future—et cetera, et cetera, et cetera . . ."

"True, true," Bragg intoned.

"Of course, you'd be more subtle than that. A little
of the old zodiacal sweet-talk . . . I see the initials
b.s. . . ."

"Don't mock."

"I'm serious, believe me. I'm serious."

Bragg thought for a moment. "How will all this help
me?"

"Listen, you great lummox. The people concerned in
this picture—they want Georgina Game very very
badly. But, for one reason or another, they are convinced she isn't going to budge. Her agent, the producer, the bloke who wrote the book, the director, everybody in Hollywood has tried." Antrobus laid it on
thick. "She won't shift."

"True, true," Bragg intoned.

"Now, imagine their amazement—their gratitude,
Waldo—if you predicted, against all the odds, that she
will do it."

There was now a half-amused expression on Waldo

Bragg's face; the other half might have been suspicion or it might have been greed. "Don't put me in promise-land, Richard," he said.

"Waldo, my dear chap—this girl believes in astrology as devoutly as I believe in the numerology of bank notes. You tell her it's written in the stars—she'll do it."

The two halves of Bragg's expression came together in a definite shape. It was greed.

"What sign is she? Aries?"

"I don't know," Antrobus said.

"She sounds like an Aries."

"Aries, Pisces, Virgo, whatever. She could have been born under a toadstool. The point is, a year from now, she could be the biggest thing in pictures since public credulity. You know all about public credulity, Waldo."

"That wasn't called for."

"Okay—but you'll be the guy who saw it all first. I shall tell everybody. You'll be her Santa Claus and swami rolled into one. You'll be able to write your own ticket."

"I'm very sincere about my gift," Bragg said. He was suddenly on the defensive.

"I know you are," Antrobus said soothingly. "But you know perfectly well a lot of what you tell a client is simple common sense—"

"I try to guide people's anxieties about the future to . . . to practical conclusions," Bragg said. "But that's only part of my gift." His eyes filled with tears.

"Most people are arsed up, or snowed in one way or another, Waldo," Antrobus said quickly.

The delicate fissures of self-pity trembled on Waldo's made-up face.

"Most people don't know where to go, or what to do next. You take the hem-and-haw out of their lives. That's great. That's fine. I don't think that's immoral. I don't happen to think it's astrology either, but I'm not knocking it. Whatever it is, whatever you want to call it, Waldo, it's a great comfort for a lot of people."

Bragg dabbed at his eyes carefully with the blue napkin. He was wearing a little mascara.

"It's a kind of liberation," Antrobus went on. Between Christ, Freud, and Waldo Bragg, he would put his money on Waldo every time. "You give a lot of people peace of mind. You give them hope. You're dealing in a rare commodity these days, Waldo. You're entitled to your Danegeld, old son."

He reached across the small table and touched Bragg's hand. He squeezed it once in a manly fashion that was neither patronizing nor amatory.

Bragg responded with a brave smile, exposing his new fluorescent teeth.

Antrobus said, "Read the book I've bought you. You know the girl we're talking about. Just read the book and see what you think."

"What's in this for you, Richard?"

"I just want to bring two of my dearest chums together," Antrobus said with a small necrotic grin. He was pleased that Bragg's tears had stopped.

"Codswallop. You're up to something no good."

"Just read the nice book and I'll arrange a meeting," Antrobus said. "All right?"

"All right," Waldo said, wondering whether his mascara was smudged. "I'll think about it."

"That's all I want you to do, Waldo—think about it."

18

Catharine Gaillard walked into Marie-Thérèse Square at exactly eleven-thirty. Alwyn Brand was waiting. He sat in his car on the far side of the square where the cool shadows were.

He waved his long arm languidly as she crossed the cobbled square smiling. He got out of the car and walked around to the passenger side and opened the door for her.

"You're a very good timekeeper," he said.

"It's essential in my business," she said.

Brand lifted a pale jutting eyebrow quizzically.

"I'm an air hostess these days," she said.

"Good Lord, I thought for a moment—"

"I know what you thought. You have a dirty mind."
They both laughed. It broke the ice.

She slipped into the car, a dusty two-year-old Citroen
which didn't suit the Englishman's image at all. A Bentley would have been more suitable, she thought. A
Rolls or a Bentley. On the back seat was an enormous
hamper.

"It looks as if you've brought enough food to feed the
five thousand," she said as he got in behind the wheel
and fiddled the car into first. They moved off at a se-
date pace, a procession of one.

"Had to borrow it from the hotel. It was the only
hamper they had, I'm afraid. It's a bit ostentatious." He
was looking straight ahead, concentrating on the road.

Catharine reached back and lifted the lid of the hamper.

"I'm pleased to see you didn't attempt to fill it," she
said. She turned back in her seat. "I should be on a
régime."

"A few choice comestibles. A little vino—"

"I always thought you didn't drink."

"*You* do."

"What a thoughtful man you are, Alwyn."

"I don't say no to the occasional glass. For thy stomach's sake, and all that."

"It *is* nice to see you again. It's been a hundred years.
What have you been up to? What are you doing in St.
Saladin? How did you know I was here?"

Brand was unruffled by the stream of questions. His
expression didn't change.

"One: a bit of this, a bit of that. Two: earning a
crust. Three: I saw you leaving the casino last night,"
he said in his orderly fashion. He has probably never
done anything really spontaneous or rash in his whole
life, Catharine thought. Even his smile seemed stuccoed
with scruples.

"Why didn't you say hello?"

"By the time I'd got outside you'd gone. Disappeared
into the night."

"How did you know where I was staying?"

"There are two decent hotels in St. Saladin. I'm in one. You weren't booked in there. I telephoned the other. And there you were."

"What a clever detective you are."

"Were you serious—about being an air hostess?"

"Perfectly serious."

"Do you enjoy it?"

"It's fine. But I tend to live behind a moat of optimism anyway."

"Avenue Foch must miss you," he said.

"When you stopped coming—it wasn't the same."

Brand smiled politely.

Catharine couldn't tell whether it was restraint or indifference.

He drove very slowly through the town; he drove like a bishop. On the open road he put his foot down and pushed the Citroen up to almost forty miles an hour.

Even in late June the roads were still almost empty. They drove with the windows half down. The air was cool and sweet. They drove north, winding their way leisurely up into the hills behind Cannes.

"I love long car journeys," Catharine said.

"They do say that traveling is the frivolous part in the lives of serious people, and the serious part in the lives of frivolous ones," Brand said.

"Surely that depends on where you're traveling to?"

"I thought we'd stop for a glass of Sancerre in St.-Paul-de-Vence. Watch a game of boule, perhaps. If you'd like that. Although it's such a glorious day, I'm quite happy to go straight to our picnic. Whatever you say."

"You choose," Catharine said in a lazy voice. She settled down in her seat and closed her eyes. "I don't want to to make any decisions today. I'm entirely in your hands."

"Then we shall proceed to our picnic without delay. I have the perfect place. Did I tell you? A stream to cool the wine, a glade to cool the brow. Have you brought a book to read?"

"Damn, I forgot."

"Never mind. You may tell me one of your stories."

"Sing for my supper?"

"Lord, no. I didn't mean that at all. I do apologize."

She opened one amused eye and looked up at him. His eyes were still nervously on the road ahead.

"Don't be silly. I don't mind. I'll tell you a story. I enjoy talking to you, telling you things."

"Yes?" He stole a quick look down at her.

"I wouldn't say it if I didn't mean it." She touched his knee gently. It was a bony knee. He wore gray flannel trousers and a cream shirt beneath a Harris tweed jacket. His shoulders were narrow and sloping. He seemed almost flimsy. With his aristocratic, overbred nose he could only be an Englishman, she thought.

After about ninety minutes of steady driving, Brand slowed down and pulled off the main highway and into a dirt track barely wide enough to take the Citroen. The hedges scraped the sides of the car.

"A secret place. How lovely," Catharine said. She sat up and started to take an interest in their surroundings. "How on earth did you find such a place?"

"Used to come here as a child," he said.

"I can't imagine you as a child. What sort of child were you, Alwyn?"

"I was not, as you can imagine, a pretty child. I never felt particularly loved—which is strange because, in truth, I never went without much."

"That's the saddest thing I've ever heard," Catharine said.

"Odd thing," he said, "I didn't feel sad. I was learning about life. Learning to be. That's the plain fact, I suppose."

"By being unloved?"

"To survive in this world we must ignore those we are supposed to love. We must give all our attention to our enemies."

"Are you being serious?"

"Oh yes. Perfectly. Surely I've said that to you before?" He smiled.

Catharine sank down into the deep leather seat again and lifted her feet onto the dashboard. Her eyes were half closed. She brushed a fly off her naked leg. "I don't think you really believe that, Alwyn," she said. It didn't sound like the truth. It was the sort of thing men said at parties when they were a little drunk and belligerent; the sort of thing some men said to girls to make themselves sound tough and interesting. It sounded funny coming from Alwyn Brand, a man who amused her and made her feel safe.

"You're not a chess player?" he said.

"Not a very good one."

"Then you're not a chess player," he said abruptly. "The world's in the devil's own mess because—"

"Interrupting—where does tolerance and—"

"Tolerance is another word for apathy. Most of the time. Apathy and inertia," Brand said. "To offer the cheek to the smiter—Matthew 5, thirty-nine. To be meek—" He didn't finish the sentence.

They were moving very slowly now. After a while he said, "You see, my dear, we must not judge others by their kindness, or by their usefulness to us."

"How then?"

"By how much they compromise or threaten our existence."

"That's very negative," Catharine said. She looked at the sky. There wasn't a cloud in it.

"It's necessary," Brand said. "It's the world we live in."

"Then it's very depressing."

"Why so?"

"If you're right then there's no sense in the world."

Brand glanced down at Catharine's legs. Her skirt had risen a long way up her thighs.

"The most naked thing about a naked woman," he said.

"What's that?"

"Thighs," he said.

"That's nice," Catharine said. She began to talk quickly. She was pleased to be on a subject she could handle. After a while, perhaps six or seven minutes, the car came to a halt.

"We seem to have run out of track," she said.

"We're there," Brand said. "The other side of that copse."

Catharine looked at her watch.

"One-fifteen. Perfect picnic time."

He smiled. "But of course."

"My lord, my liege," she said, stretching her arms above her head and pushing her fingertips onto the roof of the car.

Brand leaned across her and opened her door. "Out! I want to show you my secret garden."

"A secret garden!"

He looked pleased with himself.

There was a gap in the hedge like a porchway to a church. On the other side was a meadowed valley; at the foot of the first meadow, beneath a wild tangle of arbutus and the green cumulus of a dozen cork oaks, a narrow stream sparkled in the blazing sunlight. Along the opposite bank, amid a relentless growth of plants and shrubbery and overgrown thickets of broom and rose-laurel, ran some fifty feet of ancient wall.

"Alwyn, it's beautiful."

"I thought you'd like it."

"I love it. It's the most beautiful spot I've ever seen."

"The wall is all that's left of an old monastery. Probably eleventh century. The ivy's all that's holding it up now I should think."

"I love it. I *love* it. I love wild things. Wild flowers—"

"Gogol said that the best flowers are the ones that grow by themselves on a grave."

"Gogol said that?"

"Nikolai Gogol."

"A Russian, of course."

"Through and through."

"That's weird. About the flowers and the grave. How his mind worked."

"He was a very unhappy man. I'll fetch the hamper," Brand said.

He carried the large hamper in front of him like a huge laundry basket. He took it to the edge of the stream and set it down on a carpet of moon daisies.

"There," he said. He was breathing heavily. He sat down cross-legged beside it. His fine silver hair gleamed in the sunlight.

Catharine opened the hamper. She took out a blue-and-white checked tablecloth and matching napkins.

She spread the cloth on the grass and laid it with enameled Chinese plates and silver cutlery and heavy wine goblets.

"This is more like a banquet," she said.

"I'm a secret sybarite. Here, let me." He took the bottle of white wine and put in the stream. "Give it ten minutes," he said. He delved into the hamper and produced a roasted chicken.

"I'll carve," he said.

"I'm a hopeless carver."

"It's stuffed with wild garlic and herbs. You serve the salad. No black olives for me."

"You've thought of everything."

"Even a corkscrew," he said.

"Brilliant."

"I made them leave the hulls on the strawberries. We can dip them in the sugar and cream."

"You were just too mean to order dessert bowls," she said.

"I thought it was more picnicky," he said. "To dip them."

"I was teasing you. Take your jacket off. You must be so hot."

"In a moment," he said.

He didn't look hot. He had a prawn-colored skin that looked as if it were permanently chilled. It was such an English skin, Catharine thought. His cheeks were smooth, almost like a woman's. She couldn't tell whether it was because he shaved incredibly close, or didn't have to shave at all.

She unbuttoned her blouse.

"Do you suppose they issue PV's in this neck of the woods?" she said, hoisting her skirt.

"PV? What's that?" He could see her white panties.

"*Procès verbal.* A sort of parking ticket certain ladies get for . . . loitering."

Brand went to the stream and retrieved the wine. He opened it and poured a little into Catharine's glass.

"Did you get many?"

"PV's? I wasn't exactly in the loitering class." She smiled. She sipped the wine. "Perfect."

He filled her glass and then his own.

"No. A *courtisane d'haut vol*. That's how I've always thought of you."

"Was I ever," she said. "Now I'm another kind of high-flyer."

"Yes, you are."

"Why did you stop coming to see me, Alwyn?"

"I returned to London."

"Then I don't feel so bad about it."

"Why did you feel bad?"

"I thought I must have displeased you."

"On the contrary. You pleased me very much."

"You are a strange man."

"Strange? How so?"

"Nicely strange. I don't know—you never seemed to *need* me. Most clients need something. Not just sex."

"Then what?"

"Sympathy, authority. Mothering. Something. You never seemed to want anything. I was always surprised when you came back. I never knew what it was you wanted from me."

"Some men want to be inconsolable—it is their only solace."

"I don't believe that. Not about you. You can't cherish a place as beautiful as this place and say you want to be inconsolable."

He shrugged and smiled. He poured more wine into her glass. He'd hardly touched his own.

"So now you work for Prince Philippe."

"I didn't tell you that." Catharine's eyes were suddenly alert, almost too bright to be merely playful. "How did you know that, Alwyn?"

"A croupier at the casino told me," he said easily. "Last night."

Catharine relaxed and grinned a little.

"Thrust into the exile of respectability. Don't spread it around. I don't want to ruin my reputation."

"Your secret is safe with me."

She leaned forward and kissed him quickly on the tip of his long, slightly hooked nose.

"You are a nice man," she said.

Brand looked at her steadily for a long moment.

"How do you know that?" he asked.

"Because most men are not nice. And you are not like most men."

"Is that what you really believe—or what you pretend to believe?" he asked.

"That's a very difficult question to be putting to a girl at a picnic. I thought men liked their women to be mindless and game. Especially—"

"Do you have an answer?"

She sipped her wine slowly and thought about it.

"It's what I believe," she said. "You are not like most men I know. I feel relaxed with you. You make me forget my body. I don't have to think about my face, the way I look, when I'm with you. I mean that nicely. With some men, quite a few men, I'm seized with the most terrible apprehensions. I've never admitted that to anyone before."

"Yet you're continually putting yourself at risk, at their mercy? It's a rather dangerous masochism, don't you think?"

He spoke quietly but there was something almost brutal in the question, something not very nice in his voice. He sat with his back to the sun, facing her. Unable to see his face clearly, because of the glare, she realized how very soft and feminine his voice was.

She slowly dipped a strawberry into the thick cream.

She turned slightly and sat sideways and very straight, avoiding the sun in her eyes. Her body was a long curve, a line that started from her foot and curved right up to her throat.

"I don't think I'm a masochist. I've spent much of my working life, until recently at least, pretending to be the opposite."

"Did you enjoy that?"

"The opposite? You want me to tell you about it?"

"Yes."

"I always enjoyed whipping a man," she said. Her smile hardened a little. She knew that Brand loved her flagellation stories. But now, in the bright sunlight, she felt slightly ill at ease describing such things. They were stories to be told in boudoirs, exaggerated in the dark, in whispers. She hoped that Brand would not press her, but a cold prodding wisp of smile was already beginning to appear on his thin lips. "The first serious stroke," she said, "causes an almost instant discoloration of the skin."

She closed her eyes and lifted her face up to the warm rays of the sun as she talked. The faint smile remained on her face, like a water lily glimpsed just below the surface of a still deep pond.

"Sometimes, with some men, the back looks as if it has been sprinkled with scalding black coffee even before—"

There was a crack, barely louder than the sound of a twig breaking beneath a hunter's foot.

A red mist filled the air.

Catharine toppled sideways.

The bullet entered at the right side of her chin, traveled upward at a forty-five-degree angle, and left by the left temple. The entry wound was small and neat, like a dimple.

Alwyn Brand sat caressing the .22 rimfire Beretta between his thighs, the barrel pointing upward.

A small trickle of blood stained several moon daisies.

He wiped the revolver with his napkin and dropped it into the bottom of the picnic basket. He sighed heavily, like a man who must rise from a repast and get on with his work. He carefully packed the picnic things, including the empty wine bottle. He collected several discarded strawberry hulls and olive stones in the palm of his hand and wrapped them in a piece of the greaseproof paper the chicken had come in. He packed these in the hamper too. He picked up the cartridge case and found the bullet caught up in Catharine's bloody hair. He dropped them both into his pocket.

He looked around. Now, except for Catharine Gaillard's body, the picnic spot was was as clean as they'd found it.

Alwyn Brand was very punctilious about that sort of thing.

He carried the hamper back to the car. He took off his jacket. He opened the trunk and collected four cakes of solid alcohol, the sort that campers use on portable cooking stoves, and the spare can of gasoline. He returned to the meadow. He stepped easily with his long legs across the narrowest part of the stream. He placed the solid alcohol and the gasoline under the old monastery wall.

Catharine's body was lighter than he'd expected. He dropped her into a hollow at the west corner of the wall. He removed the ring she wore on her right hand, and the thin gold crucifix from around her neck.

He sang tunelessly while he worked, but after a while he relapsed into silence.

He soaked her hair and clothes in gasoline and packed the cakes of alcohol around her. In the silence he could hear the humming of bees. He set a match to a twist of paper and dropped it onto the gasoline. The alcohol cakes exploded into flames with a low harsh sound.

There were indentations in the grass where the picnic basket had sat, and where Catharine's body had lain.

It was nearly four o'clock when he backed the Citroen up the narrow lane and turned on to the twisty byways that would get him back onto the N202 about ten kilometers north of Guillaumes.

He was bone-tired.

Somewhere along the way he stopped the car and tossed her ring and crucifix into a ravine. The pieces of gold flashed briefly in the late-afternoon sunlight as they floated downward. They disappeared from view long before they landed in the rough undergrowth at the bottom of the gorge.

According to Risso and Ardoino, there are 2,466 species of vasculiferous plants in the flora of the Alpes-Maritime.

Alwyn Brand could well believe it.

It was a beautiful view.

19

"Sorry, monsieur. Still no answer from Mlle. Gaillard's apartment." The girl's voice had a tone of politely suppressed boredom. It was the third time he'd called in two hours.

He was worried. The worry made him sound bad-tempered. "Let me speak to the front desk," he said. The girl put him through at once.

"Reception."

"I've been trying to contact Mlle. Gaillard. Has she left any message for me? Captain Casenave."

"Mlle. Gaillard. Room 27. No, Captain. No messages."

She'd been gone two days. It was a strict rule for his crew to check in with him every twenty-four hours, or leave a telephone number or an address where they could be reached. It was fortunate that Philippe hadn't wanted the plane in a hurry.

Casenave looked anxious. And he looked angry. For two days he'd been expecting her to call any minute. The last time he'd talked to her she'd been irritable, he remembered. But it was early in the morning. "Where the hell is she?" he said out loud. He was pacing his hotel room. One theory overtook another in a rosary of possibilities. Had she just quit? Pulled the pin and returned to Paris? It was unlikely. Why pay to go home when they'd be flying back shortly anyway. Was she stranded somewhere without a telephone? On a yacht, he thought. Perhaps she'd been taken ill? Was she now unconscious, unidentified, in some hospital bed? Fragments of explanation drifted through his mind like debris in space. He had avoided reporting her absence to

Philippe so far, but he would have to say something soon. To protect himself.

It was five-thirty. He needed a drink.

Still full of brooding anxiety, he entered Giorgio's bar on the west side of Marie-Thérèse Square. It was his favorite hangout in St. Saladin. It was a small place with pictures of racing drivers on the walls; the drivers who had died were in black frames.

"The captain is well this evening?" Giorgio was a large man, an Italian, broad, with a red face and a black moustache. His hair was thick and black and glossy. He must have weighed nearly two hundred pounds, but there was no softness on his body. Before the war he'd been a mechanic with the Ferrari racing team. Casenave didn't know his last name; very few people did. He was a good barman: he listened when you wanted to talk and he had plenty of anecdotes when you just wanted to listen.

"The captain is well enough, Giorgio," Casenave said. He ordered a glass of the local red. It was a good wine, maybe a little rough around the edges, but it wouldn't travel. Ten miles outside St. Saladin it was pure horse liniment.

"Only so well? Because the captain doesn't fly, that is it. An aviator must fly, otherwise what is the point of being an aviator? Drivers the same. Drivers must die racing. There is no point otherwise."

Casenave smiled. "I don't want to die flying." He'd come close enough to know that much.

"Those ones who don't move—they are dead already," Giorgio said. His laugh became a cough. The cough wracked his whole body. The paroxysm bent him double. The cough was the legacy of a lifetime of inhaling engine fumes. He coughed and choked for almost a minute before pouring himself a glass of water and getting it down. Some of it spilled on the front of his shirt. His red face had turned practically purple. His eyes were bloodshot. "Shit, man," he said in a shaking voice. He breathed deeply a few times, like a man preparing for a long underwater swim. "That pit shit—" He shook his head, then seemed to shudder all over with a sort of self-disgust. "Never leaves you. Pit shit."

"Let me buy you a drink," Casenave said. He felt embarrassed. He sat very still, hoping the embarrassment didn't show.

"That's kind of you." Giorgio poured himself a cognac. "Here's into your face," he said.

He knocked it back in one movement and poured himself a second, much stiffer drink from the same bottle. It was the good stuff he kept for himself under the counter.

"Don't let it worry me. Useless as tits on a boar, worry," he said. He had a grin like the San Andreas fault.

"Right," Casenave said without conviction. A feeling of anger was beginning to rankle him again. Where the hell had Catharine got to? The thoughtless bitch. He knew what he felt was more than professional concern. He longed for her presence. More and more he felt the need for her. It was a long time since he'd known what it was like to miss a woman. To miss a woman's laugh and a woman's smile, to yearn to hear her voice again. He had not believed he would know such pain again. If she were to walk through that door now—

"The lady—she is joining you this evening?" Giorgio asked.

"I don't know," Casenave said.

"A beautiful woman. A traffic-stopper. Better than Mr. Ferodo's brake linings." Giorgio began to laugh and Casenave was afraid he would start to cough again.

"There was a time—such women I knew. I was leading the crazy life. Monza, Mexico City, Monte Carlo . . ." He rattled off the names like an old fighter recalling other fighters he'd fought and beaten and loved. "A lifetime in a single season. Lots of lives. Lots of seasons. Crazy. I had plenty pennies, my health. They was the good days, my flying friend. I splashed around good. Too much, maybe. But what the hell—such women. I don't forget none of them. The wild ones, the kind ones, the submissive ones, you know what I mean? The rich ones, the eager ones. Dancers, acrobats. There was even an ice skater." He waved a floppy hand chest high and grinned his San Andreas grin. "The ones I only know in the dark. I remember. I don't brag. Some of them loved

me, some not. Some loved my money. Some, who the
hell knows? Who cares? They're all the same in the end.
Reminiscences. I got reminiscences. A small bar and
plenty reminiscences." He winked. "Better than Rem-
brandts. Better than Rubens, reminiscences. What you
say, Captain?"

"What can I say, Giorgio? You're a happy man. You
got it right for you."

"You're damn right I got it right, Captain. Hoarding
the *dinero*—that's an abuse. You know what I mean?"

"Right."

"Reminiscences," Giorgio said. He tapped his left eye
with his index finger and nodded slowly.

A man and a woman came into the bar. Casenave
guessed they were English even before they spoke. The
man wore a white linen jacket, flannels, and a floppy
Panama hat of great age. He was a thin man with a dry
querulous face. They both ordered sherry. Giorgio set
them up in schooners. The couple sat at a table near the
door. They sat in silence. The sort of silence that only
needs an opening line to start an argument.

Giorgio came back and sat with Casenave.

"Your lady—"

"Catharine," Casenave said. He wanted to say her
name. "Catharine Gaillard."

"A lotta class. That sort of class, it disappeared the
year they removed the running board," he said mysteriously. "Class. You can always tell. I watch her cross the
square. The way she walk. Aceroo from head to toe.
The way she held herself. Lady written all over her.
She is wearing this simple—I don't know what you call
it. A peasant could wear what she wears but she give it
a sort of—"

"When was this?" Casenave interrupted.

"What?"

"When did you see Catharine crossing the square?"

Giorgio shrugged his heavy shoulders. "Yesterday?
No, the day before perhaps. Yeah, it was the day before."

"Was she alone?"

"Yeah, alone."

"What time?"

"I don't know what time, Captain. I like to watch the girls go by. I don't time them."

"Morning? Afternoon? When? In the evening?"

"It was the morning. I was putting out the chairs."

"She was walking across the square—to where? Which way was she going?"

Giorgio got up and filled Casenave's glass.

"On the house," he said. He looked hard at the captain for a long moment with unexpected feeling in his maroon eyes, a quiet unexpected understanding. It came, perhaps, from the same secret places as the lines that were carved deep into his face and into his thick powerful neck. "You in love with her, your girl, yes?"

"Never mind."

"She walk out on you?"

"You've got the wrong end of the stick, Giorgio."

"I don't see where she goes. Not exactly."

"How can you not—"

"But there was a car waiting. Ten-fifteen minutes. A Citroen. A black six-cylinder job. A year old, maybe two. I hear it come into the square. The engine has that sound—before it starts to miss. She was getting ignition trouble pretty damn soon. Still I hear these things."

"Catharine went in the car?"

"I don't see. I come in. To get more chairs. I go out again, the car is gone. Your girl is gone. The square is empty."

A policeman came into the bar and ordered a beer. He put his hat on the bar and wiped his brow and the back of his neck with a red handkerchief. Giorgio poured a bottle of Stella Artois and said something that made the policeman grin and shake his head. He wiped the inside of his cap and put the handkerchief in his back pocket. Giorgio went back and sat with Casenave.

"Maigret," he said, grinning.

Casenave sipped his wine. He put the glass on the table and began to drum three fingers rhythmically on the side of his forehead.

"She was going toward the car?"

Giorgio stopped grinning and concentrated.

"Your girl? Across the square—in that direction, sure, toward the car."

"Did you notice the driver?"

"I see him—but I don't pay attention. A driver, that's all. A man. The car was Italian-registered. That I remember."

The English couple were talking now. Complaining in loud voices about the French, the cost of everything, the service at their hotel and about somebody's ingratitude. Somebody named Fairfax or Fairclough. The woman was tall and rather tense and not attractive, but she acted as if she were. It was almost the same thing, Casenave thought. She looked like a woman who needed a tight rein.

"Perhaps your girl, she never went in the car," Giorgio said in a reasoning voice.

"Was she carrying anything? A case?"

"A case? A suitcase?"

"A bag, a holdall—"

"No. She had this crazy way of walking—very light, up on her toes. She carried nothing."

"Are you sure?"

"She carried nothing."

Casenave bit his lip. There was a silence in the bar now. The English couple were studying a road map the man had spread out on the table between them. The woman had a look of exasperation. The man's little finger wriggled slowly across France, following a thin broken red line.

"Haven't we had enough scenic deviations, Henry?" she said.

"I hate autoroutes," he said. "So bloody boring."

"Getting lost is bloody boring," she said. Her mouth was pursed with sulky martyrdom. The man didn't answer. A small unfriendly smile haunted his face. His finger continued to follow the red line, like a man adding up a score. Maybe an old score. Casenave wondered whether all married couples in England had that duelist air about them.

"She'll turn up," Giorgio said with an air of finality. "They always do, the beautiful bitches." He patted Casenave's shoulder and stood up. "Another drink, my friend?"

"Not now, Giorgio. I'll be back later."

Outside, the square was waking up for the evening performance. The heat had gone. A few tourists had already drifted in to look at the shopwindows, sit outside the cafés, sip beer and perhaps pernod, and write their cards home. Plan tomorrow's excursions and work out how much they could afford to risk at the casino later.

Casenave crossed the large square, walking in a hurry, leaning forward as if into a strong wind, his brow furrowed, muscles taut. He wore cream gabardine slacks and a brown suede jacket. You'd have taken him for an American, perhaps. He had that thinness California men who spend a lot of time on the tennis courts, in the sun, have. His brown-going-gray hair was cut close, not quite a crewcut, exposing a long white scar running along the left side of his head. The man who did that to him died three minutes later, baling out of a Messerschmit-109. Casenave watched him fall 4,000 feet, tugging at his jammed rip-cord all the way down. It was the first man Casenave had killed. The first man he'd seen die a violent death. He felt nothing. He felt detached. A hangover gave him worse problems of conscience. A lot worse.

"Mlle. Gaillard is not back?"

"No, monsieur," the pale-faced young manager said. He didn't even bother to check her key. But he remembered to smile the meaningless managerial smile. He had that Simonized air of a man who gets his living being nice to people he doesn't know, people he often doesn't like even when he does get to know them.

"I want to see her room, please," Casenave said.

"That is not possible, monsieur—"

Casenave placed both his strong useful hands on the reception counter. He spoke carefully, seriously, like a surgeon telling a frightened patient an operation is the only way. "My name is Casenave. Captain Casenave. I'm on Prince Philippe's personal staff. Mlle. Gaillard is also on His Highness's personal staff—and she appears to be missing. Before I officially report this situation—"

"Of course, Captain Casenave. Now I understand, of course."

He took Catharine's key from the pigeonhole and led the way upstairs.

"Room 27," he said. He unlocked the door and stood back, allowing Casenave to go in first. The windows were closed. The room had a stuffy suspended air that hotel rooms always acquire between guests. A faint smell of insecticide came from the bathroom.

"Ants," the manager said apologetically.

"And nobody saw her leave?" Casenave asked again. He spoke with the inside of his lower lip between his teeth.

"I've told you, sir—nobody. I have checked."

Her black overnight case sat on the rack at the foot of the double bed. The bed had already been turned down for the night. A paperback novel and her small dictionary were on the bedside table. A snapshot of a pretty girl—probably Catharine's sister, there was a likeness—was stuck into the edge of the dressing-table mirror. Casenave opened the old heavy wardrobe. A dress, a couple of skirts, and a white blouse hung there in the gloom alongside a few empty wire hangers. He closed the wardrobe door and went to the bathroom.

"None of her things are here," he said.

"Monsieur?"

"Her toilette things. Makeup. Women's things. They're gone."

The manager came into the bathroom and looked around. His expression had something glazed about it, as if he were determined to be uninvolved. "She must have taken them with her," he said. "If she planned to stay away for a few days—"

"She didn't," Casenave said. He didn't know why he said it. He didn't know why he believed it. But he did. He pushed his way past the manager in the doorway and went back into the bedroom. He stood in the middle of the large old-fashioned room and looked slowly around.

"Something," he said, almost to himself. "Something . . ."

"Sometimes guests book rooms for appearance's sake," the manager said from the bathroom doorway. "You understand? Perhaps she is with a friend—in another hotel, an apartment maybe?"

"Something's wrong in here," Casenave said.

The manager looked around the room and shrugged in a nervous semblance of insouciance.

"What can be wrong, monsieur?" A startled look came into his dark eyes and stayed there. He started to blink as if trying to shift whatever it was in there that troubled him.

"Something's not right," Casenave said. He felt it. He felt it somewhere between the heart and wherever that instinct sits which tells a pilot to put his nose down at a certain moment in a dogfight. He could never explain it then, and he couldn't explain it now. It was just something he felt—between the shoulder blades? In the back of his neck? Deep down in the belly? It was like having a sudden bad pain and not knowing where the root is.

"Have you finished, monsieur?" the manager asked. He was nervously playing with his cuffs. He tried a polite smile but his zygomaticus wasn't up to the strain: the muscle pulled back his thin mouth and let it go almost at once. The effect was a kind of twitch.

Casenave walked across to the window and looked out at the balcony. He turned and walked out into the corridor. "I'm finished," he said. "You'll leave Mlle. Gaillard's things where they are for the moment." It wasn't a question.

"But of course, Captain Casenave. As long as Prince Philippe's office requires the room." The manager closed the door and turned the key twice in the lock.

"Are the rooms cleaned every day—even when they haven't been slept in?"

"The maid checks them out, of course," the manager said. Casenave noticed he didn't answer the question but it wasn't important.

"Do you think Mlle. Gaillard will be back soon?" The manager asked as if he really cared.

"You got me there, pal," Casenave said.

Edouard Casenave made his way back to the square. He walked slowly this time. He needed another drink and just prayed that Philippe didn't plan on doing any flying in the morning.

Giorgio's bar was now almost full. People sat in little groups of twos and threes. Casenave sat outside at a table. It was a very small round table and he had it to himself.

"Sticking with vino, Captain?" Giorgio was at his elbow. There were now several other waiters bustling around.

"I think it's time for cognac."

"Sure thing."

Shutters had gone up on most of the shops in the square. Only the restaurants and cafés glowed, a pale sulphur-yellow glow, in the dusk. A group of young Americans sat around the fountain in the middle of the square. Casenave tried to guess their ages, but Americans were difficult. They were always a lot older or a lot younger than you imagined. An accordion was playing in one of the tourist traps on the other side of the square. Casenave hated accordions. What sort of man would want to learn to play a squeeze-box, he wondered.

Giorgio returned with the cognac. "Bust loose on that, my friend."

"I wish it was that easy," Casenave said.

"She still missing?"

"Yes."

"I don't wish to be rude, Captain, but I think you're racing your motor. A girl skips off for a couple of days—what's that?"

"Not this girl," Casenave said.

"*All* girls," Giorgio said. "She wants to throw a scare into you."

"It's not that sort of relationship."

It wasn't that sort of relationship. He thought about the day he met her. She'd been hired by the Bureau. He remembered the terse telegram saying she would be joining his crew as senior stewardess. He was given no choice, no say in the matter. He was mad as hell, but who could he complain to? Philippe? He wouldn't want to know. The Bureau? Sure. But who? It was such an insidious organization. He knew that well enough. He had been hired on a handshake by a man apparently now dead. If he wasn't, he was certainly a self-effacing gentleman. Casenave couldn't complain. Not really. Not when he thought about it. He was paid through a bank in Liechtenstein. The first Monday of every month, on the dot. His crew had the same deal. No sweat. No tax. The plane was serviced at Le Bourget, by a subsidiary of Air France. Everything was paid for by the Bureau direct. Casenave sent his expenses to a secretary called Genevieve Lacroix in St. Saladin. They were settled without question, within seven days, via the same bank in Liechtenstein. It was a smooth comfortable operation. Why make waves? They were foisting a new stewardess on him. So what? Simmer down. He'd been taking orders all his life, hadn't he? He'd just pocket his pride. Again.

A few hours later, Catharine had phoned him. He still didn't know why but he invited her to dinner at the Coupole.

"You're younger than you sound on the telephone," she said.

Casenave felt uncomfortable with women. He never knew what to say when they made personal comments like that. He just stared at her hands. Carpenter's hands, he thought. He'd never seen such *capable* hands on a woman before. Yet somehow—she held her thumb and middle finger close together—she gave them an almost tapered look. And when she smiled it was a smile worth waiting for. Beneath the extraordinarily bright lights, amid the noisy crowds of the Montparnasse smart set, she brought him out of his shell. He almost never found it easy talking about himself. He believed the only really important things in a man's life were found carved in his school desk—and on his tombstone.

"Tell me about you," she said. "The north, south, west, and east of your life."

He said he was a superannuated fighter pilot. After the war he was casting around in Paris for something to do when, out of the blue, so to speak, he was offered the St. Saladin job. He'd met Philippe a few times during the war, in London, at the French club. He seemed like a nice enough guy—for a prince. Casenave wasn't keen to continue flying but his air force gratuity was running low and there was nothing else—so here he was.

"And here we are," Catharine said.

"And you?"

"My parents died in the war," she said.

"Oh. I'm sorry. The war—"

"Oh, no—not that. I can't blame Hitler for that. A lot of things, but not that. My father died quite naturally—of pneumonia. My mother followed him soon afterward, and everybody of course said she died of a broken heart. It sounded more romantic I suppose than cirrhosis of the liver. I don't know why I drink. But, as you see, I do. I stayed at school until I was seventeen. I still had a brace on my teeth at seventeen. You see—" She leaned forward and pouted. "My mouth is permanently exaggerated."

"It's a beautiful mouth."

"Your first compliment. I think we're going to be friends after all."

"You thought we weren't?"

"You sounded pretty *anti* on the phone."

"I owe you an apology."

"No charge."

"Then what happened?"

"When?"

"You left school—?"

"I left school. A convent, would you believe? In—no, *near*—Biarritz. *In* Biarritz sounds much too smart. Then I came to the big city. I lived with my sister. I worked in a hat shop in Passy. A photographer asked me to model some millinery for a magazine. I became a model. I tried acting but—" She made a face. "I've had a fairly . . . anonymous life. Without a little wine to illuminate it, it would be easy to forget."

"Tell me about now."

"Now—I keep my roots in a tachy case. I like quick getaways."

"You've never been married?"

"No. You?"

"Once. In England. In the war."

"And?"

"Divorced. On D-Day as a matter of fact."

"A day to remember."

"Hardly." He noticed lipstick traces on her glass. It

surprised him because he hadn't realized, even under the bright Coupole lights, that she had any makeup on.

"It's a strange thing," she said. "I've never wanted to marry, to be married. But I once read a story about a tribe discovered in South America or Borneo or some godforsaken place. A true story. They all live to be at least a hundred years old and they all have this thing, two things, in common. They are all married and they practically live on honey. I'd like to live to a hundred. And if that's what it takes . . . But then the thought of all those years of conjugal boredom! I read Zola when I was eleven. Can you imagine?"

They sat in the Coupole, sat and talked and ordered a second bottle of wine, and then a half-bottle, then coffee, for a very long time. They went over their lives, their disappointments, the happy times, said what they wanted. "I learn best from lovers. My life would be pointless if I didn't," she said. "I lost my dreams of glory at ten thousand feet," he said. "A long time ago." He was, they both were, nicely smashed.

Casenave hadn't been out with a beautiful woman for a very long time, he realized. He enjoyed the quiet attention Catharine attracted. He had never felt that secure with his wife. His ex-wife. But then she was English. *Very.* He never quite trusted the English. Perhaps it was because there was no sexual tension between them that he felt so good with Catharine. It made a difference. The sex thing. There was no question of taking her to bed, of asking her back to his house in Mortefontaine. He liked her. He liked her a lot. He wanted to be her friend before he became her lover. He had no doubt in his mind that they would become lovers. Only not yet. Not just yet. He wanted their relationship to grow. It was, he felt sure, even then, that very first night at the Coupole, just a matter of time. He wanted it to grow.

But time seemed to have run out on him.

I keep my roots in a tachy case, she said.

I like quick getaways, she said.

She'd certainly warned him.

There's no fool like a middle-aged fool, Casenave thought.

He finished his cognac and paid the check and left a tip, more than was strictly necessary. All his headwork told him nothing. It reassured him still less. It added up to no calculable sum of understanding at all. *Nichts*. All the Gauloises and all the cognac . . .

Edouard Casenave wasn't drunk when he left Giorgio's. But he wasn't exactly sober either. He was what Catharine would call gentlemanly tipsy, or sack-mellow. He was about halfway down the last narrow street leading to his hotel when he became aware of the car moving toward him. It moved slowly at first, its tires throbbing like a muffled drumbeat on the rough cobblestones. His senses bristled. The drumbeat was getting faster and faster. The car was about twenty yards away when the driver stabbed on all his lights and gunned the motor.

Blinded, Casenave threw himself against the wall, flattening himself face first and sucking in his breath with the gasping sound, from the depths of his soul, of a man being smashed in the stomach by a real pro, a real hitter.

The left front fender caught his hip and spun him along the wall, palpitating him between granite and twenty hundredweight of roaring blurr, before flinging him loose like a discarded rag doll. He shot maybe twelve feet into the air. For a moment he seemed transfixed, spread-eagled in the black aspic wake of the dazzling beams. He remembered the German, frantically tugging at the chute that never opened.

Casenave hit the middle of the street on all fours, spun head over heels, and crashed against the wall like a man trying to break in a new miracle.

The car swerved with the impact. The driver overcorrected. The car careened back to the other side of the street again before he got it under control. He was good, real good, that driver. He was hitting forty when he turned the corner. In St. Saladin that's a lot of driving.

Casenave lay very still, partly because he was only half-conscious, and partly because he didn't want that bus driver to come back and try his luck a second time.

He could smell burning rubber and gasoline and blood. Especially blood. The sound of the engine seemed to be getting fainter.

Then he passed out.

20

He was falling. Falling very slowly, swinging in the wind. Seagulls flew around him. Flocks of seagulls, zinc-white, screeching like banshees, whirling and diving. Yellow bayonet-beaks going for his eyes. He looked up. There was no canopy of silk. Only a vapor-stained sky. Very blue and very high. He was already dead, swinging on a gibbet, with nobody to close his eyes.

He screamed, just once, and then he was awake.

The room was dark, almost totally black. It felt like a small room. A tidy room, the room of a child who's gone away. The faint sound of footsteps outside. The sound of something being wheeled along, rattling quietly on a hard floor. A shifting metallic sound. A cart of some sort.

He thought: a tumbril.

Then he remembered the nightmare.

The door opened and several dark figures came into the room. They left the door open and stood in the wedge of light that came in from outside.

"Well, my friend, you're with us again?" a man said. It was a friendly voice with the timbre of authority.

"Where am I?" His own voice sounded strange. It sounded unused, and uncertain how it was supposed to work. A woman laughed quietly, a friendly laugh, and a second man's voice said something inaudible.

He'd been in great pain and now it had stopped. No pain is a great gift when you have suffered a great deal of it. But then he found he couldn't move and that frightened him more than the pain and the seagulls. He couldn't feel anything. He almost wanted the pain back. At least with the pain—

"I can't move." It was a shout, a cry, full of panic and pleading.

"It's all right," the woman's voice said. "You're perfectly safe. You're in hospital and perfectly safe."

"I thought people said 'Where am I?' only in movies," the first voice said.

The woman's voice said, "Close your eyes now, Captain Casenave. I'm putting on the light."

He closed his eyes. He felt the room light up on the other side of his lids. It was like the red glow they sometimes leave on a stage curtain after the house lights have dimmed.

"You're looking better already," the woman's voice said.

"I can't move," Casenave said again. His voice was quieter. He'd got the panic out of it.

"You're all right," the woman said. "You're going to be fine."

"I can't move."

"It's only temporary," the woman said.

"A few days," a man said. "A week at the most."

"You're suffering from a sort of body amnesia," the woman told him. "It's not uncommon—you took quite a bump, you know."

"You'll be as right as rain."

"Open your eyes now please, Captain," the woman said.

Casenave did as he was told. She was holding up seven fingers.

"How many?"

Casenave told her.

"Go to the top of the class, Captain." She smiled. It was a nice smile. She wore a white coat over a tweed skirt and an oatmeal-colored sweater. She had nice breasts.

"I'm Dr. Audemare. This is Dr. Rousseau. And," she indicated the second man, "Dr. Boullet. We've been looking after you."

"Excuse me." Dr. Boullet leaned forward and lifted Casenave's eyelid and shined a pencil torch into his pupil. He did the same thing to his other eye. He turned and nodded to Dr. Audemare.

"You remember what happened?" Dr. Audemare asked.

"I got hit by a car."

She took a chart from the foot of the bed.

"How long?" Casenave said.

"Have you been in here? Four days," Dr. Audemare told him. She continued studying the chart for a moment and then replaced it in its sleeve. "You're an iron man, Captain. By rights, you should be pushing up the daisies."

"The orderlies were all for taking you straight to the morgue," Dr. Rousseau said. He was the one with the friendly but businesslike voice.

Dr. Audemare said, "You got away with five broken ribs, a fractured cheekbone, some abrasions and bruises. There's a nasty gash on the back of your head where you bounced—but it's no worse than the one you had before." She smiled at the scar on the side of his head. "Even so, Captain, you've probably mopped up as much punishment as you can take for a little while."

"Prince Philippe has been inquiring after you," Dr. Rousseau said. "Many times. Father Cornelius was here this morning."

"The police also want a word with you when you feel up to it," Dr. Audemare said. "Perhaps tomorrow."

"And there's a friend outside now if you'd like—" Dr. Rousseau began.

"Catharine? Mlle. Gaillard?" Casenave's face lit up.

"Giorgio. He didn't give his other name."

"Giorgio."

"He arrived shortly after they brought you in," Dr. Audemare said. "He's been parked outside practically ever since. I think he has no home to go to."

"Let me see him. Please."

"Very well," Dr. Audemare said. She went out and returned almost at once with Giorgio. The big Italian went over to the bed. He reached out his large hand and touched Casenave's forehead.

"You crazy bastard. You don't look where you going."

"Not long," Dr. Audemare said. She left the room followed by Rousseau and Boullet.

"Thanks," Casenave said. "For dropping in."

"You owe me for last cognac."

Casenave grinned.

"I got change," Giorgio said. "You need change. I got change."

"Who told you?"

"About the smack-up? Maigret?"

"Maigret?"

"The policeman. He's in the bar, having a Stella. I don't know his name. He see us talking. When he recognize you later, he tell me. Your friend has a big shunt." Giorgio drew the side of his hand across his windpipe. "We thought—*il est mort* . . ."

"I zigged. I should have zagged."

"Next time, please, try it in car. It's safer maybe."

"Have you seen Catharine?"

"Your girl? She don't come to bar."

"It's been three days?"

"Since you smack up? Four days. Four nights."

"No word," Casenave said.

"I don't hear. I don't know. I don't think you should be worrying about your girl now. I think you have other problems now."

Dr. Audemare returned. "That's it," she said.

"Listen, you crazy man, I come tomorrow. Maybe I bring you grapes."

"In a bottle, Giorgio."

"You see, nurse, I make him better already."

Dr. Audemare smiled. "Your long wait was worthwhile."

"It wasn't so long if you bring sandwiches." Giorgio grinned his big grin. He patted a hip flask. "And a little something besides."

"Go now," Dr. Audemare said firmly, still smiling. She put her hand on Giorgio's chest and backed him toward the door.

"I see you tomorrow, Captain," he said over her shoulder. "Your credit's okay for another day."

Casenave could hear him laughing all the way down the corridor.

A nurse came in and gave him a draught of something that tasted bitter. She held the glass to his lips, her other hand supporting his head. She put out the light as one puts out the light of an empty room, a room in which no one remains. It frightened him. He wanted to call out, stake a claim, remind her that he was still there. She closed the door.

In a little while, how soon he wasn't sure, he was flying very low over the sea, his engine dead. It was dusk and the wind and the waves made the only sound in the dark tight-fitting cockpit. Wisps of fog hung over the sea and clung to the wings. Then, in a moment of utter clarity, before the dusk and the mist and the sea engulfed him completely, he saw the book. It was a distinct impression, unbidden. A black book. It was on a bedside table in a room he didn't recognize. It was a large room. Bright and friendly. He knew the small book was important. But why? He was skimming the waves. He knew he had to impress the book on his memory. He remembered clutching the toys of a vivid childhood dream and deliberately waking himself up, hoping to snatch his spoils back to reality. He picked up the book and held it to his chest, very tight, with both hands. The plane softly silently surged into the sea. It was not bad, he thought, there in the deep, in the silence, in the immovable empty dark.

Philippe said quietly, with a savage gravity: "I am not a patient man. My father has been dead and buried now for—"

"The administrative problems, Your Highness, have been immense and quite unforeseeable—" Paul Duclos began.

"The administrative problems appear to be nothing but inefficiency or a bureaucratic plot to—"

"Your Highness, there are no plots," Duclos said hurriedly.

"You will understand my having conceived the most serious doubts," Philippe said. His voice was deadly polite.

Roberto Cheroffini looked uncomfortable and said nothing. His face was dove-gray and had a damp sheen like something recently modeled in wax. Philippe was rushing his fences, he thought. His fingers gripped the arms of his chair.

"Everything you have asked for is being prepared. Only it takes a little time," Duclos said. "We have to collate all the—"

"Twenty-four hours, gentlemen," Philippe said calmly.

He picked up a copy of *Paris-Match* from his desk. His picture was on the cover. It was a grainy long-lens shot taken at the funeral. He was touching an irritation just below his left eye with the back of his wrist: he seemed to be brushing away a tear. In the background flew the royal standard at half mast. *Inside*—the cover line read, Bodoni white on black —*St. Saladin: Sounding the Last Post?*

Philippe tossed the magazine into Duclos' lap.

"Also I want some answers to the questions raised in that," he said.

Duclos fumbled the catch, and colored. "I'll read it," he said, staring at the cover. He had a bright blank look in his eyes that reminded Cornelius of a ventriloquist's dummy.

Cheroffini looked steadily at the new Prince of St. Saladin, now sitting in Maximilien's old familiar chair, on the discreet dais, beneath the portrait of Princess Marie-Thérèse Louise at the age of seventeen. Father Cornelius stood behind him, a little to his right. His face watchful, communicating nothing. It was the moment, the scene, Cheroffini had been anticipating for what now seemed like half his lifetime. The moment, or the beginning of the day, of reckoning. What was it Duclos had said that long-ago night? We must subscribe to the safe harlotry of history? Cheroffini should have known. He should have spoken up then. No harlot is safe. He should have told the simple truth. But he'd said nothing. He kept quiet and the damage in that instant was done. How much did Philippe know? How much had he guessed? His curtness, Cheroffini felt, was not that of a man who didn't have some information, some inside wire, and an object in view. Philippe was hurrying toward a showdown, that was for sure. The war had proved he was not without courage. It still remained to be seen whether he was not the worst of fools. Cheroffini would have advised a waiting game.

"I also want to know how *Paris-Match*—" Philippe began slowly lifting the magazines and newspapers on his desk one by one, throwing them aside as he named them—"the Paris *Herald-Tribune, Le Monde*, the *Continental Daily Mail, Figaro, Nice-Matin* . . . all seem to know so much about our affairs. Where does this information come from?" He paused exactly long enough to let his words sink in, but not long enough to allow Duclos and Cheroffini to think of an answer. "Good day, gentlemen," he said evenly. He didn't stand up. The dismissal was disconcertingly naked.

When they had gone Cornelius said, "Well, the oracles came but do we know any more than we did before?"

"They are lying to me," Philippe said. "I know that much more. Have you been in touch with the clinic?"

"I drove over before matins."

"And?"

"He's doing fine. You may visit him later, if you wish. They say he's as strong as a Sabine bull."

"Do we know how it happened yet—exactly?"

"A hit-and-run driver. Probably drunk. I gather Casenave had had a couple of stiff belts himself."

"It's as well I don't need the plane," Philippe said unfeelingly. He was not looking at the priest but at the contents of the drawer he'd opened in his father's desk. "Somebody," he said after a moment, "has been through these drawers. You can tell, you know. It is odd, a certain feeling, a dead, picked-over feeling." He closed the drawer and smiled at the priest. "In the war the bodies that had been looted looked different from other bodies. They *looked* more dead." He opened his father's cigarette box. It was empty. "And when they got there, the cupboard was bare," he said. He snapped the lid down on the word *bare*. He was still smiling but it was the smile of a solitary. A smile meant for nobody but himself.

He picked up the copy of *Nice-Matin* and began slowly turning over the pages until he found what he wanted.

"Have you read this?"

"My French—" Cornelius began.

"Of course," Philippe said. He stared at the page for a moment.

"It's an article by the *rédacteur*—the editor."

He spoke hesitantly as his mind moved from the written French to English.

"The headline is: *de court plaisir—long repentir*. Short pleasure, long lament. It begins by referring to my father's timely death—"

"*Timely* death? It says that?"

"*Morte la bête, mort le venin*," Philippe read aloud with no particular expression in his voice. "Dead men tell no tales. The tangled affairs of St. Saladin, now that Prince Maximilien belongs to history, may never be unraveled or satisfactorily explained."

Cornelius moved around the desk and sat in Cheroffini's chair. The used leather arms were still damp with the Count's perspiration. Cornelius placed his own dry hands on his knees.

"It asks if I am—is Prince Philippe—strong enough —or is it already too late?—to save St. Saladin? There will no doubt, the editor thinks, be trouble ahead. Is Prince Philippe the man for the job? No, man enough . . . is Prince Philippe *man enough* for the job? The Playboy Prince—they never miss an opportunity to slip that one in—my purely social accomplishments are well known . . . my prodigality . . . et cetera, et cetera, et cetera. *Qui court deux lievres, n'en prendra aucun*—he that hunts two hares will catch neither. Ergo, I have too many social irons in the fire. I must concentrate now on the task in hand—the salvation of St. Saladin. I must be *determined* et cetera, et cetera. *Qui ne peut mordre, ne doit pas montrer les dents*. That's—" Philippe smiled, "—a man who isn't willing to bite shouldn't snarl, shouldn't show his teeth."

He read on silently for a few minutes. Cornelius felt severed from Philippe's mind. He reminded the priest of a grownup who has been reading a story to a child and become absorbed in the adventure, forgetting the child, forgetting to read aloud, yet hiding his excitement.

Finally, quoting the final paragraph from memory, Philippe said: "It is not always—*mieux vaut plier que rompre*—it is not always better to bend than break."

He dropped the newspaper, outspread, onto the desk. "So—*Paris-Match* is sounding the last post for us. The *Herald-Tribune* dismisses us as a Graustarkian anachronism, whatever that is, and *Nice-Matin* insists I get my teeth into a problem they can't bring themselves to actually name."

"If they did spell it out—"

"It would spell Stosch," Philippe said.

His eyes began to search the article again, his finger crossing the newsprint like a needle on a seismograph. "There's something also here—*oui*, here we are, *deux chiens ne s'accordent point à un os*—two dogs never agree about one bone."

Cornelius hesitated, not knowing what to say.

Philippe closed the newspaper carefully, thoughtfully, like a man who has just read a lesson in church, or a company report, that came too close to home.

"Stosch," he said softly, as if recalling some far-off memory. "Stosch, Stosch, Stosch. *Qui casse les verres les paye.*" He looked up and smiled at the priest. "Who breaks, pays."

21

It was not immediately apparent that Lionel Hammond's career as the most successful independent agent in London had reached a crucial moment.

"I don't know why, Biron. She telephoned me this morning to say she'd changed her mind. She wants to do it. Now I'm passing on that message to you. I'm as surprised and delighted as you are, my dear fellow."

Hammond leaned back in his chair and studied the ceiling.

"I do believe today's your birthday. I'm very pleased for you—for you both. It's going to be a wonderful picture. You've got the script. A fine director. Perfect casting."

It was the familiar polite prelude to the usual conflict between agent and producer negotiating terms. It always reminded Hammond of enemies who salute each other before they open fire, like the French and English before the battle of Fontenoy.

"There is just the question of money, of course."

His voice was quiet and steady, uncompromised by emotion. He tapped the ash from his cigarette carefully into a tray.

"Seventy thousand pounds."

Molly Longman stood on the other side of Hammond's desk. She could hear Biron Strauss as clearly as if he were in the room with them.

"That little lady has never collected a penny over ten before, Lionel, and you know it. You're joking with me, right? Georgina Game's a tenner, no ifs, no buts."

"I'm not joking, Biron. Circumstances change."

"Ten's her top whack," Strauss said. "Don't try to schlock me, Lionel."

Hammond pulled the telephone away from his ear.

"She likes the script, Biron. She—"

"You're giving me a fast count, Lionel. Lionel, I don't like what you're doing to me. I didn't expect a Maypole party—okay, so there are no rules . . ."

Molly held an imaginary cup to her mouth, her little finger extended in the air. Hammond smiled and nodded yes. She went out and closed the door behind her.

"That's her price now," Hammond said, bringing the telephone close and taking it away before Strauss could shout in his ear again.

"Fifteen," Strauss said. "Fifteen. That's her price. Top."

"By a marvel of abstract logic the ancient philosophers of the East originated the idea of Nirvana, the absolute nothing. Now, Biron, the most optimistic producer knows that—"

"Since when have you been in the shakedown game, Lionel? Okay, so Masters is dead and you've got to get yourself a new meal ticket—"

"That's an unnecessarily offensive—"

"Everybody in this town knows it, Lionel. But you're not doing yourself any favors pushing Game this fast. You'll be a laughingstock . . . Do you really believe there's a producer in his right mind who'll cough up that kind of dough? They'd take a drive-in waitress first."

Hammond listened with the air of a sane man incarcerated with a lunatic, obliged to humor his dangerous antics to avoid assault, dreaming of escape, longing to fly the coop. He knew that in the end Biron Strauss would give everything or nothing.

"If you won't pay it you won't pay it, Biron." Hammond spoke gently. The strain of negotiation showed nowhere about him. He might have been talking to his grocer, or his wine merchant, ordering orange pekoe tea or laying down some inexpensive claret. "Ambition must crystalize into money eventually," he said.

"Greed," Strauss said through clenched teeth. "Ambition crystalizes into greed."

"Greed is a fashionable ailment."

The fee had been Georgina's idea. It was heavy freight. He wouldn't have asked for half of that, and would probably have settled for a quarter. Yet Georgina seemed oddly confident that Strauss would throw in with it in the end. "He'll shout and scream and call me every kind of *gonif* in the book, Lionel. But if he wants me as bad as he seems to want me, he'll find the money somehow," she'd said. Hammond didn't argue with her. Strauss had sent her a copy of the script bound in calfskin, her name imprinted on the cover in gold. He was serious all right, Biron Strauss. Desperately serious. It was worth a try, Hammond thought.

"What makes you think she's worth seventy thousand pounds a picture all of a sudden anyway?" Strauss asked.

"Because we can get it," Hammond said simply.

"Cut the shit, Lionel."

"Biron, she likes the script. I'd be lying to you to say that she was anything less than ecstatic about it. The price is seventy thousand. Thirty on signature, thirty on the first day of production, ten on completion."

"Let me ask you a question. What makes you think I'm so snarable, Lionel?" Strauss sounded a lot calmer now but there was a haunting anxiety in his voice.

"You take it all too personally, my friend. I don't think you're snarable or not snarable," Hammond said. "We all know what it's like to want something very badly—to experience certain appetites and cravings we can't satisfy."

"At that price—" Strauss began.

"There is an absolute and a relative poverty, Biron. Relative poverty is our kind of poverty. The occasional failure to get the little extras in life. I'm sure you'll find a girl—even if it means a drive-in waitress, as you say yourself."

"I'm a primitive man, Lionel—"

"A primitive man will not put up with hunger in his belly for long, Biron. I know that. When the game disappears the hunter goes in search of new hunting grounds. I wish you luck. I really do, my friend."

Molly returned with a cup of tea on a small tray and three Garibaldi biscuits on a white plate.

There was a long silence on the line, except for the sound of Strauss breathing.

"I'm at the Dorchester," he said at last. "Be here in fifteen minutes."

"Do we have a deal?" Hammond asked.

"Fifteen minutes here."

"Do we have a deal?"

"You got your seventy thousand. Call it what you like."

Lionel Hammond put down the telephone and dipped a Garibaldi into his milky tea.

"Sometimes, Molly, I think Georgina doesn't need an agent at all."

22

Three hours later in an apartment on the boulevard Haussman, Georgina Game heard the news. "Well, my sweet, it's worked," she told Liz Huntington, putting down the telephone.

"You got it?"

"Yep."

"Bloody Aïda! You've got to hand it to the little rat. I should charge you commission. For the introduction."

"I'm such a lucky bugger," Georgina said distractedly. She slumped back in the deep El Morocco-striped sofa.

"What you asked for?" Liz said.

"Every red cent." Georgina grinned. "Every red cent."

"The devil you say! That puts you right up there, doesn't it?"

"Sort of, I guess."

"Sort of my eye! You *know* it does."

"I hope it does."

"To think—you almost blew it!"

"Barmy," Georgina said. "Crazy. I must have had a hole in my wig."

"I think it calls for a little celebratory drink, don't you?"

"Why not?" Georgina said in a what-the-hell tone.

Liz opened the liquor cabinet and surveyed the bottles.

"No," she said, suddenly closing the cupboard. "Champagne. Champagne on the house. There's a bottle in the fridge."

She went through to the kitchen and returned holding

a bottle of Mumm's 47 by the neck, waving it to and fro like a handbell.

"Mumm's the word," she said.

"Whose apartment is this anyway, Liz?"

"One Peglar Bernhardt. The Third. Can you imagine anyone making three of him?"

"Isn't he dead?"

"Immoderately." She made a tragic gesture.

"He died in the arms of his lady or something? In California?"

"That's the newspaper version. The hearts-and-flowers and flacks' rendition. He actually pooped out at the Beverly Hills Hotel—on Good Friday, would you believe?—playing backgammon with a call girl."

"Really?"

"Lucy Davers."

"I know that name."

"An American girl, from Texas. She was with my agency for a while. Did a little modeling in Europe and a lot of hustling in New York. I think you met her at my house once. Howard Hughes had her on coffee-and-cake money for a couple of years, so people called her an actress. But you'd be hard pushed to name a movie she's made—or an actor she hasn't."

"Poor Peglar Bernhardt."

"Can you imagine the loneliness of that guy? Having to pay a five-hundred-dollar-a-night hooker to come up to his suite to play backgammon?"

"Backgammon? Really?"

"Oh sure. That part's true. He was backgammon-nuts," Liz said in a listless tone.

"The dark miseries of loneliness," Georgina said.

"It wasn't as bad as all that. Peglar would rather have had double sixes than sex anytime." Liz made an expression disparaging all gamblers and gambling. "Backgammon bores me to extinction inside five minutes." Smiling, she spoke in her most solemn manner. Georgina found it not unpleasantly disorienting.

"Could you be a whore, do you think, Georgina?"

"When I was filming in Pompeii last year I persuaded the guide to unlock the whorehouse for me—a great honor for ladies. There are paintings outside each little cubicle and the painting shows what particular specialty that whore did, and she only stuck to the one thing apparently. The age of specialization isn't all that new, you see. Anyway, there was one lady who took it up her arse and laid belly down all day long. I thought that was the perfect magoo. You don't move all day— you can get through about eight novels a week, eat an orange, take a nap, you don't even have to look at the guy. A lot of money just to read and sleep and screw all day."

"I'm not mad about taking it up my arse," Liz said balefully.

Georgina leaned back in the sofa and watched Liz as she worked on the cork, expertly using her thumbs. She still had the studio rouge in her hollow cheeks. She really was a very striking woman, Georgina thought, studying the glistening tango-red lips, every curve of her wide mouth accentuated, the moony-pale face and the eyeliner curved up at the outer corners of her eyes. Her dark corn-colored hair had been carefully lightened at the temples to give width to her brow. A shadow of greasepaint above and below her gray eyes gave them the perilous beauty of metalled winter sky. She had the sort of looks that went well with the black and white Chinese creations both Balenciaga and Dior were pushing hard that season. It was no surprise that she was in such demand. A recent poll placed her number five among the world's top ten models.

"What are you doing in this apartment?" Georgina said for something to say, for she had a pretty shrewd idea what the answer would be.

"Well, my dear, he gave me the keys. Whenever I was in Paris, he said, use the apartment."

"No strings?"

"My specialty's broad-mindedness," Liz said giving Georgina a coquettish look under her long nylon lashes.

"Doesn't anyone object? His heirs—"

"Listen, my dear, it's going to take ages to sort out his estate. He has houses and apartments everywhere. Probably places even he'd forgotten he had. Do you know at one time he had four apartments in New York?

Four. Including a permanent suite at the Waldorf Towers."

She popped the cork.

"So you'll just go on staying here until—"

"Until they change the locks or try to charge me rent." She poured the champagne and handed a glass to Georgina.

"You've got what it takes, Huntington."

"Intestinal fortitude, my dear." She raised her glass. "To you," she said.

"To clever old Antrobus," Georgina said.

"Right. To Richard Antrobus."

It had been a snap decision for Georgina to come with Liz to Paris. Liz was working for *Elle* and *Vogue*, so Georgina had plenty of time to herself. It was exactly the sort of break she needed. Things were getting just a little awkward in London. She was finding it more and more difficult to convince herself that what she felt for Richard Antrobus was no more than infatuation. She knew all about him. He was dangerous. He was unreliable. He was as bad as they all said he was, and as good. He was both risible and resilient. His charm was calculated, but his vulnerability was real enough. His charm was old and wicked but there was something close to childhood in his vulnerability. Whatever it was, it was getting through to Georgina. Richard was aware of her comprehension—he was too smart not to be—but not disconcerted. "You must forgive my sleight-of-mouth," he had said when she caught him lying about something quite silly to some of her friends at a dinner party. He was compulsively dishonest in small ways, he told her, but he was not a hypocrite. She believed him. She believed he had a kind of integrity. In his fashion. It was the sort of English schoolboy integrity that stopped him snitching on a friend but wouldn't prevent him stealing from the church poorbox if it were raining and he needed to take a taxi home. "I lie at least once a day. To keep my hand in," he said with a complete surrender that puzzled Georgina. But she felt no real anger against him . . . only this deep inexplicable concern that was almost compassion and almost love.

She felt an instinctive happiness in his company. Yet

he had been quite happy for her to come to Paris without him. "Aren't you suspicious?" she said.

"A man never looks under the bed unless he has hidden there himself," he told her.

"And you never have, I suppose," she said. He was playing games.

"Never been quick enough. Been caught in the bed," he said. "Once or twice."

Antrobus had done something no other man had ever done: he'd made Georgina Game jealous.

"What do you think? Do you think I should offer him a percentage, or something?" Georgina asked Liz.

"There's nothing like living at Liberty Hall."

"He's not as black as he's painted. He's got more integrity than people give him credit for," Georgina said defensively.

"He's probably never taken money from a woman he wouldn't bang. Is that integrity?"

"Be serious, Liz."

"I'm being serious. *You* be sensible."

"Then what should I do? Offer him ten percent?" She was angry with herself for having started the conversation. She knew how hapless she must have sounded. It wasn't like her at all.

"I'm still not clear about what he did exactly," Liz said.

"Well, after your lunch party I saw him a few times. Right? We went to Ascot. We had dinner once or twice. The fact is, I was on a bit of a rebound and he was . . . available."

"This sounds ominous," Liz said.

"I told him about the offer. I told him I wouldn't do it because I didn't like the idea of working for Biron Strauss."

"And he said, if the money's right, grab it?" Liz smiled but there was contempt in her voice.

"No. Not at all. He was very sweet. He said it was the sort of decision that only I could make. And that was that. Until—about a month later we met Waldo Bragg. We were at some—"

"The crystal gazer?"

"The clairvoyant. He said some amazing things to me."

"Such as?"

"Like—well, everything he said really was pretty startling. He didn't know about the Siegelman book. How could he? But he described the girl so accurately—it was weird. He said I would be asked to play this girl and it would bring me great acclaim and happiness."

Liz smiled. It was a fond smile but not particularly reassuring.

"He said I would soon be working for a man, a foreigner. This man would not be a friend, nor would he be trustworthy, but he was important. I would say no many times before I said yes. And I would not regret my decision."

"You're talking like Bragg," Liz said.

"I'm telling you exactly what he said."

"Go on."

"He said he saw poetry and yet there was no poetry. He seemed a bit confused but—"

"*Biron* Strauss."

"Well, that's what went through my mind," Georgina said.

"It could be a coincidence. Or intuitive rummaging."

"He said other things. Oh Lord! My Lord! It shattered me. I made an appointment to see him again. You see, all this happened over dinner. He is an astonishing man. You must go."

"So *Bragg* persuaded you to do the picture?"

"No. But he made me think again. Very seriously."

"I don't doubt it," Liz said. "I don't in the least doubt it." A delicate, not unkind mockery flickered in her voice.

"You know, when I read the book I had to keep digging down into myself to try to discover what she really felt. Bragg told me more about this girl's feelings in five minutes—"

"I don't see why you should feel such a debt to Richard," Liz said.

"It was Richard who told me to ask for so much money—once he saw my mind was made up."

"Shit or bust. That sounds like Richard."

"He convinced me it was on. He's very good for my ego. He knows me very well."

"Never let intimacy creep into an affair," Liz said slowly and with no cynical emphasis. Georgina smiled and felt around for a suitable retort but found none.

Liz poured more champagne into their glasses. She put the palm of her hand on her kidneys and pulled back her shoulders. "It gets you there, standing around in those piss-elegant poses all day. Do you know what the photographer asked for today? He said he wanted me to give him the nonchalant posture—I quote—of a beautiful woman at the other end of a leash on which an elegant Borzoi is crapping in the gutter."

"Very descriptive," Georgina said.

"Too bloody descriptive."

"Some photographers—it's like having your face raped," Georgina said.

"What did you do today?" Liz asked.

"Moseyed around. Oh—I got the *Herald-Tribune* and the London papers in Smiths. They're by my bed."

"What's happening in the world? Just give me the headlines."

"Your friend King Farouk has had a horn fitted to his Rolls. It yelps like a dog being run over."

"He's not my friend," Liz said with a sideways glance at Georgina. "Not any more."

Georgina liked to tease Liz about her famous lovers, mainly because Liz never talked about them herself. The story went that Liz had picked up Farouk in St. Saladin. She had been losing heavily at chemin-de-fer. Farouk grandly shoved a million-franc plaque across the table to her as an introductory present. Liz immediately gave it to the croupier. "*Pour le personnel*," she said without as much as a glance at the fat Egyptian king.

Liz had style. She had that extraordinary ability of taking advantage of the most difficult circumstances.

"Did you really give a million-franc tip to the croupier?" Georgina asked her once.

"You dare a lot at nineteen," Liz said, not exactly confirming the legend and not bothering to deny it. "Anyway, I prefer guys who know how to slip bread quietly." Sometimes she could be so cool she was practically inanimate. "Anyway, anyway. Kings are far too unreliable."

"I had tea at Rumpelmayers today," Georgina said. "I've had a lovely time."

"While I've been slaving over a hot camera," Liz said.

"Canon fodder," Georgina said.

"Oh very funny. *Very* funny."

"Would you like to live in Paris, Liz?"

"If it was filled with English people and American dollars," Liz said. She was standing by the tall windows, looking down into the street. She smiled but it was a sun-lonely smile. There was a drift of secret shadows around her eyes.

"You look like Garbo waiting for her luggage," Georgina said.

"How serious are you about Richard?"

The question surprised Georgina.

"I don't know, I think he has taken a violent fancy to me," she said, carefully avoiding an answer.

"You're not going to elope with him or anything silly like that?"

"And sacrifice all those presents?" Georgina kept it light. Lighter than she actually felt.

"That's his specialty, you know. Sweeping rich ladies off their feet, riding herd on their emotions."

"He didn't invent gunpowder," Georgina said.

"He's left his pecker tracks on more sheets in Belgravia than the whole of the—"

"He has some fascinating vices," Georgina said quickly with a silencing gesture.

"And no boring virtues?" Liz regarded Georgina with the frank humorous gaze of a woman used to making calibrations of other people's misgivings . . . and millstones.

"He is nice and wicked. You have to admit. Richard is never dull. I hate dull men," Georgina said in too much of a rush. She checked herself almost at once and continued more slowly, remembering to smile an elaborate smile of indifference. "He is reckless, unscrupulous, almost utterly bad. What more can a girl want?"

"I'd hate to see you get hurt with a man like that—" Liz's words hung in midair.

"You don't like him very much, do you?" Georgina said.

"*Au contraire*. I like him very much. I don't trust him one bit. You know what Caroline Wylie said about him, don't you?"

"I don't really care to know," Georgina said. She made a haughty pass at good humor. For a moment she regretted telling Liz so much.

"Well, anyway," Liz said. "Be careful. I'd hate to see you just drifting to disaster."

That evening at dinner Georgina said, "What did Caroline Wylie say?"

Liz smiled.

"She said that enough would never be enough for Richard. He would always want more and he would always hurt the woman who gave it to him."

"Caroline Wylie said that?"

"Yes."

"Wow! Some lady, huh? Caroline Wylie?"

"An heiress's wrath is wondrously clinging," Liz said.

They were dining at Lapérouse on the Quai des Grands-Augustins. The picturesque restaurant facing the Seine on the Left Bank had the old-fashioned look Georgina liked. Nobody seemed to be sure how old Lapérouse really was. It was a favorite eating place of Robert Louis Stevenson and of Thackeray, and Baedeker gave it top billing in 1888. Harry Ogilvy first took Georgina there when she was sixteen. It was part of her sixteenth birthday present: a tour of Europe, enjoying the best of everything.

"I love this place," Georgina told Liz now. "It's just how I imagine a good Paris restaurant of a hundred years ago must have looked and felt. The low ceilings, the murals. Don't you love all that Louis Seize bric-à-brac and faded finery?"

"It's the ideal lovers' rendezvous," Liz said. "Do you think people think we're a couple of lesbs?"

"If you were my lover," Georgina said easily, "I'd be entertaining you now in a secret alcove *à deux*."

"Here? In this restaurant?"

"The entrance is behind a portrait of Madame de Pompadour on one of the landings," Georgina said.

"You ever use it?"

"No. My father told me about it. Enraged cuckolds have been known to search the place from the cellar to the eaves without discovering its existence."

"I must remember that," Liz said.

"The atmosphere here. It's so decadent."

"It makes you long for the days when young gallants would give estates for one tilt with love's lance," Liz said.

"What's the most you've been offered, Liz?" Georgina said.

"For a one-night stand? Count Zughetti—he offered a villa. He turned quite nasty when I declined. We were in Las Vegas. He drove me out of town, toward the desert. He said he was going to kill me. If he couldn't have me he was going to kill me, then shoot himself."

"Weren't you scared?"

"He was bluffing."

"How could you be sure?"

"He stopped at all the red lights."

Georgina laughed. "It was still monkeying with the buzz saw."

"Yeah, well," Liz grinned. "You've got to take a few risks in life—otherwise what would you have to talk about in the powder room?"

"Would you—just for money?" Georgina asked.

"My morals are pretty much the morals of the rich. It's a fairly ruttish society, let's face it."

"But *just* for money?" Georgina said again.

"I find my favorite mentors and apostles in the courts of Farouk, Aly Khan, Princess Margaret, Prince Philippe. . . . Sure, if the price was right and the man was right—why not? I said earlier—my specialty's broad-mindedness."

"Zughetti wasn't the right man?"

"Jesus, no. Let the cripple wed a limping wife, I say. He's so fucking fey. Do you know he travels everywhere with his own potted palm tree. In a jardinière. For his Shih-tsu to pee against. His Shih-tsu hates strange trees. How could you go to bed with a man like that—even for a villa?" Liz gave a small theatrical shudder.

"I bet that raised a few eyebrows. The jardinière," Georgina said. "In Vegas."

"I think they finally asked him to get out of town. A *toutes jambes*, or whatever it is they say in Nevada."

Georgina liked Liz's quiet humor and her easygoing style. You always knew where you stood with a girl like Liz. She was so uncomplicated. Still, it was unusual to get her talking about herself quite so freely. Naming names, as they said in Washington. She usually had the habit of letting you talk about you. She never talked about her past—her childhood past, her parents, where she came from. Liz was one of those women who arrive on the scene absolute and unconditional, with plenty of presence and no past at all. She was English, probably a Londoner, probably middle-class or close to it. Looking at her now, through the brilliant makeup, through the acquired air of elegance, Georgina thought she recognized something else. She seemed to have that special look of beautiful contempt refined by—what was it? Guilt? Insecurity? Some sort of secret? Some sort of pain? For a moment, Georgina was reminded of those lonely travel-stained children you meet in movie studios and in the theater, kids who have grown up in hotels, in rented rooms, in transit, in the fumes of nomadic ambitious parents. It had all been there, when Georgina thought about it, in that fleeting sunless smile she had seen that afternoon, when Liz stood by the tall window looking down into the street.

"See that girl who's just come in?" Liz interrupted Georgina's thoughts.

"Yes."

"Her name is Isak Girod—"

"I know Isak Girod. She's a very good actress. Who's the man with her?"

"I'm not sure. She has a lively proclivity for rich admirers. She's been very close to Prince Philippe for quite a while."

"Didn't somebody quite famous kill himself for her?"

"Yves Segni. Because of her affair with Philippe."

"I remember. The singer. I saw him once at the Tabou."

"There's a wicked story going around the studios that she's been offered a hundred thousand dollars for her memoirs. Or a dollar a dick."

"That's very cruel," Georgina said, but she laughed all the same.

Isak Girod knew they were discussing her. She talked to her companion with that indefinable expression of amused tolerance and barely suppressed boredom which is supposed to bespeak real class.

"She's very beautiful," Georgina said. "Will she marry the Prince?"

"Like a shot I should think—if she could afford it."

"How do you mean? If she could afford it?"

"The rumor has it that Prince Philippe is for sale."

They were both slightly drunk when they returned to the apartment on boulevard Haussman. Georgina sat on the bed and watched Liz undress. She undressed slowly, not reluctantly but with a sort of sensual self-absorption, a self-attentiveness.

"You're making me feel shy," Liz said after a little while. She had undressed down to her panties and bra.

"I'm sorry."

"What a waste!" Liz said. "A super dinner, this apartment, champagne on ice—and not a man between us. Who would believe it?"

"A man between us?"

They both giggled.

"I *did* enjoy this evening," Georgina said.

"It was lovely."

Georgina undressed, quickly, removing her dress and underclothes in an almost continuously flowing movement. She was naked for a brief moment before putting on a white satin peignoir.

"You have a great body," Liz said. "You bitch."

"Thank you."

Georgina sat down on the large double bed and curled her knees beneath her chin. Liz sat at the dressing table, brushing her hair.

"I'm so tired."

"I'm not at all surprised, darling. You've had a long day."

"It's a hard life for us poor little working girls."

Georgina got up and took the brush out of Liz's hand.

"Let me."

She began to brush her hair with long strong strokes.

"That's nice," Liz said. She could feel the warmth of Georgina's body through the soft satin pressing against her back. She let herself relax against Georgina. At first, and only for a moment, the satin felt cold against her bare skin.

"That's nice," she said again, softer. She wondered whether Georgina would yield, would be scared by the proximity, would back away. For a moment they became very still, staring at each other in the dressing-table mirror.

"Yes?" Georgina said.

Liz just smiled and leaned backward into her. Boldly this time. Georgina held her face with her left hand and continued to brush her hair, with slow strokes, tenderly, watching her face in the mirror.

"You like that?"

"God . . . yes," Liz said. It was almost a whimper.

Georgina's little finger moved to the corner of Liz's mouth and gently probed.

Liz moved her head sideways. She kissed the tip of Georgina's finger, then bit her nail, hard, with intent.

"Ouch."

Liz opened her mouth and allowed Georgina's finger to slide across her tongue, making slow gentle circling movements.

Liz dropped her hands to her side and closed her eyes.

Georgina put down the brush and held Liz's head with both hands now.

They fell quiet.

Liz's head rested between Georgina's breasts.

"Have you ever?" Georgina asked softly.

"No."

"Truly?"

"I promise."

"Neither have I."

"I'm glad."

"You have the look of a thoughtful lemming," Georgina told her.

They were whispering, like tourists talking in a cathedral.

"I've thought about it," Liz said. "A lot."

"I've always wanted to kiss a woman's breasts." Georgina spoke with her lips pressed against the top of Liz's head. "To kiss and be kissed. It's been one of my fantasies . . . God, I must be pissed."

Liz smiled at Georgina in the mirror and, turning slowly from their reflections, hungrily searched for Georgina's breast with her mouth.

"That's beautiful."

After a little while, Georgina took hold of her hand and led her to the bed. She reached out and switched off the light.

"You're so brave," Liz said in the darkness. "You're so brave."

"You feel good. So soft . . ."

They lay and held each other for a long time, facing each other in the darkness, entwined, discovering . . .

"How do you feel?"

"As if—it was as if somebody scooped my belly out with a large spoon," Liz said afterward.

"How do you feel?"

"Wicked. Very wicked."

"That's beautiful."

"You feel like . . . a lovely lair . . . a cave . . . warm. So damp. Sort of . . . enveloping. Velvet. It's—"

"Is it what you imagined?"

"I don't know. I didn't know what to expect."

"You're not sorry?" Liz's voice sounded very small, childlike.

"Christ, no. It was beautiful."

"I had no idea—you—"

"It's a mistake for women to be too respectable. They are only considered dull." Georgina traced the contours of Liz's lips with her fingers. "You know what happens to good little girls, don't you?"

"No. Tell me what happens to good little girls," Liz giggled.

"They get very, *very* bored."

"Here endeth the second lesson."

"It's better to enjoy yourself when you're young. Save all the goodness for your old age—when you're out of options. My father taught me that."

"The only advice my dad ever gave me was to learn to pack for a man," Liz said. "It was pretty good advice—as far as it went."

"I know so little about you."

"Not much you don't!"

They giggled again. Liz kissed Georgina gently on her lips.

"I've been to the bottom of a lot of wells and climbed a few mountains," Liz said.

"Have you ever been married?"

"Never, but sometimes . . . nearly. Those vows—like *death* do us part. They scare me shitless. Forever, for me, is next Thursday. And that's half-closing day where I come from."

"Have you ever been in love? Really in love?"

"Once."

"Was it good?"

"While it lasted . . . it was lovely."

"You never made it to Thursday afternoon?"

"No—but you should have been around on Wednesday morning," Liz said. "Wednesday morning was just perfect."

"Next time," Georgina said just before she fell asleep. "Next time you might surprise yourself."

Liz couldn't sleep. She was wide awake, remembering. Remembering . . .

Her point of departure was that night in Rome when she first met the Ambassador. He was an elegant man, not tall, with a dark pockmarked face and teeth that gleamed.

It was just another embassy reception, nothing special. He was polite, courteous and correct. A professional politician, a public-relations man through and through. Liz wouldn't have given him another thought had he not telephoned the following evening.

"Miss Huntington," he said. "I'm in the most terrible fix. I'm giving a small dinner party tomorrow evening and my sister, who usually acts as my hostess, is unwell. Could you possibly, please, stand in for her?"

His sister apparently never recovered.

Liz became his official hostess—and his mistress. Liz fell in love with him.

A year went by.

He bought her an apartment on the via Ludovisi, discreetly close to the embassy, off the top end of the via Veneto facing the Borghese Gardens.

One day she told him she wanted to visit his country.

"I can't let you do that," he told her. "That is the one thing I cannot give you."

"Why not?"

"If my King sees you, he will admire you."

"So?"

"In my country, what the King admires the King must be offered."

"You'd have to offer him me?"

"I'd have to."

"But I love *you*," she said. "I'm *in* love with you."

The Ambassador shrugged helplessly.

Some months later he was recalled and made foreign minister. Liz packed up her Ludovisi apartment and returned to London.

She felt her very soul had been gutted.

"You know why I could not take you with me," he wrote her. "I love you too much—far, far too much to make you my wife, to make you a gift to my King. This time, for the first time, I cannot allow him to put his sickle into another man's harvest."

It was light when Liz went to sleep in Georgina's arms. It was light and it was Thursday and her face was wet with tears.

23

The acrid summer dust of old carriages floated in the sunlight like molecular minnows. The train jolted and swayed across the Thames, past Battersea Power Station, traveling fast, through the sprawling south London suburbs. Dulwich was only eleven minutes and three stops from Victoria but it was another world. Richard Antrobus watched the backyards, the bombed sites, the warehouses and small factories, the rows and rows of tiny streets slip by. After a while came the larger houses, the substantial Victorian residences which were beginning to take on the kind of aging dignity that really ugly things acquire just before they die, or disappear. Soon they would be demolished by the speculative builders, these old red-brick mansions, and each one replaced by thirty-six three-bedroom semi-detacheds selling for two thousand five hundred pounds apiece. Each standing like a tiny monument, a centrally heated tombstone, to the big old house that used to be.

London was changing.

His hands resting on his knees, Antrobus stared at the changing scenery, frowning. His mind was not on London and what people like Harry Ogilvy were doing to it. His mind was on Georgina Game—and what she was doing to him. She was driving him crazy. She seemed determined to dismantle him, limb by limb, nerve by bloody nerve, intent on building a better Antrobus, a better but maybe smaller tomorrow. The problem was, Georgina's original conception of him had one serious flaw: it was all wrong. How could he become what she wanted, when she was working from faulty information? He had lied to her, and lied to her. He had cheated her and used her and fallen in love with her.

213

That was another problem. Falling in love with her. That wasn't part of the plan at all. He had not been aware that he was falling in love. Not for a minute. Very few men are, of course. Love's onset is always unsuspected, unapparent. Were it not, a man might arm himself against his destiny.

Antrobus turned from the yellow smoke-grimed window and closed his eyes.

He couldn't get Georgina out of his mind. She had, he thought now, such a commanding absence. The phrase came into his head and made him smile. The smile stayed on his face for a long time, but after a while it had a broken-down look. It looked like a wreck waiting to be towed away. Yesterday's smile.

"You will find out things about me very soon—if you want to go on, if you really want to have me. If you are at all unsure or nervous, Richard, you'd better turn back now."

For the umpteenth time he went over the conversation they'd had before she left for Paris with Liz Huntington. He knew well enough how to make a woman feel she is being cared for, which is all most women ever want, but Georgina saw through the trick and wanted more. She always wanted more. She'd admitted it herself, the first time they went to bed together.

"I don't want a ponce on my payroll, Richard. I've seen more than enough entourage husbands in this business, dogging their rich wives like haunted courtiers. You're too worthwhile to be another spongy spouse. You're too good to settle for a second-class fame." He remembered every word. "If you want to be with me, you stand on your own two feet. I won't pick up your tab—and I won't ever expect you to pick up mine."

Antrobus sighed. The wrecked smile seemed to fall to pieces on his face. At least, he thought, Biron Strauss had coughed up like a lamb. Enough to pay off the Deauville marker, with something to spare. If only he hadn't fallen in love with the silly bitch, all would be well. As it was . . . He needed money. A lot of money. Serious money.

It was an old plan, but it still might work. Once it had been a glorious caper in their minds, a caper

planned one summer a long time ago, planned like a
dirty weekend, with jokes and giggles and genuine apprehension, with tall talk and machismo swank. And
like some of the most successful dirty weekends . . . it
never happened.

He would have to go carefully. Rekindle the old
flame, the old felonious passions . . .

At Herne Hill, two women got into his carriage. They
were both in their mid-twenties, Antrobus guessed.
One, a blonde, was nice-looking but a little too plump.
She had the slightly adventurous look of a girl used to
messing about in boats, but not in the very best boats.
Her companion was torrentially talkative. She was talking when she got into the carriage and she didn't stop.
She was, Antrobus thought now, twenty-nine and holding. She had strange dead dandelion eyes and an imper-
fect American accent, probably caught like some social
disease off a GI boyfriend, or from too many bad Hollywood movies. "So I said to him, Harold, darling, sure
she's pretty. She has a very pretty smile and all. But
what does she ever *say?*" The blond girl smiled at Antrobus with a vague look of recognition, mingled with
plain saucy interest.

The train was slowing down.

WestDulwichWestDulwichWestDulwich. The sign-
posts strung out along the narrow wooden platform
flipped by. West Dulwich. The train rolled to a halt,
brakes sighing, buffer plates clanking like slow metallic
handclaps. *Alight Here For Dulwich College Picture
Gallery,* Antrobus read the familiar sign. He slammed
the heavy door behind him, watched with frank sexual
interest by the two women. The one with the dead dandelion eyes said something in her artificial accent and
they both laughed. The train pulled away.

It was a beautiful day. A perfect day for Dulwich. A
village inside London, leafy and spacious, and nearly a
thousand years old. A molten smell of sun-warmed oil
came off the tracks, glinting in the sun. An old porter
tore his ticket and called him 'sir' with genuine respect
and friendliness. He walked down the iron-canopied
ramp, right back into his childhood. He understood
Cas's love for this place. Its sense of history lingered

like wood smoke on an autumn day. The woods, where King Charles I hunted, were still there. Cut back now but still big enough for secret assignations. He'd lost his innocence in those woods, aged thirteen. To a schoolteacher, a passionate and comely Presbyterian who treated him kindly and wept afterward and prayed for God's forgiveness and Richard's discretion.

Antrobus smiled.

His step-brother loved Dulwich with a love that was deep, and rare in bank clerks. He would never leave it. And Richard could never come back on anything more permanent than a day return. That said almost everything there was to say about them both.

Cas Antrobus was waiting in the wooden ticket hall. Richard knew he would be. Cas was never late. He carried a book. The two men shook hands and looked into each other's eyes. By coincidence, the same gunmetal-gray eyes.

"Dead on time," Cas said with a proprietorial air. "Eleven minutes."

"It's good to see you," Richard said with real warmth. "How's everybody?"

"Fine, fine. Edith had a cold but that's gone. The boys are fine. Looking forward to seeing you again."

"It's been too long," Richard said.

"It's only eleven minutes on the train," Cas said reproachfully. He hated people to think he was buried in the suburbs. "No more distance than Chelsea to Kensington."

"I suppose it isn't," Richard said. "When you think about it."

"Didn't bring the motor. Thought you might enjoy the stroll."

"Good country-type air," Richard said. Cas was probably thinking about the expense, it flashed through Richard's mind. Cas had somehow become one of those middle-class professional men, bitterly principled, a member of all the right societies, and at least one good club, children at the proper schools, who lived precariously on the cake line.

Cas Antrobus was several inches smaller than Richard and seven years older. He'd put on about ten pounds around the middle since they'd last met. His face was fuller, his hair thinner. He wore white cotton trousers and a blue blazer and his old Harrovian tie with a knot the size of an acorn.

"The boys wanted to come. To the station. To meet you. But I thought you might fancy a jar on the way."

"An ice-cold lager."

"In the Greyhound."

"Like old times."

The two men walked without haste, a Sunday strolling pace, along Gallery Road. Cas walked with his hands clasped behind his back, his chin down on his neck. His eyes were solemn, a look which had become an aging habit with him.

"The old place doesn't change," Richard said.

"All the paintings are back in the gallery, you know. They evacuated them in the blitz."

"I remember."

"Watteau, the Claudes, the Teniers. They're all back."

"My favorite is the Rembrandt," Richard said. It was the perfect opening. "You remember the one?"

"*A Girl at a Window*," Cas said at once.

"Beautiful."

"Those eyes."

"The place hasn't changed one little bit in my lifetime. It doesn't matter where I go, I love Dulwich best."

"Is the tollgate still there?"

"Of course," Cas said.

"For every horse, mule, or donkey not drawing—threepence," Richard recited the table of tolls.

"For beasts per score and so on in proportion for any less number—tenpence," Cas continued.

"For sheep, lambs, or hogs per score and so on in proportion, but not less than one ha'penny, for any less number—tuppence ha'penny," Richard came back at him.

"By Order of the Board of Alleyn's College of God's Gift Dulwich," they said together.

"There's nothing wrong with your memory," Cas said.

"My party piece," Richard said. "However old one

gets, a man never forgets his childhood party piece. You used to do 'Pack Up Your Troubles'—with a very fetching military flounce, I remember."

"Don't remind me."

"How's the Hall?"

"Drafty and expensive and full of ghosts. Father knew what he was doing."

"He usually does. You'd have got it sooner or later, anyway."

"Yes—no, of course, we love it. I wouldn't live anywhere else. But the upkeep is monstrous. That and the school fees and—" He stopped and looked at Richard with a weak apologetic smile. "I'm sorry. You don't want to hear my bleats."

On the contrary, Richard thought. He said, "Things are tough all over. Going to get a lot tougher, I fancy. I'm just thankful I don't have kids, a family, to worry about."

"It is a worry," Cas said gravely.

"How's the bank?"

"Condemned to be rich."

"Lending's a bottomless business at least."

"Scoffing infidel," Cas said. It was a favorite phrase from their childhood. "Scoffing infidel."

"I have a sincere attachment to the truth," Richard said. "Tell the truth and shame Satan, Mother always said."

"Poor Mother."

"Poor you's more to the point."

"It's not that bad, old boy," Cas said.

They walked on in silence for a while. A few times Cas seemed almost to sigh as they passed the playing fields of their childhood, as if a sense of grievous nostalgia excluded conversation.

Perfect, Richard thought.

"*A Girl at the Window,*" he finally said. "Do you remember?"

"Our plot?"

"You do remember."

"How could I forget?" Cas said. "We spent an entire summer planning it."

"Casing the gallery."

"All those notes."

"The timetables."

"That rope ladder," Cas said. "The grappling iron."

"I was perfectly serious, you know," Richard said.

"So was I."

"Really? Truly? I always thought—"

"Oh I was quite prepared to go through with it," Cas said. "I was frightfully scared, of course. But—"

"The grand bravery is fear faced, and quelled."

"The wit and wisdom of Sir Wilfred Antrobus, R.A."

"Father had a saw for every occasion. But no real answers," Richard said.

"My smallest doubts grew to the size of nightmares," Cas said. "Even so, I still think—"

"I was lucky. My courage was a sort of constitutional endowment. Otherwise known as a complete lack of imagination. Would it really have worked, Cas?"

"Then. Not now. They've got new alarm systems. Very sophisticated stuff. Pressure mats, beams, the works."

"Pity," Richard said.

"We missed our chance, little brother. Imagine. We might have been rich. Master criminals. Instead of which . . ." He grinned ruefully and didn't finish the sentence.

The Greyhound was bustling with the Sunday morning crowd. Cas pushed his way through to the bar and returned with two brimming pints of lager.

"Let's poodle through to the garden," he said.

"Cheers," he said when they were outside. He raised his glass above his head, his elbow on a line with his eyes.

"Cheers," Richard said in a different tone.

They sipped their beers and said nothing, enjoying the sunshine. The garden seemed especially quiet after the dark hubbub of the bar. A couple of young men in sports jackets sat at a wooden bench with three girls, all of them pretty. An elderly couple sat at a small table with an ancient Cairn terrier sleeping at their feet. Richard preferred big dogs. Little dogs got under your feet, he always said, big dogs got under your skin. A painted lady butterfly, a flutter of carmine, sailed over the Michaelmas daisies. "The summer," Cas said. "Always keeps her most beautiful colors for the end."

The two men stood at the end of the long garden, away from the others. Richard took the book from under his brother's arm and looked at the title. "*Objects of Monetary Policy*," he read aloud. He shoved the book back under Cas's arm. "What ever happened to Shelley?"

"What indeed," Cas said, "ever happened to Shelley?"

A small breath of wind lifted a hazel bough. Cas looked with a nostalgic expression at the exposed yellowing leaves.

They sipped their beer and talked. They talked about the past, the adventures they'd shared, the apples they'd scrumped, the girls they'd known. They talked about the good times and remembered the bad times, too.

It was not just a sentimental journey: Richard was softening his brother up.

"The real sadnesses of life are mostly in the imagination," Cas said. "Don't you think? The regrets. To recall the old times, the old plans, the trivial details of ambitions gone awry—"

"To feel the slow overshadowing of time." Richard sighed, encouraging the mood of regret and dissatisfaction, in a parody of penitence.

There was a silence.

It couldn't have been more perfect, Richard felt.

"Do you remember our other plan?" he said after a longish plausible pause.

"The bank job?"

"The bank job," Richard repeated the phrase lovingly.

"Our master plan," Cas said.

"Has time overtaken that, do you suppose?" He spoke casually.

Cas frowned and thought about it.

"No, no, not at all."

"Well, then?" Richard was grinning.

"Are you serious?"

"Oh yes. I'm serious all right."

Cas shook his head.

"I'm too old, too old, too old."

"The grand bravery," Richard said.

"Too much to lose now," Cas said. "Other people to think about."

"There's everything to gain. You're not a gambling man. How else will you ever get your hands on such a load? And that's what it's going to take to keep up the Hall, to keep the boys at school—"

"I've done my own sums," Cas said almost haughtily.

"You're never going to make them come out right simply by praying," Richard said. "If God's not at home, we must go and see the Devil."

Cas's slow reluctant smile reminded Richard of a burnt-out Catherine wheel, still smoldering bravely, but dead. Cas said, "Still my little brother. Putting me up to all kinds of mischief."

"The arithmetic of adventure," Richard said. "That's what counts. Nothing or a hatful."

"It wouldn't work, you know."

"You just said it would."

"The human element. *Us*. We're not kids any more, Richard. I'm forty-one years old and—"

"You haven't got a pot to piss in."

"Come on now."

"When did you last have a holiday? In the sun, in a hotel suite, in Europe? In Morocco? Greece? Just you and Edith, without the boys?"

"Yonks ago," Cas said, reverting to their childhood slang.

"Exactly. Do you know what I've done in the last two years—in the last *year*? The places I've been, the women I've had—"

"You're different."

"No, Cas. I just live more."

"Your arsenal of abuse is—"

"I don't want to abuse you, Cas. I want to wake you up. Abracadabra! Open sesame! Do you think they really saw the lady in half? Life is a wheeze. It's all a grift, a terrible fraud, Cas, a hoax from beginning to end. There's a trick in it every time. It isn't magic, Cas."

"And it isn't legal," Cas said with a grin.

"Behind every fortune there's a crime," Richard said. "One for the road?"

After lunch they sat in deck chairs in the garden, surrounded by the Sunday papers. The boys had gone boating on the lake in the park. Edith, in long red rubber gloves, was doing something clever with liquid manure in the kitchen garden.

"It could work," Cas said. He clasped his hands behind his neck and crossed his legs.

Richard looked carefully blank, as if the whole idea had gone out of his mind, as if he hadn't understood.

"What could work?" he asked. There was a lot of Sunday afternoon lassitude in his voice, and his eyes gave nothing away.

"The bank job," Cas said. He'd been brooding about it for a long time, through most of lunch, and afterward, when he'd been pretending to read the newspapers with such care.

"Ah, the bank job," Richard said with moderate surprise.

"I've been thinking," Cas said.

"Remind me. The basic . . . mechanics," Richard said.

"Somebody inside the bank initiates a tan—a transfer advice note. And, you see, once it gets into the system it's virtually impossible to—"

"Hold your horses. One step at a time. Tan. The transfer advice note is what exactly? Slowly."

"Tan is simply a form advising a manager that an account, a customer, has been transferred to his branch."

"That's all?"

"The amount in the account is posted, plus specimen copies of the customer's signature plus an *S* stamp."

"Which is?"

"The shield sheet—his credit rating, in layman's language."

"Just that?" Richard said.

"More or less. The credit rating is indicated by a code word. The code words are changed every day. There are seven categories—covering . . . well, covering everybody from crooks to bishops. The passbook is sent to head office. The account transfer is recorded and the book forwarded to the new branch, a week or so later."

"The code word also acts as an authorization, I suppose?"

"Yes."

"Thus the daily switch."

"Yes."

"How do you get the transfer note into the system?"

"Each day between nine and two o'clock, the bank flyers—"

"Flyers?"

"The vans that carry messages, various orders, memos, credit notes, sometimes some foreign currency—but very little cash generally—between the branches."

"The internal mail system."

Cas nodded. "There are five collections during the day. Anything that has to move between branches goes into the bag—"

"The bags collected by the flyers?"

"Yes. The bags are taken to the vans, opened and sorted enroute. The flyers are really circulating sorting offices. The bags are sealed before leaving the bank and can only be unlocked inside the flyer—there's a special bench key. It's an electronic gadget that is activated by the driver. It only works when all the doors are locked."

"How many men are on the flyers?"

"Three. A driver, sorter, and the runner—the messenger."

"Where would the transfer notes appear to come from?"

"We'd have to give some thought to that."

"I mean, the forms—"

"The forms are standard. The name of the branch is typed in and the manager's signature added."

"And once it's in the flyer—" Richard said.

"Bingo!" Cas had an almost schoolboyish flush of excitement that spread right down his neck.

"It can't be traced back?" Richard asked.

"How? Once the bag is opened inside the flyer the envelopes are sorted and thrown up into the appropriate branch bag. The bag is then sealed, and delivered."

"What about the code word?"

"What about it?"

"It changes every day. How many people have access to that information?"

"Managers and chief cashiers."

"Two men in each branch. Is that all?"

"Some head-office people, of course. The security people. I don't know how many that involves."

"So—you initiate—how many transfer notes?"

"We've got six hundred twenty branches in the greater London area."

"How much time would we have?"

"Two days, I'd say. Three would be pushing it a bit."

"Then what happens?"

Cas cleared his throat nervously.

"The receiving branch confirms the tan to head office, together with the new account number which has to be registered and recorded in the passbook. But there is no passbook. Then the balloon goes up. The instigating branch reports back: account unknown."

"Two days. We could clean up in two days," Richard said.

The two men looked at each other and started to grin at the same time.

"Forty-eight hours with the keys to the counting house," Richard said at last.

"Some banks can bear more than others. Too much would look suspicious. In some of the smaller branches—"

"Why don't we just hit six of the big ones?" Richard asked.

"There's just so much a man can ask for over the counter—especially a stranger—without arousing interest, even suspicion."

He stood up and rubbed his chin and watched his wife working in the kitchen garden which had grown so much bigger since he and Richard were children. It now reached halfway down to the old croquet lawn.

"No, volume is the safest bet. Dozens of fair-to-middling hits, as quickly as possible."

"In two days, what do you think?" Richard said.

"I don't know. I don't know how you can calculate that."

Cas sat down again. He was breathing deeply, as if he'd been exercising hard.

"How many of your banks have safety-deposit boxes?" Richard asked.

"Not all of them. I'd say, at a rough guess, two hundred. Two-fifty. Why?"

"I was thinking . . . Wouldn't it be psychologically disarming . . . I mean, wouldn't they be less curious if the client appeared *not* to be taking the money out of the building at all? I mean, if he were simply——"

"We call it a tactical transfer," Cas said. "It sounds better than tax fiddle."

"It happens?"

"Of course it happens. We're not supposed to know about it."

"The client is left alone with his deed box?"

"Absolutely."

"It's getting better and better all the time," Richard said. He continued to look thoughtful.

"What?"

Richard hesitated before saying anything. "If a man kept a safety-deposit box—would that information appear on the transfer advice note?" he asked finally.

"Yes," Cas said. "I forgot about that."

"Okay, so let's concentrate on the banks with safety-deposit boxes for a start. You can get a list?"

"No problem."

"We should work inside as small a radius as possible. Once we decide which ones to hit, I'll drive over the route. Then we'll get some idea how many we can handle."

The two men talked long into the afternoon and twilight of the evening. Talked quietly, between long silences sometimes. Edith brought them tea, and, later, gin and tonic. She didn't ask what it was they talked about. She didn't try to join them. She wasn't listening. Her mind was somewhere else. She was a tall, thin, almost bony Englishwoman, with long slim legs. She was a remote, slightly crazy lady. She was a good mother and loved her garden, and Cas had once told Richard that she was amazingly good in bed. She had been beautiful at eighteen; now, at thirty-five, she was damned attractive, as Cas would say, and soon she would be handsome. She smiled. The smile came slowly out of the stillness of her face and returned into the same stillness. She put the drinks on the table between the brothers and returned to the house. The men went on with their conversation. It was like old times. The old jokes, the same nervous care, the apprehensions. Richard's role was crucial. Cas took him through it, step by step, word by word, hazard by hazard. Risks would have to be taken, he said several times. "*The Girl at the Window* would have been easier," Richard said. "The undone past is always easier," Cas said. It had always started this way. Richard putting ideas into Cas's head, egging him on, gently geeing him up. Then Cas, methodical, steady, thoughtful Cas, taking over. It was his party now, and he knew it. It scared and exhilarated him. It made him feel alive again.

He drove Richard to the station. It was ten o'clock.

"Let me ask you a question," he said. It was quite cold now and they walked back and forth on the narrow wooden platform to keep warm.

"Ask me anything you like," Richard said.

"Why?"

"Why? The adventure of it," Richard said.

"No. Once perhaps. But not now."

Richard shrugged. "The money, then."

"Yes, but why *now*?"

"I have an expensive habit to support," Richard said.

"It's going to work," Cas said. His face felt stiff with cold.

He watched the train until it was out of sight. Then he turned and walked down the ramp and got back into his car and drove slowly home.

24

Edouard Casenave woke up with the answer. The black book. The small black book he'd seen in his dream, that dream wedged between narcosis and sleep.

It was Catharine Gaillard's dictionary.

It was so obvious now. If she'd intended to be away for more than a day, she'd have taken it with her. He'd even known her to put it in her purse when they were simply slipping round the corner to dinner. It was more than a dictionary: it was a sort of talisman, an amulet.

"I hate to be lost for words," she said.

But he'd seen it on her bedside table at the hotel.

The realization thoroughly awakened him. Somebody had gone to a lot of trouble to make it look as if Catharine had gone away for a few days—removing her toiletries from the bathroom, removing her makeup. The idea had been shaping itself in his imagination for days. But now he *knew*. Somebody, not Catharine, had taken those things from her room. Only they didn't know her well enough. They didn't know that she would never have left her dictionary behind.

Not in a hundred years.

He felt both relieved and anxious. Relieved that he had finally discovered what had been nagging him; anxious about its implications.

A sort of anguish accumulated inside of him. He was thinking hard. Who would want to make it look as if she had simply skipped? And why? Somebody playing for time? Whose time? Trying to put others off the scent? What scent? It just didn't add up. It made no sense at all. Did she leave the book behind on purpose?

He began to sweat.

It was all so damn complicated. He felt lost, suffocating in the undergrowth of unreason. His ribs ached and a pain that was much sharper darted between his jaw and his left temple. His thinned cheeks burned with foreboding. I want something, he told himself, I can never have again.

He tried to calculate how long he'd been in that soundproofed imprisoning hospital room. It seemed like forever. The room was so silent, and filled with a sort of bloated blackness. He lay on his back, thinking, staring into the darkness. He knew it was over. It was almost as if it had never been.

After a while he fell into a troubled sleep. He dreamed of Catharine. He dreamed she was dead. In the distance somebody was digging. She was very beautiful in her coffin, almost smiling. Her hands were crossed across her naked breasts and on the pillow beside her head was the small black book.

Only he knew it wasn't a Bible.

Only he knew the truth.

He was woken by the sound of somebody breathing. But just for a moment the dream and the sound of breathing overlapped, merged into one: Catharine, sweet pale Catharine, was coming back to life. Her beautiful white breasts began to rise and fall, so gently. The sound of digging stopped. Her eyes opened, her unwavering smile widened . . . "You mustn't be unhappy," she said and then she was gone.

Casenave kept his eyes closed, listening, making up his mind, carefully separating the dream from reality.

The breathing was the only real thing.

It almost made him smile . . . the rasping furry breath of a man. A big man. A man who smoked too much, who drank too much. A man who couldn't keep still: a continuously searching rustle, a convulsive fidgeting . . . the soft nervous noises of a sixty-a-day man trapped in a no-smoking zone. He never stopped moving. It was a sort of St. Vitus dance played waltz time.

Casenave didn't need to open his eyes.

He knew.

"I guess a little smoke isn't going to hurt me now, Giorgio," he said, his eyes still closed. "I won't rat on you."

"You bastard. How long you been awake? How long you know?"

"Could hear you suffering. Maybe *you* should be on the morphine."

"Nicotine'll do me," Giorgio said.

A match quickly scraped against a box. The reeky smell of Gauloises filled the antiseptic air. After a little while Giorgio stopped fidgeting and settled into a quiet, almost heavy contentment. Casenave continued to lie very still, on his back. He could almost feel the big Italian's sense of fellowship, his understanding. A long time of silence passed. It was a kind of communion.

Casenave opened his eyes.

It was bright daylight.

"Giorgio?"

"Yes?"

"Do you remember—before my accident—you told me about seeing a car in the square?"

"A car?" He seemed suddenly fazed by the question.

"The morning you saw Catharine. You said there was a car waiting in the square."

"Right, right. A Citroen."

"You said it sounded odd."

"Not odd—different. It had that sound—before the engine starts to miss. It's not always a sound even. Sometimes it's just a feeling you get. A sensation sort of—in here." He tapped the side of his large Roman nose.

"How long after this feeling—"

"Before trouble?"

"Yes."

He shrugged. He studied the thick black hair on the back of his large hand. "I don't know. Don't count on any long journeys."

"What's a long journey, Giorgio?"

"Fifty kilometers could be a long journey with some engines. I don't know what to tell you, Captain."

"That noise in the engine—" Casenave said. Then another thought came into his head and gave him pause. "How many garages are there in St. Saladin?"

"Able to fix up engine? Six, seven workshops maybe—and a few cowboy outfits."

"And within—say fifty kilometers?"

"Jesus, Captain, I don't know."

"Could you find out for me?"

"Listen, Captain—"

"Please, Giorgio."

"The Michelin people in Paris—" he said, without conviction.

"What about the local gendarmerie? Wouldn't they have a list. Your friend Maigret—"

"Yes, probably."

"Giorgio, would you—"

"Captain—I know what's on your mind." He scowled darkly, but too much.

"It's worth a try."

"It would take a long time. And maybe I still come up with nothing. Anyway, I told you. I never saw your girl get in the car. Maybe the car was just a car. Maybe it had nothing to do with her."

"But maybe it did. I keep thinking . . . maybe it did."

The memory of Catharine stirred in the room like a prowling ghost, with no freedom to come and go. Giorgio felt it, too. He was a superstitious man and the sense of her restless presence made him nervous. Tiny pearls of sweat glistened in his thick black moustache.

"Have the police talked to you yet?" he asked.

"Yesterday. The day before. Sometime. I don't know. I couldn't tell them much." Casenave's eyelids were pricking and the pain in his cheek wasn't getting any better. "Would you recognize it again? The Citroen?"

"Black, six-cylinder job, coupla years old. How could I miss it? There can only be ten thousand cars like that in South of France, Captain."

"Italian registration."

"Great. Okay . . . that cuts it down a lot. Let's say two thousand or so."

"There you go." Casenave managed a smile.

"I wish I didn't mention no car," Giorgio said. His voice was low, like a mumble. He stood up. "I gotta go now. Those wop sonsabitches rob me blind when I don't watch them."

"Thanks for coming."

"Listen t'me. You sure you wanna find this car? Whatever?" he said warningly.

"Whatever."

"It's asking plenty. But I try. Be it on your own head. All right?"

"Thanks Giorgio."

"Don't thank me. Don't thank me."   /

The big man squeezed Casenave's shoulder. He turned and walked toward the door at the end of the bed. Casenave closed his eyes. The door opened and closed quietly. For fully fifteen minutes the pilot stared at the high ceiling, thinking. What would the car tell him that he didn't already know? Catharine Gaillard was dead. He was quite sure of that now. So why did he need to know about the car? The thought—no, the answer—frightened him. Killing, he thought, was like riding a bicycle, like swimming . . . once you'd learned to do it, it came easy.

"We got lucky," Giorgio told him. "The third workshop. It was still there."

"And you're sure? It's the same car you saw in the square?" Casenave asked.

"No. But it was same model, same year, same color—and it was in with ignition fault."

Casenave could think of nothing to say.

He sat up slowly in the hospital bed. He still looked very pale beneath the neon lights.

After a while, he said hesitantly: "It couldn't be a coincidence, could it?"

"Well, my friend—there is one more thing."

Casenave looked at him closely. Waiting for the big man to continue.

"The front left-hand fender is damaged. The left headlamp smashed—"

"So?"

"The car that hit you—it caught you smack on its left side. This car—its left headlamp is smashed. The glass the police picked up where you got bumped, it come from Bosch headlamp. The broken headlamp on the Citroen in workshop, it is Bosch . . . that's strange because Citroens usually have Sev Marchell or Sibié units."

"How do you know—about the kind of glass they found—"

"I asked. Maigret told me."

Casenave looked at him in silence.

"Do me a favor, Giorgio. Don't tell your friend Maigret about the car in the workshop. Not yet."

"Okay."

They fell silent.

"You want to know the rest?" Giorgio asked after a time.

"I'm sorry, I was thinking. Yes, go on, Giorgio."

"The car belongs to the Palace."

"The Palace? Who—"

"A pool car. One of six the workshop garages and services for the royal household—which mostly means senior casino personnel, people in the Bureau."

"Names? Did you get the names?"

Giorgio took a small piece of paper from his pocket. He spread it out on the table by Casenave's bed and squinted at a list written with a soft lead pencil. "We know five people who used this particular car since last service—which was on seventeenth last month—but not when they used it. It's a mess, that garage. No organization."

"It's a start. Anyway," Casenave encouraged him.

"A Paul Schill, somebody named Kun. Schill is a casino supervisor, the other I don't know exactly. They thought something in the Bureau. Leon Kun, his name. Then a woman named Genevieve Lacroix. And Dieter Stosch. Stosch is—"

"I know who Stosch is," Casenave said. "No dates at all?"

"The place is a shambles. People are supposed to sign a book when they take a car out and again when it is brought back. Sometimes they sign the book but forget to write in the dates and times. Sometimes they don't even sign the book."

"You said five names."

Giorgio squinted at the piece of paper. "Alwyn Brand," he said.

"I know."

"But Brand, Stosch, and the woman—none of their names are in the book. A mechanic, he remembered . . . otherwise you'd have just the two names."

"He was sure about the others? The mechanic?"

"He was the only one with any brains in the whole place."

"There could be more names then?"

Giorgio shrugged.

"He didn't think so." The big Italian tapped the piece of paper slowly. "But we do know one thing, my friend. Whoever was behind the wheel when the car hit you— he know how to drive. He was good, Captain. Damn good. He picked the spot right. He know a thing or two . . . about the only halfway straight in the whole of St. Saladin. It still give him under thirty meters after hitting you to make sharp right into street with a hard reverse camber—the whole road falls away from the inside. I walk it over last night. I tell you. It was a lotta driving—he didn't touch the sides outta there. We're talking about a very very competitive driver, somebody driving on the limits."

"Giorgio—you know what you're saying?"

"I don't think I tell you a thing you don't know all the time, Captain."

"The bastards."

"But professional bastards. You are a lucky man, I think."

"Poor Catharine," Casenave said.

25

They met at lunchtime on the little suspension bridge over the lake in St. James's Park. Cas Antrobus carried a leather briefcase and a brown paper bag with breadcrumbs to feed the ducks.

"We go on Wednesday," he said.

Richard Antrobus looked at his brother incredulously.

"That's only two days——"

"What's wrong with that?"

"Nothing. Only——"

"Richard, you haven't suddenly got cold feet, have you?"

"Of course not. I'm surprised, that's all. I wasn't expecting it to be quite so soon."

Cas wore his dark-gray banker's suit. It was double-breasted and the trousers were too wide, the cuffs too deep. It aged him almost more than his thinning hair. It gave him a stiff formal air of humorless respectability, an aura of steady unimaginative reliability.

"There's a B.E.A. flight from Manchester to Paris Friday evening at nine o'clock. I made a booking in the name of Anderson. James Anderson. You'll pick the tickets up at the B.E.A. desk one hour before takeoff."

"I still don't see why it's necessary to drag all the way up to Manchester when there's a perfectly——"

"If the car is noticed, if it's somehow connected with this business . . . it'll confuse the issue if it's abandoned in Manchester. Leave it in the center of the city. Take a cab to the airport."

"If you really think it's necessary."

"Also the airport currency checks are less stringent in Manchester."

"I'm convinced."

"You've acquired an identity?"

"Wilfred Charles Spicer. There's a driving license, a Harrods account card, American Express. His army discharge papers . . . ex-major, Coldstreams. An R.A.C. card——"

"That sounds very pukka."

"I've had some cards printed, too."

"Spicer's papers and things—they can't be traced back?"

"I acquired them personally. From a rather smart tweed jacket in the barber shop at the Savoy."

"Good God, Richard!" There was such a sound of horror in his voice that Richard stopped and stared at his brother in amazement.

"Stealing a gentleman's wallet offends your sense of morality, does it?"

Cas's frown was heavy, puzzled. Then he smiled. "It's odd, isn't it? Yes—I felt—it was a sort of kick in the gut . . . the family . . . a sense of shame." He tried to make a joke of it, he didn't want to unnerve Richard at this stage of the game. "I mean, the *Savoy*."

"Well, we didn't want to steal just *anyone's* identity, did we?"

"It brought it home to me, that's all. What we're basically up to."

"Lifting the wallet—that's the only really wicked part."

They continued their stroll.

"You've been over the route I mapped out?"

"A dozen times."

"How's the timing?"

"The longest lap, thirty-eight minutes. The shortest, twenty-three. That's down from forty-one and twenty-seven."

"Good man. The weather forecast is good. Dry with—"

"The weather forecast!"

"If it's raining there'll be jams. You could drop a couple of appointments in heavy traffic. We need two dry days."

"You think of everything."

"I hope so."

They crossed the bridge and turned right. They strolled along the gravel path bordering the lake toward the Horse Guards. The sound of a bugle call drifted across the ornamental lake from Wellington Barracks. St. James's was Richard's favorite park in London. It lacked the air of life and vitality of Hyde Park; it was smaller and fussier than Green Park. But it had a bygone sense of style, an Edwardian speed. He liked to watch the nurses and nannies strolling with their charges—the nurses young and shyly *knowing*; the nannies so proud, so *imperial*. They all belonged to another age. Even the pretty office girls, lazing away their lunch hours on the grass, seemed like girls from some dressmaking ateliers of the past, reading paperback romances like house-maids in love. Cas stopped in front of a group of ducks and opened the paper bag.

"I've picked Wednesday and Thursday for several reasons," he said. He sprinkled crumbs of brown bread on the water. He spoke softly. Standing there, feeding the ducks, he looked like a man living off the meager solace of careful savings of careful years. "They're half-closing days in the districts you'll be working. After one o'clock, therefore, the traffic will be lighter. Business'll be quieter in the banks. It will speed things up all around. It could conceivably add two extra appointments to the day."

"The transfer advice notes—they start dropping when? Wednesday morning?"

"Yes. Your first appointment is Wimbledon Chase. Wimbledon is an early drop—but don't arrive before ten-fifteen. There'll be customers in the bank by then. It would be a mistake to be the first in—Mr. Spicer."

"Wilfred Charles Spicer."

"Your credit balance will be £187,000 and fifteen shillings in each branch. You must decide the touch accordingly. If anything smells at all wrong—settle for twenty quid, or nothing at all—rather than provoke questions. Because once anyone smells a rat—that's it."

"Don't worry."

"Now—Friday's run."

"Friday? I thought we had two days?"

"If the manure is going to hit the fan before the weekend, we'll know by noon Friday. If Clearing Centre is still quiet by then . . . you'll have until the banks close. Another three hours, three or four hits. I'll drop the tans regardless. . . ."

He took out a blue envelope from his inside pocket and gave it to Richard.

"Here are Friday's appointments and the route. I suggest you drive over it this afternoon, and again to-morrow."

"Yes, sir." Richard grinned. He put the envelope into his own pocket.

"I'm sorry. I don't mean to be bossy," Cas said.

"It's all right."

"Your end—is that all in order?"

"I think so."

"*Think* so !"

"You don't expect me to have it in writing, do you? There are ways of doing these things. You must remember we're talking about a lot of money, Caspar. I've put out feelers in all the right places. People in Deauville, Cannes."

"How much is it going to cost, do you think?"

"It'll vary, obviously. It should average out at—oh, about thirty cents on the dollar."

"Daylight robbery." Cas grinned.

He turned the paper bag upside down and emptied the last of the crumbs into the lake. The ducks moved in, their yellow bills pecking furiously at the last of the bread.

"We can afford it," Richard said.

"How long will it take, do you suppose?"

They continued their walk.

"I figure two to three weeks. The first week will tell. It'll get stickier once they start circulating numbers—I presume they will have numbers to circulate?"

"It's pretty certain, yes."

"Pity."

"You want jam on it?"

"Why not?"

"Don't forget. American dollars or Swiss francs. At a pinch the German mark—"

"What about the Polish zloty?"

"Stay well away from the satellite currencies," Cas said seriously.

"I *was* joking." They had been through the exchange details twenty times.

"It's no joking matter, Richard," Cas said irritably.

They walked slowly, in silence. Around the lake, along the Birdcage Walk side of the park.

"Let's sit here for a moment," Cas said.

They sat on an empty bench. Cas opened his briefcase and took out several forms. "You'll have to sign these, Mr. Spicer," he said. "Keep a copy for yourself. Remember the signature."

"I've been working on it," Richard said.

"Good. This is the specimen signature that will go out with the tan." He returned the signed papers to his briefcase and zipped it up.

The two men continued their walk.

"So—that's it. We're all set then?" Cas said after a little while.

"All set."

"Good luck, Richard."

"Good luck yourself." He patted his brother on the shoulder.

"So, anyway . . . How's Georgina by the by?" Cas said.

"Fine. She left for Hollywood last Tuesday."

"A picture in Hollywood? The boys will be thrilled! Do you think she could get them John Wayne's autograph?"

"It might be arranged."

"Bit sudden, wasn't it?"

"Hollywood? Yes, it was rather. The Biron Strauss picture—the one she's been doing in Spain—the studio work was switched to California. Union problems at Elstree, or something. Apparently Strauss, in a misplaced effort to please the workers, served the crew cold salmon and champagne on the flight out to Spain."

"How could that possibly cause union trouble?"

"The electricians said they were entitled to a *hot* meal."

"Ah," said Cas.

"It was such a rare act of generosity on his part—it would have been almost funny, if it wasn't so bloody pathetic."

"Never thank your staff for anything, Father says. Gratitude only convinces them that they are doing too much."

"Poor Strauss. He's learned that lesson the hard way."

"Is that good? Hollywood? For Georgina."

"I don't think it really matters. The experience, I suppose, will be good for her."

"Will you be joining her?"

"That's the plan. After this business is . . . out of the way."

"She's a nice girl."

"Yes."

"Serious?"

"Oh you know, Cas. Once bitten . . ."

"Actresses can be a bit difficult, I imagine. Still, a nice girl . . ." Cas said. His mind wasn't on the conversation anymore.

They reached the suspension bridge where they had started their stroll.

"Something's bothering you, Cas. What is it?"

"There is just one . . . *tiny* danger."

It was the first time in all the weeks they'd been discussing it, planning it, that he'd used such a heavy word. He'd talked about the *difficulties*, the *problems*, even, once, the *hazards*. But he'd never talked about *danger* before. Even a *tiny danger*. It was enough to unnerve Richard.

"You see," Cas said. He was obviously picking his words carefully. "A manager getting a tan on a customer with such a healthy credit balance, with a recommended priority status—he might just be tempted to pick up the blower and have a chat about him, get filled in on the personal details—golf handicap—"

"You mean call . . . the other manager?"

"Exactly."

"Christ Almighty!"

"It's a risk."

"I'll say it's a risk!"

"If we could put the phones out of action," Cas said reflectively.

"This is getting a bit hairy, isn't it Cas? A bit out of our line. I mean—"

"You see, the thing is—he would ring on the managerial hot line. The private line, the ex-directory number."

"Cutting lines—"

"We only have to put one line on the blink. All the tans will originate from Bloomsbury West. A big branch and the manager's name is Jay—an easy signature to imitate. So—"

"Cas, I—"

"I had a bit of a fling a couple of years ago—"

"You!"

"A girl in my Foreign Department. It never came to anything, but while it lasted it was fairly intense. She was an extraordinarily jealous lady. One of her less attractive habits was to telephone me on Saturday mornings and put my line out of action for the whole weekend—"

"What happened?"

"I got her transferred to Beirut."

"No, I mean how did she put your phone up the spout?"

"That's it, you see. She simply dialed my number and when I answered, or Edith answered, she wouldn't replace her receiver. She said it made her feel closer to me. All the same, bloody inconvenient. Every weekend."

"An open line—"

"Exactly. So. Dial Jay—sorry wrong number—don't replace the receiver. We've got him."

"He'll report a fault on the line—"

"It'll take days."

"Banks have other lines."

"Of course, but managers only speak to managers on hot lines. It's one of those things. Snobbery, one-upmanship, class distinction—"

"You think it'll really work?"

"I don't know. Exciting, isn't it?"

Richard grinned. "What do you really think?"

"I think—I think maybe my whole life will be a little less dull from now on. Who knows—I might even take a little trip to Beirut!"

26

The long ghost-blue motor launch cut through the calm glistening water, moving at high speed. Count Cheroffini and Paul Duclos sat close together alongside the young sailor who stood straight behind the wheel. The courtiers had the fixed look of old men, stricken with gathering doubts, going to a funeral.

It took eight minutes to reach the *Grunden Tief II*. The slender black wooden clipper—which once, a long time ago, crossed the Atlantic in eleven days and four hours—sat at the entrance to the bay.

In seven years Stosch had never been farther from St. Saladin than aboard the *Grunden Tief*, and the *Grunden Tief* had never been more than a day's hard driving from where she was now anchored.

Stosch, in black linen trousers and a black Breton sweater, waited for the courtiers in the saloon. It was a seagoing room, practical and masculine, with a hum of muted affluence. A heavy Black Watch tartan carpet covered the floor. The sofas and chairs were upholstered in the same dark hunting cloth. A blue marlin, about three hundred pounds of stuffed lethalness, its tail curved like a scimitar, stretched out along the top of one wall. Nineteenth-century drawings of schooners, brigantines, and full-riggers covered the opposite wall. A big brass lamp hung over the center of a teak table which ran down the starboard length of the saloon.

Genevieve Lacroix sat at the far end of the long table. She wore blue silk slacks and a blue sweater over a pale-green silk shirt that matched her eyes. She wore no makeup. She looked at her best, Cheroffini thought, without makeup. He found her slightly-sunflawed skin charming. It gave her an almost tomboyish look. He knew how deceptive, how dangerously deceptive, that look was.

"Welcome aboard, gentlemen," Stosch said. He did not offer to shake hands. "I trust you have no objection to Mlle. Lacroix being present. I think—in the circumstances—a record should be kept."

Cheroffini nodded his agreement.

"Mlle. Lacroix." Duclos gave her a small smile.

Genevieve Lacroix acknowledged the two men with a level look that would have been supercilious on a plainer face. She smiled slowly. It was the smile of a woman whose heart wasn't in it.

"A drink, gentlemen?"

"A Scotch, thank you," Cheroffini said. "Ice and water."

"A bullshot," Duclos said.

The courtiers sat opposite each other at the long table.

Stosch gestured to the steward. He was a small bald man with a batik patch of pink flesh, clover-shaped, on his left cheek. He mixed the drinks without a word and offered them to the courtiers on a silver tray. He left the saloon at once. Nothing in his face suggested he had heard a word that had been spoken.

Stosch gave a look to Genevieve Lacroix. She took a notepad from a small canvas duffle bag by her chair. She clicked a gold Parker pen and Stosch started to talk.

Cheroffini and Duclos stared at him in disbelief.

St. Saladin, he said, was falling.

He was not given to dramatic emphasis. Neither Cheroffini nor Duclos could read the expression in his pale star-cold eyes.

Cheroffini's mind leapt back a long way. To a night in 1933—when Maximilien admitted something similar. Then it was a matter of fraudulent bookkeeping concealing the royal extravagances, driving St. Saladin to the edge of bankruptcy.

But now?

"Falling," Stosch said again in his quiet voice.

A slow subversive smile began to appear on his face, like the first crack in the earth before a violent quake.

It was a voracious smile that seemed to say: I am the only man who can save us now. I am the only one ruthless enough, with strength enough and vision enough, to do what must be done.

Cheroffini remembered him at that first meeting. He remembered that elegant conqueror's uniform made for peace and promenades. He remembered the powerful black-gloved hands. The same metallic face, the same glint in the eyes. He still looks, Cheroffini thought, as if he scours himself every day with steel wool: he is hard and clean and cold with the same compulsion, the same instinct, that makes vultures predatory . . . it is simply the thing to be.

Stosch had been hired to be ruthless. Maximilien had picked his man well.

"Falling," Stosch continued. "But not yet fallen."

Genevieve Lacroix continued to concentrate on her note-taking. It was almost as if she weren't there at all; a biscuit-colored hand sliding across the paper her only movement.

The *Grunden Tief* moved almost imperceptibly on the swell, as if she were breathing, sighing, waiting. In the distance, through the porthole behind Duclos, Cheroffini could see the houses in the hills with their sunlit rose-pink washes, the old crooked walls of burnt sienna. Here and there on the steep slopes were scars of red rock in the parched yellow scrub.

"In a world so altered from that in which St. Saladin flourished in the beginning, and in the war—" Stosch suddenly stopped and considered the courtiers dispassionately, with deliberation.

"Philippe's criticism—" Cheroffini began in the unexpected silence.

Stosch held up his hand.

"Facts not criticism are our concern, gentlemen. That is not a question one can argue about," he added smoothly, stressing the strict chilling economy of his smile. "His Royal Highness returns with the posturing spirit of a crusader. It is picturesque but it is not enough."

He paused.

"Facts, gentlemen."

He opened a green folder on the desk in front of him. He extracted a sheet of foolscap full of figures.

"It is a fact that Monte Carlo now attracts eight point five percent more international high rollers than St. Saladin—against six point four percent two years ago. I do not have to remind you that, unlike Monaco, St. Saladin has only its casino revenues on which to depend for survival.

"Facts, gentlemen.

"It is a fact that the rich no longer come eventually to St. Saladin. We are no more the natural pre-eminent resort of the rich."

"The rich no longer wish to advertise their wealth," Duclos said, with his nervous squirm. "It is considered vulgar now to be seen to have money to burn."

Stosch ignored the interruption. He went on in his quiet spring-loaded voice: "It is also a fact that not a single new hotel, restaurant, theater, road, church, school, beach, or entertainment facility has been built here since 1945. St. Saladin is stagnant, gentlemen. *That* is a fact.

"Las Vegas is now taking eleven percent of our prewar North American business—against three point two percent of Monte Carlo's."

He looked up from his notes.

"There is, too, an accelerating fall in our hot money inflow. . . . There is a variety of external causes for this decline which does not concern this conversation directly."

He took a sip from his glass of Sancerre.

"Before long, two years, three years—five at the very most—the English will legalize gambling. The impact on the gambling markets will be critical, in some cases fatal. The structure and revenue potential of the business throughout the world will be transformed. When that time comes—"

He stopped dead and looked from Cheroffini to Duclos. His smile was as hard as Siberian ice.

After a long silence, which neither Cheroffini nor Duclos attempted to interrupt, Stosch continued slowly:

"According to the figures Leon Kun has got out . . ." His forefinger moved slowly across the sums set out on the foolscap sheet. "Taking the year ended May thirty-one. The casino paid out an average $269,000 a month in salaries, commissions, and pensions. Add to that the interest on the Bourse loans of 1933 and 1939 . . . water, heating, lighting, insurance, taxes . . . et cetera, et cetera . . . the total deficit is increasing at the rate of one point eight percent a month.

"I will not trouble you with the various projections for the moment, gentlemen. Suffice it to say it is an arithmetical fact that even after consolidation and revaluation of intercorporate holdings, casino revenues, capitalization of reserves, and the transfer of the SS Memorandum surplus—"

He hesitated, returned the foolscap sheet of figures to the green folder.

"It is a fact, gentlemen . . . the Princess Royale Gaming Casino and Sporting Society—St. Saladin itself—will be bankrupt by the end of the present decade."

Cheroffini looked at Duclos. Duclos had gone white. His dry white tongue moved across his marmoreal lips. The northwest corner of his jaw seemed to have collapsed. He looked very old and very tired. Cheroffini suddenly felt the pitying repulsion he always felt for anything near to death. Poor Duclos. His thin transparent hands began to flutter with age, with shock. He had the look of a man shaken by something half remembered.

"We belong to the old dispensation," Cheroffini said almost involuntarily. He was suddenly aware that the Stosch faction, created by Maximilien, had finally overwhelmed the power that gave it being. Stosch, Kun, Genevieve Lacroix alias Mlle. Chaire . . . they were the new elite. They were St. Saladin now. "The old order—" Cheroffini's voice echoed with the spectral agony of dismantled glory. "Paul and I—"

"We cannot survive the present decade—unless action is taken at once," Stosch sliced into his sentence.

"If I may be permitted to mention one other fact your summary spares us." Cheroffini's voice was suddenly firm again, hardened with anger. There was a look of unfamiliar animus on his seamed, still-handsome face. "You, Dieter, are not entirely inculpable, not entirely unerring in this—"

"Geologists are always at their best the morning after the earthquake," Stosch said. He had expected the thrust. He had prepared the answer. It was glib, a parry. He knew it. He knew he had to hurry on. "We are at the great watershed of change, gentlemen. We face a time of challenge. But it is also a time of promise, of privilege, a time for expansion and daring. We have no time to stop and apportion blame. There are new horizons, new peaks, new liberations. . . ."

The courtiers listened, stunned, silent, as Stosch outlined his intricate financial theories, his complex pragmatic scheme for the salvation of St. Saladin. It was a most lawyerlike presentation: concise, cunning, and persuasive.

Dieter Stosch, Cheroffini thought, was no longer a German: he seemed to belong to no race at all. The casino was his country; the SS Memorandum his birth certificate, his passport, his visa and *pièce justificative*. Stosch, Kun, Mlle. Chaire, the ringmasters; Alwyn Brand, even the priest Cornelius . . . they were all citizens of the casino now, incorporated in its entity, driven by its force. Germany, France, the United States, England, and Italy—they were simply lands from which they came. Lands seldom talked about, lands seldom returned to, unbidding lands, lands unmagnetized by nostalgia or loyalty or childhood dreams. They had turned their souls and their spirits to St. Saladin.

But Dieter Stosch—self-instructed, solitary, shorn of history, secretive and dangerous Dieter Stosch—he was the most puzzling of them all. For he was finally more wrapped up in himself than Tutenkhamon. "I have this nightmare," Cheroffini once told Duclos. "One day I'll finally unravel that enigmatic sonofabitch and find nothing but a heap of grinning dust."

Stosch stood up and poured himself another glass of Sancerre. He placed a paracodeine on his tongue and sipped the wine.

"The Alpes-Maritime Treaty of 1911," he said quietly. He stared at the two men with an expression a poker player would give his eye teeth to possess. "It is now a matter of concern."

Cheroffini acknowledged the statement with a small movement, less than a blink, of his eyelids. Duclos made no visible sign. His hands continued to tremble even though he clasped them together in his lap. He looked very unhappy, yet detached from the events going on around him.

Stosch returned to his chair at the head of the long table.

"If His Royal Highness does not produce an heir—in lawful wedlock—St. Saladin becomes extinct by absorption. Swallowed up by France. Gentlemen, our annexation will be swift, lawful, and unlamented in the outside world."

"Italy—"

"Italy might get a bad case of indigestion—but that's all. The Alpes-Maritime Treaty is possibly vindictive but it is certainly valid and unquestionably watertight." Stosch spoke in a smooth cadence, an evenness of tone that gave an edge of authority to his words. "An Heir Apparent is precariously overdue."

"Aren't we jumping the gun?" Cheroffini asked.

"First we must provide His Royal Highness with a bride," Stosch continued as if he had not been interrupted. "A bride who will bring something to St. Saladin."

"An alliance?" Cheroffini asked with surprise in his voice.

"An alliance of a kind. An asset. A new . . . attraction."

"Philippe is a headstrong man," Duclos said, slowly coming out of his state of shock. "What if he prefers to . . . to obey the dictates of his heart?"

"Are you guessing?"

"Not altogether."

"The Isak Girod woman?"

"Exactly so," Duclos said.

"She is not suitable," Stosch said. He was rapidly clenching and unclenching a small hard muscle in the side of his jaw.

"Will that be your argument?" Cheroffini asked. "When you confront His Royal Highness?"

"Princes cannot expect to marry to please themselves," Stosch said. "They must marry for posterity, for money—for their land, their family. That is their duty."

"The dictates of one's heart don't always consider duty . . . or suitability," Duclos said with an old man's air of ruminative revelation. "The Duke of Windsor once told me a long time afterward—"

"Philippe cannot be allowed . . . it is too clumsy, too risky," Stosch said abruptly. "His marriage must first and foremost be an act of consolidation. There is no room for love, no room for romantic manuever. We are not in the hearts-and-flowers business. We are talking about money. We are talking about the power-and-prestige business. All very negotiable commodities, gentlemen. We cannot afford to squander them on a profitless love match, a senseless zoological passion."

"Mlle. Girod—"

"A ritual heartbreak won't hurt Philippe's romantic image, I fancy," Stosch said. "It will do St. Saladin no harm."

"I take your point," Cheroffini said. "But it is perfectly clear that Philippe plans to rule—with total sovereignty."

"He wishes to be the cock in the basket?" Stosch said. "By the gift of Heaven?"

"By the grace of God."

"Ah. By the grace of God. You make being a prince sound like a prize for learning one's catechism, for being a good boy at Sunday School. How long is one expected to keep this prize?"

"God's word lasts forever," Cheroffini said stiffly. "*Ertragen muss man was der Himmel sendet.*" He deliberately lapsed into German, reminding Stosch of his outsider origins.

"What Heaven sends we must endure," Stosch repeated slowly. He was unruffled. "Like some hereditary disease? Is that it?"

"If you wish to put it that way."

"But—these noble sentiments—isn't it difficult to tell where piety begins and self-preservation ends?"

Roberto Cheroffini saw the danger. He tried to change his position.

"All are not huntsmen who can blow the huntsman's horn," he said cryptically. It was an old statesman's ploy.

Stosch knew it. He didn't bite. "Is it not possible that relations between the Almighty and the Palace have . . . well, let us say, gone downhill since the old rules were made? So many peculating princes . . . so many . . . expensive poseurs."

Cheroffini said nothing.

Stosch turned to Duclos.

"What do you say, Paul?"

"Lookers-on see most of the game," Duclos said, fastidiously evasive again. Old habits, Cheroffini thought, die hard.

"Mlle. Lacroix?" Stosch looked to the end of the table.

She looked up from her notepad and smiled easily.

"The victor is always in the right," she said.

"That is my point," Stosch said. "Exactly. Great thieves hang little thieves. In business, I suppose, one would simply call it a takeover. A board-room reshuffle—"

"Dieter, how can you compare one of the oldest royal families in Europe with—"

"Let me put a question to you," Stosch said quickly. "You see, I have never been sure— Where in the dark reaches of our royal family's past did God first intervene? In what absent moment did He first bestow His favors, His warranty? Perhaps we should invite Father Cornelius to explain it to us. Or do you have an answer, Count Cheroffini? No? Paul?"

"The idea that—" Cheroffini began.

"You see, I have this odd suspicion," Stosch cut across him again with the cynical air of pseudo-simplicity. "This gift ordained in Heaven . . . when you come right down to it, isn't it a polite way of saying that some arboreal ancestor simply murdered— *plundered*—his way to the top of the heap? Doesn't the royal franchise start with the dirtiest gang in town?

Surely it was ever thus? St. John was wrong. In the beginning was the sword."

"Today a man is much likelier to commit a crime to avoid a crown than to claim one," Cheroffini said uneasily. There was no conviction in his eyes.

"Princes have to foster that impression," Stosch said. "It is all they have left."

"There is no peace in a crown," Duclos said.

"You understand what I'm saying?" Stosch went on quietly, with the same level intonation. "If I am right—and I have a feeling I am right—every mutineer, every rebel, every traitor and upstart and anarchist, every revolutionary becomes a prince, a king perhaps . . . if he wins. The crown is merely a testament of providential crime. One egg is like another, surely?"

"And the will of the people?" Cheroffini asked. "What of that?"

"The will of the people? Like the voice of shareholders, it is manipulable. Tell them there is doubt and compunction about the Prince. Tell them loud enough and often enough and they'll believe it." Stosch shrugged slowly. It was a very French shrug, Cheroffini thought, for a very German philosophy.

"When you come right down to it, what right have princes to complain when they are displumed?" Cheroffini noticed how cleverly Stosch avoided the obvious word: usurped.

Cheroffini had seen this all coming for a long time. Perhaps before even Stosch knew it himself. This was what it was all about: Stosch wanted St. Saladin. To own it. That was his ambition—vast, simple, pathological.

"Or has God Almighty changed the rules, gentlemen? Does He no longer approve of insurrection? Of a man's right to fight for the crown? Does He now frown on the duplicity of court intrigue? On backstair deals and betrayal?"

Nobody spoke.

Stosch smiled. He looked slowly from Cheroffini to Duclos and back to the Count.

After a long silence he said with a kind of somber amenity, as if to signal the end of his provoking display of power: "But, gentlemen, the Divine invention or otherwise of our royal family is of no consequence. I am simply musing aloud. Manipulation is better than . . . revolution. We shall let the Prince keep his fine plumage. Napoleon remade the bed of the Bourbons. I merely offer to plump up the pillows for Philippe."

The smile stayed on his face but it wasn't the same smile. The light had gone out of it. It was like looking at the impression of a face petrified on an ancient shroud.

What fascinates the child is the puppet. What matters to the man are the wires. Philippe must be securely wired. Maximilien's words came back to Cheroffini now as he watched the man chosen—destined?—to pull those wires.

"Gentlemen, point number one," Stosch said. "We cannot win on a dead horse. We must therefore take every precaution to keep His Royal Highness alive and well."

"You think his life might be in danger?" Duclos asked incredulously.

"There are those in the Elysée Palace, at the Quai d'Orsay, who would not shed too many tears at his funeral—the funeral of a man who has bequeathed them a sovereign state."

"You don't think—"

"It's always possible. Anything is possible. It would be dangerously naïve to put too much trust in the sanctity of treaty obligations, don't you think? But if the Prince is going to receive the consecration of an assassin's bullet—it is more likely to be fired by a cuckold . . . or an abandoned mistress."

"Isak Girod?"

"She is on the list."

"List?"

"I have made a list of people to be watched, those to be guarded against," Stosch said mildly.

The old courtiers stared at him disbelievingly.

He went on evenly, "I have also taken the precaution of issuing instructions that he is not to fly again—either in the *Ambassador* or aboard any commercial airliner—until a constitutional heir is conceived and delivered."

"May I inquire whether your instructions have anything to do with the absence of Mlle. Gaillard—or Casenave's unfortunate accident?" Cheroffini asked.

"Nothing."

"Strange coincidences then?"

"You think it is necessary to contrive at the disappearance of a stewardess in order to restrain the Prince? Count Cheroffini, you underestimate me."

Stosch stared at the courtier for a moment and shook his head slowly. "No, sir. Forty-eight hours ago the *Ambassador* was grounded by order of the FCAA. The plane is now undergoing extensive maintenance work and tests, which will last just as long as is necessary . . ."

"And how do you propose to keep His Royal Highness from simply walking onto any Air France or—"

"You and Paul will sign this." His voice had a tone of injunction. He lifted his right hand, palm upward. Genevieve Lacroix stood up and walked the length of the table with the superior air of a girl on a catwalk. She put a second green folder in front of him and returned to her seat. Stosch waited until she had clicked her Parker again before he continued.

"I have already signed," he said, extracting a large cream-colored document from the folder. "Three Executive signatures are needed to bring in an Emergency Proclamation restraining the Prince's movements during a crisis of State—"

"Under what provision—"

"It is covered by the Order for the Maintenance of Self-determination under the discretionary clause of the 1911 treaty."

"Might we not be accused of acting provocatively— so soon after Maximilien's death?" Duclos asked.

"We must discharge that responsibility which is ours and ours alone," Stosch said.

"But morally—"

"We have no time for moral debate, for moral dubieties."

"There is a legal precedent," Cheroffini said.

Stosch smiled genially. "Princess Marie-Thérèse Louise used a similar stratagem to restrain Prince Tullio at a particularly delicate moment in 1887," he said. "I know my history."

He handed the pen and the document to Duclos. Without a word, without reading a line of its contents, the courtier signed his name beneath Stosch's.

Stosch reached out and slid the document across the table to Cheroffini. Duclos handed him the pen.

"This is the festival of Michael the Indomitable, who expelled the Devil from Heaven," Cheroffini said quietly as he signed the document, not with any flourish but slowly, like a man signing his own death warrant. "And if the Devil had expelled Michael, this would be the festival of the Devil."

"In the hangman's house," Stosch said with genial rebuke, "nobody speaks of the rope."

27

It was seven o'clock in the evening. The two courtiers had been gone for more than an hour. Philippe got up from the club chair by the French window and switched on the lights in the study. He was alone, lost in thought. He stood behind the raised desk and slowly turned over the pages of the Proclamation the way one turns over the pages of an out-of-date newspaper. It contained nothing he didn't already know. There were no surprises. "No personal feelings weigh in this matter: it is an order of common sense and of true mutual interests. It is an order for the repose and security of St. Saladin," Cheroffini had said with the precision for which he was renowned and which prevented him from taking sides.

The Proclamation, on the face of it, set out merely to secure the future sovereignty of St. Saladin. Between the lines, it put the axe to the very root of Philippe's power.

"It still leaves you looking good," Duclos had told him.

"A mummy probably looks good if you're a necrophiliac," Philippe said, staring hard at Duclos' old chamois-colored face.

"I can assure Your Highness that Dieter Stosch is impelled only by the deepest interests of St. Saladin."

"You will forgive me for observing that the methods employed do not appear to match the noble motives you imply."

"I am an honest intermediary, Your Highness. I assure you I would tolerate no machinations against the safety and quiescence of St. Saladin," Cheroffini said.

"You regard this . . . German as the regenerator of our land—"

"Perhaps a tactical meekness—"

"The meek inherit earthworms."

"Our economic and political future is simply compromised by want of an heir to the throne. There is an absence of investment in St. Saladin because the public and the Bourse are uneasy about our future . . . but imagine what would be the strength of His Highness's throne today if it were guaranteed by the existence of a son. It would be useful, would it not, sir, to be supported by a direct heir?"

"You take away everything—my freedom, my power, the woman I love—"

"Love, duty—they both exact their measure of pain, both exact their measure of sacrifice," Cheroffini said quietly.

"I am being shunted into a political ghetto," Philippe said. "Stosch's thirst for instant submission is—"

"Time is of the essence," Duclos chipped in. "That is all. A swift and suitable marriage would conciliate all parties—"

"Stosch is moving too fast," Philippe said. "Just remember men who want to be rich in a year usually get themselves hanged in six months."

"The Proclamation is merely a temporary expedient—" Duclos began.

"Isn't that what they said when they cut off King Charles' head?" Philippe asked drily. "Where would Stosch's maneuvers end if I were not so necessary to St. Saladin?"

"It does not behoove us to set ourselves up as judges

of what might happen in different circumstances," Cheroffini said shortly.

It was interesting, Philippe thought, that Dieter Stosch continued to stay in the background. He held the best cards, but still he got others to play them. Philippe stroked his throat and studied the ceiling. It was like a quarrel between a shark and an eagle, he thought. They couldn't destroy each other so long as they stuck to their own elements.

He closed the pages of the Proclamation.

He didn't blame Cheroffini and Duclos. In their way, they were necessary. They were there to be used by either side. He smiled at the thought. Poor Cheroffini and Duclos. Old men protecting their privileges, fearing for their existence. Worn out by their political passions; victims of their own cunning and misplaced patriotism. They had simply been outmaneuvered by Stosch, and by time itself. What the lion wills, the jackals must not resist. No, even that was unfair. It was their loyalty to Maximilien that had brought them to this. Stosch may have come to court through their influence but it had always been Maximilien's policy they were pursuing, his schemes they were bolstering. Now they were like soldiers, cut off behind enemy lines, acting out old orders long after the plans have changed, long after Command HQ itself has been overrun and destroyed. They were too old for new campaigns, too slow for new strategies.

Philippe paced slowly around the room. Any moment now, Father Cornelius was due. Philippe needed somebody to talk to, somebody he could trust. He stood in front of the Picasso lithographs of the copulating couple. He smiled. That, he thought, is what Stosch is doing to me now.

Cornelius arrived a few minutes late, sweating slightly from the long walk from his rooms on the other side of the palace. He came in and closed the door after him. He sat down in the club chair.

"Out of condition, Father?"

"As Cardinal Newman said, health of body and mind is a great blessing . . . if we can bear it."

"Scotch?"

"Please."

The Prince poured the drink and handed it to the puffing priest.

"Drink that—and read this," he said. He dropped the Emergency Proclamation into Cornelius' lap.

"An Order restraining the movements of His Royal Highness Prince André Antonin Philippe, Marquis d'Murat, during a crisis of State," Cornelius said aloud. He read on in silence until the end.

"It sounds impressive. But, then, what official document in St. Saladin doesn't sound impressive?"

"It's flowery—but it's legal."

"It sounds like the Ten Commandments rewritten by Machiavelli. What does it mean?"

"It means exactly what it says. I've been ground-reined." He told Cornelius what Cheroffini and Duclos had said, what Stosch wanted.

"What are you going to do?" Cornelius asked when he had finished.

"I'll survive. I've never really been free. The only free man is a man with no charge, with no mission. You know that, Father."

"You're taking it very well."

Philippe grinned and took Cornelius' empty glass.

"The truth is, I wasn't planning to go anywhere anyway. I travel only for pleasure. Now it's time for business, wouldn't you say? My business is St. Saladin."

"Where did this come from?" Cornelius asked, lifting the Proclamation.

"Duclos and Cheroffini delivered it."

"Cheroffini with Stosch. That surprises me."

The Prince shrugged. He refilled the glass and handed it to Cornelius.

"He is set in his ways. He is too tired to learn the modern choreography of circumvention."

"Surely men who dance attendance will always learn new steps. . . ."

"Is that what they teach you in the Vatican?"

Cornelius grinned and shook his head.

"We all play the same game but some more piously than others," he said.

"Stosch uses all the legal niceties, but he is still demanding a self-destructive price for my title."

"The meanness is—"

"He wouldn't put his hand in his pocket to scratch his balls, Father."

Cornelius smiled, but he could see that Philippe was wound up tight as a golf ball.

Philippe poured himself a Scotch and moved behind the desk. He opened a drawer and took out a silver coin.

"My great-great-grandfather designed the coins of St. Saladin. On one side of the pieces he inscribed *God Grant It*. The other side of the coin bore the legend: *St. Saladin—Jeu de hasard*."

He tossed the coin to Cornelius.

"I suspect God and St. Saladin have been on opposite sides ever since."

Cornelius caught the coin in his left hand.

"What are you doing here, Father? In Godless St. Saladin? In this game of chance?"

"Mother Church and Lady Luck—there's always been a strange affinity," Cornelius said slowly. "They gambled for the Robe at the foot of the Cross." He didn't want to argue with Philippe. He waited, hoping that the Prince would change the subject.

Philippe hesitated a moment, swirling the Scotch in the bottom of his glass.

"I have discovered everything now—except God," he said finally. "Let me ask you a question, Father."

"Go ahead."

"Supposing the soul is nothing more than a mirage of the mind—and God merely a figment of the soul?"

Cornelius managed a loose-fitting grin.

"A man can build on a well-constructed fiction," he said.

"You answered very quickly."

"Don't think I haven't thought about it."

"I can trust you," Philippe said.

Cornelius leaned forward and put the piece of silver on the desk. "I would like you always to remember that," he said quietly.

"My moods may change, but never my mind," Philippe said.

He picked up the coin from the desk.

"I have the perspective of seven centuries of history. Stosch is merely a temporary threat. . . ."

28

At fourteen minutes past ten o'clock, Richard Antrobus entered the bank and joined the shortest line in front of a window manned by a beaky-nosed clerk with a small gray toothbrush moustache fir-cone-stained by tobacco smoke. The girl in front of Antrobus, paying in several small separate amounts of money, had got her sums wrong. It took a little time to sort out.

Finally Antrobus was at the window.

"Morning." He used a clipped bright military tone. "Spicer. Wilfred Spicer." He placed his large tachy case with the gold initials *W.C.S.* on the counter. "My account is being transferred to you from Bloomsbury."

"Mr. Spicer? Just a moment, sir. I believe we had your notification in this morning."

"Good show," Antrobus said. He wore a double-breasted camel overcoat and a brown felt trilby.

The clerk went and talked to an older man behind a high desk in a glass cubicle at the back of the bank. Documents were produced. Examined. Conversation. The two men suddenly looked up and regarded Antrobus for several moments. More low serious conversation. Antrobus started to sweat. He took out a handkerchief and blew his nose, casually wiping his palms. The older man picked up the telephone and dialed. Antrobus tried not to watch. Who was he calling? The police? Head Office? Jay? Was Jay's phone still . . . diffused? Antrobus tasted the dryness of fear in his throat. A cold spasm of panic, like cramp, caught his stomach. His fingers jerked like legs freshly torn from a frog's body.

After what seemed like an interminable time, the older clerk shook his head and replaced the receiver. He gave the clerk some papers and dismissed him with a small shrug.

"The manager isn't in yet," the clerk said, returning with several pages of documents. "But the advice note's here. That's the important thing." He studied the top sheet for a moment. "Yes, it all seems to be in order."

"How very efficient," Antrobus said cheerfully. "May I see my passbook?"

"We're not quite that efficient I'm afraid, Mr. Spicer. The passbook comes via the clearing center at head office. It takes a little longer."

"There's always some small snag."

"Not really, sir. If you want to know the amount of the balance transferred—"

"It should be about one hundred and eighty-five thousand," Antrobus said. "Give or take a few bob."

"If you can identify yourself, sir, I can let you know to the penny."

"Wilfred Charles Spicer," Antrobus said, taking out his wallet. He extracted a business card, driver's license, a Royal Automobile Club membership card. He slipped them under the grill. He held his wallet open. "My discharge papers, American Express . . . if you want them, too—"

The clerk inspected the driver's license cursorily. "That's all right, Mr. Spicer. You do understand—"

"Of course, dear fellow. I like a man to be careful when he's looking after my money."

The clerk smiled his appreciation. "Your credit balance is one hundred and eighty-seven thousand pounds fifteen shillings."

"Mustn't forget the fifteen shillings," Antrobus said jovially. He had adopted the voice of a much older man. He carefully replaced the driving license and R.A.C. card in his wallet.

"I'd like to pick up my new checkbook while I'm about it," he said. "Can do?"

"If you could just wait a few moments—"

"No tearing hurry," Antrobus said, looking at his watch.

It was ten thirty-one.

He had been in the bank seventeen minutes. He had calculated twenty minutes for each transaction. He had only three minutes left. Shit. He would have to revise his schedule. If he allowed thirty minutes for transaction time, thirty minutes traveling . . . one bank an hour—four and three-quarter hits, with a bit of luck. Two days, nine and a half banks. Say ten. He'd counted on thirteen or fourteen. Well, it wasn't so bad. He'd simply have to up his withdrawals. Say an average of seventy thousand a bank, ten banks—seven hundred thousand pounds. And there was always the chance of a few more on Friday . . .

"If you could sign here, Mr. Spicer . . . and here." The clerk pushed two forms under the grill.

Antrobus signed each one, dotting the *i*'s in Wilfred and Spicer with small neat circles.

The clerk examined the signatures, then compared them with the transfer specimen signatures in front of him.

"Fine," he said.

It was ten thirty-nine.

He gave Antrobus a new checkbook, a paying-in book, and several leaflets on the history and wisdom of banking.

"Good, good," Antrobus said, slipping the leaflets and the paying-in book into his briefcase.

"Now, a safety-deposit box."

"A deposit box, Mr. Spicer?"

The clerk looked at the transfer advice note in front of him. "Yes, you had S.D.P. facilities in Bloomsbury, I see."

"The safest way to fly," Antrobus said.

"That shouldn't be a problem," the clerk said. "If you'll wait just a moment."

He went back to the older man at the back of the bank. More conversation, more consultation of the paperwork. Another phone call . . . engaged. Antrobus felt the hollow panic in the pit of his stomach, prickly sweat ran down his back.

The clerk returned.

"That's all in order, Mr. Spicer."

"Good show." Slowly Antrobus began to write out a check for cash. He pressed down hard to stop his hand shaking.

"If you could just arrange for this—I'd like to put it downstairs now," he said slowly as he completed the signature.

"Eighty-eight thousand pounds," he said quietly handing over the cheque.

"Just a moment, sir." There was a look of concern on the clerk's face.

It was ten forty-five.

The clerk had disappeared into a back office.

Ten forty-seven.

A man appeared at Antrobus' side. He was a swarthy, low-built man with a broken nose. His gray gimlet eyes had an enamel-like glitter.

"Mr. Spicer?" The voice was soft.

"Mr. Wilfred Spicer?" It sounded like an allegation.

Antrobus jumped.

"Yes?"

"My name is Partridge. James Partridge. I'm the manager."

He held out his hand.

"Welcome," he said, "to Wimbledon Chase. I'm sorry I wasn't here when you arrived."

"That's all right. Your Mr.—" Antrobus read the name block in front of the position "—Mosley has been looking after me very well."

Antrobus could feel his heart beating inside his rib cage like a berserk sparrow.

"He is getting your money together," Partridge said. "I'll show you downstairs."

He led him down a flight of narrow stone steps to the basement. They went through an iron-bar door at the right of the stairs, through a narrow hallway into the vault. Inside, Partridge withdrew a long green steel box from a bank of boxes built into the end wall.

"We only go up to a size six here, I'm afraid Mr. Spicer. I see from Mr. Jay's note you had a nine in Bloomsbury."

He placed the heavy deep green box on the plain wooden table in the middle of the room.

"I'm sure that will do," Antrobus said. "I won't usually want to put more than today's total in at any one time." He took a sealed legal-looking envelope from his tachy case. "And this," he said.

"I think that should go in all right," Partridge said. "The annual rental for a six box is twelve pounds a year. So you're saving nearly five pounds on your old nine."

"Every little helps."

"These days," Partridge said with the nicely calculated air of professional commiseration.

Mosley arrived carrying a deep wooden tray of fresh bundles of notes.

"If you'd care to count that, Mr. Spicer—then we'll leave you to it," Partridge said.

"Eighty-eight thousand, sir," Mosley said.

"In fives. There should be one hundred and seventy-six packets of five hundred."

Antrobus made a show of counting the packets.

"Only just," he said. "Old boy."

He started to open the envelope.

"Then we'll leave you to your business," Partridge said hurriedly, handing him the key. It was strict bank policy to leave customers alone with their boxes. There were no doubt very good legal reasons for such discretion.

"When you're finished, just leave the box on the table. The bell is on the left by the door. Ring when you're ready. Mr. Mosley will come and let you out—and do the necessary."

Partridge extended his hand.

"I'm very pleased to have met you, Mr. Spicer. If there is anything, anytime—"

"Thank you."

"When you've settled in over this side of the river, perhaps some lunch—"

"I'd enjoy that."

"There's rather a good little Italian place just opened—"

"Splendid, splendid." Antrobus was getting anxious

about the time. He looked at his watch, remembering to give a military twist of the wrist.

Ten fifty-eight.

"We must let you get on," Partridge said. He began to back toward the door. Mosley followed him.

"Leave you to it then," the manager said.

"Yes. Suddenly I'm rather behind schedule."

Left alone, Antrobus worked fast. He packed the bundles of flimsy white five-pound notes into his case. He put the sealed envelope—it contained nothing more than a folded front page of the *Times* and the card of Mr. Wilfred Charles Spicer, Investment Consultant—into the box. He locked the box and dropped the key into the bottom of his case.

He rang the bell.

It was three minutes past eleven when he stepped into the street again.

The whole business had taken forty-nine minutes.

"California here I come," he started to hum under his breath on his way to the next appointment.

29

Isak Girod had made love all that hot summer's afternoon with her dress on. She felt deliciously tarty. She gave the taxi driver Philippe's address. He looked pointedly at her and then at the *hôtel de passe* from which she had emerged. He repeated the Île-St.-Louis address in a leering Belleville accent without removing the smelly cheroot from his mouth.

"That is correct," Isak said. Her voice had an icy authority. It put the driver in his place. *"Oui, mademoiselle,"* he said. His flat East End voice was no longer leering. "L'Île St.-Louis, quai d'Anjou."

Isak settled back as the cab pulled slowly away from

the curb and filtered into the heavy traffic on the rue Beaubourg.

The driver studied Isak in his rear-view mirror, trying to pigeonhole her. He knew the hotel well. She didn't fit. He finally figured she was another la-de-da dame on the fly.

"This traffic," he said, casually adjusting the mirror to look at her legs. "Soon Paris is going to jam tight. Nobody's ever going to get it moving again."

Isak said nothing.

She opened her purse and took out a gold flapjack mirror and examined her face.

She smiled.

She looked well fucked. She glowed with it. Her blond hair was tied straight back with a brown velvet ribbon. She leaned forward and rolled down the window of the cab and felt the cool stale breeze of the city on her face and on her bare arms and legs.

It was almost five o'clock. The rush hour was getting under way. It would take at least forty minutes to get to the Île St.-Louis.

She closed the compact and replaced it in her purse. She settled back in the seat and closed her eyes. She was aware of her body beneath the thin silk dress. She felt swollen, she felt slightly sore. The soreness actually made her feel sexy again, needing, wanting it again.

She thought about the sordidness of the small room of the hotel in which she had spent the afternoon. A small shudder of excitement passed through the pit of her belly.

The idea of picking up a stranger in a bar had originally been Philippe's but she knew he would be astonished that she had actually done it. She had done it for Philippe, she told herself—but she knew that wasn't really true. She wanted to do it. She wanted to act out the fantasy every bit as much as Philippe had wanted her to.

The paradox was that while needing constant adventures to satisfy her body, the adventures only made her need Philippe more. She saw her peccadillos only as the material, the inspiration for the passions she ultimately shared with Philippe. The lovers she took were peripheral creatures chosen to torment and tantalize and arouse him. "You must understand . . . I crave the excruciating excitement of flaunted unfaithfulness," he had once explained his feelings to her. It had never occurred to Isak that they had fallen into the worst possible trap that lovers can be in: they had abandoned the art of imagination. They had lost the erotic gift, the erotic charge, of fantasy. Her lovers now dominated their love life. Her adventures were more and more reckless and wanton. They had become indispensable.

Her lover that afternoon was rough trade. Muscular but rather short, he'd smelled of tobacco and *vin du pays* and something else besides, something she couldn't place. Something male and musty, a dry-goods sort of smell. He had been crude but amazingly durable. He had no surprises, no imagination. He made love to her silently, with clumsy determination. He made no effort to please her. He didn't try to understand her. She felt like a day that had to be got through. She was being *used*. The insides of her thighs were bruised, there were finger marks where he'd gripped her forearms. Isak had picked him up in a bar in one of the pinched little side streets off the rue Lombards.

He'd shown no surprise when he discovered that, except for the thin gold chain she always wore around her waist, she was naked beneath the silk dress. He'd assumed she was a whore, or perhaps a housewife trying to make ends meet, or simply doing it for the thrill. It had angered him when she refused to remove her dress. He'd offered to pay more if she would take it off. The cheap lasciviousness of it, she thought, the sheer exhibitionism, the tartiness of what she'd done! Her throat felt constricted with excitement.

The taxi turned left into the rue de Rivoli. The traffic was much heavier. They moved a few yards and were stopped by a policeman, although the signals were green, pointing his long white baton at the front of the taxi.

A large American car crawled out of a side street in front of them.

"Yanks. They're everywhere, making trouble," the

taxi driver grumbled. "Those big cars shouldn't be allowed into the city."

Isak knew it would be quicker to walk, but she was too exhausted, even though she could almost see the Pont Marie.

Traffic jams usually made her nervous. This one didn't worry her at all. She felt as relaxed as if she'd swallowed a couple of downers. For the first time in her life she had made love to a complete stranger, a man totally and obviously beneath her. She didn't know his name, or where he came from, or what he did for a living. She just hoped he was clean, that was all. The thought didn't particularly bother her. In the morning she'd arrange for a checkup with Dr. Péritti. Péritti was Philippe's physician; if she had picked up anything he'd assume that Phillipe was to blame. Her reputation was safe enough.

She was surprised at how shameless she felt. It had been an exciting afternoon. A memorable one. A first. Afterward she had closed her eyes for a few minutes; she wasn't asleep, but she wasn't awake either. It was a timeless time. The iron lattice gates clanged. A motor started up with a life-weary growl. The narrow cage slowly descended to the streets of Les Halles.

She was alone.

The smell of him hung in the air. Isak lay on her back on the narrow bed and slowly opened her eyes. There was a trancelike quality about the room, a luminous blur. She smiled at the ceiling, thinking how he must have been congratulating himself as he disappeared into the crowd. Her lover! He'd got it for nothing! It was a rotten trick to play on a working girl! That would certainly excite Philippe. Her heart beat a little faster.

Her flesh began to tingle again as her mind went back, relishing that squalid little room on the third floor of the old cliquart-stone hotel.

The taxi driver was trying to get around the jam. He turned into a street of tall narrow houses that leaned against each other. "It's worth a try," he said, looking at her naked crossed legs.

"Very well," she said.

She was in no hurry. Isak loved the occasional irony of the names given to the maze of streets and courtyards and alleyways of Paris. The rue Réaumur, bordering the hotel she'd just left, marked the beginning of the most concentrated prostitute population in the city. It was named after the man who measured the heat and ice points in a thermometer. She would mention that to Philippe when she told him about that afternoon. Her talent for trivia was one of their running amusements.

The taxi got a move on through the side streets, but to no avail. They were trapped in a maze of one-way diversions. They rejoined the rue de Rivoli at the point where they'd left it. The driver swore under his breath but didn't bother to point out the failure to Isak. Her eyes were closed.

She was back on the bed, staring at the patch of clear Italian sky through the crooked window above her head, imagining all the bodies that must have used that cubicle, all the years of violation and sweaty foreplay and copulation and coming on that hard acquiescent bed.

The decadence of the thought excited her.

She was pleased her pickup lover had disappeared. It was the best exit there was, the perfect comic *coup de grâce*.

Then, in a world of her own, she had unclasped the chain from around her glistening waist. She wrapped the chain inside her silk Hermès head scarf and pulled it up between her legs, her thighs still seeping . . . the stranger's jism, their mutual sweat, the sweet damp fever.

She turned on her left side, facing the smeared distempered wall. Slowly, thinking only of Philippe, of the things she would tell him, of his responsive, almost liturgical passion, she'd worked the silk scarf back and forth, deeper and deeper. On her face was a small smile of sensual insolence. Philippe loved to watch her doing what she was now doing. He called it her silken saddle.

Her pale green absinthe-colored eyes squeezed tight, then opened wide, thinking of Philippe. The black iron bedstead began to squeak softly, rhythmically. Her soft mouth, misshapen now by abrasive and abandoned narcissism, made loving gasping sounds, thinking of Philippe. . . .

When she came, she called his name, just once, a branding beseechment, a cry of atavistic, almost spiteful fulfillment.

Somewhere along the corridor a man's voice cheered. *"Ma foi! Madame se meurt! Madame est morte!"* And then there was silence.

It was a remote nocturnal silence made by nocturnal happenings, by nocturnal thoughts of nocturnal people.

Isak lay very still.

A fly suddenly buzzed into activity and flew into the closed window a couple of times, then retreated to nurse its sore head on the naked light bulb hanging from the center of the ceiling.

The silence returned.

Isak continued to lie very still. She was not thinking of Philippe now. She was not thinking of anything, or anybody. After a while, she turned from the stained wall and slowly stood up. The worn brown linoleum felt cold beneath her naked feet, it felt almost like marble. The texture of marble had always frightened her.

She clasped the chain back around her waist.

She slipped on her white sling-back shoes and smoothed down her silk dress.

The fly flew down onto the faint patch of hair oil the man had left on the pillow.

Isak remembered the snarl on the man's mouth when he came, the noise he made, but she couldn't remember now what he looked like, whether his hair was black or fair, whether his eyes were blue or gray, cruel or kind.

She tied back her hair with the brown velvet ribbon.

She picked up her purse from the washstand and looked slowly around the room, as if absorbing the atmosphere, memorizing its meager contents, item by item: the narrow iron bedstead, the chipped ewer, the chest of drawers, the brown bedside cabinet with a split plywood door that wouldn't close.

She wouldn't forget that room. It existed outside time, beyond reality. She ran a finger along the wall as she left, lingeringly, as if taking leave of a childhood place, as if not to do so would bring her bad luck. One day she would bring Philippe there, to that very room.

She had closed the door quietly and walked slowly along the narrow corridor full of other doors leading to other rooms just like the one she'd left. She didn't hurry. She walked down the three flights of stairs to the reception desk and ordered the concierge to telephone for a taxi. There was something about Isak Girod that told the concierge, an old mulatto woman, not to argue the toss.

It took, as Isak had guessed it would, more than thirty minutes to get back to the apartment.

Escalle, Philippe's manservant, opened the door to her almost at once. The Prince, he said, had called from St. Saladin. He wanted her to return his call as soon as she came in.

"Thank you, Escalle. Any other messages?"

"That was all, Mlle. Girod."

"Nobody loves me," she said.

"Will you be dining at home this evening, Mlle. Girod?" he asked. He was watching her closely but without desire, and almost without interest. Isak sometimes felt that he was a man who'd never had a dirty thought in his head in all his life.

"At home?" She had to think for a moment. He meant, of course, there, at Île St.-Louis. That was where she spent most of her time now. Although she had never quite established her authority over the staff, it was plain that in every other sense she was the mistress of the house. Philippe had not brought another woman back to the house to sleep for more than a year, despite the fact that the newspapers continued to refer to other women in his life.

Isak still kept her own flat in Saint-Germain-des-Prés. It was one of three studio apartments in a small, pretty courtyard behind the Café Flore. She still half thought of that as her home. It was where she kept many of her clothes, entertained her lovers. It was where she retreated when she'd fought with Philippe. Philippe wanted her to decorate it like a bordello but she'd refused, although she'd given way—often quite literally—on the big brass bed he'd bought her last Christmas from a Marseille whorehouse.

"I'm not sure what I'm doing this evening," she said to Escalle. "It's been such a frantic day. I've been up to my eyes in charity meetings. I haven't had a minute to myself." She spoke with exaggerated exhaustion. It was almost the truth.

"Then I shall inform Cook there is a possibility you will be in for dinner," Escalle said smoothly.

"What time did His Highness call?"

"He telephoned at three twenty-five," Escalle said with his usual precision.

Escalle was probably no more than forty years old but already he had acquired that aura of grave forebearance, a serenity that stops just short of submission, that one usually associates with old retainers. Isak noticed that he displayed no curiosity about her appearance whatsoever, although she was aware that the wear-and-tear of the afternoon must have shown in more ways than one. The taxi driver had noticed it. Why not Escalle? What did he really think, Escalle? Was he so completely trapped inside his own class and calling? He was dutiful and efficient, but there was something about him that always disturbed Isak. He was too smooth. He was a man with no scars on his ass.

Her mouth felt dry.

It was a warm deep-breathing sort of evening. She walked to the window. Three black barges with white funnels were passing in a slow straight line, like nuns going to vespers.

"I would like a long gin and tonic, Escalle," she said, turning from the window. A small involuntary shudder went through her body. Now she was safely home, she began to feel afraid, aware of the risks she'd taken in Les Halles that afternoon.

"A gin and tonic," Escalle said. He had the faintest possible smile, as if he'd been stabbed with a discreet pain that he knew well and almost enjoyed.

"Plenty of ice and lemon."

"I shall see to it at once," he said.

"I'll have it in my room," she said.

"Yes, of course," he said.

Alone, she suddenly thought of the fly crawling on the hard gray pillow, licking up the man's cheap hair oil. It gave a disfiguring edge to the element of fantasy. She tried to shake the image from her mind. She rubbed her bare bruised forearm. She felt the gooseflesh that had suddenly appeared there. She felt resentful that one housefly could threaten her determined dream.

She went to her room. She adjusted the shutters, opening the slits between them to increase the soft slanting evening light. The light sliced through the slits making a caged pattern on the floor and walls. She stood in the middle of the room and undid the clasp of her dress at the nape of her neck. She slipped the dress over her shoulders and let it fall to the floor. She stepped out of the circle of crumpled silk, naked except for her gold chain and white slingback shoes. As she prowled across the room, undoing the ribbon and shaking out her hair, she looked like a tall stripteaser at the end of her act. She went into the large bathroom. She didn't bother with the lights, she ignored her reflection in the full-length mirror. She showered for five minutes, her face held up into the cold spray. She used Philippe's soap; the spicy masculinity of its scent satisfied her more than her own Chanel No. 5 at this particular moment.

She soaped herself from head to foot, slowly.

Afterward she patted herself dry and slipped into a white silk robe with Philippe's crest and initials on the breast pocket. She combed her wet hair straight back and close to her head like a boy. She was stroking a cream into her throat when Escalle tapped on the bedroom door.

"*Entrez* . . ." she called out in a businesslike voice.

Escalle came in carrying a tray covered with a white cloth. Beside the highball glass of gin and tonic were a bowl of Sterlet caviar, a plate of extremely thin buttered black bread, and a sliced lemon.

"My goodness! I might just faint away with pleasure," she said. She smiled, sidelong and sweet.

Escalle placed the tray on the table on her side of the bed. On his way out he picked up the careless heap of Pucci from the floor and folded it over the back of an armchair.

"Will that be all?" he asked politely. He looked around the room with a professional air.

"Thank you, Escalle," she said. "This is divine."

She dipped a finger into the caviar and licked it with a long slow sweep of her extended pink tongue. The unborn fish reminded her that she had to make an appointment with Dr. Péritti.

"Such a civilized thought," she said to Escalle. She knew that beneath the robe her naked body was silhouetted in the slanting evening light. Escalle went out, his back ever so slightly stooped, like a man leaving a church just before the collection is taken. Isak almost expected him to turn and genuflect.

She sat on the bed and sipped the drink. It was perfect. She always judged a barman on how well he could mix a gin and tonic. Escalle got full marks.

She was spreading the caviar on the *tartine* when the telephone rang.

"Isak?" Philippe said almost at once.

"Darling. Yes. I've just got in and got your message."

"Are you all right?"

"Yes, of course. I was just about to call you. Are *you* all right?"

"You sound strange," Philippe said.

"Strange? No. I'm sitting up in bed with a very long, very cold gin and tonic. An Escalle special. I was just making myself comfortable to call you."

"You sounded—I don't know," Philippe said.

"Well, I'm fine darling."

She lay back and looked at the ceiling. She was prepared for a long lovers' chat, although she had already decided not to tease him with her afternoon's adventure. She would save it. For a time when she could reap the benefits physically, and without delay.

"I've missed you," she said. "Really, really, really. It's been *ages*."

"One week and five days."

"An eternity."

"For my father, yes."

"That's sacrilege—or something," she said. Philippe was unmoved by his father's death; it was as if a distant relative had died, or a famous stranger. Isak made no effort to be solemn.

"I'm sure you've found plenty to do while I've been away," he said in a half-prompting voice.

She made a clicking noise with her tongue on the roof of her mouth. "Writing my life story on the dungeon walls of night," she said in a melodramatic tone.

"The graffiti of the guilty."

"The graffiti of lovers."

"What are you wearing?"

"A robe. One of yours. It smells of you."

"Then you should have it cleaned at once."

"Certainly not. It's my only consolation." She slipped her hand inside the large robe and felt her smooth talcumed armpit. God, she missed that man. She was suddenly aware how cool it had become in the room; the light had turned a tawny color that was almost gold.

"Your letter was lovely," she said. "Brown ink. I'm sure that means something."

"Mourning, probably. The whole palace supply was changed last week."

"The inky mysteries of protocol. And I was hoping it was something dreadfully romantic."

"Perhaps that too," Philippe said. There was a detachment in his voice.

"You hardly sound like the man who wants me— wants me so much it hurts," she said, using a phrase written in brown ink.

"Isak, I want you." He appeared to make a great effort to get the words simple and right, but his voice was false, filled with a hoarded strain, an uneasy sense of concentration.

"You sound dead to the world, darling," Isak said. "Has it been too terrible?"

"There are problems, Isak—" The end of the sentence was lost as someone cut in on the line and went away again.

"I've been away too long."

Isak stared uncertainly at the ceiling. The palms of her hands were suddenly damp with premonitory misgiving.

"Where are you calling from?"

"The palace—my suite."

She slowly sat up, sat up very straight, and very still, with a blank pharaohonic stare.

"Darling, listen to me," he said. "I want you to come as soon as possible."

"Yes, of course. Will you send the plane?"

"No. The plane has—It isn't available. Don't ask questions. I'll explain everything when you get here."

"I'll catch the first Air France flight in the morning."

"The eight o'clock. From Le Bourget."

"You'll meet me at Toulon?"

"If I'm not there, go straight to the Résidence di la Pinède in St. Tropez."

"My sweet darling—"

"Book the flight yourself, direct with Air France. Don't go through the agency. Do it yourself. Avoid the press."

"Darling—what *is* going on, *please*?"

"Not now, Isak."

"I love you," she said.

"Take care."

"You take care."

Philippe replaced the receiver but the line was not immediately disconnected; Isak waited for the second click. It was like waiting for a blow to fall. It was very gentle, a few seconds later.

"You take great care, my darling," she said softly into the dead mouthpiece.

30

"What time is your appointment tomorrow?" Dieter Stosch asked.

"Twelve forty-five," Genevieve Lacroix said. "At Fouquet's. She's arriving today on the Golden Arrow. She's not too fond of flying."

"She's good, this English girl?"

"Exceptionally. Since Catherine Gaillard . . . I'd say probably the best we have." Mlle. Lacroix waited for Stosch to comment, but he just stood very still, with an air of cold preoccupation.

"She's also beautiful," Mlle. Lacroix said to break the silence. "She has that luminous pallor one associates with good breeding—and bed."

"She comes from a good family?"

"She behaves as if she does."

"Just so!" Stosch said.

They stood on opposite sides of the marquetry table containing Stosch's priceless Bustelli collection, the porcelain figures set out like tall frail chess men. He leaned forward and slightly adjusted the angle of the Donna Martina.

"You'll catch the six o'clock flight this evening?"

"I prefer that—but if you wish I could still leave in the morning," she said. "The nine o'clock plane gives me enough time—if it isn't too delayed."

"I have a better idea. Go with Leon Kun. He is taking the Memorandums to London this evening. It is a simple matter to take you to Paris first."

"Thank you."

"Casenave complains he doesn't get enough flying hours. It will please him to log Paris. But return Air France. It'll be quicker than waiting for Kun to return, I think."

"I'm booked back on the five o'clock flight."

"This particular product interests me very much." He returned to his desk and sat down. He put a paracodeine tablet in his mouth. "Talking of Casenave. How is the captain these days . . . privately?"

He's changed since Mlle. Gaillard's . . . absence."

"How so? Changed?"

"Changed . . . more morose. Sort of . . . it's hard to explain. It's as if he always has something on his mind. As if he's somewhere else."

Stosch looked knowing. "On autopilot?" he asked.

"Exactly." Mlle. Lacroix smiled. "On autopilot is exactly it."

"We must watch him," Stosch said. His lips tightened. He still hadn't discovered exactly who was to blame for the bungled attempt to silence Casenave. The order hadn't come from him, and that kind of initiative was dangerous—especially when it failed. Genevieve Lacroix's reminder that Casenave perhaps still had the dead stewardess on his mind renewed Stosch's concern. There had been no need to try to eliminate the pilot, no need at all; the attempt on his life only underlined the fact that there was something somebody wanted to hide. Still, it had been a long time ago and Casenave had proved nothing, discovered nothing, not even the truth about his own unfortunate accident. The police had lost interest in both Catharine Gaillard's disappearance and Casenave's accident almost at once. The charred remains of an unidentified woman's body in a field near Guillaumes six months ago got an inside-page paragraph in *Nice-Matin*.

"Paris," Stosch said. "The usual arrangements?"

"George Cinq. Mlle. Chaire. Our friend'll be at the Tremoille. Under her own colors."

"Has she given you any indication—about the product?"

"No."

"But you say they've been close?"

"For a year, or more. Very."

"Well, then," Stosch said in an expressionless voice. He was still half-thinking about Casenave.

"At least we know that our rich American friend doesn't have a family who'd expect titles and subsidies," Genevieve Lacroix said lightly.

"Half American," Stosch said. He was again giving his attention to the conversation. "Georgina Game is half American. Half British."

"Most people think of her as an American, a Hollywood star—"

"Even so," Stosch observed in a dry, slightly reproving tone. "She probably has better blood than half the princesslings we've been considering."

"Not merely blue but Technicolored," Mlle. Lacroix said softly. "A genuine Hollywood princess."

Stosch showed no sign that he'd heard the remark. It was perhaps fortunate, Mlle. Lacroix thought in the dead silence that followed her small wry joke. For she suspected that he was rationalizing the failures of the past year. His attempts to induce one of the more established royal houses of Europe to provide Philippe with a bride had not been successful. Even Queen Juliana of the Netherlands, the only monarch to show anything more than official politeness toward St. Saladin's royal matchmakers, refused to consider the question seriously for a moment. Her daughter Princess Beatrix, she pointed out frostily, was a headstrong girl, not yet eighteen, and certainly not prepared to be given to a prince more than twice her age and—although Queen Juliana didn't actually spell it out—in quite a different sovereign league altogether.

For some time now Dieter Stosch had been planning to advance a solution to the gathering crisis in St. Saladin with an unexpected twist—a sensation, not merely to secure the country's fragile independence, but to put it back in the public eye, back in the money. A short secret list of potential brides for Philippe had been drawn up. It included six names: two American heiresses, the daughter of an English duke, one of the more attractive Blandenberg princesses, an Italian contessa, and Georgina Game. The duke's daughter had had one abortion too many and could no longer bear the vital heir. The contessa could not for the moment be parted from a German politician with whom she was having a passionate affair. One of the American heiresses died in a plane crash in Kenya and the other declined even to meet Father Cornelius, who had been dispatched to Palm Beach to discuss the matter. One way or another, Georgina Game had gone to the top of the list.

"Trying to reconcile the demands of our hunger and our honor . . ." Stosch said. He picked up the report on the Blandenberg princess. She had been a frontrunner, tipped by the press, approved by public sentiment, until Stosch received the product: she had syphilis. "It's amazing how many people who live behind moats have waterfront morals," he said wearily.

He dropped the report as if it were something dirty.

Genevieve Lacroix studied him with sympathy and amusement in her eyes. She sat down in a deep arm-

chair next to the barred windows overlooking the courtyard. She was pleased to be getting away for even a few
hours, to be going to Paris this evening and not tomorrow. The more the crisis grew the more claustrophobic
St. Saladin seemed to become. It had been almost a
month since her last visit to Paris. Then it was to collect
product on the contessa, and to check on Isak Girod.
Philippe's refusal to give up his French mistress did not
help the present predicament. He had bought the
French actress a lavish villa just outside Grasse where
the couple now spent most weekends. Isak had kept her
studio apartment in St-Germain-des-Prés and was still a
frequent "guest" at Philippe's house in Paris during his
enforced presence in St. Saladin. Isak was still convinced
that she would one day be princess of St. Saladin. Speculation about the couple filled the gossip columns of
Europe and America. In Paris a rough left-wing scandal
magazine published a series of photographs of Isak sunbathing in the nude by the pool in Grasse. Isak's lawyers
dismissed them as "the fakes of garbage journalism" but
failed noticeably to sue. "Prince Philippe, as ever, takes
no pains to hide his mistress from public view," crowed a
subsequent editorial in the magazine above another nude
shot of Isak. It was all part of the quiet desperate power
game between the Prince and Stosch. Stosch had ordered
and planted the nude photographs to discredit Isak Girod, to embarrass the Prince, to make their relationship
less tenable. But he badly miscalculated Philippe: "What
do I care what people think?" the Prince shrugged off
the episode. "One likes one's possessions to be admired."

It had been a difficult year for Dieter Stosch.

"He turned the throne into a back seat," Count Cheroffini had said. "But he forgot one thing. He forgot that
the world is full of back-seat drivers."

"You have good hopes of Georgina Game?" Genevieve Lacroix asked gently. The whole marriage question had become a touchy subject inside the Bureau.

"She looks the part," Stosch said slowly. "There's
something . . . cold there, something hard. An education, style, a superior sense of culture. She's got reserves
a man'll never reach."

"Is that good? I mean, couldn't that be awkward for us?"

"She's ambitious and she's famous. Famous women with ambition will always negotiate to become even more famous."

"But a marriage? Negotiate—*bargain* over a marriage?"

Stosch just smiled.

"*Especially* over a marriage. The popular pretext for marriage is romance. In reality marriage is a business arrangement, a deal, based on selfish motives, on the needs and satisfactions of the principal signatories."

"The idea that love—" Genevieve started to say.

"There is no more a place for love in marriage than in contracts between corporations, or in treaties between nations. Only the poor and the foolish marry for altruistic reasons. For *love*, as you call it. The rich marry out of egotism, to consolidate, to make life more agreeable."

"Forget the vows, the small print's what it's all about. Is that it?"

"Exactly," Stosch said in a quiet reasonable tone.

"How long do you think—"

"Marriage is seldom the sacrament of a long affair— the kind of marriage we have in mind," he said.

"Georgina Game has prestige. Her pictures make a great deal of money. She has the credentials Hollywood likes. But St. Saladin is hardly Hollywood," Genevieve said slowly. She had to tread carefully. "She's perfect collateral when it comes to financing movies. But is it enough to—"

"Maybe we'll give her a chance to play something a lot bigger than she ever expected," Stosch said as if he hadn't been listening to a word Genevieve had said.

"That's really my point. Can she handle it?"

"We shall see what we shall see," Stosch said. His eyes suddenly narrowed as if somebody had opened a furnace door. "Go to Paris, talk to the girl, get the product. We don't know anything until we see the product."

It was shortly after twelve-fifteen when Liz Huntington left the Tremoille, crossed over to the rue Pierre Charron, and began to walk slowly toward the Champs-Élysées. She loved Paris but now she felt a strange despair, a sadness. She thought about the last time she had been there, that beautiful week with Georgina. It seemed a long time ago. She thought about that first night in the apartment on the boulevard Haussman. She tried to transfer her sense of sadness to poor dead Peglar Bernhardt whose flat they'd shared, but it didn't work that day, dammit.

She was too early for her appointment but couldn't bear to stay in her hotel room any longer. She sauntered as slowly as she could without being mistaken for a prostitute, looking in the windows of the small fashion shops with unseeing tear-filled eyes; she had avoided wearing mascara. She kept remembering what Georgina said that first night they'd slept together:

"Love can give you a lot of happiness but it can also give you a lot of grief. But real friendship, friendship between two women, is something much more special. You feel like the sister I always wanted. Really good friends, I guess, are just like sisters—they know all the weak spots, all the chinks in each other's psyches. It's a fatal knowledge, if you think about it, a weapon, an irresistible inexhaustible temptation. You have to watch out for it all the time, I guess . . . but it's the gift you give to each other, the power, the trust. I've had a lot of lovers, Liz, but I tell you, you're a real friend and I've had precious few of them in my life."

Liz found herself resenting Georgina's confidences, her trusting revelations, those intimate disclosures. *That fatal knowledge,* Georgina called it. Christ, how right she was. If it were possible to die from an overdose of remorse, Liz thought, she wouldn't make it through lunch. Her throat ached with tiredness and crying. She hadn't slept for more than a couple of hours that night. She ordered black coffee and cognac for breakfast. She had never drunk cognac at breakfast before in her life. But her mind was very clear, and made up.

She arrived at Fouquet's ten minutes early and ordered an Americano. She was determined that this would be her last assignment for Mlle. Chaire—and whoever the hell was behind *her*. The request for a Priority One product on Georgina was the end. Positively. The whole business had gone crazy. And coming out of the blue like that . . .

Mlle. Chaire had been quiet for a year or more. Liz smoked a cigarette and tried to recall her last report. It was either on the German diplomat, she decided, or Richard Antrobus. They came pretty close together. But since then—nothing. The money continued to arrive on the second Monday of each month in a registered envelope, a thousand dollars in one-hundred-dollar bills or, occasionally, in Swiss francs.

She opened her handbag and checked that the envelope was safe. She lit another cigarette. She was nervous, but it wasn't the nervous excitement she'd felt at the beginning of her assignments. Then the idea of espionage, of spying, of working for Mlle. Chaire and the mysterious Principal Consumer had thrilled her, and scared her a little bit too. But now she simply felt cheap, and done for. She finished the Americano and looked around the restaurant. She didn't especially care for Fouquet's, but it was the regular rendezvous. It was too full of expense-account Americans these days, she thought. The old intimacy had gone, although the food was certainly as good as ever, and it was conveniently close to the hotel.

Mlle. Chaire arrived exactly on time. The two women kissed each other's cheeks. Genevieve admired Liz's new brown Balenciaga suit, stroking her arm: it was almost an intimate caress; a man would have done it a little harder and held it for a little longer.

Liz ordered a second Americano. Mlle. Chaire said she would wait and have a glass of wine with her lunch.

The two women talked about fashions, the new movies, the price of things in London and Paris. They talked about Rubirosa, Rainier, Hayworth, Zanuck, Lollobrigida—the sort of people with instant one-name recognition. They talked in English, in voices that carried to the surrounding tables, all of which were now full. It was the familiar playacting preamble. Their girl talk would continue until the main course arrived, then their voices would drop almost imperceptibly, but enough, enough to keep their secrets.

Liz always admired Mlle. Chaire's appearance. She was, when she was dressed up, one of those women who didn't seem to have any particular age. She had that look that said: *Class, Experience and Down Boy,* all at the same time. It was a look English and American women could never quite achieve, and Italian women always overplayed. Very rich South Americans got closest, Liz thought, but their scent was usually wrong.

Both women ordered sole maison and green salad.

Mlle. Chaire studied the wine list knowingly and finally ordered a bottle of Chevalier-Montrachet. She always, Liz knew enough to notice, chose not just a good wine, but the right wine. It was a rare talent in a woman, even a Frenchwoman.

"How long will you stay in Paris?" Mlle. Chaire asked when the fish arrived and the waiter had taken it off the bone for Liz.

"Two days."

"Only two days. That is a shame."

"I have to go to America."

"America? How nice for you. New York?"

"Los Angeles. I'm going to visit Georgina."

"Are you now?" Mlle. Chaire said in a suddenly interested tone. "Then you must let us know what you think."

Liz took a deep breath and said, "No."

"No? What do you mean, Elizabeth?"

"I've decided. I don't want to continue with—with our arrangement."

"What is that exactly?" Mlle. Chaire asked. She had a clever way of raising her voice, of putting an air of amusement into her tone, whenever she said anything innocuous, of no value to people at the other tables. But Liz noticed the quick change in her green eyes. They were eyes that would probably chill those on whom they never smiled.

"I just feel so badly about this—" She touched her handbag on the empty seat by her side with her fingertips.

Mlle. Chaire looked quickly sympathetic. She lowered her voice. "But the arrangement is a satisfactory one, surely? Principal Consumer is pleased with your work. He asks for very little, after all. Five products in how long? Four years? Not that even, I think. The return is good, no?"

"The money's fine. But this particular . . . she's like a sister. She trusted me." Liz closed her eyes.

"You know, my dear, there is nothing quite so delicate as the malice, the tenderness, the jealousy and love of one sister for another. I understand your feelings, but it is human nature to—"

"She *trusted* me, Mlle. Chaire."

"But it is done now. It will never be so—what is it you say? Close to home? It will never be so close to home again."

"We can't be sure of that." Liz opened her eyes as if from prayer. Her face had an almost pious, almost tragic look.

"No, that is true, but it is most unlikely, wouldn't you say? How many sisters do you have, after all?" Mlle. Chaire smiled knowingly, suddenly guessing the depth and nature of the relationship.

"You were lovers?"

"Georgina and me?"

"Yes."

"No."

"Don't be ashamed, *chérie*. I think it's very beautiful. Two beautiful women—"

"We weren't lovers."

"Oh come on now, Elizabeth."

"What can I tell you?" Liz said with a pretense of amiability but her voice sounded different, as if she had difficulty keeping it natural.

"Who—who took the initiative?" Mlle. Chaire persisted. "You? No, I don't think it would have been you."

"Mlle. Chaire!" Liz looked nervously around the restaurant. "Please!"

"Yes?"

"Don't bully me."

"Audacity in a beautiful woman is so . . . so exciting."

"But not imprudence." Liz moistened her lips.

"Is it in the product?"

There was a moment's pause.

"No," Liz said in a small unresisting voice. Why deny it? Why fight this hard sophisticated clever woman? What did it matter, after all?

"It doesn't matter," Mlle. Chaire spoke softly. "Just so long as I know. Would you like to go to bed with me, Elizabeth?"

"I don't know."

"But you enjoyed going to bed with Georgina?"

"Yes."

"Did you come?" she asked in a matter-of-fact tone.

"Yes."

"Did she come too?"

"Yes. I think she did. Why are you asking these questions, Mlle. Chaire?"

Mlle. Chaire gave a small smile. "You didn't mention her—her weakness for ladies in the report? There's no suggestion of it at all?"

"I told you. I didn't think—"

"She has been with other women, then?"

"I didn't say that. No . . . I don't think she has. It was just that once. The circumstances were right . . . it happened. We both wanted it to happen, I suppose."

In the silence that followed that admission Liz started to break then crumble the roll on her bread plate.

"It was just the once?" Mlle. Chaire said, watching Liz knead the crumbs into small pellets.

"We spent a few days together. Here, in Paris. We shared an apartment—"

"But after that—no more?"

"No."

"Did you have other opportunities?"

"I suppose so. In London—"

"So she isn't what you would call a lesbian?"

"I hate that word."

Mlle. Chaire sat very still and just smiled.

"You haven't answered my question."

"She isn't a lesbian—and neither am I. I prefer it with men, if that's the distinction. I'm sure Georgina does too . . . prefer it with men."

Mlle. Chaire continued to smile.

"And so do I," she said. "It is only nature. But sometimes, with another woman, that is good too. Were you both a little high?"

"Yes, a little, the first evening."

Mlle. Chaire reached across the table and touched Liz's hand.

"Don't be nervous, Elizabeth."

Liz pushed aside the demolished roll. Then it was over. She felt Mlle. Chaire withdraw. The pressure was off, the questions stopped. It came to an end as abruptly and as strangely as it began.

"The fish is good?"

"The fish is lovely," Liz said in a polite voice.

Minutes passed and neither woman spoke. It wasn't an embarrassed kind of silence. It was just a silence while both women ate, and thought. Liz's mind worked slowly back to the beginning, to the point at issue.

"I just wish I knew what this was all about. Who the dickens would want this kind of information about—" she realized she had raised her voice and quickly went into a lower key "—you know, Georgina?"

"I can't answer that question. You know that, Elizabeth."

"Can't?"

"There's no point pursuing it, my dear," Mlle. Chaire said in a bright new brittle voice. "Just think of it as helping some interlocking interest groups." As she said this she gave a hard hostile smile to three men at the next table who seemed to be more interested in trying to listen in than in pursuing their own conversation. The hard smile worked. It was the sort of set smile you often see on the faces of very rich women, women anesthetized by affluence. The trio turned away and got on with their own discussion. One of them, he looked like the youngest one, blushed darkly and dropped his fork onto the floor.

"You do understand, Elizabeth, don't you?"

"I have to think about this . . . whole sticky business."

"Too much introspection will only confuse you."

"Don't patronize me, Mlle. Chaire—or whatever your name is," Liz said. There was a sharp edge to her

voice that hadn't been there before. Her anxiety had
turned into resentment and then into anger.

"You've got it wrong, Elizabeth. It's simply that—"
Mlle. Chaire lowered her voice but kept the hard contained smile on her lips. Her eyes moved sideways, then
back to Liz. "Knowing too much—it's like going back-
stage in a theater . . . you see how it is done. You are
robbed a little bit—of the magic, of your innocence—it
is never the same again. Keep your illusions."

Liz pretended to think about it.

"The theater has never thrilled me too much," she
said after a pause. She wasn't quite sure where the conversation was going, or even what it meant. It was an
uncomfortable lunch, but not in the way Liz had expected it to be uncomfortable.

Mlle. Chaire softened the line of her mouth. She had
a gentle look now as she said, "The Principal Consumer—he always helps his friends. You've made a lot
of money—"

"I don't dispute that."

"It has not required a great deal of effort beyond
what you would have been doing anyway?"

"No."

"Accept the magnitude of your luck. Don't gripe.
We've never interfered with your private . . .
arrangements? Asked you to sleep with anyone, anyone
too . . . unattractive?"

"No—but, look, listen to me for a minute please: if
you skate on thin ice long enough . . . I finally got
cold feet, that's all. Maybe it's not just the Georgina
business, maybe it's not guilt, not some big deal
about—"

Mlle. Chaire reached across the table and touched
the velvet sleeve of Liz's jacket. Her eyes glinted with
something, but it wasn't humor, and it wasn't exactly
kindness either. "Information, an occasional document
. . . It pays for many beautiful things. Tickets to California, your independence, the best—"

"Of course it does. I know that. I'm simply saying—"

"You can't have your cock and eat it!"

Liz finally smiled. It was her first genuine smile all
through lunch.

"This product—you think it harms your friend in some way? Is that it?" Mlle. Chaire asked quietly.

"Harm? No, I don't think it'll harm her. It betrays some trusts, some things that . . . I just feel so fucking disloyal."

"You have a loyalty to Principal Consumer, too. You must get your priorities right. It's not as if . . . there's no ethics committee . . ."

The wine steward refilled their glasses.

"It just seems so very strange," Liz said when he'd gone. "I mean, the other products—fine, I could understand why somebody might want information on . . . those sort of people. But Georgina—"

"You mustn't be too inquisitive. I don't think Principal Consumer approves of curiosity . . . people who are too curious are often too talkative." A blunt warning wouldn't do any harm. "Just remember, my dear, you're paid to supply information, not to puzzle your pretty head why it is required."

"I would be inhuman not to wonder, not to think about it sometimes."

"Enjoy your theories, Elizabeth. Just don't talk about them."

"This one. It's ruined all my theories," Liz said.

"Leave it at that," Mlle. Chaire said very quietly.

"I'll try."

"Good girl."

Mlle. Chaire glanced around the restaurant. The tables around them were now nearly all empty. "Now. Give me the envelope now," she said quickly in a tight voice.

Liz was startled by the suddeness of the demand. She had never handed over a product in the open before. The exchange was usually completed at the end of lunch, in the ladies' room. Liz took the envelope from her purse and obediently slipped it across the table. Mlle. Chaire put it into her own purse in a casual unhurried way.

"That's fine," she said. The hardness seeped out of her smile. She was relaxed now, and all politeness. She asked the waiter for the check. "Where can you be reached—should there be any queries?"

"Well, the Tremoille until Thursday. Then the Beverly Wilshire."

"If there's any change of plan, let the concierge at the Tremoille know your new address. I hope you have a pleasant stay in California. How long will you be away do you think?"

"I don't know exactly. A month perhaps."

"Get a nice tan. Don't worry about a thing."

"Thanks a bunch."

"The Americans have a saying: Look after number one."

As usual, Liz left the restaurant first. She didn't want to go back to the hotel immediately. She walked in the direction of the Arc de Triomphe. It was just beginning to rain. That fine, almost languid rain you hardly notice, that Paris rain that soaks you through to your skin. Maybe it was the wine, maybe it was Mlle. Chaire's reassurances—maybe it was the knowledge that it was done and there was no going back—but Liz felt better after lunch. After all, she told herself, it was perfectly true that there could hardly be another request for a product so close to home. And it would certainly be foolish to give up such a lucrative arrangement because of something that was already done. Who was it who said that a precedent always buried a principle? Whoever he was, he was wrong, she thought. Principles aren't buried at all. They are drowned. In wine, in tears, in the rain. In Paris.

She walked aimlessly for a very long time. If she kept on walking, she thought, she would eventually grow tired. It seemed inconceivable she'd slept so little the night before. When she grew tired she would go back to the hotel and go to bed. She wanted to sleep for a very long time.

Book Two

31

"She's had journalists stumped ever since she first arrived in Hollywood eighteen months ago. There is no single insightful phrase that sums her up. The Arctic Sphinx? The million-dollar enigma? Such phrases only compound the mystery that is Georgina Game. Not since Garbo has an actress bedazzled and stunned the senses with such style. She is sudden sunlight on an icy bend, beautiful and unexpected and perilous. . . ."

Dave Jarrup stopped typing and looked at his watch. It was almost ten minutes to six. He stood up and went to the door of his office in the publicity department. He felt stiff. He suddenly noticed the bitter smell of cold coffee in the room.

"Esther, sweetheart, what time's the wrap?"

"Six straight up—unless Fowler's called the half," his secretary said. "You want me to check?" She was already reaching for the phone.

"Please, sweetheart." He straightened the bronze plaque by the door and read for the nineteen-hundredth time:

> If we shadows have offended,
> Think but this, and all is mended,
> That you have but slumber'd here,
> While these visions did appear.

He lit a cigarette.

"Stage four. *Babylon Is Burning*," he heard Esther say in a voice she'd modeled on Katie Hepburn's.

He felt like a condemned man hoping for a last-minute reprieve.

He had a six-fifteen appointment with Georgina Game.

It was crazy. In thirty-two years as a Hollywood press agent, Dave Jarrup had never before been apprehensive about keeping an appointment with an actress. *Never*. He'd taken shellackings from Bette Davis, dealt with the tantrums of Crawford, handled the scandals of Turner. He'd been best man at two of Veronica Lake's weddings, and a witness in one of her divorces. He'd driven at ninety miles an hour in the middle of the night to stick his fingers down the throat of a love goddess who'd thoughtfully called him to say good-bye, she was checking out with barbiturates and booze. . . .

But Georgina Game—*milady* Game—she was something else. She was the only one he'd ever really disliked, the only one he couldn't figure at all.

Like most press agents, Dave Jarrup had a love-hate relationship with all his clients. "Civilians," he wrote in an anniversary number of the *Hollywood Reporter,* "think movie stars are gods. Gods expected to pronounce on politics, religion, morality, birth control, on African affairs, the economy, and the price of bread. You name it. At Santa Anita, people ask them what's going to win the next race. Let me tell you right now, folks: actors are just the same as anybody else—some of them know what's going to win the next race, but most of them don't."

At fifty-three, Jarrup was one of the best unit men in the business. He could have been publicity director at Fox, Metro, any one of the majors. He preferred to work at the coal-face, as he called unit publicity. "I'm a pit man," he told them when the big offer came around every two years or so. "I'm a face worker from way back." He was a rambly-looking man of average height. He had a used leathery face you almost expected to creak every time he smiled. The bridge of his nose had been broken once or twice and never fixed. It was the kind of face that women liked: "a landslide of sensuality," Rita Hayworth called it once. He had tired fawn-colored eyes. A thin scar started just above his craggy left eyebrow and traveled up into his graying brown hairline: a legacy of going to the aid of Errol Flynn in a

nightclub brawl in Montreal a few years back. "One or-
nery flack like Jarrup, he's worth a dozen arty-farty directors," Flynn said later. "He knows how to protect
the profile."

"He'll be scarred for life because of you," Bogart
said.

"That face of Jarrup's, sport, it'd be incomplete without a Heidelberg slash or two," Flynn said.

Esther poked her head around the door. "Fowler's
called the half."

"Thanks honey," Jarrup said.

The secretary smiled. They both recognized the relief
in his voice.

"The sun's over the yardarm," she said, looking at
her watch. It was as if someone had wired their minds
together.

"Good thinking, my little Rocky Mountain canary."
He used his W. C. Fields growl. "Think I'm gonna need
it."

"I think you're right."

She went back into her office and returned in a moment with a glass of bourbon.

"One Old Grand-dad coming up." She cleared a
space on his cluttered desk.

"I hope you put some water in that?"

"Pure Kentucky branch water—straight from the
cooler."

"I want all my wits about me for Milady," he said.
"Could you remove that coffee, please. It offends me."

"You let it get cold," she said accusingly, picking up
the beaker of untouched coffee.

"Sorry, honey," he said vaguely.

He sat down and rolled the sheet of paper out of the
portable Olivetti and read over his afternoon's work.

"She is sudden sunlight on an icy bend, beautiful and
unexpected and perilous." He sipped the bourbon and
thought about the word perilous. He put a clean sheet
of paper into the machine and typed:

"But look deeply into those tawny brown eyes. There
is something there that could explain her mystery after
all. They are the eyes of a woman who has always been

alone. The eyes of a woman who does not regret her history . . . only, perhaps, her destiny."

Jarrup ran his fingers through his thick short-cut hair and grinned at the sentence he had just written. It was bullshit. But it was the sort of bullshit the public wanted to hear, the sort of bullshit he was paid four hundred bucks a week to spread around thick. Anyway, the truth was far less interesting. The truth was—what? Georgina Game was a rich photogenic bitch who'd gotten lucky. Period. Only that didn't sell movies and it didn't sell newspapers and it certainly wasn't worth four C-notes a week to write about either.

Jarrup read the piece through and crossed out the word perilous. Milady had approval of everything the studio put out about her, everything Jarrup wrote, every item that was planted in the columns. She was a stickler for maintaining what she called "a standard of reticence." He called it The Game Doctrine. In a world where exaggeration and invention are par for the course, it didn't make his life any easier. "I don't want you trespassing on my reservation. Publicity's baloney no matter how thin you slice it, Mr. Jarrup."

He stubbed out the cigarette in an ashtray stolen from the Brown Derby.

"Esther. Come here a minute, will ya, baby."

She came in and stood against the wall with a bottle of Coke in her hand. She wore a brown tunic dress, only slightly darker than her tan, and large dark glasses pushed to the top of her blond head. If she hadn't been playing around with one of the most successful producers on the lot, he could have fancied her quite seriously.

He read her the piece on Georgina Game.

"What do you think?"

"I like the word *stumped,*" she said. "Very English."

"Her eyes *are* brown, ain't they?"

"You haven't noticed?"

"I don't look. She'd say I was getting too personal. Invading her goddamned privacy. If she could keep a couple of state lines between us she'd be happy as all hell."

"Brown to black with tawny highlights."

"Sometimes I think I don't know that limey dingbat at all."

"Just goes to show."

"Show what?"

"Actresses are not always to blame."

"For what?"

"Their images. It's the publicity caricature that sticks."

"Stardom, sweetheart. It's a kind of character assassination."

Esther looked at him quizzically.

"You ought to invest in a couch. You're wasted in publicity."

"Stardom's a self-inflicted wound," Jarrup went on. "She *wants* to be a fucking mystery. If I went in there now and told her the jig was up—I knew all about her—she'd crap her britches."

Jarrup's poolroom language was a blind, an instinctive defense mechanism hiding several skeletons including a genuine sensitivity and a Blair and Cornell education. He'd written several successful ballads and the book of a musical that folded after a couple of weeks on Broadway. His poetry had been published in some of the little literary magazines back East. It was no accident that he had been put on the Georgina Game picture: he had acquired a reputation, over the years, for being able to "handle" difficult actresses, a few of whom he'd bedded in the line of duty. "A lay is a lay is a layout," he once told an editor who wanted to know how he'd persuaded a particularly unco-operative actress to do an "at home" spread for *Look* magazine.

He lifted his glass and studied Esther through the bourbon.

"Lissen, beebee. I tell you something for nossing. Secrecy—Milady's first article of faith."

"And the second?"

"Ah—then she gets just like all the rest. We're down to naked egotism."

Esther smiled. "She still isn't going to like—" She walked across the room and picked up Jarrup's copy and read: ". . . bedazzled and stunned the senses with such style."

"It's not inaccurate, for Christ's sake," Jarrup said, going on the attack. "Just the standard sacramental hyperbole of Hollywood, honey."

"Too enthusiastic. You forget. She has a rich girl's antipathy to enthusiasm."

Jarrup grinned and sipped his drink.

"I don't need a ballyhooligan, thank you, Mr. Jarrup," he said. It was Georgina's famous put-down at Chasen's the night they first met.

"You handled that very well."

"You mean I took it lying down."

"I don't mean that at all."

"Then tell me this. Why don't I just blow the whole fucking myth once and for all? Don't be surprised if one day I just go stool—"

"You won't."

"No? And why not?"

"Because you take in whitewashing for a living," Esther said. "Remember?" She smiled with amused encouragement. "Why louse things up?"

"Came the dawn." Jarrup grinned into his bourbon. "Sure. Never let 'em break your heart—or bust your ass."

"You're just a cuddly old teddy bear at heart."

"My tolerance, sweetheart . . . an old man's indolence."

"Balls."

"Well, thank you for that." He looked at his watch. It was six-twenty.

"Have we arranged flowers for that dame we booked into the Beverly Wilshire for Milady by the way?"

"Elizabeth Huntington. Sure. Flowers, fruit, firewater. All done. She's due tomorrow."

"Booze, too? Was that—"

"I found out that Miss Huntington is also a very dear friend of our Mr. Bobby Rivkin. Any good friend of the studio boss, I figured . . ."

"You figured right, sweetheart. You people here in California sure know how to live."

Jarrup finished his drink and put on his jacket.

"It's going to be formal, is it?"

"It's always fucking formal with Milady Game."

"You have to admit it works. She gets more fan mail than Lassie gets condition powders."

"Fans don't ask for much. Just the last word in mediocrity."

"It's the fans that make the star. I quote David Jarrup, if my memory serves me right. A star doesn't have to be a great actress."

"I said that?" He looked incredulous. "It's ironical, ain't it?"

"Yeah. What?" Esther adjusted the Venetian blind to stop the late-afternoon sun from blinding Jarrup. "What's ironical?"

"The night Norma Talmadge retired. She dismissed a bunch of fans waiting for her outside a restaurant," he said. "The Vendome, I think it was. 'Go away,' she told them. 'I don't *need* you any more.' "

Esther smiled. She'd heard the story before.

"This tarantula," Jarrup said. "She doesn't even *wait* to retire. Already she's hanging crêpe on their noses."

"Is Mr. Omnibus about?"

Jarrup grinned. "Richard Antrobus," he said. "I hope so. She's easier when he's around. Not so feisty."

"Not such a cow, you mean."

"You said it, not me."

"What's his story?"

"Who the hell knows?"

"Aren't you interested?"

"Not especially."

"The breeze in the powder room—"

"Let me give you two bits' worth of advice, honeychild."

"Go ahead."

"First rule of Hollywood survival: Don't believe anything unless you've seen it with your own baby blues."

"Is that it? The lesson for today?"

"And if you see it with your own baby blues, keep your trap shut."

"I'm never sure whether you're being serious or not," Esther said.

"You fancy him?"

"Do I fancy him? A bit of an English pantywaist

but . . . yeah, I wouldn't kick him out of bed exactly."

"He seems to be well-heeled."

"Hers, you think?"

"The money? I don't think so. Louella says he's talking a deal with Paramount. Nothing to do with Milady."

"As what?"

"Producer."

"They'll eat him alive."

Jarrup shrugged. "He's tougher than he looks. They always are. Milady listens to him—and she ain't done so bad."

"Don't you think that Oscar was a bit of a fluke? You could spit out of the window and hit half a dozen actresses who could've done as well."

"Hush your mouth."

"No, seriously."

"She deserved it, but the timing didn't hurt none. Not much opposition, the town desperate for a new face . . . have I got time for another one?"

"I think I can warm up the ice cubes," Esther smiled. She took his empty glass and he followed her into the outer office.

"What d'you have to see her for?"

"*Life.*"

"You make it sound more like a sentence than an appointment."

"What's the difference?"

"What do they want this time? Let me guess. Hollywood's New Garbo? No, not that again. How about— The Elusive Game?"

"That's very good."

Esther polished her nails on her lapel and studied them admiringly.

"No, believe it or not, *Life* actually wants to do a piece on Hollywood's most eligible bachelor girl."

"Well, you know what they say. The old tunes are the best tunes. Will she do it?"

"Like fun."

Esther handed him his drink.

"You can only ask, I guess."

"I miss the days when stardom was pure exhibition-ism."

He smiled. It was the smile of a businessman having his margins squeezed.

"If there's one thing I don't hardly need now it's a hot, loaded, temperamental actress—erudite in five languages."

"Refusing to give out the time of day in any one of them."

"The trouble with building pedestals for actresses—they always end up pissing on you from a great height."

He swallowed his drink.

"And now, dear lady, I'm going to suck ass. A language everybody understands."

"Good luck," Esther said.

"The Elusive Game—that's very, very good. I might try to sell it to *Look*. The stars are golden fruit upon a tree, all out of reach. George Eliot."

"Wasn't that the guy who used to head up publicity at Fox?"

"I think that was two other fellas, sweetheart," Jarrup said, handing her the empty glass.

Georgina Game's dressing room was over on the West Pico side of the lot, next to the low white stucco-walled executive block. It had been built especially for her in Old English cottage style. It stood in a thicket of rhododendron and laurel with deep crimson Frensham roses around the front door. A picket fence enclosed a small front lawn.

Georgina was taking a shower when Jarrup got there. Her maid, Josephine, offered him a drink and he accepted. He knew it was a mistake but he was too emboldened by the first two bourbons to decline the third.

"Is Mr. Antrobus about?"

"Not yet, Mr. Jarrup. I believe Miss Georgina is expecting him though." The maid looked at her watch. It was a very good watch. "And I believe Mr. Rivkin is also expected to drop by after rushes."

"She's certainly the belle of the ball," Jarrup said.

"She's a very lovely lady," the maid said, giving him a hard look. "You're not going to rushes?"

"Not tonight, Josephine," Jarrup said. Gottfried

Rilke wouldn't let him into rushes if he offered to buy a ticket. Rushes, the director proclaimed, were sacred: he watched them with the cameraman, the producer, assistant director, film editor, and script girl. Sometimes a favored actor was also admitted. Georgina Game never watched her own rushes. It gave her complexes, she said.

"It's kinda warm in here, ain't it?" Jarrup said.

"Miss Georgina don't like no air conditioning," the maid said. "It's bad for her skin."

"It's like an oven in here."

"Depends what you're used to," Josephine said. Josephine was an old Hollywood hand. She belonged to that special breed of mechanics—secretaries, chauffeurs, hairdressers, photographers, gofers—trained in the art of salutary compromise. Never snipe the star, kid.

Georgina came into the living room about fifteen minutes later. She was wearing beige slacks and a white blouse. Her breasts swelled against the silk like soft ripe fruit.

"David," she said, holding out her hand.

"Miss Game," he said, putting down his glass and taking her hand to his lips. "I saw a French movie once," he said.

"You make me feel positively regal," she said.

"Your Majesty." Jarrup bowed low.

"Now I think you're after something."

"But a small request," he said.

She gave him the sort of smile that flickers on sleeping lips.

"Ah, a small request."

"A smidgen." Jarrup held up his thumb and forefinger barely apart. "A flea's instep."

He wanted to test the temperature a little more before plunging in. She seemed to be in a good mood, but you could never tell. It was the final week of the picture and people were saying she was even better than in *Danger East*. Biron Strauss, who had been given an option on fifty thousand shares of studio stock plus a five-year contract on the strength of *Danger East*'s returns, was offering three-to-one she would collect another Oscar nomination for *Babylon Is Burning*.

"Pour yourself a drink," she said.

"You?"

"No thanks."

It was a nice-sized drawing room, not much larger than a small ballroom, furnished by a man who'd won a couple of Oscars for his production designs. He'd cannibalized the dressing rooms of several English actors no longer on the lot. A deeply upholstered chesterfield and a writing table came from Ronnie Colman's old dressing room. A card table, a Georgian mirror, four tapestried armchairs, and an oil painting of Napoleon were taken from Rex Harrison's former suite. The yellow velvet draperies, carpets, the fireplace, and a Steinway concert grand came from Greer Garsons's bungalow. There were pewter mugs, brass lamps, a cabinet full of bone china, a large glass jar full of English barley sugar. Somehow it all worked. Georgina had added a few mementoes of her own—a snapshot of her parents, a painting of a favorite horse, a color photograph of herself and Richard Antrobus looking at each other through a racquet at the Beverly Hills Tennis Club.

Jarrup was pouring a bourbon when the front door began to chime like cheerful village church bells. Josephine admitted Gottfried Rilke. He was a small fat hard-looking man with a round shaven head and a thick beard. It gave him the uncanny appearance of having put his face on in a hurry and upside down. He advanced to the middle of the room and held out his arms toward Georgina. He shut his eyes and sighed deeply. He was always careful to hail a rising star.

"I come from rushes," he said finally. The careful California cadence didn't hide the Teutonic origins of his accent. "Darling tochter, I am in the presence of an actress of genius." He opened his small eyes and looked at her like a sly fat cat watching a mousehole. "I am going to tell you something now I should not tell you. Tonight I show the café scene to Bobby and Spence Tracy and, I tell you, baby, tonight you were magic. Everybody said you're the biggest thing to hit this town since the Santa Fe line. Spence said, 'You don't direct this girl. You just pour celluloid over her.' That's what Tracy said and, Jesus, tochter, he's a hard man to please. I made three pictures with that son of a bitch and I never heard him praise another actor yet."

Rilke crossed the large room and hugged Georgina. She stood stiffly in his arms.

"I know I give you a hard time on the set. I know that. Ten, twenty takes. But I know what's inside you. Greatness is inside you. I make you sweat. I make you ache. I make you weep. But I promise you I give you Oscar to bite on to ease the pain."

He unclasped her and stood back.

"I'm pleased you're happy," Georgina said simply.

"I like a *still* actress," Rilke changed gear. "I don't like busy-busy actresses. Tracy said the same thing. With a still actress—you see what's in the eye, what's in their head. You know what's happening inside of them. Discipline, you have discipline, sweetie."

"What did Rivkin say?" Georgina asked with cool interest, unswayed by Rilke's gushing praises. She knew he was probably only trying to soften her up to do his next picture with Tracy.

Rilke helped himself to a handful of pistachio nuts from a bowl on the coffee table. "He says the picture'll play like Paderewski. It'll outgross *Danger East* by—"

"What would you like to drink, Gottfried?" Georgina asked quickly. She disliked the fierce immoderation of box-office speculation.

"Thank you. Just a ginger ale."

"Would you be a dear, David?"

Jarrup fixed the drink and handed it to the director.

"Jarrup," Rilke acknowledged him for the first time. "This girl you handle different. She's not like the others. No pin-ups—I want the audience to use their imaginations," he said sharply.

"Mr. Rilke, we've always handled Miss Game with dignity," Jarrup said. "She's not the sort of actress who has to live off her divestments."

Rilke looked grim. His last picture had starred Jane Russell whose famous cleavage plunged almost as breathtakingly as the box-office returns.

"*Time, Newsweek, Look, Life* magazine," Jarrup went on in a quiet, telling voice. "New York *Times,* the

London *Times* . . . Miss Game gets the best. Nobody gets near her who can't spell Eisenstein."

"I guess that cuts out most of the publicity department," Rilke said.

Jarrup shrugged and smiled. "The movie business is full of people who know all about publicity."

"Just you make sure they can also spell Rilke," the director said. His small face had turned dark. He put his unfinished glass of ginger ale on the Steinway. He paused to examine the portrait of Napoleon for a moment. He wondered whether he could buy it from props.

"I won't need you till eleven-thirty in the morning, little one," he said, turning to Georgina. He kissed her on both cheeks. "We shoot you coming out the bank—where you see Errol getting into the cab across the street with the girl."

"An eleven-thirty call and no dialogue to learn," Georgina said. "Heaven."

"But made up and on the set eleven-thirty, pretty and pronto, yes?"

"Yes, sir." Georgina stood back and saluted.

"He's not so bad," Georgina said when Rilke had gone. "He has his moments of megalomania but he can be v. amusing."

"He's about as amusing as a hole in the heart."

"But he *is* a good director."

"There sure as hell's nothing wrong with his directing," Jarrup said.

"He sometimes rubs people up the wrong way."

"He wants a finger in every pie."

"Every pie except the humble ones," Georgina said.

Jarrup smiled. He suddenly felt easier. "Yeah, well—trouble with being a press agent is that everybody thinks they know your business better than you do."

"And the trouble with the cinema business—" Georgina began.

"Don't call it the cine*mar*. This is Hollywood, kid," Jarrup said in a fake tough voice. "The movie racket, see, not the cine*mar*. Call it the cine*mar* and people get confused and start talking about *art*. And art's murder on a press agent's column inches."

Georgina laughed.

"Okay, kiddo, whaddya want?" she said out of the side of her mouth, picking up Jarrup's crude conspiratorial tone. "But no bathing suits and no lingerie, see."

Jarrup outlined, as carefully as he could, *Life*'s idea.

"Jesus H. Christ, David," she said when he had finished.

"I already told them no," he lied smoothly.

"I should hope so, too." The earlier humor had gone out of her voice. To Jarrup's American ear, she now sounded almost prissy. It was a weakness of hers. She had spent a month in dubbing getting rid of the prissy bits in *Danger East*. She learned fast. Her voice was an octave lower now and, most of the time, without any trace of Mayfair.

"But I do have another idea," Jarrup went on in a reflective way. *"Life* magazine is keen to do a piece on you. We just have to make sure it's the right piece, a good piece, at the right time. A big break just before the picture opens in New York—"

"Get to the idea, David. Don't bullshit on your own doorstep."

"Well, it's *just* an idea at this stage. We can always have second and more sober thoughts if it isn't quite right," he said cautiously. His instinct for survival grew stronger as he grew older. He wanted all the room he could get to duck out of trouble if the idea didn't meet with her approval. "I was thinking—a feature called The Elusive Game. There's a very good George Eliot line they could peg it to: *The stars are golden fruit upon a tree, all out of reach . . .*"

Georgina looked at him for a long moment, saying nothing. He was a very surprising man, she thought.

"It has a touch of class," he said. "The sort of thing *Life* goes for . . ."

"I think even Mr. Rilke would have to approve of George Eliot," she said, smiling faintly.

"The beauty of it is," Jarrup said with a little more confidence. "You'd hardly need be troubled at all. Plenty of long-lens shots—coming out of Tiffany's, walking alone on the beach, musing in the woods, going to church, a lot of production stuff, naturally . . .

studying your script on the set, surrounded yet alone. That sort of . . . *feeling. Mood* pictures, capturing a whole atmosphere . . . an *aura.* The idea is to show the essential *aloneness* of Georgina Game."

"Well—"

"We'd get picture approval, a guaranteed publication date," Jarrup hurried on. "A day's work is all we're talking about. A million dollars' worth of publicity—minimum."

"I'm not sure about Tiffany's. Isn't that rather obvious?"

"Tiffany's. Cartier. I. Magnin. Teitelbaum. The supermarket, a Thrifty Drugstore. It doesn't matter. The idea is that you are *alone,* a solitary star, unrecognized . . . people pass you on the street and don't recognize you because you are a *very private person.* You are your own woman. You choose to live your private life unseen."

Jarrup was pulling them out of the air now.

"One day, you say?"

"Cross my heart," he said, crossing his heart. "See, it's not just a picture spread. It's not just one magazine layout. We're encapsulating an entire philosophy. The essential you—the star, the golden fruit, out of reach. The Elusive Game. It's an irresistible idea. *Life*'ll love it. It's beautiful. Perfect. It'll be picked up everywhere."

Jarrup was really flying now. He suddenly knew, he just *knew*, how to handle her. Play along with her reticence. *Use* her reserve.

Jarrup went on for about ten minutes, elaborating the idea. Georgina listened, she didn't try to interrupt.

Finally he stopped and studied Georgina for a long serious moment. He knew he had her hooked now. "I've given this a great deal of thought," he said somberly. "If you agree, it'll be the basis—the major thrust—of our postproduction campaign. I know it's been a very hard picture to shoot and I've purposely kept out of your hair, kept publicity requests to an absolute minimum. But we're going to need one big one in the bag and I really do believe this is it. Give me this one and I got it all covered."

"We could shoot the beach stuff at Santa Barbara

next weekend, if you like," Georgina said, making up her mind. It suited her perfectly.

"Terrific," Jarrup said. "And there has to be a little church up there someplace we could use."

"There's one very pretty one. *Tiny*. They actually have sheep in the churchyard."

"Sheep!"

"I thought you'd like that, Mr. Jarrup. After all, aren't you dealing in wool a little bit yourself?"

Dave Jarrup was halfway across Coldwater Canyon when he realized that he had stopped hating Georgina Game, and started loving her.

Almost.

32

At seven-thirty in the morning, Leon Kun was summoned to Stosch's office. Stosch continued to study the papers on his desk with a fixed stare. There was something about the product that puzzled him. He woke up that morning with the idea that there was something wrong. It went around and around, seeking outlet, expression, in the circuits of his mind. But what could it be? The product was interesting but not especially revelatory. It added little to other reports on the same woman, except . . . except what?

Although more personal, Liz Huntington's product lacked subtlety. It was a no-nonsense catalogue of facts, figures, friends and lovers. There was some mildly mischievous gossip, a reference to a numbered account in Zurich that would cause Georgina Game a great deal of trouble if the revenue people in London were to get wind of it. There were a couple of risqué anecdotes that had also turned up in one other product, and reference to an affair with an unnamed English politician which was new, but of no real interest.

No, there was something else. He had a sixth sense about these things.

Leon Kun stood silently in front of Stosch's desk, a faint look of consternation on his pale smooth face.

"Leon?" Stosch looked up, as if noticing the little bald finance controller for the first time.

"Yes sir?"

Stosch closed the report and tossed it to Kun's side of the large desk. "Read that, please."

Kun opened the report and began to read carefully, still standing up, turning over the pages quickly and quietly. When he had finished he closed the report and carefully placed it back in front of Stosch.

"It's—it's very interesting," he said in a voice that couldn't settle on a precise tone.

"You think so? Why?" Stosch said coldly.

"It—" Kun looked uneasy. "It seems straightforward enough."

"I read it last night. I woke up worrying about it. Nothing strikes you as . . . odd?"

"Odd?"

"Something in there worries me, Leon. What is it that worries me?"

Kun leaned across the desk and retrieved the report and began to read it again.

"Take it away, Leon," Stosch said. "Study it. Think about it."

"Yes, Dieter. I'll—"

"I'm lunching aboard the *Grunden Tief*. Join me at one-thirty."

"Thank you, sir." His voice had the grateful sound of a rewarded hero-worshiper.

"Leon."

"Controller?"

"It's in there somewhere. Find it."

Leon Kun was puzzled, and worried. There was nothing. He was beginning to wonder if Dieter Stosch's remarkable intuition had finally let him down. It happens, he told himself. It had to happen sometime. Kun

had read Liz Huntington's product five or six times and
found nothing disturbing, nothing out of the ordinary.
He continued to stare at the closely typed pages in an
uncomfortable frame of mind. Stosch's interest and favor meant everything to him. He rubbed his soft hand
across his soft face: it was a face that carried no history
at all—no scars, no rebuffs, no regrets, no sense of success or failure. It was a face that never tanned in the
sun, nor grew paler in winter. "He looks," Edouard Casenave said once, "like an unoccupied Hilton bedroom."

Kun was just about to close the report when the
name hit him. His pale, almost invisible eyebrows suddenly lifted. Of course. One name buried among so
many. Of course. A thin smile skittered across the shiny
blank eyes. Although of no great significance in itself,
that name, wedged between those particular dates—that
was the key. The reason for Dieter Stosch's instinctive
concern.

Kun buzzed Registry. He ordered up files, tran-
scripts, product. He called the Casino Records Office
and specified ledgers and returns. He sent for the Bureau's bound files of English and French newspapers,
going back over the last eighteen months. He locked
himself in his office. He told his secretary nobody, except Dieter Stosch, was to disturb him. Then slowly,
methodically, mouth pursed, Leon Kun went to work.
He worked for a long time and his expression did not
change. A man of imperturbable dedication, unani-
mated by Stosch's intuitive brilliance, he patiently built
his dossier, his proof. He ignored nothing, however
seemingly insignificant. He followed his standard con-
sectary technique, assembling his evidence from double-
checked facts and unimpeachable sources, constantly
testing it, exemplifying and changing it as new information came to light. He applied himself assiduously, with
all his ponderous skill and patience, to the task. He was
factual to the point of finickiness.

It wasn't surprising that the name hadn't come to
light inside the Bureau before in connection with this
particular episode, he thought as the picture began to
emerge.

Laundering was a common practice in most casinos

around the world. But for obvious reasons, only the briefest, most basic details were ever released to the Bureau for circulation in the SS Memorandum. It was always useful to know how much hot money was on the market—it naturally affected the "interest" a casino charged—so most casinos played along. To a point. The laundry business was more discreetly called Exchange Marketing Progression Studies, or EMPS, in the Memorandum. Used in conjunction with information supplied from sources other than management—croupiers, pit bosses, accountants—the EMPS gave the Bureau a fairly accurate picture of any given casino's laundering operation, including details of the currency being cleaned—and the rate charged for the service.

Kun, with almost an air of mysticism, burrowed on. He drew up a list of seventeen casinos that filed EMPS during those weeks. Then he checked them against the names appearing on the separate situation reports that casino security officers file every five days: a list of clients whose movements casinos like to keep a particular eye on—high rollers, crooks, celebrities, big-time whores, and anyone who has ever been the subject of a Red Alert.

Thirteen of the seventeen casinos which returned EMPS during the weeks examined that morning by Leon Kun also reported the presence of the same man. . . .

Leon Kun boarded the *Grunden Tief II* with a few minutes to spare before his one-thirty lunch appointment with Dieter Stosch. He went straight down to the saloon.

"It's the Englishman Richard Antrobus—your fingerspitzengefuhl," Kun said, placing his completed file on the long teak table.

The two men were alone in the saloon. Stosch picked up the file and opened it with no air of surprise, or satisfaction.

"The product mentions the upturn in his fortunes starting last—" Kun began.

"I remember," Stosch said. He handed the file back to Kun. "Summarize."

"Seventeen months ago, a massive swindle was perpetrated on about a dozen branches of an English bank."

"I remember."

"Two hundred thousand pounds of that money—the numbers were known and circulated by Interpol."

"Go on."

"Before the massive defalcations were discovered," Kun continued in his fastidious way, "a number of deals were completed with member casinos—"

"Laundry deals?"

"Yes, sir."

"Richard Antrobus?"

"Yes, sir."

"No doubts?"

"None." Kun consulted the file. "He also settled his Deauville marker. With money laundered in casinos in Belgium and Italy."

"Continue."

Kun consulted his file and gave dates, places, amounts, batches of serial numbers, and the rates charged by each of the thirteen casinos that laundered substantial sums of sterling shortly after the London job. He also named three illegal operations in Portugal and Switzerland which plunged heavily into the laundry business at that time.

"Altogether he cleaned four hundred and twenty thousand pounds," Kun said, looking up from the file.

"All in Europe?"

"I concentrated the search in Europe," Kun said in a hurt voice with which Stosch was familiar. "The time factor—"

"His take on that would be?"

"Two hundred and sixty-four thousand six hundred pounds."

"They charged him dearly."

"One hundred and fifty-five thousand four hundred pounds," Kun said at once. "An average of thirty-seven percent."

Stosch could not help smiling.

"According to Scotland Yard sources, the total amount stolen was a little over seven hundred and fifty thousand pounds," Kun continued. "Antrobus is presumably still sitting on the rest."

"Waiting for laundry prices to come down," Stosch said. "Who can blame him?" As he talked, he picked up the telephone and asked for Genevieve Lacroix. A few moments later he said:

"Mlle. Lacroix. An Englishman named Richard Antrobus appears in the Game product. We already have a thorough Red Alert file on him but I want the answer to one question: who does he know in banking circles?"

He put down the telephone and smiled at Kun.

"Thank you, Leon," he said. "You have done well. Are you hungry?"

33

" 'ere, I dun 'alf fancy you," Georgina Game said in a very good cockney accent.

"You's a bit tasty yerself, missus," Richard Antrobus answered in the same tone, but not quite so accomplished.

"D'yer loves me then?"

"I fucks yer, dun I?"

They stood by the pool. They could see the city of Los Angeles spread out below them, beginning to sparkle in the evening light. A small breeze came from the west, from off the ocean. Their profiles were silhouetted almost black against the setting sun. Their heads leaned in toward each other.

"What time is dinner, darling?" Antrobus said. He kissed her forehead.

"I said we'd pick Liz up at about eight-thirty. I've booked a table at Romanoff's for nine."

"*Romanoff*'s? You *hate* Romanoff's." He stood back a step and stared at her incredulously.

"I thought Liz would enjoy a taste of Early Hollywood Awful," Georgina said. "It's her first time out here, darling."

"Is Bobby Rivkin joining us?"

"Later."

"The later the better."

"He isn't so bad. There are a lot worse."

He moved toward her again. They stood close together for a long time, talking in low intimate voices, enjoying the animal comfort of each other's body warmth. It had become a small ritual in their day, when they returned from the studios. Occasionally they went to bed for an hour, but mostly they walked to the end of the long terrace above the pool, above the city, and talked about their day.

Suddenly an absolute silence settled on the garden. The automatic sprinklers had stopped turning, stopped their swishing sound.

They noticed the sudden silence at the same time and smiled.

"Civilization as we know it has just ended," Antrobus said in a *March of Time* voice.

"The earth smells so . . . so new, doesn't it?" Georgina said. "I love the smell of fresh wet earth. It reminds me of England."

"I mentioned the new sprinkler system this morning at the studio," he said. "It was a *terrible* mistake."

"Don't tell me! Let me guess! It's unlucky to mention sprinklers inside a studio? Like an actor actually saying the name of *that* play—"

"*Macbeth*," said Antrobus, who thought that was a silly nonsense.

"—or whistling in a dressing room," Georgina went on. "It's an old Hollywood superstition?"

"Not yet—but I think it's going to be. The moment I mentioned it, naturally Dore Blomberg wanted one installed in his backyard. His backyard, as he calls it, has a nine-hole golf course, would you believe? Had no idea what I was starting, did I? The whole day was just about taken up with the great sprinkler crisis. He went apeshit because it was to be shipped from Pennsylvania or some such place and can't be delivered for a couple of weeks. Even for the great Dore Blomberg!"

"Such deprivation." Georgina sighed an exaggerated sigh.

"He had that poor little English queen Bryan Foulis, his personal executive aide, in tears."

"Chewing the Bigelow on the floor."

"But in front of everybody, darling. It was grotesque. What was so strange was how everybody just sat there, looking on, as if they were watching a play. I almost expected them to stand up and applaud at the end of it all."

"I suppose you would need to have lived in courts to really comprehend Hollywood. I mean, to understand how an insignificant remark—like *sprinklers*, for God's sake!—can blow up into such a how-do-you-do."

"Kings and studio moguls . . . they can only vent their displeasure before an audience, perhaps," Antrobus said. "Does Bobby Rivkin carry on like that?"

"I haven't seen it. If he did in front of me, I'd be out of that studio like a shot."

They turned away from the view of Los Angeles and made their way slowly back toward the big pink house the studio had rented for Georgina. It was a very old house by Hollywood standards, built in Italian Renaissance style in 1920 by Theda Bara. Her famous line— or, rather, subtitle—"Kiss me, my fool" was still carved in the tall iron gates that led into the palatial gardens on the south side of the house. The beautifully tended lawns were protected against the occasional mild California breeze by windbreaks of cypress and cedar trees and beautiful live oaks with dark dense glossy egg-shaped leaves that never lost their color.

"It's a beautiful evening," Georgina said. "I like the way California evenings sort of . . . dwindle into warm nights."

"Where are the snows of yesteryear?" Antrobus smiled. He wrapped his arm around her shoulders and kissed the top of her head.

Georgina walked on for a few paces then suddenly stopped and turned and snarled scornfully:

"Kiss me, my fool!"

"I'd much rather lay you right now, if it's all the same to you."

"Oh, all right, you sweet-talking bastard," she said. There was contented capitulation in her voice.

They kissed, open-mouthed, lingeringly.

"You always were a pushover," Antrobus said when they broke free. "With a bit of the old chat."

"Do you remember that first lunch, at Liz's?"

They continued to walk slowly along the terrace. Georgina put her arm through his.

"*And* the afternoon."

"God, the afternoon! Will I ever forget the afternoon! I thought you'd never stop!"

"Me!"

"Yes, *you!* You dirty dog! Your breath smelled of red wine."

"And you weren't sure whether you wanted to see me again," Antrobus smirked.

"Oh I wanted to see you again—I just wasn't sure whether it was very wise. And don't smirk."

"And now?"

"The jury's still out."

"Fink-face. I was just beginning to feel confident." She stopped again and brushed her fingers lightly against his crotch.

"You still feel confident enough to me, sir."

"Unhand me, madam!"

"You have a hot-weather crotch. Has anybody ever told you you have a hot-weather crotch before, Antrobus?"

"Probably."

"Are you happy, darling?"

"Yes."

The lights inside the house went on, followed by the pool lights.

"You know," Georgina said as they continued their stroll back to the house. "I'd like to buy Liz something special while she's here. What shall I get her?"

"How about a bridesmaid's dress?" Antrobus said. There was something in his voice that hadn't been

there a moment ago—a nervousness perhaps, an un-
quiet. .

Georgina stopped and looked up at him.

"Darling?" she said softly. She wasn't sure.

"I'm . . . I mean it, Georgina," he said. "Let's do
it. We could fly to Vegas next weekend or—"

"Richard, darling darling Richard, I do love you."

"Then you'll marry me?"

They stood facing each other, their faces inches
apart. He held her hands light and close to her side. In
that moment everything stood still.

"Yes, I rather think I will," she said at last.

Then very softly, very deeply, she began to cry.

Richard held her tightly in his arms.

"Oh, Christ," he said quietly over and over. "Oh,
Christ." He sounded relieved and surprised and
strangely remote.

They went into the house.

"I must fix my face," Georgina said.

When she came back into the large paneled oak
drawing room, Richard had already opened a bottle of
champagne. He handed her a glass.

"To the next Mrs. Richard Antrobus," he said.

"Don't make it sound like a bloody production line,"
she said with a feigned air of magnanimous tolerance.
She still looked slightly shattered in a joyous sort of
way.

"To us," she said.

"To our future—together."

They drank the toast.

"How do you feel, Miss Game?"

"It's . . . it's all slightly unreal, like a dream, drinking a toast to our engagement, our future, in Theda
Bara's old mansion . . . in Hollywood. I mean, it's all
a bit . . . *ghostly,*" she said abstractedly in a quiet
voice.

"Ghostly!" he said indignantly.

"*Haunting. Romantically* haunting," she said quickly
with more conviction. "I *love* it."

He smiled.

"Now I have some news for you," he said. "A surprise."

"Make it a very small one please. I don't think I'm up to taking any more—"

"I clinched the Paramount deal. This afternoon."

"You didn't!"

"Yes I did." He spoke slowly, putting little pauses between each word, the way they read the news on the BBC World Service.

"Darling!"

"Isn't that good?"

"Good? Good? It's marvelous. Oh, darling, I'm so proud of you. I'm so . . . *proud* of you."

"Well, you can take a bow or two yourself, you know."

"Me? Why me? You did it, darling."

"You told me you had no intention of marrying a bum, so—"

"I said no such thing, Antrobus."

"Huh!"

"Anyway, who found the property? And developed it?"

"The amazing thing is," he said. "I find it truly hard to look modest. How does one look suitably modest, Georgina? I must work on my shy boyish smile."

"Sweetheart, listen. Be serious. When do you go? Who've you got? Who'll direct?"

Antrobus finished his drink and held up his left hand. "One." He bent back the pinkie with his right index finger. "I'll be executive producer, whatever that means.

"Two." He smacked his ring finger. "The studio'll put in a producer to watch over the day-to-day stuff—a sort of glorified production manager, according to Dore Blomberg. But it'll be my baby. I'll be calling the shots, as they say in the trade.

"Three." he moved on to his middle finger and held it. "They want William Holden. He's not completely what I had in mind for Coburn but apparently he's got a commitment to Paramount, so—"

Antrobus shrugged. Then he grinned. "I feel quite light-headed."

"He's not really old enough to play Coburn, is he? But he's a marvelous actor. And good box office."

"That's what Blomberg keeps telling me. He has an extremely glossy face—"

"Blomberg?"

"Blomberg. With those spaniel-wet eyes—with those ready tears of really bad actors. Actually, he could easily have been an actor. He has the vague age of an actor who has faded too soon."

"And four?" Georgina pressed on.

"And four—probably George Seaton to direct. He's got the script now. We'll know in a couple of days. He's worked with Holden before. A picture called *Apartment for Peggy—Apartment for Peggy?*"

"I don't know," Georgina said, smiling. She put down her glass and slowly hugged him.

"I knew it. I knew it. I knew it. You'll be another Irving Thalberg!"

"Irving *who?*"

"Oh, darling, I'm so happy. I'll help you. It'll be my turn to help you. You will let me?"

"Let you? My darling child, I'm depending on it."

"Tell me exactly what happened today. Who was at the meeting? What did you say? Begin at the beginning. I want to know everything."

The butler, a small Hungarian improbably named Cholmeley, arrived with a bowl of cracked crab and placed it on the malachite table in front of the hand-hewn Egyptian granite fireplace. "A little *hors d'oeuvre* with the champagne," he said in a grave murmur. He silently refilled the glasses and left.

Antrobus went over the details of the deal. He told her about the jokes that were recited, the terrible suggestions that were made, he mimicked Blomberg's pompous philosophies ("he rules with iron platitudes: *Go over budget, what does it matter if you gotta grosser? Come in a million under and the picture's a pizzicato—ya come outta the small end of the horn*"), he told her about the brilliant impractical idea, the incredible misunderstandings. . . .

Georgina sat on the sofa and rested her elbows on her knees. The tips of her fingers made small floating circles on her temples. She looked amused, alarmed, concerned, stunned; she laughed, listened silently, nodded wisely, didn't interrupt. She had never seen Antrobus so completely happy, so completely *involved*.

"You handled it just right," she said when he had finished. "Did you wear that suit?"

"Yes." He looked mildly surprised at the question.

"Good. English tailoring. It impresses men like Dore Blomberg. You know they judge everything by weight out here. The weight of the worsted, the weight of an actress, the weight of a script. I swear to God. These people!"

"Us limeys have got to stick together, right?"

"Now?" said Georgina.

"We haven't got time."

"A quickie. To celebrate."

34

They arrived at Romanoff's at nine-thirty but there was no difficulty about the table, although groups of people were milling at the bar, waiting to be seated. They were given the second booth from the left, just off the main entrance. It was Humphrey Bogart's favorite table and, naturally, in Hollywood's caste seating system, was recognized as the best in the restaurant.

Bobby Rivkin got away from the studio earlier than he'd expected. He sat on the left of the semicircular booth next to Georgina. Antrobus sat on the right with Liz on his left-hand side. The headwaiter stood at the front of the table, smiling, with two waiters in support, also smiling. The people at the bar, and those in the other booths who had to crane their necks to do so, concentrated their attention on Georgina. She was the hottest lady in the business and she wasn't seen on the town that often.

"I'll have my usual," Rivkin said. "And Miss Game will have?"

"Orange juice, please."

"Miss Huntington?"

"An Americano," she said.

"Richard? What's your poison?"

"A very dry Martini straight up," he said, to Georgina's surprise.

The headwaiter went away, followed by his entourage.

"Georgie Jessel said a man could bring his wife and kids here and have a really very pleasant meal for less than two thousand dollars," Rivkin said to Liz.

"Who's Georgie Jessel?" Liz said.

"A comic," Rivkin said with a small surprised grin. He was a dark good-looking man with an aquiline nose, a high still smooth forehead, and wistful eyes when he wanted, which he happened to now. Liz had met him in London just when he was getting out of his second marriage.

After the drinks arrived, Georgina said to Antrobus: "Shall I tell them, or will you?"

"You," Antrobus said.

"Okay. Richard and I are getting married."

"Darling!" Liz's napkin flew out of her hands into the air like a frightened bird.

"Shhh!" Georgina said. "We don't want the world to know."

"Hey, congratulations, you guys," Rivkin said. Then, "Have you told Louella?"

"No we haven't," Georgina said firmly. "And we're not going to—and neither is the studio."

Rivkin leaned back in his seat and raised his hands in surrender. "Okay, okay, okay. A joke. I wish to hell I hadn't made it." He grinned. It was a devastating grin with a lot of teeth and a lot more charm.

"When?" Liz asked in a low voice, full of suppressed excitement.

"The picture finishes next week. We thought days to Mexico, or Vegas or maybe Nassau, for if you're free?"

"If *I'm* free?!"

320   *Peter Evans*

"I'm going to need a maid of honor."

"We'll be free," Rivkin said, rowing himself in.

"We've just got to sort out the tax situation," Antrobus said. "Where we do it can make a lot of difference later on, to both of us."

"Richard's doing a picture for Paramount," Georgina said, turning to him proudly.

"Oh Christ! It's all too much," Liz said. "Everything's happening at once."

"Congratulations again," Rivkin said. "But you should have brought it to us."

"I didn't want it to look as if it had anything to do with Georgina," Antrobus told him. "I didn't want people to think I was using her to——"

"Screw what people think," Rivkin said. "I'd have given you a better deal than Blomberg."

"Thanks. I'll remember next time."

Rivkin leaned across the table and patted Antrobus's hand.

"It's a tough business, kid. You're diving in at the deep end. I don't envy you. I came up through the ranks, so——"

"Just how do you learn to be a mogul, Bobby?" Georgina asked with wicked solemnity.

Rivkin took the question seriously.

"Well, I started out with L.B., as you know. My title then was executive assistant. In the old days I guess the word would have been valet. I was his majordomo, his deckhand, chief cook and bottle washer, half friend, half servant. In the old days I'd have been the poor schmo, the guy with the round haircut who slept on straw at the foot of the great man's bed, the schmuck who carried his *billets-doux*, who shined his boots, punched his pillows, who rode by his stirrup in battle, who nursed him in sickness and lied and perjured myself to hell to support whatever he wanted. . . . I tell you, I learned everything I know from L.B."

There was a small silence when he'd finished. Antrobus admired his head in a gesture that could have been wonderment, anything. He didn't look at Georgina.

In the next booth a man with a loud gravelly complaining voice was saying:

"He'll wind up borvis, the bum. I tell ya, I did a movie with Gable, a sweet man, I gotta Utrillo. I did a movie with Peck, I gotta Utrecht. I did a movie with that son of a bitch, all I got was an ulcer. Jimmy Dean? I couldn't look ya in the face again if I unloaded that little squirt on ya. . . ."

"What's *borvis*?" Georgina whispered to Rivkin.

"Barefoot," Rivkin said.

"Oh."

"Well, you finally did it," Liz said. "You're finally going to take the plunge." She kissed Georgina gently on the cheek.

"You next," Georgina said.

"It's not for me. For *you*, it's great—"

"C'mon now," Rivkin said.

"Well, to tell you the truth . . . I haven't had that many offers lately!"

"Lately—like in ten days," Rivkin said.

"Ah but there was a time," Liz said in a voice brimming over with nostalgia and lament. "Rejected suitors fell like autumn leaves at my feet."

"It's all true, it's all true," Georgina said, picking up the same sighing satirical tone.

"Jesus," Antrobus said. "Bring on the fiddlers."

Liz pretended to look hurt.

"I lie not, sir. Once, I was afraid to open the *Times* for fear of seeing the announcements of their suicides." She changed her tone and grinned. "Usually all I ever saw were photographs of their weddings. Oh, I tell you . . . one day I'm going to publish an anthology of all their heartbroken farewell letters. It'll put Art Buchwald in the shade—not to mention Mr. Messel."

"Jessel," said Rivkin.

Between courses, an elegantly dressed man with close-cut gray hair and a wide tumorous nose came to their table.

"It's good to see you, Bobby," he said to Rivkin.

"Prince Romanoff—I'd like you to meet Miss Georgina Game."

"Welcome," Romanoff said, bowing slightly and, as

he did so, smacking the side of his black trousers with
an alligator riding crop.

Rivkin made the introductions.

"*Prince* Romanoff," Liz said when the restaurateur
had gone. *"Prince?"*

"Why not? If he wants to be," Rivkin said. "In a
town of great pretenders why be plain Harry Gerguson
from Brooklyn if you can be a Russian prince from
Ashkhabad? Do you know, he actually sends his shirts
to Sulka's in New York to be cleaned?"

"I should think," Georgina said, "*that* is more likely
to make a man a pauper than a prince."

"Pongee shirts," said Rivkin, who noticed things like
that.

During the evening, several people dropped by the
table to say hello to Rivkin, and be introduced to Georgina. Jerry Wald, a producer at Fox, came and told
them a long story about somebody called Sid Grauman
that wasn't very funny because nobody except Rivkin
had any idea who Sid Grauman was.

"Grauman's *Chinese*," Rivkin said afterward.

"It doesn't sound Chinese to me," Liz said.

"Grauman's Chinese *Theatre*," Rivkin said. "On
Hollywood Boulevard."

A journalist with a weak chin and a weak mouth
shaded by a heavy moustache came over and made a
fuss over Rivkin but kept looking at Georgina. Rivkin
didn't introduce him to anyone.

Coop came over and made a big impression on Liz
with his shy shit-kicking grin. Rivkin called some people *sweetie*, and some people *doll*, and others *kid* and
honey. But he called Coop *Mr. Cooper*.

"Now that man *is* a star," Georgina said when he had
gone.

"So are you, kid," Rivkin said.

"I don't know . . . when you meet a man like that
. . . a legend like that . . . *star* seems to be just a
word assumed as a sort of gratuitous title by most other
actors," Georgina said.

"It casts a narcissistic radiance over their basic lack
of talent," Antrobus said.

"In a lot of cases the word star is unjustified," Rivkin

said slowly. "But audiences tend to take actors at their own valuation—"

"Like 'learned' lawyers and 'gentlemen' of the press."

"And 'ladies' of easy virtue," put in Liz.

"Absolutely," Georgina said. "And 'ladies' of easy virtue."

"Something like that," Rivkin said. "Unfortunately, after a time, producers get suckered in, too. They start believing that a lot of very ordinary actors are stars— and up go the prices."

He looked at his watch. "It's ten after eleven," he said, straightening his back.

Antrobus looked around for a waiter to pay the check.

"It's done," Rivkin said.

"Well, thank you, Bob—but we invited you—"

"It was my pleasure."

"Thank you again."

"There's just one more thing I wish you two guys'd let me do for you," Rivkin said, looking straight at Georgina. His voice took on a sudden tone of paternal gravity. "I'd like the studio to pick up the tab for the wedding. Give you a bit of a send—"

"Thanks," Georgina said quickly. "But no thanks, Bobby. No jamboree, no bean feast—"

"I wasn't suggesting—"

"The studio gets involved, straight away, whether we like it or not, we're into plugging the picture, setting up—"

"I don't think that necessarily follows—"

"*No,* Bobby."

"You're the star," he said reluctantly.

"And promise me one thing . . . no leaks."

"The Rivkins have never been wanting to their word," he said in a strangely old-fashioned way. He offered Georgina his hand.

"I think you should tell Dave Jarrup though," he said as an afterthought as they shook on it.

"Jarrup? What the hell for?"

"Because when this story does break, the press'll be down on him like a ton of bricks. Why didn't he tip them off? Where are you? When will you talk? Where are the pictures? The poor s.o.b. . . . those vultures'll beat the can off of him."

Georgina hesitated.

"He's a nice man, Jarrup," she said, touching Antrobus' cheek with the palm of her hand. "I think we can trust him."

"You're gonna need him at some point," Rivkin pointed out. "A real helluva nice guy."

"I'm a stranger here," Antrobus said. "Do whatever's best. If he can keep them off our backs, that's fine with me."

"Okay, we tell him—but not until we're ready to leave. Is that reasonable?"

Rivkin considered for a moment. "I'd say so," he said. "But I have to tell you kids now. It's the hardest thing in the world to keep a secret in this town. You better believe it. Four people already know—right? It's a heavy responsibility on Liz and me. It gets out—who do you immediately suspect? Me? Liz? You'd be wrong. Do you know who first told me that Libby was divorcing me? The pool man. The fucking guy who comes twice a week to clean my pool. He said he was sorry to hear the news. 'What news?' I said. I didn't know, I swear to God." He grinned. "And, shit man, Libby, she didn't even swim."

Nobody laughed. Georgina looked at Antrobus. Liz opened her purse, looked inside, and closed it again.

Rivkin said, "All I'm saying is that very soon, if not already, servants, telephone operators, taxi drivers, waiters with big ears—a lot of people are gonna know, others are gonna suspect. A lotta people in this town get paid a lotta money to find out these things. I mean, a *lotta* money."

"Let's change the subject, shall we?" Liz said. She looked pale. "This is very depressing."

"Are you all right, Liz?" Georgina asked. She looked concerned.

"Yes. The flight's just catching up with me, that's all." She made a quick calculation. "Do you know it's half past seven in the morning in London."

"Let's go, gang," Rivkin said.

They'd come in their own cars. Rivkin and Liz in his

Cadillac; the others in a Rolls. They said their good-nights on the sidewalk outside the restaurant with lots of hugs and kisses.

"Good luck with your picture," Rivkin said, gripping Antrobus by the hand. "And take care of my little girl."

"Didn't you think Liz was . . . I don't know . . . rather *distant* tonight?" Georgina asked as they drove back to the mansion in Coldwater Canyon.

"Distant? No, she seemed fine to me. She was very happy about us."

"Oh, I think she was happy about us," she said. "There was just something . . ."

"She was just tired."

"I hope that's all it was."

Georgina was silent for a long time. The chauffeur turned off Sunset at the Beverly Hills Hotel. Georgina didn't speak until they began the climb up Coldwater.

"It's not true that actors change when they become famous. They're just the same," she said quietly. "The people around them change. Their attitudes—"

"You imagine it."

"In little ways," she said. "They change. In little ways. It's sad."

Rivkin dropped Liz at the Beverly Wilshire. He walked her to the elevator. "I won't come up," he said. "You're beat and I've got a seven-thirty start."

He kissed her on her lips without forcing anything.

"Take my advice. Take a tablet, switch off the phones till lunchtime. I'll call you at twelve."

"Yes, teacher," Liz said. "I'm sorry I'm so whacked."

"Just get a good night's sleep. I'll call you at twelve."

He stood smiling at her until the attendant closed the elevator doors. Then he turned and walked swiftly through the lobby to the drugstore. He bought all the papers and ordered a coffee and sat at the counter and read the headlines. He always saved the columns till the morning.

He drove home slowly, thinking about Georgina Game's next movie. Game and Tracy, he thought. The

idea pleased him. Then he thought about Antrobus. He
hoped he wasn't going to be a problem. Husbands, especially *new* husbands, usually were. But . . . Georgina
Game and Spencer Tracy . . . he started doing sums
in his head.

Liz Huntington sat down on her bed. The impulse to
confide her misery to someone was so strong in her that
she was glad that Bobby Rivkin had decided not to
spend the night with her.

She picked up the telephone.

"I want to place a call to the concierge at the Tremoille Hotel in Paris, please. Yes, Paris, France. No,
I'm sorry, I don't know the number."

She spelled Tremoille.

The operator said the call would take about half an
hour to put through.

"In that case, my dear, would you do me a favor?
Would *you* talk to the concierge for me? The concierge.
Tell him to ask Mlle. Chaire to call me. Mademoiselle
Chaire, yes. That's very kind of you. No, that's all. That
she should call me here as soon as possible. Yes."

She gave the operator time to write the message
down and read it back to her.

"Thank you, my dear. And I don't want to take any
calls until noon—unless there's a call from Mlle.
Chaire. Fine, yes, thank you. Good night."

Liz went into the bathroom and removed her
makeup.

She stared at her naked face, the pale lemon skin, in
the mirror for a long time.

"If you stare in the mirror long enough," her mother
used to tell her, "you'll see the Devil."

35

"Controller?"

The voice was so considerately gentle it was hardly audible.

"Yes," Stosch said. It came from a long way off, from the depths of sleep. Then, as he unclotted his throat and brain of slumber: "Yes?" More firmly.

"I'm sorry to disturb you," Genevieve Lacroix said.

"What is the time, please?" Stosch asked. He wanted time to clear his head.

"It's twenty minutes to five o'clock."

"Yes, Mlle. Lacroix. What is it?"

"I have just spoken to California. To Elizabeth Huntington. Georgina Game is getting married."

"To the Englishman?"

"Richard Antrobus."

"When?"

"Sometime in the next ten days."

"In California?"

"More probably Mexico."

Stosch paused. He clenched his eyes tight and opened them wide. The sea seemed to take a deep breath.

"We don't have much time. I want a meeting in my office at seven o'clock. You and Brand and—no, just you and Brand, I think. Bring all the product on Antrobus—and the new material on his brother."

"Caspar Antrobus."

Stosch smiled, but as if it were an all-but-forgotten thing to do.

"Are we ahead or behind California?" he asked.

"Ahead," Mlle. Lacroix said. "Eight hours."

"Get Brand onto the first possible flight to Los An-

geles. Call Casenave. Get him to fly Brand to Paris.
Does he have a visa?"

"I'm sure he has," Mlle. Lacroix said. It was a strict
Bureau rule that visas to the United States, to all major
gambling capitals, be, in Bureau jargon, "loaded" at all
times.

Stosch did not sleep again. His leg ached. He had
many things on his mind. At five o'clock he went to his
gymnasium. Slowly, purposely, with the almost submissive air of a communicant, he worked out for forty-five
minutes. He set his mind to ignore the pain that sliced
like a cold blade through the back of his *biceps femoris*
and cut into the muscles of the lower part of his abdomen. He took a needle-point shower, extremely hot,
then very cold. He slipped into a black hooded robe,
shaved, and returned to his *petit appartement*. He was
pleased it was early. There was nobody about to notice
his heavy limp that morning. At six o'clock a pale blond
young man dressed in white with jet black eyes brought
him coffee and grape juice. He left the tray on the refectory table and departed noiselessly. Neither man
spoke. Stosch took several parocodeines with his juice.
He was up to a hundred a day now. Four grains of morphine. It was still not a large dose, he told himself. But,
he recognized, it was an undeniable habit. In 1945 when
his source mysteriously dried up—Hermann Goering, he
discovered later, had bought up all available supplies
in Germany for his personal use—Stosch had done without paracodeine, without morphine, for many months.
He could do it again. If he had to.

Stosch was in his office at six forty-five. It was very
quiet. No sound came from the casino or from the sea.
There was not even the sound of a clock. It was still
night and he waited for the day to come, enjoying the
smell of darkness, the obscure monastic sweetness of
the hour. It was a time of waiting. He sat behind his
large desk, his face impassive. The pain in his leg had
almost gone. He sat very still. He wanted to think. To
work things out. He fed on the energy of silence. He
understood very well the forces of solitude. It was his
habit, when working on a difficult product, to begin the

day in this way—thinking only of the product, of the man or, sometimes, the woman, it concerned. The ashy dawn light slowly lit up the large room. He had a look of great serenity now—the look Buddhist monks often have just before an act of self-immolation.

Genevieve Lacroix, in a black cashmere sweater and tweed skirt, walked briskly, a small familiar smile of pleasure and wonder on her face. It never failed, she thought. Even at that ungodly hour of the morning. Love it or hate it, the Old Palace building—"that opulent onion shed"—was damned impressive. She hurried past the old throne room, its walls encrusted with *lapis lazuli*, the ebony floor inlaid with floral designs in mother-of-pearl. Prince Tullio had certainly had a barbarian taste for the gaudy glitter of wealth. Yet it was extraordinary how so much of it actually worked . . . the oriental tapestries, the hit-or-miss combinations of marble and parquetry and ormolu, the chairs and sofas in Kyoto silk in soft shades of gray and rose. Ahead of her, in the long wide white and gold corridor she saw two Palace guards in their scarlet and gold uniforms. The smaller, younger one quickly put out his cigarette and retrieved his pikestaff from the floor. Only the bulge on his hip showed where the most unornamental Webley-Frosberg automatic was packed.

"Good morning, Mlle. Lacroix," the first guard said. "An early start!"

"Good morning, Keeper Devoluy," she said brightly. She knew most of the eighty-five men of the Palace Guard by name. René Devoluy was one of the seven Keepers of the Regalia.

She started up the winding marble staircase to the galleried heart of the palace. Two floors above the casino and once the private apartments of the royal family, it was now the headquarters of the Statistical Bureau. Every office in these beautiful galleries opened onto enclosed courtyards. At the far end of the longest gallery of them all, beyond the royal christening chamber with its famous font of gold and silver, was Dieter Stosch's office.

She arrived a few minutes before the hour. She didn't

look like a woman who had been awake and working since before five o'clock in the morning. She greeted Stosch with a smile as she opened her document case and placed the thinnest of the enclosed files on his desk.

"Caspar Antrobus," she said. "The brother."

"The contact?"

"Yes. His step-brother."

Stosch opened the folder and glanced through the contents.

Alwyn Brand arrived at exactly seven o'clock. He had the lean unkempt look of a reclusive archivist who habitually lived and worked to a system—a system now severely and unpleasantly disturbed. He wore a Norfolk jacket and gray flannel trousers, which he would probably call "bags." He was dabbing at his chin with a large yellow handkerchief.

"Am I late?" he asked breathlessly in his affected Balliol voice, seeing Stosch and Mlle. Lacroix. "I'm not late," he added almost petulantly, consulting a hunter watch he took from his breast pocket.

"You're wounded," Mlle. Lacroix said with amused concern.

He removed the handkerchief from his chin and studied it critically.

"A nick," he said. "Shaving," he added as if some further explanation were necessary.

"Please sit down," Stosch said.

Mlle. Lacroix sat by the window. Brand took a straight-back chair against the wall opposite the controller's desk.

Stosch directed his opening remarks to the tall Englishman.

"We have a problem," he said. "A small problem but an urgent one. Georgina Game—"

Stosch saw the look of bewilderment come into Brand's eyes.

"Georgina Game is a film actress," Stosch added for his benefit. "She is on a list of possible brides for His Royal Highness."

"Ah," said Brand.

"Mlle. Lacroix learned early this morning that Miss

Game is about to marry an Englishman named Richard
Antrobus."

Stosch stood up and walked around his desk to Genevieve Lacroix and held out his hand. She selected files
from her document case and gave them to him.

"This man Antrobus is known to us, Alwyn," he
said, passing the files to Brand. "It's all in there."

Brand took the files and held them on his lap. He
looked like a man oppressed by a premonition but determined to look aloof.

Stosch returned to his desk.

He quickly outlined the details of the English bank
robberies and the almost certain involvement of Antrobus' brother.

"Are these two gentlemen by any chance related to
Sir Wilfred Antrobus the sculptor?" Brand inquired with
an arched plucked eyebrow.

"He is their father, yes."

"Oh dear," said Brand. He looked at the files in his
lap. "I'd say, what with one thing and another, we had
young Mr. Antrobus over the proverbial barrel."

Stosch sat motionless at his desk.

"Perhaps a few words—" Brand began.

"We want him gone," Stosch said. "We want him off
the scene. How you do it, that is up to you," he added
with a small amount of fractious vehemence in his
voice. "That's your business."

"Absolutely," Brand said.

"Casenave will fly you to Paris at nine-thirty," Mlle.
Lacroix broke in. "You're on the one o'clock Pan Am
flight to Los Angeles. I've booked you into the Chateau
Marmont. The English seem to have a particular affection for it. It's very convenient. On Sunset Boulevard."

Brand nodded his approval. "I was there for a tiny
while during the war," he said.

Genevieve wondered what on earth Alwyn Brand
was doing in Hollywood during the war, but she let it
go. Nobody really knew his history. "You'll pick up
your tickets at the Pan Am desk in Paris."

"We have a number for Antrobus in California?"
Stosch asked.

Genevieve said she had put his home number and the number of the studio in the files Brand now held.

"In the green one," she said. "That's the California folder." She smiled at the tall Englishman. "Everything you want to know about the West Coast."

"I do know California," Brand said disdainfully but with a bleak smile.

"It should be an easy matter to make contact?" Stosch asked.

"I knew his father—a little bit, in London," Brand said. "Not the chummiest of chaps but a man of brusque intellect all the same. He is capable of taking in the most perplexing and abstruse ideas with immense insight yet he's still a dyed-in-the-wool—"

"But you will . . . *economize*, if necessary?" Stosch spoke with emphasis, watching Brand's bloodless face closely.

"Certainly," Brand said huffily.

Stosch only frowned.

"It is a measure required—a precaution to remove possible difficulties later on," he said carefully. He nodded at Brand. "It is a necessary act of discretion."

Genevieve Lacroix looked at her watch.

"I think you should move, Alwyn. You have to pack."

"I travel light," he said, standing up. "I don't need a lot."

He made a move toward Stosch as if intending to shake his hand, then changed his mind and turned back toward the door.

"Cheerio, then," he said. He wore the smile of a good-natured man being sent on a meaningless and tiresome errand.

"An extraordinary man," Dieter Stosch said when Brand had gone. "Who would ever believe it?"

Genevieve Lacroix smiled.

"He should feel at home in Hollywood," she said. "With all those actors. Even they would never guess."

"Let us be thankful for that," Stosch said in his even, dispassionate tone.

"What happens now?"

"About Miss Game?"

"Yes."

"Count Cheroffini, Duclos—I don't think that is the right approach," Stosch said after some reflection.

"According to the product she is close to Charles Emerson."

"Emerson?"

"There was a Red Alert on him from Vegas last October. Perhaps we could . . . impose on Mr. Emerson?"

Genevieve took a file from her case.

"He might be approachable. The family's fortune has suffered several reverses. . . ." She studied the file. "New York, New Haven & Hartford Railroad stock . . . an unfortunate natural gas investment in South Dakota . . . a long tax litigation has just gone against them . . . and his own predilection for roulette, of course . . ."

"Emerson? I remember."

"Charles Tobias Emerson. An old Boston family. He was once expected to marry Georgina's mother, but nothing came of it in the end."

"It's a thought. We shall keep it in mind." He looked amused. "Although I'm not sure that our . . . reward money will be enough to interest Mr. Emerson's kind. Those proud old-money families in America . . ."

"It would depend on the timing—on the urgency of Mr. Emerson's needs," Genevieve said. "Don't you think?"

"Is he still active, Mr. Emerson?"

"He was in Baden-Baden in January, and—" She turned over a few pages and quickly found what she was looking for. "Both the Desert Inn and the Sands filed situation reports last month. He was down a little at the Desert Inn, breaking even at the Sands."

Stosch looked thoughtful.

"The dowry. The details again, please?"

Genevieve smiled at the word *dowry*. It sounded so much more polite than *bribe*, she thought.

"Basically, two hundred and fifty thousand dollars to be paid in Switzerland, or as directed," she recited from memory. "One hundred thousand on the day of the wedding. Then fifty thousand after one year, and the final one hundred thousand paid on the safe delivery of a felicitous male heir. The money to be secured in New York on property worth one million dollars. If the princess should die before Philippe and be childless, one-third of the total dowry to be repaid within eighteen months of her death. Free of interest."

"A *felicitous* male heir," Stosch said. "You can almost hear Cheroffini's voice."

"It does have a certain aesthetic prudence about it," Genevieve said with genuine amusement.

Stosch stood up and walked to the window.

He turned and faced Genevieve.

"It has also occurred to me that we might try using Cornelius in this matter—of approaching Georgina Game."

"Would he do it? Philippe's man?"

"If he saw it as a practical sensible solution, why not? Her credentials are good. She is not a Catholic, of course, but she's never been married. Comes from a respectable background. With sound American connections—that should appeal to the good priest's sense of patriotism . . ."

"Father Cornelius," Genevieve said slowly.

"We appoint him ambassador of goodwill. . . . Our friends in Las Vegas will ensure he is taken to the film studios, an introduction to the woman will be no problem, a few discreet dinner parties . . ."

"Cornelius would actually put the proposition to her—just like that? A few pleasantries and—"

"He would merely lay the groundwork. He is not without wiles—and a certain American charm. He need only . . . intimate, hint at—you understand. She is not a stupid woman. She is perceptive. She would see the possibilities. . . ."

He looked at Genevieve gravely. He was, she thought, not for the first time, the most striking-looking man she'd ever seen. With his close-cut blond hair, that hard lean face—he looked like a man who, by right, by class, by providence, was born to command.

"I think Cornelius is a very good idea," she said. "I really do."

"Anyway, it is a thought," Stosch said. "I think we could convince the estimable priest that it is his duty . . . for the Prince . . ."

The smile was only momentary.

36

"He's a friend of my father, apparently," Richard Antrobus said. "An art dealer, or some such. Anyway, I said I'd have a drink with him in the Polo Lounge this evening."

"What time?"

"Six."

"What's his name again?" Georgina said. She slipped slowly lower in the bath until the water was on a line with her nipples.

"Alwyn Brand?"

"Never heard of him."

"He didn't claim to be a *famous* art dealer," Richard said.

"He'll have to do something about that, if he wants to do any business here. *Everybody* is famous in Hollywood. Even our gardener is famous. The *maid* is famous—"

"Apparently, we've also got a good mutual friend at Deauville. Bernard Ledoux at the casino."

"Your gambling friends," Georgina said with a dismissive sniff.

"I forgot. You don't approve of gambling."

"At least it keeps people away from television."

Antrobus finished shaving. He put on a bathrobe and sat on a stool above the sunken onyx bath. He looked down at Georgina, who was examining her breasts.

"The least I can do is have a drink with the fellow."

He sounded like a man who has been obscurely wounded.

"Darling, *of course*."

"I thought you had that *tone* in your voice."

"What *tone*?"

"*That* tone. He's-off-boozing-with-the-boys-already tone . . . suspicions of a little *cinq-à-sept* . . ."

"Don't be an arse," she said. "Do you really like my breasts? Should I have them enlarged? There's a doctor on Bedford Drive who does marvelous things with foam rubber—"

"Silicon. No." He stretched out his foot and touched her nipple with his big toe. "You have perfect breasts. I love your breasts."

"They're very . . . *Japanese*-looking."

"Miniaturized mammaries?"

"You see! You *do* think they're too small."

He gave her a quelling look.

"Why is it that being straight with a woman always makes a man feel guilty?" he said.

"I don't know. Does it?"

"He sounds *molto simpatico*—"

"Who?"

"Mr. Brand—one of the chaps."

"How did he get this number?"

"He called me at the studio."

"Do you know that Marlon Brando has to change his number every fortnight?"

"Probably to avoid his ex-wives."

"Ha-de-ha-ha," Georgina said in a flat humorless voice, but smiling.

"And don't say fortnight. Americans don't say fortnight."

"Oh I forgot. You're the great American producer now."

"I heard at the studio today—your idol Bette Davis—"

"What about her?"

"They say she's planning a one-woman show on Broadway. Doing scenes from her divorces."

"It really is . . . *unsettling*—the horrid obsession this town has with divorce, for ill-natured gossip . . ."

"Listen, darling, get out of that bath—"

"And into a dry humor—"

"Put your glad rags on and come down to the Polo Lounge with me. Meet Mr. Brand."

"You know I hate that place."

"One drink?"

"No."

"Two drinks?"

"No."

"I am prevented by the exigencies of pride to offer you three drinks. So what d'you say? I swear by San Simeon we won't stay more than half an hour. Just put on a nice frock, an amiable face and—"

"Please darling, don't make me. I really really would rather not."

"Really really? Or just really?"

"Really really."

"Very well." He sighed. "You're a great trial to me, woman."

"You know what I really fancy now?" she said.

"Surprise me."

"A nice cup of tea."

"You've surprised me. The fabulous Georgina Game drinking not champagne but a cup of tea in her sunken marble—"

"Onyx."

"—bathtub."

"It's very English."

"It's excessively homely. It's not your actual Jean Harlows, is it?"

He picked up the telephone and buzzed the kitchen.

"Merla? Miss Game would like tea. If you would be kind enough to bring it to her in the bathroom. Yes, Merla."

He replaced the receiver.

"She sounded quite shocked. I suspect you have broken some great Hollywood taboo. Perhaps she'll report you to the Hays Office. Such Bacchanalian goings-on—"

"I love you, Antrobus."

"I thought her smile was beginning to slip its moorings this morning when—"

"You might have to have an ear job."

"An ear job?"

"Actresses have nose jobs, tit jobs—producers have ear jobs. There's this very good man up on Hillcrest who specializes in unheeding ears for producers—he did Mayer's, Strauss's, Schary's—"

"What's that you say? I can't hear you."

"I said *I love you.*"

"No thank you, I'm trying to give them up."

"You sod!"

She splashed him, soaking his bathrobe.

"Serves you right," she said. "Serves you bloody well right."

"Just for that I'm going to pee in the bath."

He stood menacingly above her.

"You dare, you rotten swine!"

There was a polite knock on the door and Merla came in with the tea.

He got there shortly before six o'clock. Nobody had been asking for him, the headwaiter said. Would he like a table? He said he would have a drink at the bar first and go to the table when his guest arrived. "Yes sir, table three, Mr. Antrobus, whenever you're ready," Antoine said. "Will Miss Game be joining you later?" Perhaps, Antrobus said vaguely. He didn't want to jeopardize his good table. Unlike Georgina, Antrobus rather enjoyed the swank hokum, the pure snobbery of the Polo Lounge. He liked the twilight aura. It was one of those Hollywood shrines where the conversation ran the gamut from sweet nothings to ten percent.

He ordered a Scotch and water and stood at the bar, listening to the babble of bull-shooting, the alibis, the ninety-four-point-four-proof confidences flowing around him:

"So I know where to put the leaves in a samovar, Duke, I tell him, does that make me a commie . . ."

". . . in Vancouver in just two situations the second week, nine-five. In Peoria, the best Wednesday opening since . . ."

"It's a shame. I was a real close personal friend of Lou's."

"Then I thought . . . what the hell am I running for? My house ain't on fire . . ."

"I tell ya . . . that switchboard lit up . . ."

"Listen, you dumb fuck, I said . . ."

". . . so apart from Game . . . where are the new great leading females . . ."

"I did everything for that douche bag. Okay, she was the bread-winner . . . I even pressed her goddam dresses when her maid was off . . . she's a very very mixed up broad . . ."

"What's Lou gonna do now? Jesus, I just wish I could help him but . . ."

Antrobus noticed him at once.

He stood in the doorway, in a crumpled tweed suit, glaring into the deep gloom with an apprehensive air of transgression.

Antrobus finished his drink and walked over.

"Alwyn Brand?"

"Yes?" Brand peered closely at Antrobus.

"Richard Antrobus. How d'you do?"

"Goodness me, how can you see anything in here, Mr. Antrobus," Brand said in a querulous voice. "Anyway, thank you for rescuing me so promptly."

Antoine appeared and led them to the banquette opposite the bar.

"What will you have, Mr. Brand?" Antrobus asked when they were seated.

"I don't usually have anything—anything of an alcoholic nature, that is. Perhaps, on this occasion, a glass of sherry. A dry sherry."

"Dry sherry for Mr. Brand, Antoine. I'll have a Scotch. Water, no ice. Haig."

"Yes, sir."

"How do you like Hollywood so far?" Antrobus said.

"The only Hollywood person I'm on speaking terms with is a very decent sort. He is the lift attendant at my hotel. He knows Greta Garbo."

"You have to have connections in this town." Antrobus grinned. "Anybody who knows Greta Garbo—it's a start."

The drinks came.

"Ice?" the waiter said to Brand.

"Certainly not." He looked pained, like a great auk with some private grief. "Ice in sherry, indeed," he said to Antrobus when the waiter had gone.

A waiter came around with a silver tray of hot cheesy morsels and cocktail sausages. Brand took a sausage.

"How's my father?"

"Oh very well," Brand said easily. "He's just started a bust of Churchill. He's pretty bucked about that."

"Oh? Who's that for?"

"Been commissioned by the General Apothecaries' Company, I believe."

"He's finally finished off Eisenhower then?"

Brand nodded.

"He was never really happy with it," he said when he had finished the sausage. "Three sittings were all the President ever gave him, you know."

Alwyn Brand had studied the product well.

"Wilfred finally got his manservant, old Wilson, to sit in for the hands. Unfortunately the poor fellow has arthritis rather badly in the joints of his fingers and they don't look at all right for a former supreme commander of all allied forces of sea, land, and air, your father says. Although I'm sure they're perfectly passable as the hands of a President of the United States."

"But still not golfer's hands?" Antrobus smiled.

"Hardly golfer's hands. Even a golfer renowned for his consistent inability to do a hole in single figures," Brand agreed solemnly.

"Call for Ava Gardner." Johnny the page boy paraded through the lounge. "Miss Gardner—telephone."

The room was crowded now. The multifarious conversations had become one loud indistinct murmur, a sort of galvanized purr punctuated by an occasional loud laugh, a single distinct line, a sharp oath.

"Are you," Antrobus asked, "planning to do some business here, Mr. Brand?"

"Actually, you are my business. The sole reason for my being here, sir," Brand said courteously.

"Me?"

Brand took out of his jacket pocket an envelope and gave it to Antrobus.

"Don't open it now. But when you do, you will see I am most sincere in what I am about to say to you."

Antrobus picked up the bulky envelope and smiled. "You make it sound very mysterious, Mr. Brand."

"Forgive me, sir. Melodrama is the last thing I wish to convey."

". . . she just wants custody of the money . . ." a plaintive voice rose above the general hubbub around the bar.

Antrobus smiled.

"Then what do you wish to convey, Mr. Brand?" he asked.

"I represent certain people who wish you to leave Miss Game."

"I'm sorry I—*leave* Georgina? You mean—"

"Get out of her life, Mr. Antrobus."

Antrobus laughed. "What an absurd idea," he said.

"I do urge you to take this matter seriously, Mr. Antrobus."

Antrobus followed Brand's eyes to the envelope between them on the table.

"These people, my principals, they are most anxious that you leave Miss Game immediately."

"I think, Mr. Brand, you'd better be a little more specific—or have I missed the joke?"

"It is no joke, sir."

"Then I think—"

"There is a particular bank in London most anxious to discover the whereabouts of a rather large sum of money, I believe. A sum not unadjacent to three-quarters of a million pounds."

A small quiver of silence, it was almost like a sudden chill, seemed to pass through the banquette.

Eyes almost closed, Alwyn Brand quietly, very slowly, reeled off the essential details with an air of regret. When he had finished, he said:

"You will discover, in that envelope, Mr. Antrobus, more precise information as to the background of that most impressive crime." He spoke with a pedantic and provoking slowness.

"Laurence Harvey—telephone. Call for Mr. Harvey."

Antrobus looked as if a smile had died on his face and rotted there.

"Mr. Brand—I need—I have to talk to you."

"Mr. Antrobus, we *are* talking. There really is nothing you can say to me that will alter the course of future events—nor, indeed, change the quiddity of your somewhat baleful behavior in the past." He studied Antrobus with a look of genuine sorrow in his eyes. " 'Fraid that is the quandary with felonious prosperity—it imposes so many inescapable conditions."

"Who sent you, Brand?" Antrobus removed the carcass of the smile from his face.

"It is of no matter."

"The studio?"

"I cannot answer that question."

"I just want to know who is trying to hand me my hat."

"I believe you have a brother . . . Tom?" Brand reached out a bony finger and tapped the envelope. "I shouldn't leave that lying about, if I were you, by the by."

"Brand, for Christ's sake—"

"Nobody, I assure you, wishes to deprive you of your money. All you have to do is—I believe the colloquial—the slang expression is . . . make yourself scarce. Vis-à-vis Miss Game."

Brand sipped his sherry.

"It is necessary, well, let us say desirable, that you do exactly as I suggest, Mr. Antrobus."

"And if I don't?"

"My dear fellow, I don't wish to discomfort you more than is necessary but I must point out to you the . . . extreme vulnerability, not to say the hopelessness, of your situation."

Antrobus ordered another drink.

"Not for me, thank you," Brand said politely.

"What we are really talking about here is . . . a shakedown."

"A shakedown, Mr. Antrobus?"

"Blackmail. A squeeze—"

"Not in the ordinary sense. I like to think we are essentially talking about your future travel arrangements."

"Blackmail, Brand."

"Thievery, Mr. Antrobus."

"It's the studio, isn't it? Who else would want me to leave Georgina?"

"I am merely the messenger, the postman. Motives are not my province."

The waiter slipped a fresh drink in front of Antrobus. "Listen Brand, I'm a reasonably well-off fellow—"

"Bribery, Mr. Antrobus? An overture? A subvention? Deary me. That's very common—and very foolish."

"Just let me meet these people." Antrobus fought to keep the panic out of his voice.

"That is not possible."

Antrobus swallowed almost half of the fresh glass of Scotch.

Brand took out his watch and peered shortsightedly at the time in the gloom. He slipped the watch back into his pocket. "Between time and us it is as to which shall kill the other," he said gently.

"If it's not the studio—"

"It's an old French saying, I believe."

"Brand, for pity's sake—"

"You are a handsome young man. You have money. Plenty of money . . . and not much conscience. You have already amply demonstrated that. Don't imperil your whole future with a momentary passion. Don't be in too much of a hurry to make a romantic gesture. Love is an absurdly overrated pastime, you know."

"But my work's here—I have a movie—you're cutting me off at the knees, Brand."

"There is much in what you say, sir. However, think things over a bit. You will find that the action I am proposing is the only practical solution."

"Practical! I might as well be dead!"

"Ah," Brand said softly.

Perhaps it was the way he said it; perhaps it was something in his face . . . but Richard Antrobus was suddenly very afraid.

"Think things over a bit," Brand said. "I think you'll realize that the . . . middle course I am propounding is best. However abhorrent and personally hateful one may find it, one must always adjust to circumstances. It is the first law of self-preservation, sir."

Brand paused and sipped his sherry. He looked around the room, an opaque smile on his lips. He studied the people at the bar as if they were strange but amusing natives of an unexplored hinterland.

Without looking at Antrobus, he said, "Be assured of one thing, sir. My people respect your independence. The deal they are proposing is an honest one—or, let us say, a straightforward one. But there are other people in the world—perhaps more lawful-minded people, but constitutionally and unimpeachably vindictive people, the eye-for-an-eye establishment, shall we say?—people who might become marshaled against you, against your brother, if certain . . . beastly information should fall into their hands."

The smell of cigars and L'Aimant came from the next banquette.

"I'd like to know one thing, Brand. Do you really know my father?"

"I haven't seen him for some while. We are both members of Boodle's."

"You stink, Brand."

"Malodorous incivilities will resolve nothing," Brand said amiably. "Now I really must toddle."

He stood up and looked down at Antrobus.

"I shall telephone you at your office tomorrow at twelve o'clock. Mr. Antrobus . . . I do urge you not to be tiresome—and remember you have other people to think of." He nodded toward the envelope. "Put it away, there's a good chap. Before you forget it."

37

Antrobus asked a waiter to bring a telephone to the table. He ordered another Scotch. When the telephone was plugged in, he asked the operator to get him the Beverly Wilshire Hotel.

"Miss Huntington," he said after a few moments. "Miss Liz Huntington."

"Miss Huntington doesn't answer, I'm sorry."

"Did she leave a number where she might be reached?"

"No, she didn't, sir."

Antrobus sat and thought. The waiter brought his drink. He picked up the phone and gave the operator Bobby Rivkin's Malibu number. The call went through almost at once.

"Mr. Rivkin's residence," said a Mexican voice trying hard not to be.

"Is Miss Huntington there, please. This is Richard Antrobus."

"Just one moment, please, sir."

"Hello, Richard. How are *you*?" Liz said in a bright voice after a couple of minutes.

"Liz, I have to talk to you."

"Where are you? I hardly hear you. Is there a party going on?"

"I'm in the Polo Lounge. I have to talk to you, Liz."

"Whenever—Bobby's gone to a sneak preview in Westwood. Then he's got dinner with some boring people from New York—I pleaded a headache, or the Fifth Symphony, or something."

"I could come out to the beach now. Is that all right?"

"Come on over. You know where we are. Watch out

for the fire station on the right—about two hundred yards past that." She gave him the number.

"I'm leaving now."

He put the envelope in his pocket. He signed the check and added twenty percent.

"Thank you, Mr. Antrobus," Antoine said. His eyes glistened with the metallic sincerity of *maître d's* and movie stars. He was pleased to get the table back. Cary Grant and a party of four were expected any minute. "My regards to Miss Game. Hope to see you again real soon, Mr. Antrobus."

"Thank *you*, Mr. Antrobus," said the parking lot attendant who had the Rolls out front almost before Antrobus got to the end of the red carpet which runs from lobby to driveway. He slipped the bill away like a magician. "Have a nice evening now."

Antrobus drove much too quickly down the sweeping palm-tree-lined driveway, turned right onto Sunset and west toward the beach. He drove fast, thinking of the extraordinary meeting with Alwyn Brand. Alwyn Brand who looked like an academic and talked and behaved like an aesthetic assassin. He thought of the rumpled tweed suit and the old-fashioned silver pocket watch and the aura of Puritanism with which the Englishman sipped his sherry. Antrobus kept trying to figure out what sort of organization would use such a man. Where would anybody *find* such a character? Richard Antrobus had no doubt in his mind, no doubt at all, that Alwyn Brand was capable of murder. Would be quite *happy* to murder to get his way. He hadn't threatened physical violence, of course . . . but surely it was implicit in everything he said? It was always there, the threat, the air of menace, just beneath the surface, subliminal, oblique, malefic. Yet he *had* given Antrobus a choice. If he had been sent simply to kill him, why bother with all the talk? Why set up that meeting, why come out into the open?

"Jesus," Antrobus said aloud.

Beyond Beverly Hills, Sunset started to twist and turn dangerously. Antrobus kept his foot down, even on the hairpins. He kept in top gear all the way. If he'd thought a bit more, if he'd had just a little less to drink, he would have taken Santa Monica, which is a straighter road, though less exotic maybe, and twenty minutes faster.

The Pacific appeared abruptly, looking cold and foreboding in the fading evening light. The air got suddenly cooler. Antrobus touched a button and the windows closed without a murmur.

The signal was green. He turned right onto the Pacific Coast Highway, below the tall cliffs. *Slide Area* signs warned the unwary of falling rocks. *Drive Carefully*, admonished alternate signs. Antrobus noticed none of them. His mind was still fixed on Brand.

It was obvious that Brand knew a great deal about his background, aside from its more incriminating aspects. What, he wondered, if Brand had been hired to kill him then discovered he was the son of a friend . . . was that sufficient to give him qualms—scruples? That made a sort of sense. The brotherhood of Boodle's, he thought. It was one possibility. It was one feasible scenario. He smiled as he caught himself using the Hollywood word.

He saw the fire station and slowed down and started watching for the numbers. The Rivkin shack—that's what Rivkin called it and that's what it looked like from the road—was just about where Liz said it would be. He did a hard U-turn and parked tight against the neglected ranch-boarding that ran between the houses. It took a little while to find the bell in the faded sand-specked garage-like door. He pressed the bell but could hear no sound inside the house, so he kept on pressing. The door was opened by a small dark man. There was the smell of fresh cologne on his face, and a smile like a crack in an earthenware jug. He wore a butler's getup that wouldn't have raised an eyebrow in Belgravia, or the best parts of Washington, D.C. He showed Antrobus down a narrow dark corridor and into an oak-beamed living room not much larger than a small-town pool hall. The far wall was floor-to-ceiling plate glass and beyond that was nothing but the ocean and Hawaii. The other walls were covered in tan suede and smothered with framed autographed photographs of actors, politicians, royalty, sportsmen. There were plaques and diplomas and awards from various movie magazines. A flattering portrait of Rivkin dressed as a U.S. Cavalry Officer in one of his early movie roles hung alongside several Rouaults, a Modigliani, and a garish poster advertising the first movie Rivkin produced.

Liz had her back to him. She wore a long silk gown in brilliant jade, slit to the thighs. She was peering through a huge brass telescope.

"Mister Hantrobbuzz," the butler announced, bowing slightly as he stood aside to let him in.

"Darling, that was quick!" Liz turned and came toward him. "I was just looking to see whether I knew anybody on the beach . . . in Waikiki."

"Oh," Antrobus said after a pause.

"Usually, though, all we ever see through that are people screwing their asses off on their boats off the Santa Monica Pier."

She wore hardly any makeup. Her skin looked fresh, and was already beginning to tan. She kissed him on the mouth, but not as if it really meant anything.

"Come and sit down and tell me all about it. You sounded *terrible* on the phone." She stood back and studied his face. "And you don't look so hot, either."

She went over to the mahogany bar that ran the length of the right-hand wall. Antrobus sank into a curved brown suede sofa.

"We've got White Horse, Chivas Regal, J & B—"

"Chivas, thanks, with a little water. Don't drown it."

She fixed the drink, not too strong, and made an Americano for herself. She came from behind the bar and handed him the Scotch. She walked around the room, switching on the lights.

"So what's so important that you have to drive like fucking Fangio to talk to your old Auntie Liz?"

"It's serious, Liz—and I'm . . . I don't know what to do."

"You and Georgina?"

"Yes—and no."

"You always were the boy for a straight answer."

She sat at the other end of the long sofa. "How's the drink?"

"I love Georgina. She loves me. Nothing's changed," he said.

"So—"

"Tonight I met a man—"

"Fucking Wellington boots! You haven't gone queer?"

"For Christ's sake, Liz! Shut up for a minute! This is serious!"

"I'm sorry, it just sounded so . . . go on." She took the smile off her face. She half-turned away from him and took a cigarette out of a heavy gold box on the Spanish coffee table. She got up and went over to the bar and lit the cigarette with a heavy table lighter. She took her time, waiting for Richard to begin. She avoided looking at him.

He sat staring at the tan tiled floor.

"Does Georgina know you're here?" she asked finally, not so much because she was interested in whether Georgina knew or not, but because she wanted to get him started.

"No," he said, taking his eyes off the tiles. "I came straight here after he left—"

"This man you met—at the Polo Lounge?"

"Yes." Slowly, hesitantly, nervously, he told her the whole story up to the point of the ultimatum.

"But that's preposterous," Liz said. "It has to be one of those elaborate Hollywood jokes, surely? Somebody's pulling your leg, Richard."

"No, Liz."

"Come on, now. A man telephones you out of the blue, says he is a friend of your father and whoever in Biarritz—"

"Deauville."

"—and the next thing is, he's up and warning you off Georgina!"

"You don't understand. I've been a very naughty boy—"

"We all know that, darling."

"No, Liz. *Very* naughty. I have done something which could get me—and other people—into a great deal of trouble. Big trouble, Liz. I'm not talking about traffic-ticket stuff . . . I did something very . . . wrong. Something very big."

Liz stood up and took the empty glass out of his hand. She poured him another Scotch, only stronger this time.

"I don't believe it," she said, handing him the Scotch. "Not you, Richard, you were always pretty lethal with ladies in a drawing room, but—"

"This man tonight—he knows everything."

"Do you want to tell me—"

"No," he said sharply. Then gently: "I can't, Liz. It doesn't just concern me . . ."

"This man—" She sat down on the sofa beside him. "How could he have found out—whatever it is he's found out?"

"I don't know," Richard said in a quiet flat voice. "But he knows. He knows . . . where, how, who—"

"Now let me get this straight in my head. He just wants you to leave Georgina? To go away and never see her again?"

"Yes."

"He doesn't want money?"

"Apparently not."

"It's bizarre. It's . . . irrational."

He waved a hand in the air.

"Did he know about next week—the marriage?"

"He didn't say. It wasn't mentioned."

"All the same—it's a bit odd, isn't it? The timing . . ."

"Do you think it's the studio, Liz?"

"Bobby?"

"Bobby . . . Strauss . . . Rilke . . ." He spoke in a small hopeless voice.

Liz just stared at him in silence for a long moment.

"But why? For what reason?" she said finally. Her eyes had a watchful thoughtful look.

"I don't know, Liz," Antrobus said slowly. "But somebody—"

"This—this *thing* you've done. Can they actually *prove* it? I mean, they might know you did it, but—"

"It's no good. They know. They've got all they need—" His hand involuntarily patted the envelope in his inside breast pocket.

"Are you absolutely sure they're not just blowing smoke?"

"They have an inside wire, Liz."

She didn't say anything for a long time and when she spoke again there was exasperation in her voice.

"And yet they're using this information just to scare you off Georgina? Nothing else? They don't want money, they don't want . . . I mean, it's just crazy."

"It *has* to be the studio, Liz."

"Not Bobby," she said firmly. "Not Riv. He's a lot of shades of shit—but not this."

"I heard a story a little while ago. Isn't there mob money in the studio now?" Antrobus asked.

"They say that about every studio, Richard. You know that."

"But this is the sort of thing the Mafia would do—the way they behave, isn't it?"

"Your man hardly sounds like a Mafia representative, Richard."

Richard made a noise that wasn't a laugh or a word or a sigh. It might have been the sound of pure misery.

"Anyway," Liz said. "Don't you think the studio has enough corporate muscle to get what it wants legally without—"

"Christ, Liz. What am I going to do?"

"Stop feeling sorry for yourself for a start."

She hated that sound of whipped gloom in his voice.

He stood up and stretched his mouth wide. He walked across to the window and stared at the darkness where the sea was.

"So anyway . . ." He spoke in a consciously stronger voice. "What do I do? Laugh in their faces? Tell them to do their worst? Throw in my hand? What do I do?"

He looked down at her, biting his lip. The slit in her gown exposed her thighs up to where her panties would show if she were wearing panties. Any other time, he would have made a pass . . . he'd had her once. He couldn't remember how good it was . . . It was a pity he'd had so many women he couldn't remember . . . not because they were unmemorable but because he was so often fried to the gills at the time. He guessed she was probably very good. . . .

Liz smiled and shifted the angle of her legs, closing the slit in her gown. She knew him very well. *She* remembered how good it'd been.

"What do I do, Liz?"

"Well, if you're sure they're not bluffing—"

"They're not bluffing."

"—and whatever it is you're supposed to have done really is heavy—"

"Heavy," Antrobus said. "The heaviest. Short of actually killing somebody."

"Then either you're all wrong or you're all through, Richard. In this town . . . with Georgina. What else can I tell you?"

His face had a fixed look. The look of having been wrapped up, ready for shipment to some other, colder, more remote expression.

"You wanted me to tell you the truth, Richard," Liz said. "I've told you the truth. I've leveled with you."

"Thanks," he said resentfully.

Liz didn't say anything.

"I'm sorry, Liz," Richard said. "Don't be upset. I didn't mean to sound ungrateful. I know how you must feel . . . you were the only one I could talk to."

She lifted her face and gave him a faint smile.

She was thinking of something else. Something that suddenly worried her a lot. Something she didn't want to think about at all . . .

Mlle. Chaire.

Mlle. Chaire had asked for a report on Richard Antrobus. It was the last report she did before . . . the report on Georgina Game.

Jesus Christ. Did Mlle. Chaire—

"Whoever it is," Richard said, rolling the glass between his palms. "Behind this business. Whoever it is, they're more interested in Georgina than me, or plain money."

"Her father?" Liz said on an impulse.

Antrobus passed a hand across his eyes.

"My God!" he said quietly.

"I don't know," said Liz.

"My God!" he said again in a shattered voice.

"It's a possibility," she said. "It has all the earmarks of a tough determined *independent* mind, right?" Liz said, warming to her new theory. "A mind just the teensiweensiest bit crooked."

"Harry Ogre," Antrobus said softly. "Harry bloody Ogre."

"Had Georgina told him?"

"About us?"

"About getting married?"

"She talked to him last night . . . he seemed to accept it—"

"Too soon—even Harry'd never get you flagged down, have somebody whispering in your ear *that* fast—"

"—with all the goods—I mean, Liz, this guy . . . he had *documents*, for God's sake!"

Liz wanted it to be Harry Ogilvy. She wanted it so badly to be Harry Ogilvy. In her heart, even then, she knew it wasn't, couldn't be. . . .

"Well, darling. Take your pick," she said. "Somebody means business, right? As far as I can see, you have a couple of choices. Do as they say. Skedaddle, scram, P.D.Q. They probably don't mess about, right?"

"Or?"

"Take a chance. Tell Georgina as much as you can, as much as you have to—let *her* decide."

"Is that fair? On her, I mean."

"She does love you, Richard. I don't know why, but she really does."

"It's not much of a choice, is it?"

"The consequences—if you stick around—will be pretty hairy. If it's as bad as you say, Richard, and you really do love Georgina—well, you've got to put her first. You've got to think of what it'd do to her career . . . those morality groups out here, the Legion of Decency, the women's guilds . . . they could bury her . . . the League of Catholic Mothers . . . she's not immune . . . those people, Christ, look what they did to Bergman . . . just for sleeping with Rossellini. He made some pretty godawful pictures, but I guess your hustle's more serious than that. . . ."

"You could say," Antrobus said without smiling.

"I think you're playing with the big boys, Richard. You've got yourself in up to your ears—but at least they seem to be handing you a shovel to dig yourself out—"

"Or dig my own grave."

"My feeling is—pack your bags, just piss off."

"What about Georgina?"

"She'll hurt—but she'll hurt a lot more if you stick around and this thing really does blow up—"

"You're right, Liz."

"You don't have much time."

"He's calling at midday."

"I'm glad I didn't buy the bridesmaid's dress," she said.

"This is what's called making a mess of one's life, I suppose," he said.

She felt sorry for him, but this wasn't the time to show sympathy. She knew he was on the ledge. She took the glass out of his hand and went to the bar. She fixed two drinks and took them back to the sofa. She handed him the Scotch.

"Here's looking at ya, kid," she said.

He grinned, not much, but it was a grin and he meant it.

"I don't have to show you no stinking badge," he said, just like Bogey.

38

She had a sweet musky kind of odor. It wasn't sweat and it wasn't scent. Philippe had never smelled it on any other woman in his life. Isak claimed it was the result of omnific endocrine glands and the sign of a highly sexed woman. It permeated the bedroom, and often lingered in Philippe's car for days.

He stood by the deep-embrasured window in the bedroom of their villa in Grasse.

"You smell good," he said.

"You love it, don't you?"

"Yes."

"It excites you?"

"You know it does."

"You love watching me?"

"Yes."

She was naked beneath the finest cream satin chemise, on the bed, on her back. Her fingers played impudently, lovingly over her gently glistening body.

Philippe moved around the room, barefoot on the dark oak floor, and stood at the foot of the bed. Her unashamed air of erotic deshabille, that akimbo sense of insolence . . . she reminded him of Lautrec's drawing of the exhausted prostitute.

"God, you were so good today."

"May I have a drink, please?"

He filled two glasses from a jug of champagne and peaches that stood on a chest by the window.

"You spoil me," she said. She took a sip from the glass and put it on the table by the bed.

Philippe put on a pair of Levi's. He sat on the bed and gripped her ankle.

"Don't stop," he said. "What you were doing."

"You are such a voyeur."

"Yes."

"You are so beautiful," she said. "You know so much. About *me*. You are the essential conjunction of my happiness. Do you know that, Prince André Antonin Philippe, Marquis d'Murat, member of the Supreme Cross of the Order of Croissy, winner of the Croix de—"

"And you are . . . you are such an explicit amalgam of . . ."

"Of what? You don't know what to say," she said. "You start things you don't know how to finish." She wanted him to think of something good to tell her.

"Of redeeming vices," he said finally.

"An amalgam of redeeming vices," she said slowly. "Yes, that's very good. I like that."

"I thought you would like that. You see, I know how to finger the mainspring of your vanity."

"You do. What's your secret?"

"I practice a lot."

"Darling." She sat up and curled herself into his arms. "I do miss you. We see each other so seldom . . . these moments . . . the feeling of isolation . . . the threat of depression is always so close now."

"You mustn't worry, my little *mec*," he said. "We must play the waiting game. You understand the need for that?"

The pale panoplied greenery of her eyes darkened with distilled malice.

"I hate that man. I hate what he is doing to us."

"You mustn't take it personally."

"He has the morals of a medieval gangster. I hate him. I hate the—"

"Be patient. I have years of strength ahead of me." He smiled at her. "Even with you sapping it—"

"Do you also have years of patience?"

"If need be."

"You do still want to marry me, Philippe?"

"I want to marry you," he said, expressionless.

"You see, my mind is instinctive. It isn't a very logical mind and sometimes . . . I heard a terrible story in Paris and—"

"What terrible story, Isak?" Philippe tightened his grip on her wrist.

"Raoul Richelieu is saying there is a secret list . . . a list of women, eligible women, moneybags—"

"For *me*?"

"Yes."

"I take this woman and her tobacco scrip to be my wedded wife—"

"He says it's true!"

"He has an imaginative mind for a hairdresser. Evil but imaginative. Tell me, does he know who is supposed to be on this . . . *secret* list?"

"You know he hears everything. You said so yourself."

"But no names?"

"That rich American girl who died in the air crash. She was on it."

"Naturally. And?"

"Princess Marguérite Letessier."

"Of Blandenberg?"

"Yes."

Philippe thought about it.

"Did you know that Blandenberg has forty-seven princesses? Forty-seven. That's only thirteen less than it has square miles. She is probably the prettiest of them all, little Marguérite," he said slowly, in a teasing thoughtful voice, ignoring the signs of restiveness in Isak's eyes. "Come to think of it, she is just the sort of woman I like. She has class, breeding. She looks dangerous—schizy and very dangerous—"

"She has the pox," Isak said matter-of-factly. "Is that dangerous enough?"

"Richelieu told you that as well, did he?" Philippe said, still in his slow amused voice.

"No."

"Who told you?"

"Igor Boissard. She gave it to him—and if you don't watch out, I'll give it to you!"

"Boissard? You've been with Boissard?"

There was sudden excitement and anxiety in Philippe's voice. It came like abrupt thunder out of nowhere on a sultry day.

"He wants me," Isak said quietly.

She felt the tables turning. She rolled out of Philippe's arms and displayed herself on the bed in an aura of sensual abstraction.

"And you? What do you want?"

"The days are long . . . interminable hours in which there is little to do but kill time as best one can. He pleases me. Igor the terrible—"

"You have been to bed with him?"

Philippe's face was rigid.

"Not yet . . ." The movement she made was almost a writhing, as if she had been suddenly unleashed from some voluptuous paralysis. Her chemise clung to her body, high about her waist.

"I let him watch me dress . . . I tease . . ."

"Tell me, Isak."

"I let him touch me a little—here . . ."

"You let him touch you? Tell me, Isak. How—"

"I take his hand—like this."

She rolled across the bed and pushed into Philippe with her back against his bare chest. She took hold of his hand and guided it down, around her waist, and down, down between her thighs.

"How long, darling . . ." Philippe's voice was thick with excitement and open jealousy.

"Tell me. Tell me what he did, how you felt, how you—"

"I was wet. As wet as I am now. Yes, there, my sweet. That's my baby. Oh yes, that's the spot, that's the—oh, darling . . . he didn't do it—not yet—"

"You lie to me. He took you—"

"Not yet—I wouldn't let him, he tried, he tried . . . I want *you*—" Her fingers clawed at his hair. He bit her lips.

"Was it good? *Tell me*—"

"I only teased him . . . darling, please, now, I want you. Please put it in me. You're so big, so hard. Slide it into me . . ."

He helped her undo his Levi's, breathing hard.

"Don't take them off. I like it when you keep them on . . . it makes me feel like such a whore . . . so cheap. Yes, yes . . . into me. Hurt me." They were mouth to mouth, flesh to flesh, incoherent and animal, entwined in sweating straining limbs. "Darling, you're so deep . . . oh God! I feel you so deep inside of me."

"Will you let Boissard do it to you like this?"

"If you tell me to. If you want him to. If you order it."

"I think so."

"Yes, yes . . . I'll do whatever you want, darling . . . Tell me you want me to—"

She screamed and she came. She never knew what came first, the cry or the climax. She had never been able to work it out.

"You are a wild beautiful woman," Philippe told her

tenderly afterward, mouth pressed against her throat.

"I have never been wild. I have often been lonely. Do you know what I mean? Sometimes, I think . . . if that's what it takes not to be lonely for a few hours . . . a few days, a few weeks . . . well, it is cheap at the price. I can't bear to be alone, Philippe."

He held her close. He held her tight.

"You're not alone," he said "Don't talk."

"Promise me. Promise me you won't leave me?"

"I promise."

"I want you to know that I want *you* . . . I want to be with you . . . I'll wait for you."

"I know, I know," he said softly. "Shh now."

"Forever."

"Yes."

"I do want you so," she whispered. "You are so good."

"I once had an English nanny," Philippe said. "She always used to say, '*Iwant* never gets.' "

"Nannies don't always know best, do they?" Isak said in a small child's voice that wasn't acting.

"Not always, darling."

"You turned my life around, Philippe." She stroked his face. Her hand might have been Victorian, except for the tan: sinewy, soft, with short unpolished nails. Polish was for Paris, for the city.

"We mustn't be sad," Philippe said.

Isak sat up and sniffed loudly and smiled.

"You're right," she said in a brave big-girl's voice that *was* acting. "It is a tragic business—we must not make the mistake of playing it tragically."

"No."

"Here." Isak handed Philippe her glass of champagne from the table by the side of the bed. "Don't take all the peaches."

He sipped it and handed the glass back to her.

"I keep telling myself I can't take this any longer," she said smiling. "But I can take it. That's my problem. I have a will to live. I have such a strength to live."

"That's important."

"Is there . . . a secret list, Philippe?"

"I don't know. Stosch has always one invariable answer to a problem and that answer is secrecy."

"But you do know, don't you, that something—or someone—has to break soon?"

Philippe shrugged.

Isak got off the bed and went to her dressing table. She sat down in front of the mirror and started to brush her hair.

"Don't do that," Philippe said after a few minutes.

"Not brush my hair?"

"The way you do it—it's as if you're angry about something."

She smiled automatically at his reflection in the mirror. "I'm not angry."

"Come here," he said.

On the way back to the bed she picked up a copy of *Newsweek* magazine from the top of the chest next to the window.

She dropped it on the bed beside Philippe.

"What's that?"

"Have you seen what the Americans are saying about you now?"

"No," Philippe said in a careless way.

She opened the magazine and said, "Do you want to hear?"

"Do I have a choice?"

"There is a picture of you playing tennis with Baron Gottfried von Cramm. The caption reads, 'Prince Philippe: forever trapped in the Saladin days between tutelage and responsibility.' "

"Is it a good picture?"

"Do you want me to read the rest?"

"It isn't necessary. Unless you have some missionary compulsion—"

"Darling," Isak said sadly, as if trying to teach the alphabet to a backward child. "They're virtually calling you a deadbeat."

"Let 'em."

"Two tigers cannot share one hill. When your father died—that's what you told me. But still up there on that hill live two tigers . . ."

Philippe stood up with sudden energy. He lit a cigarette and walked to the window and looked out. Isak could see the tension in his lean naked back. But when he finally turned and faced her, he was relaxed again. Physically relaxed, at any rate.

"My mother, Her Serene Highness the Princess Bianca, once owned a coat of jewels worth, it was said, two hundred and fifty thousand dollars. It was estimated that it cost her three hundred dollars just to put it on. Because, you see, every time she ventured out in it small precious stones would invariably fall off and be lost forever," he said in his gentlest voice. "It was an uncomfortable coat to wear, as you can imagine. But my mother wore it uncomplainingly, diligently, with self-denying passive fortitude. Why did she wear it? For St. Saladin. It attracted attention, you see. It was outrageous, absurdly magnificent. She hated that coat . . . but it was something she had to do. It was good for business. It was expected of her. It was her duty."

Philippe stubbed out his cigarette.

He walked to the foot of the bed and looked down at Isak with a sad smile on his lips.

"Now I have to wear a coat. It isn't a bejeweled coat any more. But it is very uncomfortable all the same. Some people may say it looks rather like a coat of sackcloth and ashes, but it is the only coat I have for the moment. The coat I must parade in, prowl in, be seen to be proud in. It is my duty, you see."

Isak knelt at the foot of the bed and held Philippe around the waist.

"Darling, I'm sorry. It's just that—it's so very difficult for me to understand sometimes."

"I know."

"I get very confused."

"It isn't an easy game to play and there are no set rules, except those inculcated from birth . . . by contagion, maybe. Perhaps they are supernaturally communicated, I don't know."

"Our children will be born knowing them?"

"Yes."

"Then they can teach me," Isak said.

Pensive twilight shadows moved across the bed. A vesper bell began to toll in the distant village. A sweet musky odor filled the air.

39

Richard had left the Polo Lounge, Antoine said, oh, more than three hours ago. Georgina wasn't angry. Thank you, she said politely and replaced the receiver. It had been an unnecessary call. She just had this strange indefinable instinct . . . it wasn't mistrust, or skepticism, or even uncertainty. She didn't want to examine what it was, perhaps because she knew. At least she didn't feel jealousy, as she feared she might. And she wasn't angry, as she had a right to be. She wasn't even anxious for his safety. If there had been an accident, driving her car, she would have been told soon enough. No, it went much deeper than that. She was waiting now . . . locked in that primal penitentiary of the spirit, banged up in that preparatory coop . . . waiting for the waiting to end. And then? She sat alone in the dark, just thinking and trying not to think, remembering and trying not to remember.

"Shall I see you again?" he'd asked after that first time.

"I don't know. I must think about it," she'd told him honestly. She'd hesitated then because she hated losers. Losers scared her, like the lepers she'd once seen in Lambaréné. It was nobody's fault. Nobody wanted to be a leper, and nobody wanted to be scared, and nobody wanted to be a loser. But she knew from the beginning that Richard Antrobus was what he was: the worst kind of loser, the kind that knew it, felt it, and could do nothing about it. He'd tried so hard. But even in the good days, even now when he was in the money and paid his share and bought her beautiful things . . . something always lingered in those eyes, something damnable, like a bloodstain that you can sponge and swab and scour and still it stays, a little fainter perhaps, but a little deeper too, always there.

Lovers always want from one another more than they can or ought to give, perhaps. But at least she had no illusions. She always saw him exactly the way he was: unscrupulous and headstrong and funny. She saw him with all his weaknesses and follies and dreamy schemes and social bigotry and mercenary charm, his paradoxical generosity and selfishness, and the diverting malice from which nobody was ever exempt, not even Richard Antrobus. With patience and imagination, a woman can always excuse and idolize and perhaps even still fancy such a man. It isn't so easy to need him, to want him, to love him.

He came in very quietly through the side door at the opposite end of the house. He didn't see her, sitting in the hugh armchair facing the terrace. Only the lamp on the sunken bar was on. He mixed a drink. He gave a deep sigh.

"Why such a big sigh, Richard?" she said quietly.

It scared him, her voice coming out of the dark like that. The tumbler made a crackling thud as it hit the top of the bar.

"Georgina?"

"Who did you think it was? The ghost of Theda?"

"Christ Almighty, this can be a spooky house sometimes," he said.

"I like a house that's worthy of ghosts," she said.

"Do you want a drink,"

"No thank you, darling."

She was very controlled.

"Have you eaten," she said in a neutral tone.

"No—I'm sorry—I—"

"Do you want Merla to get you something?"

"I'm not hungry."

"Well, you haven't been off screwing—"

"Darling—"

"Screwing always makes you hungry. I've changed my mind. I will have a drink, thank you," she said in exactly the same level tone.

"Scotch?"

"Is that what you're having?"

"Yes."

"Is that what you've been having?"

"A few. I'm—"

"Then I'll have Scotch."

The icebox started to grumble and shake as he opened the door.

"No ice, if that's for me," she said. "We really must get the man in to fix that bloody thing."

He closed the door. She heard him pour the drink, then splash a few more fingers into his own glass.

"Saving on the light bills?" he asked. He walked slowly, a drink in each hand, to the dark part of the big room.

"I thought I'd just sit here and wait for you," she said. "It was perfectly light when I sat down."

"Darling." He handed her the drink. "Are you all right?"

"Am I all right?"

"I'm so sorry."

"Do you have any idea what time it is?" Her tone was simply inquiring, without censure or reproach. She hated scenes of incrimination at any time.

"It must be after eleven. I can't see my watch," he said.

"My call's at nine. That's not too bad. Nine on the set. I've asked Merla to call me at six. This is very good Scotch. Did you have a nice evening?"

"Jesus Christ, Georgina!" Anger and frustration suddenly surged into his voice. "Shout at me! Scream at me! Throw something! Lose your fucking temper! Go for my eyes! *Do* something!"

"No, Richard."

"Give me something to fight against." He dropped to his knees and began to cry. "Give me an excuse, Georgina. Give me a reason."

She reached out and stroked his hair.

"It's really bad," she said.

"Really really," he said.

"Really really? Or just really?" she asked tenderly.

He held her around her waist and buried his head in her lap. They stayed like that, in the dark, for a very long time, not talking.

"I like the dark," she said after the tension had finally gone out of his body.

"What is it they say? Love is a great source of economy in a household . . ." He lifted his head from her lap.

"Would you like to go for a walk in the garden?" she asked.

"That'd be nice."

"Shall I put on the lights?"

"Let's leave the dark on."

They walked slowly to the end of the terrace and looked down on the city.

"It always reminds me at night of thousands of tiny diamonds on a black velvet cloth in Cartier's window," he said.

"All this can be yours, baby," Georgina said.

"You're stepping on my lines," he said.

"Do you think people ever said things like that? *All this can be yours, baby!* I mean, *real* people?"

"Theda probably said it all the time."

"Kiss me, my fool—and all this can be yours, baby."

He smiled and kissed her forehead tenderly.

"Theda is an anagram of death," he said. "Her real name was Theodosia Goodman."

"That's a nice name. Theodosia."

There was a long silence.

"When I first met you, first really fancied you . . . I had such audacity—"

"Atavism, I think, is the word you're looking for."

"—but the day I realized I was in love with you . . . sheer terror set in."

"Can't say I noticed," Georgina said.

"It's true. I found it amazingly difficult to . . . to tell you how I felt."

"I think I always knew."

"Even now, when it's important . . ."

"Don't worry about it, Richard."

"I have to tell you."

"I knew this evening. I knew—"

"What? What did you know?"

"You're going away. You're leaving me. It's all over, isn't it?"

"I have to go."

"I know you do."

"It must be as if I'm dead . . . beyond your reach, beyond—"

"*Shh*. Maybe . . . you won't seem quite so lost . . . the less I know."

"It'll never be over."

"No."

They talked softly in short expiring sentences.

"Why do people take to loving one another?" he asked.

"It's silly, isn't it?"

"It ruins everything."

"It's an old story."

"Do you think it was ever not . . . an old story?"

"I doubt it."

"That's very sad."

"Yet the people in it still manage to get their hearts broken," she said.

"With monotonous regularity."

"People never learn, do they?"

"People never learn."

He squeezed her hand.

"The sadness about happiness is that you never know you actually had it until it's too late," she said.

"You should only make comedies now," he said.

"Rivkin's got a comedy he wants to do. With Tracy in the South of France this summer."

"You should do it."

"Yes?"

"You haven't done a real comedy. You'd be marvelous in a sort of Lubitsch—"

"Christ, I'm going to miss you." Her voice hovered on the brink of tears and panic. "What am I going to *do*?"

They stood very close, side by side, looking out over the city in a sort of stricken stillness, a silence that was not uncommunicative.

"I went to see Liz tonight."

"I'm pleased she's around. I think I'm going to need her."

"On the way back, I decided . . . I was going to make you hate me."

"*Hate* you?"

"I thought it'd make it easier if—"

"You are funny, Antrobus. A funny, silly, astonishing man."

"I've done some terrible things. I—"

"No, Richard. I told you."

"You don't even want to know why?"

"No."

"I'd rather tell you at least a little . . . not just about . . . I'd hate you to make painful discoveries when I'm—"

"No."

"You are an astonishing woman."

They continued walking. They went down the terrace steps and through the tall iron gates that led to the wide palatial gardens on the south side of the house.

"There are just some things in life that you know will happen," Georgina said. "It may just be going to a movie, or having dinner with a friend, or taking a plane trip, or a holiday . . . weeks ahead they are already events in your life, *faits accomplis*, unavoidable pieces of future. But there are other things—just as well planned, just as looked forward to, just as seemingly definite—that you *know* will never happen. There's something inside of you that can't *feel*, can't *imagine*, that particular bit of tomorrow. You never have that feeling?"

"No."

"I've always had it. Since I was a small child. My father would talk about things we were going to do together, the trips he'd planned—I just knew they would never happen. In the end, I learned to figure out one from the other—it saved a lot of disappointment, a lot of tears."

"Didn't you ever figure wrong?"

"No."

"That's extraordinary."

"Well, anyway, that's how I felt about us. I kept telling myself I was wrong this time. But, as you see . . ." She shivered a little bit.

"Are you cold?"

"No. It's all right," she said. "I knew that something would finally get in the way. I knew that somebody would come along and upset the applecart. Tonight, waiting for you, I knew it'd happened. There were no ominous omens . . . I just sort of knew it had happened."

He took off his jacket and slipped it around her shoulders.

"But, you see, in my heart of hearts . . . I never set much store by our future together."

"I don't know what to say," Antrobus said.

"You don't have to say anything. I know. You know me, an old Aries witch from way back."

"One thing I will tell you. Will you let me tell you one thing?"

"If you promise it won't make me cry."

"Most of my life I've been a loser—a charming loser. In fact, losing was half the secret of my charm, and at least my debts were extravagantly incurred. I got by very well. I've always known how to use my friends, especially my lady friends—as you know. Oh, the odd frayed cuff, the occasional bailiff banging on my door . . . but it all had a certain romantic decadence that some ladies seemed to rather like."

"Yes, so I noticed."

"You once told me I had a mercenary charm—"

"It's true," she said with hardly a falter. "You're a terrible user of people."

"But for about twenty minutes of my life I got lucky. For twenty minutes of my life I was on a real winning streak . . . and I was lucky enough to have shared that twenty minutes with you. End of very boring speech."

"It was a very beautiful speech. And I'm grateful. Thank you."

"I don't know. Maybe it'd have been kinder—more eloquent—to have kept my trap shut," he said in a different kind of voice.

"No. I wanted to hear it. I needed it."

They turned and walked back to the house.

"I'll sleep in my dressing room tonight," he said. "I've got some work to do. I don't want to disturb you."

"You won't disturb me."

"I'll see, then. When I'm finished."

He walked her to the bedroom and took his jacket from her shoulders.

"Thank you," she said.

She turned and held up her face to be kissed. She opened her mouth, waiting for the loving moist pressure of his tongue, but it never came. It was a good-bye kiss from a man who had already gone.

At exactly six o'clock Merla woke her and gave her a glass of hot water. In two minutes she returned with tea.

"Bath's ready, Miss Game," the maid said. "Six o'clock."

"I'm awake," Georgina said.

"I've put out your slacks and a blue sweater. And I should take a jacket—"

The word jacket triggered it.

"Thank you, Merla. Fine," Georgina said, getting out of bed faster than Merla had ever seen her get out of bed in her life.

"Something the matter, Miss Game?"

Georgina was still putting on her peignoir when she entered his dressing room. He had gone. His suits, his shirts, shoes had gone. All the cupboards were empty, the drawers open and cleaned out.

"Merla—Merla—" Georgina rushed back to her room.

"Yes, ma'am?"

"When did Mr. Antrobus leave?"

"Mr. Antrobus gone? I didn't know he'd gone, Miss Game."

"Check if he's taken his car, will you please?"

Georgina went through to the drawing room.

She noticed it at once.

On her script was an envelope.

"Darling," he'd written on the back in his terrible handwriting that was part script and part block capitals, a child's scrawl.

This is why. You don't have to read it. But it explains everything—and excuses nothing. It can also hurt other people—badly!!!—so don't go leaving it on a number eleven bus—or in any strange beds! This may not sound very much like a love letter . . . but it is. It is. —R.

She put the envelope inside the script as Merla returned.

"He's taken the Jaguar, Miss Game."

Dave Jarrup took the call at the studio a few minutes after eleven o'clock that morning.

"Jesus," he said after listening for a long time. "The poor bastard." He listened some more and then he said, "And it's a positive identification?"

Another pause.

"No, no—but I'd hate to—"

He reached for a cigarette.

"Sure. Thank you, Captain."

He replaced the receiver slowly and forgot about the cigarette.

"Esther."

His secretary came in smiling. Her blond hair was tied back with a little-girl bow.

"Antrobus is dead," he said.

"Oh my God," she said. "Did they get a confession?"

"Don't be a smartass, Esther. The guy's dead."

She looked contrite.

"Sorry, Dave. He was never my favorite people. How'd it happen?"

"An auto accident—over in Venice."

"Venice? What the hell was he doing in Venice?"

"They figure he was on his way to the airport and turned off Lincoln too soon . . . he had a couple of suitcases in the car."

"See Venice and die," Esther said.

"Naples," Jarrup said. "It's see Naples and die."

"It doesn't really matter, does it?" she said.

"He severed his spinal cord. Mentally, he was killed instantly. Physically he died about an hour ago—"

"What are you going to do?"

"Tell Rivkin, I guess."

"Who's going to tell Milady?"

"Any volunteers?"

"Rivkin should do it."

"The thing is to move. The press'll be down here like a yellow streak."

"You think they'll connect?"

"Does a bear shit in the woods?"

He picked up the phone and asked for Bobby Rivkin's office.

"You'd better put me through, sweetheart," he said in a tough voice when the secretary said he was in conference. "Because, believe me, the studio's gonna be on fire any minute now and Mr. Rivkin likes to know about these things."

She put him through.

"This had better be important, Dave."

Rivkin listened quietly.

"Okay, Dave. I'll go on the set myself and tell her. Come up to my office at—" he looked at his watch "—twelve. Prepare a statement. Something short and dignified. I guess we'll have to suspend production a coupla days."

"She has only three more days anyway, doesn't she?"

"Yeah."

"Lousy timing," Jarrup said.

"It was almost perfect timing," Rivkin said softly.

Book Three

40

Lionel Hammond arrived first. He chose a table in the shade on the terrace. He ordered a Perrier water. He sat with his back to the sun and to the large lily-white hotel which, from the pavilion, with its brilliant yellow blinds and blue shutters, looked like a fairytale palace. It was probably his favorite hotel, the Grand Hôtel du Cap, Hammond reflected. It could barely have changed an iota since Scott and Zelda were living it up here in the twenties. It was the hotel Fitzgerald used as a model for Gausse's Hôtel des Étrangers in *Tender Is the Night*. The thought that Georgina's next role would probably be the heroine of that book pleased him immensely. For it seemed to emphasize more than anything that he was again the most successful independent agent in London. Georgina Game was already earning fifty thousand pounds more per picture than Warren Masters was getting when he died. Even allowing for inflation, that was pretty damn good. He was asking $400,000 plus ten percent of the gross for her to play Nicole. "They bawled and bitched but they didn't say no," he told her. "I think, my dear, it's in the bag."

It was going to be a fairly typical luncheon party, he thought. A Bobby Rivkin special. The problem with men like Rivkin, and Biron Strauss, was that they couldn't distinguish between company and a crowd.

Rivkin arrived with Dave Jarrup. They looked like visitors from a rather grand yachting party, endorsed by the Prince of Wales and Edith Head. They wore dark blue blazers, white flannel trousers, and Gucci shoes. Rivkin also wore the yachting cap he'd worn in *Night on the Waves*, back in his acting days.

"Lionel, how're ya, fella?" Rivkin greeted him from ten yards away.

"Robert, good morning."

"You know Dave Jarrup, don't you?"

"Yes, of course. How are you, Mr. Jarrup?"

"Still trying to rescue your client from her legend and restore her to humanity," he said without a smile.

Hammond gave him a slow thought-concealing grin.

The two Americans sat opposite him, facing the sun. They wore sunglasses.

"She's giving Dave a pretty hard time," Rivkin said. "She hasn't given a single interview since the press call the first day of shooting. Isn't that right, Dave?"

"You got a lot of coverage out of that," Hammond said in his mild voice. "All those pictures of her and Tracy at the casino—"

"Pictures but no words," Jarrup said. "She won't *talk* to anyone."

"Personal publicity jars horribly on her, it always has," Hammond said. "It's a style that suits her best, reticence, and she is suited to—"

"We've got NBC down here, and the BBC. Spence couldn't be more co-operative if he tried. He sat down with R. T. Française yesterday for thirty-five minutes. Georgina—a *clam* has more repartee."

"She just feels she has nothing to say," Hammond said.

"Every actress should possess some viewpoint—ideally one of chat-show length," Jarrup said.

"She is just a very reticent lady."

The Americans ordered champagne cocktails.

"I guess she doesn't do so bad," Rivkin said when the drinks had come. "She got the cover of *Time*—"

"Yeah—Hollywood's New Ice Maiden Age," Jarrup quoted the cover line.

"It still wasn't exactly a hatchet job," Rivkin said. "I've read a lot worse."

"You'd better tell *her* that."

"It upset her," said Hammond. "There were a lot of inaccuracies."

"What the hell did she expect?" Jarrup said. "She

gave the guy twenty minutes on the set in Hollywood. He didn't even get up to the house, he didn't—"

"What was that great quote—about applause? Something about applause," Rivkin asked.

"I do not need to be constantly fanned by popular applause," Jarrup said in an English accent. "That one?"

"Yeah. A great quote," Rivkin said. "And that other thing about pin-ups—what was that one, Dave? Pinups are something—something—"

"Some banana oil about paradise having to do with the presence of innocence as well as the absence of clothes," Jarrup said.

"Great quote. Great quote. Everybody picked that up. Did you make that up for her, Dave?"

"Who the fuck could write dialogue like that?" Jarrup said with a smile like a small muscular spasm. "She writes all her own material."

"I thought it was a good piece," Rivkin said more confidently. "An ice maiden with an inner fire . . . that's what they called her. Right?"

"Well, they could hardly say she was just a beautiful doll whose old man was a self-made millionaire—"

"You can understand why she holds herself so aloof from the press," Hammond said, keeping the actual note of disapproval out of his voice. "She's a sitting target for these people. Anyway, Harry Ogilvy was never a—"

"I'm not going to throw her to the wolves, Mr. Hammond," Jarrup interrupted in a new, reasonable voice. "I like her a lot. And that's the truth. There are newspaper guys in England I wouldn't let within ten miles of her *stand-in*. But she has to learn to trust me. If you could just have a word with her—"

"I'll have a word," Hammond said. "There's no reason at all why everything shouldn't right itself in time. At the end of the picture—"

"The picture's going just swell," Rivkin said. "Everybody's happy."

Biron Strauss, wearing white duck pants, a French matelot's striped jersey, and Gucci shoes, joined them. Rivkin ordered a bottle of champagne.

"What time did you tell Georgina?" Rivkin asked Jarrup.

"One o'clock."

"And Spence?"

"Spence's not joining us. He wants to ride over to Grasse. Look at the cathedral there. The paintings."

"*Washing of Feet*," Hammond said in his curious expressionless voice. "A beautiful Fragonard."

"Yeah?" said Rivkin.

Hammond knew he was angry that Tracy was ducking the lunch. Rivkin was only in for the weekend. "From the factory." This was to have been his party. Like most movie moguls, his commanding presence meant nothing if it didn't command the presence of the stars. Stars determine the very existence and economy of moguls as well as movies: *gelt by association*, Warren Masters used to call it.

Maybe Jarrup knew what was going through Rivkin's mind, too. He said: "I think Spence's really worried about the rumors going around—about him and Georgina."

"Nobody pays any attention to that shit any more—except Parsons and Hedda."

"Well, Spence does. He's pretty touchy about it. The age thing—"

"She's free, white, and twenty-one. He ain't gonna go to jail."

Jarrup shrugged.

"Is there anything in it?"

"A few dinners together. They went dancing in Juanles-Pins and somebody got those pictures—"

"I saw them," Rivkin said. "Pretty close, huh?"

"Well, anyway, he's keeping outta the way."

It seemed to work. Rivkin smiled.

"That old shitpoke," he said with affectionate admiration. "I bet he's been there. That sly old bastard's been there, what's the betting? He's been there, right?"

"Could be," Jarrup said in a casual mollifying voice.

Rivkin narrowed his eyes so that they seemed to see great distances.

"Don't discourage the rumors too hard, Dave," he said. "Know what I mean?"

"Unless we had something better going for us," Biron Strauss said in a quiet voice, joining the conversation for the first time.

"Better?"

"I was over in St. Saladin the other night—playing a little chemmy with Jack and Darryl. We met some people from the palace."

"You're gonna get a title, Biron?" Rivkin ribbed him. "Lord Biron of Burbank—"

"I met a priest—" he went on, ignoring the gibe.

"A priest!"

"*The* priest. An American. Father Cornelius. He's the court holy guy, but a real poo-pah, *very* close to His Royal Highness."

"The Prince?"

"Like that." Strauss held up entwined fingers, one of them badly deformed.

"Oh good," Rivkin said. "I like the Church to be in touch with the common folk. What is he? A Mick?"

"I've invited him to lunch."

"You've invited a priest to lunch?"

"Uh-huh."

"Here? Today? With us?"

"I thought it wouldn't be such a bad move . . ." Strauss said. "Think about it."

The realization began to spread across Rivkin's face like the shadow of a cloud slowly drifting over the land.

"Jesus, Biron," he said. "Dave?"

"The Prince and the Movie Queen," Jarrup said slowly, already thinking in headlines.

"Maybe it won't come to anything—but, then maybe it will," Strauss said with a modest shrug.

"Why the hell didn't you think of it, Dave?" Rivkin turned on Jarrup with a playful show of anger.

"It'll look like a stunt," Jarrup said. "It's too good to be true."

"Who the hell cares—if it comes off," Rivkin said.

"Right," said Strauss.

"I'm afraid, gentlemen, you've overlooked one tiny thing," Hammond said.

"Yeah?"

"Georgina."

"What does—"

"She'd never go along with a—"

"Lionel—sweetheart—what's to go along with?" Rivkin said "We're just surmising—what if? Right? What if Georgina was introduced to the Prince? What if she happened to be invited to lunch at the palace? What if she got an invitation to tea? Know what I mean?"

"Put ideas in people's minds," Strauss said.

"Your client's got ten percent of this picture. And you've got ten percent of that. Don't forget that, Lionel, sweetheart."

"That, I must say, sounds a little incongruous coming from you. After the philosophy you were expounding in the New York *Times* a week ago."

"Baby, I only expound a philosophy when I'm talking to critics. Deep down, I'm a born opportunist."

"A pragmatist," Jarrup said automatically.

"All I know is you can't miss a trick in this racket. You gotta play your hand for all it's worth."

Hammond looked thoughtful. "I haven't heard any of this. I'm not even here," he said after a long pause.

"That's my boy," Rivkin said. "Like I always say: if the booty fits, you might as well steal it."

Georgina sat between Father Cornelius and Bobby Rivkin. Liz Huntington sat between Rivkin and Biron Strauss. Dave Jarrup put himself between Cornelius and Waldo Bragg, the clairvoyant. Bragg was a personal friend of Georgina's, he kept reminding people. He was the first one to predict her success in *Danger East* when *everybody*, including Georgina herself, said she wouldn't even *make* the picture. "That's right," Strauss said without enthusiasm. In the space between Strauss and Waldo Bragg at the big round table were Lionel Hammond and eight or nine assorted people Rivkin had asked to lunch for reasons that probably were no more important than an instinctive need to dress the set, an ingrained need to ensure that his was *the* luncheon party in the Eden Roc pavilion at Cap d'Antibes that day.

Georgina talked to Cornelius. They talked about the movie she was making, about Hollywood, the hotel, its history, Scott Fitzgerald, Zelda, St. Saladin, Spencer

Tracy . . . Mr. Tracy was a dear man, the most professional actor she'd ever worked with. Had Georgina ever been to St. Louis? Cornelius came from St. Louis. Yes, he still got homesick. Honest to God? Honest to God.

"I miss London and I miss New York but I don't miss Hollywood at all," she said. "I'm sure I'll never be a Californian—but I'm told everybody says that at first."

"I read the article on you in *Time* magazine," he said.

"Ugh," she said.

"Does it upset you? What people write about you?"

"I'm long past caring."

"They say some pretty personal things about the Prince, too. He feels the way you do about it. I guess it's the only sensible way."

"The Prince?"

"He isn't nearly as—I was going to say stuffy—as they make out—but stuffy's not the word. Sulky, perhaps. He just comes out of all those pieces they write about him as a kind of sulky playboy. He's not like that at all."

"Okay. What's he like—I've given you all the dirt on Mr. Tracy. Now give me the lowdown on the Prince," she said out of the side of her mouth.

"He's a great guy."

"No dark guilty secrets?"

"Oh, sure—but not from me. He has to tell me everything. Sooner or later. That's one of the perks of being a priest. You get to hear a lot of interesting stories."

"I guess that's why Catholics don't need analysts the way the poor Protestants and Jews need analysts. Catholics get it off their chests in the confessional, right?"

"Think of the dough they save, too. A few collection-plate pennies—nickels and dimes is all it takes." Cornelius grinned and sipped his wine. "Get off the couch and get on your hassocks. That should be our new slogan. Maybe I'll put it up to the Vatican."

"Then again . . . maybe you won't," she said.

"All that papal bull . . . maybe you're right."

They talked for a long time, their heads together,

laughing and making jokes, looking serious sometimes,
their voices low, then more laughter, more tooth-and-
nail conversation. Cornelius said the wine had made
him light-headed.

Rivkin finally turned to Georgina and spoke in his
actor's voice: "What are you guys talking about?"

"I was telling Father Cornelius about you."

"Yeah?" He looked pleased.

"I said you have this particular talent."

"Yeah?" Rivkin used his special smile. "What's
that?"

"You have this talent for convincing other people
that you have talent," she said.

Rivkin laughed, but she could tell he didn't like it.

"I'm not sure that it's a talent," he said. "But I figured out a long time ago that you can call most people's
bluff if you call it loud enough."

Georgina leaned over and kissed his cheek. She liked
him for saying that. She had been unnecessarily mean
because she knew that deep down Bobby Rivkin had no
sense of humor at all. Especially about himself.

"I'm a terrible tease," she said.

"You surely are, ma'am," he said in a slow Southern
accent. "You surely are a tease."

41

Bobby Rivkin was furious.

He put the telephone on his desk and closed the
door. He went back to his desk and sat down before
picking up the phone again. He was taking his time,
trying to control his temper.

"Have I got this right, or what? You're telling me
that she's been seeing the goddamn Prince for three

fucking weeks and nobody knew? Jesus Christ! You're *paid* to know about these things."

Dave Jarrup stood looking out of his window at the sea. He listened for nearly five minutes without saying a word. He despised Rivkin's actory excess.

"Liz Huntington must have known," he pointed out when Rivkin had finally stopped. It was the best shot he had. "I guess she didn't mention it to you, Bob."

"If she knew about it, I'll personally . . ." The shot went home. After a few more choice expletives and a short eloquent passage about the mendacity and deviousness of women in general, Rivkin said in a more reasonable tone:

"Well, Dave, it's obviously been a well-kept secret. But she always was a furtive bitch."

"I thought we might do something with . . . you know, clandestine rendezvous—it sounds more—"

"So the priest finally delivered, huh?" Rivkin said.

"He set it up a coupla days after you left, after that lunch."

"Yeah. I thought they were pretty chummy. So that cocksucker Strauss pulled it off. He must be feeling pretty damn pleased with himself?"

"He doesn't know yet."

"Don't tell him. Let me tell him. I'll talk to him."

"We have six o'clock here. He should be back from the location in about half an hour. They're shooting up in the pine forest with Spencer and the French chick."

"Well, what are we going to do with it, Dave? Now we've got it."

"We leak it."

"Immediately? Hold it? What?"

"Well, I only just got on to it. She told Spence and he mentioned it to me. He thought I knew. I phoned you right away."

"Yeah."

"If we hold off, let it ride, it'll get out in its own sweet time—"

"Will it, though? She's a *very* underhanded woman."

"So we leak it to Earl Wilson, or to one of the girls. We go that route."

"Yeah. Well, think about it, Dave. Let me know. I won't talk to anyone here until—" He had a sudden thought. "Dave, stick around, could it come out from the Palace? Would they spill it?"

"He has an aversion to the press," Jarrup said.

"They make a fine fucking pair."

42

"We don't do a thing," Dieter Stosch said. He stood in the middle of his large office. "We sit back. We wait. We let it take its natural course."

"Philippe knew what Cornelius was doing?" Cheroffini asked.

"Pimping," said Duclos with contempt in his voice. "The pimping priest."

"I should be careful of using such words," Stosch said, deceptively quiet.

"At least Count Cheroffini and I endeavored to arrange a proper liasion, a royal connection, at least an illustrious name . . . not a Hollywood film actress . . ."

"We cannot afford to be doctrinaire," Stosch said calmly. "You failed in your quest. Now we must see."

"Film stars! The whole thing stinks of expediency," Duclos said.

"No alliance can be too expedient if it gives us—"

"The whole business appears to have been kept remarkably discreet," Cheroffini said.

"I have no doubt the film people will let the cat out of the bag in due course. We are in no great hurry . . . give them time," Stosch said.

"How often . . . have they met?"

"On seven occasions. Three times alone."

"A film star!" Duclos said.

He looked at Cheroffini, who stood very upright

against the wall, his arms folded across his chest, betraying nothing.

"You knew she was on the list," Stosch said. "Your righteous display is barely supported by the facts—"

"I never thought we'd come to . . . to this," Duclos said, dismally shaking his head.

"Then you miscalculated—or you mismanaged," Stosch said calmly. "The choice is yours."

Cheroffini seemed to smile inadvertently.

"Did Philippe know what Cornelius was up to?" Cheroffini asked again after a silence.

"Cornelius met her on his own time," Stosch said.

"But he knew she was on our list?" Cheroffini wasn't willing to let it go easily.

"I understand that Alwyn Brand had mentioned to him the merits of this particular woman," Stosch said. He limped a little as he walked back to his desk.

Cheroffini had to admire Stosch, who had so adroitly involved the priest in an affair whose purpose was in no way godly.

It was almost as if Stosch had read his mind.

"Cornelius knows well enough that there is a time for praying and a time for politicking," he said, looking straight at the Count.

"It would have served no . . . *earthly* purpose for him to have inquired too deeply—whether or not the woman was on our list."

"The priest is off the hook then?" Cheroffini said.

"He made sure he was never on it," Stosch said.

"An honest broker," Cheroffini said. "Just like us."

"Almost," Stosch said.

"A film actress!" Duclos said, his voice heavy with lament, and recurring contempt.

From below came the distant sound of rolling dice and spinning wheels and the perpetual petitioning prayerlike murmur of people selling their souls to the Devil. . . .

"A Hollywood film actress!"

43

"I must admit, I've kissed a lot of toadies in my time, but never the Prince," Liz said that evening.

They were in Georgina's suite. It was late, but Georgina was only on stand-by call for a scene that would be shot inside a pottery in Biot the next morning if it rained. It wasn't going to rain tomorrow. It probably wasn't going to rain all that summer.

"He's a very interesting man. I really do like him," Georgina said. "Terribly good-looking . . . he probably knows exactly what he's doing. But he has no . . . he has no meaning for me."

"You haven't slept with him yet?"

"No."

"Has he tried?"

"Not so's you'd notice."

"He's probably a little afraid, too, you know. Georgina Game . . . It must be just a little bit unnerving for a man. Even a prince."

"The Ice Maiden, you mean?"

"You know what I mean. Just the . . . the whole image thing."

"Well, *he's* a little bit unreal too, you know. He has an unreal quality—he has this style—I mean, that *palace*—the whole thing is such an anachronism."

"An agreeable anachronism—wouldn't you say, my dear?"

"If you like that sort of thing."

Liz had spent all that summer with Georgina; she'd barely left her side since Richard's death. She had managed to do a little modeling in New York and some in Paris when Georgina had to be in those cities for business meetings and wardrobe fittings and the dozen and one other things that go on before a movie gets onto the studio floor. But mostly she modeled to keep up appearances, out of vanity, perhaps, or female pride. She told Georgina that it was important to keep her name in front of photographers and fashion editors, and that was true too. There were a lot of new girls coming up, new faces, and new styles. It was easy to lose touch. Her money continued to arrive every month from Mlle. Chaire and her hotel bills and traveling expenses were picked up by the studio. Rivkin had got her on the production budget as Georgina Game's voice coach.

Georgina, in a long flowery green Fath housecoat that would have got her into the Royal Enclosure at Ascot, lay on the sofa with her eyes closed. Without makeup, she looked very pale. Because of the claims of continuity, she was forbidden to sunbathe or sit too long in the sun. The lighting cameraman examined her face every morning with anxious eyes, a horticulturist monitoring the adumbrations of some rare and exotic lily. Next to her, Liz looked nearly native. "Your nipples are exactly the color of those beautiful mango flowers Gauguin loved to paint in the hair of his girls," Georgina had told her one morning, studying Liz with admiring eyes. It was the most intimate thing that had passed between them since that loving time in Paris, so long ago. It awakened no aches, aroused no desires in either of them. It was the moment that released them both from all the accumulated misgivings, from the hoarded self-doubts. Their understanding was now complete, their friendship absolute.

"A penny for them," Liz said.

"I was just thinking . . . there was always such a sense of . . . *hazard* about Richard. He once told me I only loved him because he had an air of license. . . . He was probably right."

"Richard was something special," Liz said because she knew that was what Georgina wanted to hear. Liz looked like somebody out of a thirties movie, in printed dinner pajamas, an original Chanel that the art director had found for her in the Flea Market in Paris. She sat on the floor painting her toenails geranium red.

"I haven't slept with a man since Richard died."

"Have you wanted to?" Liz asked quietly.

"Not very much. I haven't seen much I've fancied."

"I thought you and Tracy—"

"We talked about it. That was all—the chords of conscience, maybe. Anyway, it was that close, but we didn't."

"Well, I'll tell you. You might just as well have—because everybody thinks you did."

"Sure," Georgina said exactly the way Tracy said it. "Do you know he's got one of the best private collections in Hollywood?"

"What's that got to do with anything, Georgina?"

"The other day. He wanted to go and look at the paintings in Grasse instead of having lunch with us. Remember? Everybody thought he was embarrassed about being seen with me, after all the rumors. It wasn't that at all. He really did want to go and look at the paintings in Grasse. Screw Bobby, screw his lunch party, screw what people thought—"

"There's a lesson there."

"How do you mean? A lesson?"

"You have to decide what it is you want to do—and go right ahead and do it. Screw what people think."

Liz stopped concentrating on the fine brushwork on her nails and looked at Georgina closely.

"What's the matter?" Georgina said, aware of the sudden scrutiny and opening her eyes.

"Can I say something to you?"

"Be my guest." She closed her eyes again.

"You see, you now have to decide whether you want to be a woman—or a fucking monument. If you want to be a woman, you can't go on thinking how marvelous it might have been with Richard. Richard's dead. You're alive. You can't go through the rest of your natural life feeling guilty. There comes a moment when you must leave the past behind, even if you have no place to go. You're not a shrine, a memorial, you're a—"

"I know. I'm silly, I know," Georgina said quickly. She smiled, a sad smile, but when it had gone there was a harder, sharper expression on her face.

"You say things like the Prince has no meaning for

you. You've got to stop thinking like that. You're a very rich lady, you—"

"Do you think that happiness automatically accrues to savings? Like interest? Seven percent per annum willynilly—"

"Why shouldn't it?"

"It just doesn't work like that, Liz, that's why not."

A waiter came in to clear the dinner table.

Georgina sat up and retrieved her script from the floor beside the sofa. She opened it to her last big scene in the movie—where the princess has to tell Tracy who she really is, the moment when the movie stops being a comedy and becomes a poignant love story. It was her favorite moment in the whole script. She stared at the page for a long time, not seeing the words. It didn't matter. She knew the scene by heart. Tracy has the last line in the picture, after she asks for his forgiveness: "I won't forget you, if that's what you mean, Princess. I guess for people like us . . . the only password we'll ever know is good-bye." Spence had read the line to her at dinner one night and actually made her weep.

She put the script back on the floor. She sat thinking for a while. There was still a certain stubbornness in her face but it was now only the remnant of a mood that had passed.

"Know what's most . . . touching about the Prince—under all the show?" she said suddenly to Liz. Her voice had a special gentleness that Liz had noticed she usually reserved for conversations about Antrobus. "His insecurity. He said to me last night: 'Being a prince and being a movie star—they're both a solitary business.' I must say I warmed to him a whole lot after that."

"It was very perceptive of him."

"He said that somebody once said that princes were like stars—they rise and set. They've got the worship of the world but no repose."

"Shelley. Shelley said it. Only I think it was about kings. Kings are like stars . . ."

"The brain from Main."

"I'll tell you . . . I think Philippe is basically a very nice guy. And *very* dishy. He has that hardness—"

"He has a mistress—" Georgina began.

"Isak Girod. Don't you remember? That night at Lapérouse—we saw her."

"Oh Christ, yes! Do you know, Liz, I'd completely forgotten? The lady who's been offered all that money for her memoirs."

"A dollar a dick."

"Probably a terrible calumny," Georgina said. "Well, a small exaggeration, anyway."

"Why his mistress? Why don't they marry?"

"He wasn't too clear about that. He's obviously very fond of her . . . but—as you would say, Liz—he was ducking and diving a bit—"

"Isn't she supposed to be considered unsuitable by— what would it be? His Council of State? Anyway, his advisors. Didn't they put the block on her?"

"That would account for his brooding air, I suppose," Georgina said.

"A prince with a brooding air! How divine!"

44

"I still think it's ill-advised," Georgina said in a low voice, glancing around the small but crowded restaurant near the village of Salis.

"No, no," Philippe said easily. "The people know me here. They are discreet."

"Is this where you bring all your women?"

Philippe hesitated for a moment, then grinned.

"Of course. All of them," he said with a small smile of self-mockery.

It was the first time they had been out in public.

"I cannot keep you to myself forever. We must behave like other people sometimes."

"Don't you hate being recognized all the time? I do," Georgina said.

"Fame is a kind of vulgarity. It cannot be helped."

"Mademoiselle Game . . . Your Highness . . ." The *patron* handed them the menu cards with a small bow and departed.

"They say that love affairs lose their piquancy when they're no longer a secret," she said.

"Are we having a love affair?" he asked, giving her a quizzical look.

"I was simply generalizing," she said.

"You raise my hopes only to dash them to the ground," he said with feigned pathos, his eyes assuming a sudden deadness, as if they had foreclosed on their own future.

"I suppose we'll have to make up our minds soon enough—"

"Perhaps some frog's legs meunière ou Provençale—"

"—whether we're having an affair or not—before we deteriorate into old chums."

"Ah." He spoke the word softly, reflectively.

She lowered her voice and went on in a Swedish accent. "I haf no mittleground in my emotions. I dunt vant to be average. I dunt know how to be lak osser people. I am a *star*."

"Old chums?"

"Just good friends." She resumed her normal voice.

"What lovers are at airports?" he said.

"What lovers pretend to be at airports."

"I see," he said with solemn understanding. "Just good friends. Very boring."

His eyes were alive again. There was something both wanton and omniscient about those pale-blue eyes with the strange metallic luster.

"Bow-ring," Georgina said. "Have you noticed how *chic* people always say bow-ring? *Gstaad was so* bow-ring, darling . . . Have you noticed?"

"Bow-ring people are so boring," he said in a grave, sexy, faintly forbidding tone.

"Before they even open their mouths, you know they are going to be bow-ring people," Georgina said with a continuous smile. "You simply have to look at their accessories—"

"This season Yorkshire terriers and Hermès scarves," he said.

"Exactly!"

"I remember my mother used to tell a story about a very bow-ring lady. During the Prussian siege of Paris, this poor thing was obliged to consume her little pet dog—it was the year of the poodle, I believe. Anyway, it was baked in red wine and when she had finished the meal she shed a few tears. 'How my dear little Tchou-Tchou would have enjoyed these bones,' she said."

Georgina was happy and amused. But more than that she was comfortable in the company of this tall unexpected man who was still almost a stranger to her—although it was true that she had been to bed with many men she knew, or understood, a great deal less. But not since Richard died had she been so relaxed—yet so quickened with coquetry and flirtatious intent—with a man. Slowly the fences of formality and discretion which had been erected between them in those first weeks, during those secret meetings in his palace, in secluded villas and hotel suites, were finally coming down. It was true, as Liz had said, he had a hardness in him, but it was the hardness Georgina liked to see in a man: the blunt-boned angles of his face, the taut, almost barbaric grace of his movements, the dark sensual swoop of his smile. It was a face somehow beyond its time—a Medici face, she thought at once. It was a face of indefinable age, carnal yet almost messianic, too. His hair was so perfectly black, black as a crow's belly, she guessed it had been dyed: it was an interesting vanity, she thought, in such a man.

They ordered the same meal from the small menu— sole chambord with a simple *salade tomate*. Philippe asked for a bottle of Corton Charlemagne without consulting the list.

"This is a very pretty place," Georgina said, slowly nodding her head.

"It was from here that de Maupassant wrote that he had never seen anything so wonderful or so lovely as the sun setting over Antibes—it was as unforgettable as the memory of happiness, he said."

"Is happiness unforgettable?" she said.

"Most of the happy times in one's life can never be repeated. It is best to forget."

"That's very sad, if you believe that. Is that truly what you believe?"

"Yes," he said. "I make a point of it."

"I cling—" she said.

"Most people spend their lives trying to restore old times—as if old times were a damaged canvas." He sipped his wine slowly. "One must move on to new canvases—even if one knows the pictures will be less pleasing."

"That's strange. That's almost what Elizabeth said to me the other evening. You must leave the past behind . . . even if you have no place to go."

"She is right. The alternative . . ." His voice trailed away.

"What is the alternative, Philippe?"

"To be scuttled on a ghost ship," he said. "In oceans of past."

"You make it sound horrid."

He looked at her searchingly in the candlelight of the restaurant.

"You talk about your father a great deal. You never mention your mother."

"She's dead. She died in a plane crash."

"I'm sorry."

"It was a long time ago. I was a child."

"My mother killed herself. In 1939 in a suicide pact with her lover. I sometimes think she also knew this thing about happiness—only she could never erase the memories. So—" he smiled "—as I say, it is best to forget—if you can."

"You really think that? Really really or—"

She caught herself in mid-sentence and froze. She felt wretched and . . . unfaithful. But how can you be unfaithful to the dead? Every affair, every romance, develops its own special language, its own secret signs and symbols and looks, its own silly words and familiar exchanges—an idiom of intimacy that joins two people far more than the solemn vows. . . .

"Tell me about St. Saladin," she said quickly.

"It's a long story," he said.

He talked so knowingly and wisely about his land, its history since the founding of the dynasty in 1274 when Henri Carigbresci, a Savoy nobleman, was awarded St. Saladin for his courage and resolution in defeating Saracen pirates. . . .

He talked with passion and with pride. But as he came to his own times, a kind of regret came into his voice. Things are different now, he seemed to be saying. Things will never be the same again. For a moment she knew that he was on his ghost ship, adrift in those oceans of past.

It was extraordinary how close she felt to him. Without his history, except for his nobility, they were not so unalike. They both had fame, money, a kind of notoriety even. "People like you and me," he had said. "We'll never know the refuge of the common or garden." That was the real link, perhaps. Their differences in temperament and country did not matter at all. At that moment they were joined in an intimacy that was less than lover and mistress, and much more than brother and sister. Naked in bed, Georgina had felt less close to some men than she now felt to Philippe across this table in this restaurant.

They drank Calvados and coffee.

"I've enjoyed this evening more than I can possibly tell you."

"Thank you."

"It's true," Georgina said. "It's been a divine evening."

"You make it sound almost like a confession."

"Father Cornelius tells me you confess everything to him. Is that true?"

"There is one aspect of my life that is none of his damn business." Philippe grinned. "Sinful or not."

"I won't ask," she said, modestly lowering her eyes.

"Cornelius is at his best confessing ladies of high lineage—"

"The higher they are the lower they fall," Georgina said.

"Those society ladies arrayed in the most sublime *dernier cri*—who give you crabs."

"But *dressed* crabs," Georgina said with shocked maidenlike earnestness. "Surely?"

"But of course." Philippe grinned.

"I like Cornelius," he said. "That craggy face. He looks so . . . used—"

"And wise."

"For a priest."

"He had the good sense to introduce us," Georgina said.

The restaurant emptied around them, but still they sat and talked. The *patron* brought fresh coffee and departed: a man of the world who understands, who never gets familiar.

"I can't get too worked up over it," Philippe said at one point.

"Sometimes you don't sound . . . European at all," Georgina said.

"I was with the U.S. 1st Division for a lot of the war," he said.

"There is so much about you I don't know."

"I hope so," he said.

"I vant to find out alls your sekrets," she said in her Swedish accent.

"Leave me some. There's nothing sadder than a secretive man without secrets," he said.

"Tomorrow the boys are coming to tea. We shall see what we shall see," she said suddenly.

"What's that?"

"I found a diary I kept when I was eleven. It was totally empty except for one entry. In June."

"Tomorrow the boys are coming to tea?"

"We shall see what we shall see." She smiled. "A pretty interesting childhood, huh?"

"Are you happy doing what you're doing now?" he asked.

"Being an actress?"

"Yes."

"Not completely. I hate so much of what goes with it. The privations of being a public personality——"

"Then why don't you just stop? Find a way of life that you'd enjoy more?"

"A girl must think of the arithmetic as well as the art of living," she said. But even as she said it she knew, in her case, that it was no longer strictly true. She was rich, and she was as independent as everybody said she was.

They were the last couple in the restaurant.

Philippe finished his coffee.

"You know something very interesting?" Georgina said.

"Tell me something very interesting," he said.

"I'm not afraid of you any more."

"You were afraid of me?"

"Terrified."

"I was afraid of you."

"And now?"

"I'm not afraid of you any more, either."

"I'm pleased."

"Will you sleep with me tonight, Georgina?"

"The answer is yes—but I was hoping for a more romantic approach . . . from a prince," she said guile-lessly.

"It's my desire to break my lance with you in the sweet combat of love," he said with grave splendor.

"We'll print the *first* take," she said.

45

Dave Jarrup hurried through the lobby of the Grand Hôtel du Cap and up to the suite on the first floor that had been turned into the production publicity office. He noticed several new faces hanging about the lobby and wandering outside on the grass-covered terrace. The sort of faces you wouldn't usually find in that sort of hotel. They all had that anxious, slightly suspicious, misanthropic look he'd seen a hundred times before when a big news story was breaking and nobody was certain of its strength, or accuracy, or exactly when it would break. He didn't know any of the faces—and fortunately, for the moment at least, they didn't know his—but he thought there were at least five Italians, a couple of Englishmen, maybe one American, and four or five Frenchmen. At this stage, he figured, they were probably mostly local stringers, but that wouldn't last.

"Where were you when I needed you?" Esther said when he walked in.

"That bad, huh?"

"Hasn't stopped."

It was five o'clock. Nine o'clock in the morning in California.

"Okay," he said. "Let's go, men."

He put a call through to Bobby Rivkin.

"Wanna warm up the li'l ol' ice cubes?" He grinned. "For you and me both, baby."

The call came through within ten minutes.

"Bob. How are ya?" he said. Then he said, "Jesus!" He looked at Esther and opened his mouth and eyes wide with mugged-up astonishment while he listened.

"Radio *and* television?" he said.

He held the telephone out for Esther to hear what Rivkin was saying.

". . . minutes NBC news. CBS ignored it first time, but slipped in a sixty-second item in the next bulletin, and ABC gave it about the same. . . ."

Esther smiled and walked away, stirring her drink with her finger.

"Right," Jarrup said finally. "Well, we were shit out of luck with the timing—but I guess nobody can be blamed for that. Sure. No, not Jonahed, Bobby. Just the time difference. D'you want me to call her? She had that stuff five days ago, for Christ's sake! She can't squawk . . ."

He listened for a few more minutes, shaking his head.

"Not take it lying down! Louella told you that? She's

spinning her wheels, Bob. A coupla days, she'll cool
down. . . . Well, not *hard*. But implicit. Pretty damn
implicit. I even sent a covering note— . . . I'll call
her. I'll square it away."

Jarrup listened.

"Well, we've got the first of the bloodhounds and a
few porch-climbers downstairs, but just the beat guys.
My own guess is that the gentry will be here before the
end of the week. . . ."

He looked at Esther and lifted his eyebrows. He nodded, squandered a few smiles, said "sure" a few times
and "just watch me" once.

He put his hand over the mouthpiece and whispered
to Esther.

"Where's the piece that started it?"

She delved into a mound of newspapers and magazines on a coffee table in the middle of the room and
finally came up with a French newspaper. She spread it
out on his desk. Jarrup stared at the big front-page
story and pictures, continuing to listen to Bobby Rivkin.

Jarrup laughed softly and said:

"We're getting some translations . . . sure. Everywhere. Of course, London. London, Paris, Rome . . .
a home run all the way, Bob, an out-and-out mortgage-
lifter . . . The French break seems to have set the
tone. . . ."

He translated slowly from the newspaper on his desk.

"They were holding hands in a candlelit restaurant
and, ah, they were, ah, they were . . . audaciously
contemplating the kisses . . . the kisses upon each
other's lips . . . ah, lovers . . . with an eagerness to
live . . . and to love . . ."

He closed the newspaper.

"That's more or less the line in all of them as far as I
can see, Bob. They don't pull any punches."

He listened some more.

Esther placed a list of messages in front of him.

"Well, I've been out at the location all day. But Esther says Wilson's been on, and Bob Considine . . .
yeah. And some guys in London . . . Zec, Gour-
lay . . ."

Esther held up the front page of the London *Daily Mail*.

"The headline in the London *Mail* is: *Georgina and Philippe—More Than a Dalliance*? Big picture across five columns. Front page . . . I just know it, Bob. What does Liz Huntington tell you?"

He gave a big wink to Esther.

"Well, you certainly know more than we do this end," he said after a long silence.

Esther took the glass and freshened his drink. He nodded thanks.

Then he said:

"Oh, the usual line about the Ice Maiden . . . Yeah. They're calling *him*—are you ready for this?—a 'sexual conquistador' . . . no, *conquistador*. Sure they mention the film. A million times. We've got more space than Buck Rogers'd know what to do with."

Esther put some more London papers on his desk with passages ringed in red grease pencil.

"Here's one you'll love, Bob. Listen to this . . . *Prince Philippe's terminal case of satyriasis seems to—*"

He winked at Esther again and leaned back in his chair, listening.

"No, Bob. It just means he can't get enough."

He shook his head in genuine amazement.

"No, Bob—enough pussy, tail, snatch—"

Jarrup grinned. He sipped his drink and turned over the newspapers Esther had marked.

"Here's another one. *Prince Philippe—a romantic savage*—Not bad, huh? These—I'm just picking these at random . . ."

The transatlantic conversation came to an end after about forty-five minutes.

"He approves," Jarrup said.

"He's going to give his blessing?"

"According to Liz Huntington it's all true."

"What is?"

"The pair of them have been screwing like a coupla butterflies in heat—I quote—"

"Georgina and—"

"—the Prince."

"Do you mind if I take notes!" Esther said. "For my novel."

"How guys like that pull it off in the first place beats me. A prince and a Hollywood movie queen . . . ?"

"Nothing to it," Esther said. "A breeze. He, you know, makes a royal proclamation and she says 'Your palace or mine?' "

Jarrup grinned. He was feeling very relaxed now.

"Well, I tell ya. They live in a world of their own— the tribal arabesques of stardom . . . the ritual pavans of power. I mean, *the protocol!* Like, who makes the first move? These people—they have different preoccupations from you and me."

"They still get it on in the end."

"But you see the problem," Jarrup said. "Does a Hollywood movie queen, Goddess Incarnate to three hundred million movie fans, take precedence over a Riviera prince?"

"Call the palace," Esther said. "Get a ruling."

They sat in silence, sipping their drinks, waiting. Waiting for the telephone to ring, the sky to fall in, anything . . .

46

Philippe was the first to sleep afterward. She felt him slipping away from her into those drowsy drowning luscious depths. Lying entwined, immersed in the anonymous delicate darkness, now half-thinking, now half-dreaming—such yielding dreams with their irenic illusions of distance—Georgina was smiling. The sweat was still on them. She loved the special pearled wetness that swamped their bodies with that strange sweet saline of exhaustion and quenched excitement. The smell of scent and climax on silk and skin and in their hair. I've worn him out, she thought smiling in the night of the strange room. I've utterly exhausted him. It was amazing, all those months without it, she had built up inside herself a genuine belief—it wasn't even a fear—that she would never need sex again. The less you have it, she had said to Liz, the less you need it. She didn't know whether it was a biological fact, true of all women, but it was certainly true of her. She didn't even masturbate. She simply didn't think about it. She went through all the motions in her love scenes, and nobody complained, not the actor, not the director, not even the critics, but she felt nothing inside. Nothing except that emptiness, that complete complaisant void. But now her unleashed needs . . . her hoarded carnality, the suppressed exigencies of her flesh—had worn him out. Poor Philippe. She stroked his face. She loved the sleeping faces of men. Faces that concealed nothing, faces that claimed nothing. She moved gently out of their last drenched caress and turned on her back. Her thoughts drifted. Sometimes when she came she felt such a fierce fatality within her. She had told Richard that once. And he had said that strange thing: there is nothing quite as mocking as a dashboard saint in a wrecked car. Why did he say that? I don't know, he had answered . . . I suddenly saw the future, and that was it. They told her the Jaguar was a complete write-off. She wanted to ask them but knew she never could. She tried to remember the last time she had made love with Richard. Sometimes she thought it was an afternoon—just like the first time. But there were other times when she was sure it had been at night. It was strange how one could always remember the first time, but never the last . . . perhaps because one is never sure when the last time will be. Was tonight the last time with Philippe? No, she was sure of that. Richard was smiling at her now. So clearly. It was strange because sometimes . . . sometimes his face completely eluded her. Even when he was alive, there were times, making-love times, in-the-dark times, when she couldn't remember what he looked like. Once it had frightened her, so frightened her that she had to get up and switch on all the lights in the house and just look at him, pierced by such a sadness as she'd never known. I keep forgetting what you look like, she said. It hurt him so much. Dear Christ, why had she told him that? That night she woke up and he was crying. In absolute silence, just the tears pouring out of his gray eyes, like warm raindrops.

She was wide awake now. Why was there no immunity against the intrusion of dreams? she wondered.

Philippe stirred with a small satiated sigh, almost a moan. He moved his leg in his sleep, forcing his knee up between the backs of her thighs. She succumbed to the pressure, opening her legs, letting him in. Even in sleep, she thought, he was self-assertive, confident. He was a very good lover, although at first she couldn't come with him at all. "You should have heard me fake those coital cries," she had told Liz. "It was so exciting. I almost convinced *me*."

Now Philippe knew the places to touch, knew the words she liked to hear. Sometimes he made love to her in French, but she preferred to hear the things she wanted to hear in English. French was very beautiful in drawing rooms, by candlelight, French was a table tongue, but a woman needed Anglo-Saxon between the sheets. English was a basic language, a bed language.

After a little while she turned toward him again. His arms went around her and she felt him stir.

"It's all right," he said in English.

"I get frightened sometimes."

"Yes."

His hand moved down her body and stroked her soft moist hair, then his fingers entered her and curled the way she'd taught him to do it.

"Give me your tongue," she said.

He started to slide slowly downward, kissing her neck, then her breasts . . .

"No," she said urgently in the dark, tugging at his thick black hair. "Not yet. Now now. My mouth. Make love to my mouth. I want to feel your mouth open on mine."

He found her mouth with his.

She felt him grow harder. Unbelievably harder.

"*Now*," she said into his mouth.

He moved astride her and into her with such seething ease.

"Oh yes," she said.

"I know the way," he said.

"You do. Darling, you do."

He licked her face, teased her tiny nostrils with his fluttering tongue, explored her ear.

"Spit into my mouth when you start to come," she whispered. "I want to know the moment it starts for you."

"I don't want to . . . I don't want to abuse you," he said.

"You won't. I want you to do it. Please do it for me."

"Yes."

"Ejaculate into me with mouth and cock."

"You are extraordinary," he said, pulling back his head to look into her face.

"What?"

"Saying cock."

"Prick, then. Prick? Do you prefer prick?"

"Whatever pleases you."

"Joy stick?"

"Ugh."

"John Thomas?"

"No!"

"Now, darling! Please soon!" she suddenly cried out.

She thrashed beneath him like a wild thing fleeing from ghosts. . . .

He whimpered as the spit moved from his mouth into hers, as he poured his come into her cunt.

"Your spit and come, the sweat and spume of you . . . how divinely sullying," she said after the long silence that followed.

"Yes?"

"Oh, yes. On my breast and on my belly . . ."

He held her very tight.

"Kiss my nipples. Yes. Yes. Bite . . . not too hard . . . oh yes. Your teeth are so . . . more, a little more . . . yes. My nipple is so *hard* between your teeth . . . feel how hard you've made me . . . you're such a beautiful lover . . ."

He licked her slowly, from the tip of her nipple to her throat.

"I think—" she started to say. A fresh wave of contortion burst like a fist in her face. "I'm coming. Oh darling darling I'm coming. It won't stop. It's going on and on and on. Sweet darling Philippe . . ."

"I wasn't even inside you, you know," he told her afterward.

"No?"

"I just held you and you came."

"It was beautiful."

"I just held you," he said again. There was wonder as well as pride in his voice.

"It was magic," she said.

"I wonder what time it is."

"It's daylight."

"What time do you say it is?"

"Six o'clock," she guessed.

He reached for his watch.

"Twenty to eight," he said.

"Christ! We've been making love all night! I'll make the coffee," she said, getting out of bed with the abrupt movement she had learned at boarding school.

"Whose villa is this, anyway?"

They were having breakfast in a small courtyard, smelling of honeysuckle, beneath a single very old, very beautiful olive tree.

"You won't laugh?"

"It depends," Georgina said with a threatening look. A cool shadow fell across them in the hazy morning heat.

"It was my mother's."

"Your mother's?"

"It's where she brought her lovers for . . . assignations."

"Dirty weekends?"

"Princesses don't have dirty weekends," he said. "They have assignations—trysts."

"Nothing like keeping it in the family," she said.

"It's hardly ever used now. I don't even bother with

staff. A woman comes up from the village, and a man to do the garden. . . ."

"It's very remote. I love it."

She sipped her coffee. She looked around the beautiful old courtyard. It was so quiet. There was a sense of stillness about the place. It was as if it had been sealed in the nineteenth century, perhaps, and soundproofed with Pre-Raphaelite curls of ivy.

"Just for a moment I thought perhaps it was *the* villa."

"*The* villa?"

"Mlle. Girod's villa . . . the trysting place."

"No. Isak has her own place," he said easily.

"Will you continue to keep a mistress . . . after you marry? You are going to marry one day aren't you?"

He shrugged.

"Do I embarrass you?"

"Certainly not."

"I'm afraid I've acquired this very American habit of asking direct questions—"

"You don't embarrass me."

"Then why don't you answer my question?"

"It is not an easy question to answer. I want to be truthful. . . ." He spoke in a quiet deliberate voice, unaware that he was being teased. "It is too complicated."

"I'm a pretty bright girl," she said.

"It's not a question of being bright or not being bright. It is a question of . . . experience. You would have to have lived in palaces to know the difficulties."

"I've lived in studios," Georgina said. "I know all there is to know about court intrigue."

"You are not taking me seriously," he said.

"How can I when you speak to me in that grave *princely* tone at breakfast?"

"I'm sorry. I didn't mean to sound . . . princely."

"In bed you sound . . . almost human."

"Ah," he said, beginning to smile.

"Maybe I should ask you about it in bed?"

"We have other things to talk about in bed."

"I'm not a jealous lady, Philippe."

"Good."

"Your mistress doesn't bother me."

"Good."

"She is very pretty."

"Yes."

"Do you love her?"

"It's more complicated than that. May I have some more coffee, please?"

"Nothing's more complicated than love."

He shrugged.

She poured more coffee.

"You don't want to answer?"

"If I told you . . . you wouldn't believe it."

"I could try."

"One day . . . I would like to tell. Not now."

"Perhaps one day I won't want to listen."

He looked angry, just for a minute, then he smiled.

"Screw you," he said.

"That isn't very *princely*," she said. "You're a very contradictory man, Philippe."

"I am?"

"Your blend of coolness, vehemence, quixotic chivalry, vulgarity, gentleness, and cussedness . . ."

"Go on. I'm fascinated."

"It makes you a very hard man to fathom."

"You make good coffee, Miss Game."

Now she smiled.

"You see! I am contrary but I always know how to pay the important compliments. Tell a woman she makes good coffee . . . you've got her for life."

"I think we are very similar in a lot of ways, Philippe."

"You do?"

"I noticed it that night in Salis."

"What did you notice? Exactly?"

"We both need so many . . . confirmations, demonstrations . . . tests of . . . feelings . . ."

"I just need a good cup of coffee in the mornings."

"That's what you pretend. But underneath—"

"Ah underneath—a cauldron," he said self-mockingly.

"No—but you do feel more than you want people to think. You have a vulnerability—"

She saw the amusement go out of his eyes.

"You have made me very happy, Philippe," she said quickly. She reached out and touched the back of his hand. "We can amuse each other, please each other, we can even excite each other—"

"Oh yes," he said. "We can certainly do that. Even when we are being hunted down like animals by the press. With their prying thousand-millimeter lenses and—"

"Screw 'em," she said. Then: "See, now I'm picking up your vulgar expressions."

But he didn't smile.

He said, "You see this wall around us—this is how I have always lived. Incarcerated, besieged, behind high walls. I am encircled by the demands of others, by the claims and cravings of . . ." He stopped and looked at her intently. It was a look she'd grown used to, but it still made her uneasy.

"What?" she said.

"The life you have today—you made it? You are almost totally responsible for what you are?"

"I suppose so," she said.

"You created the circumstances of your fame?"

"Yes, but—"

"With talent and makeup and wigs, with dressmakers and diets and scripts and agents and producers and all the other paraphernalia . . . you made somebody, a woman, a star, called Georgina Game?"

"In a sense, yes."

"And at any one stage, at any given moment, you could have stopped it? Stopped the process?"

"I guess I always had that choice," she said.

"You see, Georgina, you, other people, always have that choice. The options are almost always open. I don't have any choice. There are no options. I'm a prince. I didn't make myself a prince. The way you made yourself a star, or the way a man makes himself an engineer. Six hundred years made me a prince. Not scripts but history books, not producers but princes and princesses made me a prince."

It was hard to know what to say and Georgina said nothing.

"I live within a system, a set of rules, that permits no choice, tolerates no change in the status quo. History haunts my soul. Even Cornelius cannot . . . exorcise history."

Georgina smiled. She prodded the bottom of her empty cup with a spoon.

"My father died in the same room and the same bed he was born in. It is the bed and the room I was born in. It is the bed and the room I shall probably die in. *Rigor mortis* is a way of life with princes, you see."

The cool sustained sense of frustration and anger, the tiny hint of unpleasantness and hostility in his voice astonished and disturbed Georgina. The argument seemed to be so much a part of the extraordinary anachronism she'd seen and felt in the palace.

"I envy you," he said in a tone that was just a shade lighter. "This year you are playing at being a princess. Next year, you will be a prostitute, or a famous . . . whatever you choose to be. That must be nice."

"It's a living," she said, not quite sure how to play the line.

"Now and yesterday and tomorrow, next month and next year and for the rest of my life—I can be only what history expects of me."

"You see, you are so . . . bloody contradictory," Georgina said, suddenly on the attack. "You cannot restore past happiness one minute—you must paint new pictures. Who said that? So why do you now talk as if the dead can dictate to the living all the time? It's crazy. No, Philippe, I can't let you get away with that. All you do is extol the past and bitch about the present."

"All I do is my duty."

"Bullshit. You don't have to suffer everything else for . . . duty. Why put up with a—"

"I told you you'd never understand."

"Last night . . . in bed . . . the incoherent passions of a man made a lot more sense—that I understood, but this . . ."

Philippe stood up abruptly, wiping his mouth with the damask napkin.

"I think we must soon be going."

"I'm sorry, Philippe."

"For what?"

"For—" No! She damn well wasn't going to apologize for saying the things she'd said. "—for getting angry," she said. "It's really none of my business."

Philippe simply smiled.

"You make love beautifully," he said. "You make excellent coffee. And you argue like a woman. Two out of three can't be bad."

47

"Let us say they have warmed their hearts a little more than is considered strictly . . . punctilious in polite society," Count Cheroffini said.

"They have behaved outrageously," Duclos said. "Outrageously."

Dieter Stosch smiled.

"It is exactly right," he said. "We shall present it as a love match. As much a love match as any village maid's. I see no serious obstacles."

"The whole business is about as subtle as Ashanti face carvings," Duclos said. The old courtier had been sleeping badly and his tiredness was telling. His lips were very pale and there were dark marks under his eyes. They were no longer the eyes of a playful snake, Cheroffini thought sadly. Just the eyes of an aging anaconda. He had stopped a long time ago being the man who liked to say he aspired to the depths of diplomacy. Now he was too blunt, too bitter. "I've said it before and I'll say it again. This business with this girl Game smells—"

"Isn't Philippe . . . obeying the dictates of his heart?" Stosch asked gently. "I seem to recall that was a phrase somebody used—"

"But this is wrong," Duclos said. He shook his head slowly. "It's too . . . obvious. Too cheap—"

"Cheap?" Stosch picked up a newspaper clipping from his desk. "He appears to have given the lady a teardrop diamond of seventy-nine carats. I wouldn't say that was cheap. The New York *Herald-Tribune*—" he dropped the clipping back onto the desk "—doesn't seem to think it's cheap."

"You know exactly what I mean," Duclos said. "The whole country is gorged on rumor and the buzz of unpleasant innuendo and—"

"You exaggerate, surely. Philippe has had more lurid . . . liaisons before without upsetting—"

"This one is being handled like a carnival show," Duclos said bitterly.

Stosch noticed how the two old courtiers never stood together any more. Cheroffini had moved to the opposite side of the room. A crook with an airtight alibi detaching himself from a framed accomplice.

"Nobody, as far as I know, is *handling* anything," Stosch said. "It is elemental, a perfectly spontaneous combustion between two extremely combustible people."

"That's what it appears to be," said Duclos.

"Whatever we have discussed in this room in the past, gentlemen . . ." He didn't finish. He smiled his cold smile. "Let us accept matters at their face value."

"Our hands are clean, are they?" Duclos asked sourly. There was a rumor that he was dying. It was almost certainly true, Stosch thought. It would be easy to check, but it would serve no purpose.

"The film people are using it," Cheroffini said. "For all it's worth."

"Naturally," Stosch said.

"*The Princess and the Cowboy*!" Duclos said in the same sour tone.

A smile passed from Cheroffini to Stosch.

"It can't . . . rebound on us?" Cheroffini asked.

"I think we can insure that it doesn't."

"Meanwhile, we continue to wait?"

"The royal yacht," Stosch said. "It's still at Kiel."

Tt wasn't a question.

"It won't be finished now before the end of summer," Cheroffini said. "There have been problems with the new turbine—"

"As a gesture of goodwill, I will offer His Highness the *Grunden Tief*. Count Cheroffini, you will suggest a short cruise to Capri or Sardinia. His Highness will appreciate the opportunity to get away from the photographers and reporters."

"With Georgina Game?"

"She finishes her film in one week from tomorrow. She will be pleased to accept an official invitation . . ."

Cheroffini gave him a sharp look.

"An official invitation?"

"We should make it clear to Philippe now that the Council of State approves of his choice. An official invitation from the Lord Privy Seal's Office—that should be sufficient indication, don't you think?"

"We inform the press?"

"No. Let it come out from the other side. The press will learn soon enough."

"You seem to forget that this might still be just another . . . another Philippe escapade," Duclos said in a more reasonable tone.

"When a man gives a woman a seventy-nine-carat diamond, you can hardly dismiss the friendship as an escapade."

"Are you planning to be along?" Cheroffini asked.

"Along?"

"The cruise?"

"No. It must be . . . very *intime*."

Cheroffini shook his head.

"There must be other guests," he said. "If we wish to present a genuine love match—what did you call it?"

"A village maid's romance," Duclos chimed in.

"A certain propriety—"

"Aren't we locking the stable door a bit late?" Duclos asked predictably.

"—let us maintain a sense of etiquette," Cheroffini went on.

"What do you suggest?" Stosch asked.

"I think a small party . . . a dozen people or so. The Aldobrandinis, perhaps. Billy Wallace, von

Cramm. Philippe is fond of von Cramm—and Barbara, if she's around."

"Onassis?" Stosch said.

"Yes, and perhaps the Thyssens or the Sciarras."

"Very well," Stosch said. "See to it."

He got up and came from behind his desk and stood over his Bustelli collection. He stood with his hands clasped behind his back, his feet six inches apart, like a soldier at ease but still on parade. He still looked like a fighting soldier. He probably hadn't put on more than a couple of pounds since the day he first came to St. Saladin, Cheroffini thought. His hair still blond and scythed-looking, the same strange gun-barrel kind of smile.

That smile was on his face now.

"Put the priest on the invitation list," he said slowly. "It should contribute considerably to the sense of decorum . . . and what's a shipboard romance without a priest?"

He moved the figure of Harlequin like a grand master moving his queen.

"Mr. Waldo Bragg?"

"Speaking."

"Mr. Bragg, just one moment, sir. We have a call for you from New York."

"Waldo?" The voice was friendly and unfamiliar.

"Yes."

"Waldo—this is Carter Vanaman. The New York *Daily Mirror*."

"Yes."

"Waldo, we'd like you to do . . . ah, make a prediction for us."

"What sort of prediction?" Waldo asked warily.

"You're a pal of Georgina Game, right?"

"She is a very dear friend of mine."

"Well, everybody here was damned impressed with the way you predicted the Oscar for her and her success and everything."

Waldo preened at himself in the bronze-tinted mirror above the telephone.

"Yes," he said. "She always comes to me. Whenever

she has to make an important decision, she comes to me. In fact, I was in the South of France with her only a week ago."

"Yeah, so we heard, Waldo."

"Yes?" The thought that people in New York followed his movements so closely made him almost shiver with pleasure. He smiled at his reflection. He pursed his lips and tilted his head slightly upward. He parted his lips and showed his newly capped teeth. The caps had cost a fortune but they improved his smile tremendously. Bill said it reminded him a little bit of Turhan Bey's smile in *Prisoners of the Casbah*. Bill was a great fan of Turhan Bey.

"Here's the situation, Waldo. We've got a coupla very good pictures here of her hand—"

"Whose hand?" Waldo had lost the thread completely.

"Game's hand, Waldo. Georgina Game—your friend?"

"True, true."

"And Prince Philippe's hand. Their palms, you know. Waving shots."

"Pictures of their hands?" Waldo asked blankly.

"We've had them blown up and they're very clear. All the lines are there. Now we'd like you to read these palms for us—"

"I don't read palms," Waldo said haughtily.

"But we *cross* them, Waldo. A thousand dollars."

"A thousand dollars?"

"You should be able to buy yourself a speed-reading course in palmistry for a thousand bucks, old buddy."

"Fifteen hundred," Waldo said automatically. He always tried it on with newspapers. It was, he said, one of the few principles he had.

"A thousand," Said Carter Vanaman. There was something in his voice that told Waldo that he'd never get more than the grand.

"How will you get the hands to me?"

"I've already air-freighted them to London. Our guy there'll have them at your place by nine-thirty in the morning. We'll need your copy by midday our time."

"I'm not sure that—"

"A thousand bucks," said Vanaman.

"Ask your man to bring a letter confirming our agreement," Waldo said. "A thousand dollars."

"Sure. And, by the way, our people on the inside over there—in St. Saladin—they tell us that that little relationship is warming up just swell."

"Yes?"

"I mean real cosy."

"True, true."

"If you'll take a tip from me, Waldo, you'll see a lawful conjunction in those palms pretty damn soon."

"What?" said Bragg, who'd been rehearsing his Turhan Bey smile again.

"A marriage," said Carter Vanaman. "Georgina and the Prince."

"True, true," said Waldo.

48

"Dave Jarrup thinks it's worth trying," Georgina said. "Esther's been fixed up in a wig and I've loaned her my blackamoor Balenciaga number. With dark glasses and a swift gait—it might just work."

"Better give her a bottle of your scent, too," Liz said. "Those guys seem to be able to sniff you out."

Georgina smiled. It wasn't a happy smile.

"They're going to make a swift showy getaway in the Roller at twelve. We'll take the staff entrance and make our escape in the launch at exactly the same time. Trala!"

"It's like a fucking commando raid," Liz said.

"Don't joke! Do you know Jarrup was up here this morning and actually made us synchronize watches!"

"The poor bastard. He's getting a lot of stick from ss."

"Poor Jarrup! What about poor me?"

"And you, darling," Liz said soothingly.

"They're so . . . *sick,* those photographers. Do you know that one of them—that common little Glaswegian one with the squeaky voice. He carries a child's doll in his camera case. If he has to cover an air crash, or comes across a road accident and a child has been killed or injured—he throws the doll onto the wreckage and photographs it. Poignancy, you see."

"The public loves a few tears with their cornflakes—"

"It's true. Ask Jarrup. He was in the bar the other night when the guy took it out—"

"Took it out?"

"The doll, you fool. He was a bit pissed. More than a bit pissed. He sat this grotesque thing on the bar and told everybody the whole story. He reckons it's made him over five thousand pounds. It's been photographed in coach wrecks, on burning rubble, in plane debris, earthquakes. . . . He calls it Pauline. After *The Perils of Pauline,* I suppose."

"Sick," said Liz.

"A real creepy-crawly."

"Is he the one who keeps sending those flowers with the pathetic notes?"

"Dear Miss Game, sorry to trouble you again but if you could give me just one little picture with His Royal Highness I could go home and everybody would stop chasing after you both," Georgina said in a whiny accurate Glaswegian accent.

"He was limping rather badly the other day, I noticed," Liz said.

"He fell out of a tree, I'm pleased to say."

"Has the luggage gone?"

"At six this morning. They sent a tender and four ratings! They certainly do things in style in St. Saladin!"

"So that's it," Liz said. "Anchors aweigh!"

At two minutes to twelve, Georgina and Liz left the suite and took the back stairs down to the kitchens. A slim young man dressed all in white was waiting for them at the back door. Without a word he took their hand baggage and led the way down the graveled path to the small jetty used by tradespeople and staff. A long, fast-looking motor launch was waiting, its engine humming quietly. A second young man, also slim, also dressed in white, helped them aboard without a word.

At two minutes past twelve Georgina and Liz were speeding across the bay toward the *Grunden Tief*.

It was a beautiful day. One of those clear sharp days you get in the South of France when time seems to be suspended and when the sea at the horizon is of the purest palest blue and faint pink clouds like silky muslin glide leisurely high in the sky.

Liz looked back.

"Well, we seem to have shaken off the pack," she said.

"Fingers crossed," Georgina said grimly.

"They won't be able to get at you in the middle of the Med!"

"Tracy told me they found him in the middle of Alaska once."

"What the hell was he doing in the middle of Alaska?"

"Trying to get away from the press!"

"Well," said Liz, stretching the word into something long and significant.

"What does *Grunden Tief* mean?" Georgina asked the tall blond boy who'd met them at the back door of the hotel.

"Wun dip," he said with a thick German accent. "*Stille Wasser grunden tief.* Still vaters wun dip. The wessel of Herr Dieter Stosch."

"Run deep," Liz said pleasantly.

"That is corwect."

"And Herr Dieter Stosch is who exactly?"

The young man looked startled.

"Herr Stosch is—is Herr Dieter Stosch . . ."

"The head man," said the second young man who spoke English with a slight American accent. "He's the chief of St. Saladin Statistical Bureau. The controller."

"Deutsch?" Georgina asked.

"Deutsch."

The two women exchanged looks. Liz made a face. The launch sped on through the glass-calm sea.

The *Grunden Tief* was now very clear, her beautiful black lines stark against the blue sky, about five hundred yards ahead. Several figures appeared to be preparing to leave in two launches that were alongside her.

After just a moment's hesitation, the launches pulled away from the schooner at high speed, made an arc, and raced for the shore. The second launch followed closely, almost as if it were in tow.

"Are they having a race?" Georgina asked as the sleek launches sped diagonally toward them.

"Herr Stosch cannot swim. He has a . . . distrust of the sea," the boy with the better English said. "He always likes another boat close—in case of accidents."

"*Wer hängen soll, ersäuft nicht,*" the first boy said quickly and quietly.

"What was that?" Georgina asked. "What did your friend say?"

The one with the English grinned and looked at his companion.

"He said that Herr Stosch shouldn't worry." He continued to look at his companion as if threatening him with something, something that amused him.

"*Ja?*" he said, still grinning, "*Ja?*"

"*Nein!*" the boy who'd spoken the German said nervously.

"He said that . . . the man born to be hanged is never drowned," the one with the English said deliberately.

"Is Dieter Stosch born to be hanged?" Georgina asked.

He didn't answer. He stared straight ahead as if he suddenly couldn't understand the language.

The two launches were speeding toward them. They were now less than fifty yards away and would pass very close.

The small figures they'd seen climbing into the first launch were now plainly visible, with definable features. The taller of the two, a thin man in a white linen jacket and trousers, with a crocus-colored silk scarf around his neck, stood next to the young sailor behind the wheel. His back was to the bow and he had a hunched look as if he hated the speed and the sea. His wispy hair was blowing in the wind, like a woman's. Opposite him was a blond man. He was handsome but Georgina could only think that he looked like a man you shouldn't bother. He wore a dark outfit that looked vaguely military. The woman by his side wore large sunglasses and a supercilious smile. Her skin was tobacco-colored. Her nose was acquiline. It was an intelligent face, not quite aristocratic, but certainly privileged.

All this Georgina took in as the launch approached them, passed alongside, and disappeared toward the shore at great speed.

"Who are those people?" she asked, looking back.

Their own launch bounced and rocked in the double wake.

"The man with the blond head. Dieter Stosch. The thin man. English. His name somebody . . . Brand. The woman. Mlle. Lacroix."

"Who exactly is Mlle. Lacroix?" Georgina asked.

"Works for Herr Stosch."

Liz was silent and filled with foreboding.

She fought to rid her face of expression, but she couldn't stop the panic and guilt that bleached her cheeks like a sudden fever.

She breathed in deeply.

Mlle. Lacroix, she knew, was Mlle. Chaire.

The implications she didn't want to think about.

The chocolate-brown Rolls-Royce with the Swiss license plates followed the coast road at the foot of the Chaîne des Maures, twisting around the little rocky bays all the way from Carqueirane to Cavalaire. They had done an almost complete circle. And still the carloads of newspapermen and photographers followed them.

"Jesus, Dave. They'll skin you alive. When they find out—" Esther began anxiously.

He stopped her with a careless wave of his hand.

"What's their beef? The boss making a little time with his secretary—"

"She's well away by now," Esther said. "Why don't we just stop and give—"

"It's a nice day. We got the limo. We got all the time

in the world—hear that clock ticking? Let's enjoy it. We'll have lunch in Cavalaire. Beautiful. The bay is just sensational. Eucalyptus, mimosa, pine trees right down to the beach—"

"Jesus, Dave," Esther said. "They're gonna be looking for eveners when they find out. They're gonna be be pretty damn sore."

"Let 'em."

"I hope it's worth it." Esther had now taken off the wig and slipped out of Georgina's coat. "Because those guys back there—I gotta be truthful with you—they're *body snatchers*, Dave. They're real mothers. They're not your Hollywood and Vine blacksmiths . . . they're gonna be awfully unpleasant."

"They can go to hell," Jarrup said pleasantly.

"You're an obstinate bastard, when you want to be."

"Uh-huh."

Esther pushed the sunglasses onto the top of her head.

"What d'you think'll happen, Dave?"

"To us?"

"To Georgina."

"With Princey?"

"Yes."

"Well, the way I got it figured this could be where he presses his suit."

"Proposes?"

"Offers her the old fraternity pin."

"I don't know," Esther said. She played with the blond wig in her lap.

"They buyer interest's there. Everybody knows he's got to get started *bientôt*. She's eligible. Why not?"

"This weekend you think?"

"Uh-huh."

"A great talent wasted," Esther said, relaxing a little, smiling. She threw the wig into the front seat.

"I didn't exactly cut my eyeteeth on a scepter but the way I got it figured, sure, it's in the cards. The official invitation . . . it's not exactly one of Errol's screwcruises to Catalina, is it?"

"I wouldn't know," Esther said.

"It's not *Sirocco* time."

"You know what they say—a rowboat by any other name!"

"Rivkin's pipeline says it's at least a possibility, right?"

"I don't know how much Liz Huntington really tells Rivkin and how much he makes up," Esther said.

"All right, even putting aside Rivkin's playbacks . . . this broad doesn't hop in the sack with just anybody. Since Antrobus—who? Name one! I sure as hell can't."

"Liz Huntington?" Esther said.

"You've got a very dirty mind," Jarrup said.

"She wouldn't be the first movie queen who likes to make it with girls."

"I can't see it. Not with Georgina Game. Milady Game."

"You sound like the little boy who doesn't want to believe that his mommy and daddy ever do it."

He stared out of the blue-tinted window reflectively.

"It sure ain't the publicity she's after."

"Did you show her the *Mirror* story?"

"Which particular one?"

"Royal wedding bells."

"The Bragg prediction? Are you kidding?"

"Wouldn't he have checked something like that with her first?"

"He may be gay, but he's certainly no gonif," Jarrup said. "She would have put the block on a story like that quicker'n look at you."

The Rolls slowed down almost to a walking pace as it started to move through the narrow streets of the village. The chauffeur pressed his chest against the wheel looking for the name of the street with the restaurant Jarrup had heard about.

Esther turned and looked at the press caravan winding behind them.

"Maybe we should've booked," she said wryly.

"I did," Jarrup said.

"This boy is bright," she said. "Oh, this boy is very bright."

He grinned and leaned back in the deep-cushioned comfort of the Roller.

"I wonder," he said, adjusting the air-conditioning, "what the poor people are doing now?"

"Quite a few of them," Esther said, "are following us."

"How was it?"

"Yes," he said. "You know."

"I didn't have to ask."

"No."

"Many men have entered my body but you are the only man who has . . . possessed my soul."

"Darling." He spoke softly, tenderly.

"You know the one thing that hurts me? Honestly hurts me, cruelly torments me? The thought of not being loved by you any more . . ."

"Don't—"

"Last night—" She put her index finger on his lips. "Last night—the awful terrible thought that you would soon be gone hit me . . . I felt as if we were . . . suddenly . . . estranged."

"I told you. I told you I was going today."

"I know. It just felt . . . different this time."

"How . . . different?"

"How is one darkness different from another darkness? You just . . . *feel* the difference. Sometimes the dark doesn't worry me at all. Sometimes I'm scared of of the dark."

"You must never be scared of us," he said.

"You are going to be with Georgina Game, aren't you?"

"Yes."

"Your infidelities . . . I have always been able to live with your infidelities—"

"They mustn't be—"

"I have been unfaithful to you, many times."

"Yes."

"But I have never been dishonest with you . . . or false. I have never been . . . disloyal."

Isak got up and found her ochre-colored lace negligee on the sofa. She slipped it on and went to the window. It was a beautiful morning. There was a haze almost like fine silk gauze across the countryside.

"It's going to be very warm today," she said.

Beyond the lawn was a wild jungle of garden and beyond that the woods. Sometimes, at night, in the quiet, she could hear the stream babbling in the heart of the woods. It always reminded her of a baby chuckling to itself in an empty nursery. Why, she wondered now, didn't she let herself get pregnant with Philippe? She'd been crazy not to. She'd been too fair, too scrupulous. It would have been so easy. She thought of the abortion in Louveciennes. Would Philippe have let her go through with that, had he known?

She heard him get up and go to the bathroom.

She lit a cigarette and continued to look out of the window, her nakedness silhouetted through the old Victorian lace. She stood with her legs a little apart, her left arm folded across her breasts, her hand tucked beneath her right armpit.

Philippe came out of the bathroom.

She could hear him getting dressed. Slowly, with the care and attention of a man putting on a ceremonial uniform.

"I don't want you to go," she said quietly. She continued to stare out of the window. "I have never said that to you before, have I?"

"I have to go," he said.

"Duty calls?" she said, hopelessly unable to keep the taunting wretchedness out of her voice.

She could feel his cool immovable composure. It was almost like a chill draught on her spine.

"Ah . . . the *amour-propre* of princes! The pride . . . I'd almost forgotten. The abysmal egotism . . . it overrides everything, doesn't it? Subordinates everybody to your purpose, to your pleasures, and whims . . ."

She spoke very softly, her back to him, looking at the distant woods. The wretchedness had left her voice. Without the wretchedness, the words were less taunting, sadder rather than colder. But she still didn't turn into the room. She still couldn't watch him preparing to go.

"You're going to ask her, aren't you?"

She waited, hoping, not breathing, but Philippe said nothing. No words of comfort, no lies, nothing.

She could hear him buttoning his shirt. His hands

moving over the silk, buttoning, moving up, buttoning, cool methodical composed Philippe . . .

She took a deep breath.

"They've won, haven't they? They've finally beaten you?"

He still said nothing.

She heard him zip up his fly, slowly.

"I knew." She spoke in the same quiet steady voice. "In the night I woke up and I knew."

She put the cigarette out in the ashtray on the chest by the window, turning it slowly into the glass. When she had finished she said, "Will you still need me . . . as your mistress?"

"I'm not—"

"Please, Philippe. Not with me."

"You know the situation."

"Oh yes."

He'd finished dressing. He was picking up his things from the table by the side of the bed now. His Cartier watch, the crocodile wallet she'd bought him at Asprey's, car keys . . .

"Do you love me?" she asked.

"Yes."

"You do?"

"I love you."

"How strange."

"Strange?"

"Sad."

Their voices had the same unrevealing mechanical tone, like a conversation between speak-your-weight machines, or talking clocks.

"Where's the *but*?"

"But?"

"The royal *but*? Like the royal *we*. It's always been there, hasn't it? Even when you haven't uttered it. In your heart, it's always been . . . yes, *but* . . ."

"I expect you to be understanding . . ."

"You're leaving me. Why don't you tell me?"

"Why do you persist? We both know . . ."

"*Noblesse oblige.*"

Philippe said nothing but Isak could almost feel him shrug.

"So it all ends on Stosch's yacht, proposing to the woman Stosch has designated—"

"That isn't true at all."

"Isn't it?"

"I still love you, Isak."

"But . . . but you simply have to marry somebody else! The noble Prince is reduced to the expedient of choosing a rich and famous—"

"No!"

"No?"

"Isak—"

"Will you tell her, Philippe? Will you tell her you don't really want a bride—just an ace in the hole? A new tourist attraction? A baby machine? Will you tell her everything, Philippe? All the . . . complex delicacies of your sexual needs? Do you think she'll understand? Do you think she'll be as . . . *willing* as me? You never know your luck, I suppose. She may love it, your little personal aid program."

Philippe stared at her back with a blank look.

"I'm sorry, Philippe," she said. She leaned her forehead against the window. "I meant to be so good about it. I've just said all the things I vowed I would never say."

Philippe didn't move.

"I might kill myself," she said.

"You can still wound me, Isak."

"I know."

"But you can never intimidate me."

"You think I wouldn't do it? Do myself in?"

"Don't let your dramatic imagination run away with you."

"But you're not sure, are you?"

"You always surprise me."

"Thank you."

"I will call you in Paris. When I return."

"Will you. Will you call me in Paris? How kind of you, Your Highness. How very . . . very considerate."

He crossed the room and kissed her just where her shoulder joined her long neck. She wanted to turn and hold him and kiss him. . . . She stood quite still, controlling her need to clutch him, staring into the woods where the hidden stream babbled like a baby.

"I want you to know that this has been—" The door closed quietly behind her. In a little while she heard the obedient morning growl of his red Ferrari and the dry cornflake crackle as it rolled across the gravel driveway. "—a very rewarding experience," she said aloud to herself in the cadaveric silence of the empty room.

She turned away from the window.

Her face was as wet as if she'd just come in from the rain.

49

The *Grunden Tief* weighed anchor at five o'clock. By seven o'clock that evening, she was being trailed by a flotilla of boats of various kinds carrying photographers and newsmen.

"Now I know what it must have felt like to have been hunted by U-boats in the war," Count Cheroffini announced at dinner that night.

"How do these people find out these things?" asked Baron Gottfried von Cramm.

"Up periscope," said his wife, Barbara Hutton. "It's all done with mirrors, Gottfried darling."

"Didn't you know?" smiled Prince Jean de Broglie, a small soft-eyed man who looked as if he'd been stuffed with swansdown.

"Mirrors are everything. You must always know who is behind you," said the Marquis de Portago, the racing driver.

"Mirror mirror on the wall who is the fairest of them all?" said the pretty heiress Talitha Helme. She had a long Florentine flow of red hair and the kind of spidery eyelashes that invited quarantine at every port. Behind the lashes were a nice pair of not very intelligent chrome-colored eyes. She was already a little drunk, or maybe on dope. Liz had noticed she had a slightly glassy-eyed look before dinner, when they had drinks on deck.

"There is an old Greek saying," Aristotle Onassis leaned across the table and touched Talitha's hand. "Modesty is the citadel of beauty and virtue."

"Ha!" said Maria Callas.

Onassis withdrew his hand.

"Modesty?" Talitha looked puzzled. "Is this guy for real?" she asked Alex Leggatt, the young American on her left.

"What do you think? Ari is an oil painting?" Maria Callas said in a Scala-scaled voice.

Everybody laughed.

Georgina sat at the head of the long table with Philippe on her right and Jean de Broglie on her left.

Liz sat at the opposite end, between Alwyn Brand and Cornelius.

"I think," she said, "this has to be about the most elegant dinner party I've ever been to. Two princes, a racing-driver marquis, a German baron, a tycoon, a count, a couple of heiresses, a film star, and a gen-you-wine prima donna."

"A class joint." Cornelius grinned. "That just leaves us three little lambs who've lost our way. A priest, a papyrologist, and—no! Liz, you can't be included with the lost sheep. A famous model! What the heck! You're in there with the quality folk. How would you say that, Alwyn? The *uppah clahs*?"

"Approximately," Brand said.

"What is that? A paper—what Father Cornelius said," Liz asked Brand.

"A papyrologist. It simply means I like to read musty old manuscripts. It's a bit of a hobby of mine, that's all."

"I feel I know you," Liz said. "Have we ever met?"

"I assure you I would remember if we had," Brand said. From a man less effeminate, it would simply have been gallant. From Brand, Liz didn't know what to make of it. His womanish English accent made the remark sound faintly unpleasant.

"I saw you in the launch today—with the blond man and . . . and the woman."

"That hardly qualifies as a meeting," he said.

"No. I didn't mean that. You seem familiar in . . . the oddest way."

"Thank you," he smiled.

"I didn't mean that either. I'm sorry . . . I'm putting it badly. But you know the way you sometimes feel you know an actor you've never met before—because you've seen him on the screen. Do you understand what I mean? It's that sort of feeling."

"How extraordinary," Brand said in his fastidious voice. "I assure you, my dear, I have never acted in a cinema picture in my life."

"How would you cast him, Liz—in a *cinema picture*?" Cornelius asked mischievously.

Liz was embarrassed by the question.

"As . . . as a papyrologist," she said quickly enough.

"Wrong," said Cornelius. "Mr. Big. The Brains. He'd have a front, of course. The headmaster of a finishing school for young ladies, perhaps. People in movies are never what they seem. Haven't you learned that yet?"

"It sometimes happens in real life," she said.

"One must always live by one's own truth," Brand said.

"Ah, watch out, Liz. I smell argument on his breath. Alwyn loves to argue, especially when he smells whisky on my breath. Isn't that the truth, Alwyn?"

"When people start telling the truth, my dear Cornelius, the sage shuts up, fools believe, and mountebanks reap."

"You see, you see," said Cornelius, triumph in his voice. "He's looking for a fight."

"Mountebank!" said Liz. "I didn't think people used words like that any more."

"Sure. Papyrologists—all the time," grinned Cornelius.

Liz caught Georgina's eye and smiled. Her own misery and misgivings were temporarily forgotten amid this

truly sybaritic scene. She let the talk flow around her
like a shallow stream of sparkling wine, following a familiar course of money, sex, scandal, risqué stories and
back, always back to money. Absent friends were
damned, approved of, ridiculed with acidic vigor and
vituperative splendor. Silver and diamonds and the exquisite baubles of wealth, real wealth, gleamed in the
candlelight amid the scent of gardenias as servants in
white gloves moved about the saloon with proper stately
ceremony, their faces impassive.

Liz kept the smile coming as she tried to work it all
out. . . . What did she really feel about men like Philippe? And women like Talitha Helme? These people
with lineage but no foundation at all . . . it was almost as if they were without pasts, as if they had only
pedigrees. Was it possible to have so much genealogy
. . . and no roots? Perhaps tomorrow, in the sun, they
would have no shadows, she thought, these beautiful, ephemeral, supremely insolent chattering creatures
around her. Cornelius was real enough, and Georgina
. . . but after them . . . Well, perhaps the race driver.
He looked like a man who lived for the next lap, the
next bend.

"We are talking about *serious* things," Talitha suddenly said above the babel of English and Italian and
French being spoken around the table. "We are talking
about *death*. Fon—" she looked at Portago "—has already written a letter to his mother in case he should
die."

The race driver looked embarrassed by the sudden
proclamation of their private conversation.

"It's just a note," he said carelessly. "Reassuring her,
you know. If I should have a bad shunt one of these
days . . . to say that she had made me very happy."

Georgina thought of the note Antrobus had left her:
the envelope she'd refused even to open before putting
it with some of his special things in her safety-deposit
box in L.A. Perhaps one day she would have the courage, or the curiosity, to see what was inside. . . . With
her thoughts already, unexpectedly, on Richard, what
came next was extraordinary.

"Death has never touched me," Talitha hurried on in

her smart transatlantic accent. "The closest I ever got was when old Willy Antrobus was doing the bust of me in London and his son was killed out in California. The poor man went to pieces. I watched it happen right under my nose. I'm sure he carved death into my eyes after that. I could never look at it again. Even when it was put into the Guildhall exhibition, I never went to see it. Isn't that strange?"

Georgina paled a shade, but said nothing.

Liz noticed and she didn't think she was the only one. Several people around that table knew about Georgina and Antrobus but nobody said a word, or tried to stop Talitha. It was what they would call *sang-froid*, Liz thought. Right now she was pleased they were exactly the sort of people they were.

The talk moved from death to drugs and settled for a moment on the lost art of homicidal poisoning.

"The Victorians were awfully fond of slow-poisoning each other," said Alex Leggatt, whose family owned the third largest pharmaceutical company in the United States. "Poison is very rarely used to murder today—"

"Perhaps the practitioners are just getting better at their art," suggested Cheroffini.

"No," said Leggatt, who was a very serious, very handsome and rather boring young man. "The big deterrent today is the giant advances we've made in biologic research—"

"How would you poison a rich aunt?" Philippe asked quickly, heading off a public-relations speech.

"White arsenic in porridge," Leggatt said, almost smirking with satisfaction. "If you really want to bump off a rich relative, that's—"

"But how many rich relatives do you know who eat porridge?" Jean de Broglie asked. "Unless one is unfortunate enough to be a Scotsman."

"Slow-poisoning has gone out of fashion because people are now in too much of a hurry—and don't seem to mind the noise of firearms quite so much as they once did."

The speaker was Alwyn Brand.

He was joining the general conversation for the first time and Onassis, Maria Callas, and the others at the opposite end of the table looked up in surprise. Nobody appeared to be quite certain who he was, or where he fitted in.

"It is perfectly true, young man, that a considerable amount of albescent arsenic could go undetected in *some* porridges. However, I suggest that thallium—"

"Thallium?" Leggatt eyed Brand suspiciously.

"It is more easily acquired. The cheap rat bane Rodeath paste will give you all you need. Enough to rid yourself of an entire army of opulent aunts and uncles if you so wish. Thallium doesn't disturb the color, odor, taste, or flavor of tea, coffee, or even malt whisky."

"We know about thallium," Leggatt said.

"You must agree then, sir, that it possesses traits and characteristics which fulfill most of the criteria of the consummate bane?"

"It has no smell, it's colorless—but, okay, so are several other substances I—"

"Its heinous goal is delayed at least forty-eight hours. Time enough for the miscreant to be on the other side of the world when . . . the bird falls off his perch. Moreover, there are no palpable mutations to excite postmortems. And, sir, by that time the bane introduced into the system will have been naturally expunged. A toxicological dissection will bear no more fruit than a neutral result at the very best."

There was a long silence.

The Princes, the Count, the Marquis, the film star, the heiresses, the prima donna, and the tycoon looked steadily at Alwyn Brand . . . then, like overadorned spectators at an existential tennis game, turned their attention to Alex Leggatt.

"A-huh. Well," Leggatt said. He looked around the table, nodding his head knowingly, biting his long lower lip. "That's a pretty good run-down on the . . . ah, thallium problem. And you can bet your sweet life that right now there's somebody over in New Jersey working on that headache."

"I'll say this for you, old sport," Cornelius said when the multilingual gossip got flowing again. "You certainly know how to stop a party dead."

"How do you know such things?" Liz asked. There

was admiration as well as amazement in her voice. "Where do you get all that stuff?"

"Odd scraps of information one discovers here and there," he said vaguely.

"In old parchments?" Liz asked, smiling.

"The pharaohs had poisons Mr. Leggatt and his whole apothecary industry *still* don't know about, my dear."

That evening Dieter Stosch sat alone at his desk in his office above the casino in the old palace of St. Saladin and read through all the product Liz Huntington had ever filed from her first days with the Bureau. Apart from the product on Richard Antrobus and Georgina Game there were reports on a German diplomat, a Persian ambassador, and several men who could loosely be described as captains of industry. She had been of considerable value to the Bureau in the past. Her product was sharp, accurate, reliable. But the need for maintaining absolute secrecy about the magnitude and the methods of the SS operation was uppermost in his mind. If Liz Huntington had recognized Genevieve Lacroix, it would be only a matter of time before she saw through the whole setup. It would mean a serious breach of security, a dangerous precedent—especially after the unfortunate business with Catharine Gaillard—to permit a field operative to get so close to the Principal Consumer. She would foolishly incriminate herself, of course, if she discussed the matter directly with Georgina Game. And Liz Huntington was not a foolish woman. But they were undoubtedly close and, he knew from experience, circumspection in such relationships could not always be relied upon.

He read Liz's product on Georgina several times: there had, he was sure now, been a loving relationship between the two women . . . there was material in the later reports, small asides, incidental observations, predictions, that could only have come out of an *intime* knowledge. Her reports on Georgina differed in many ways from her product on other pigeons.

He closed the file and took a tablet from his drawer.

He looked at the ceiling.
There was no doubt in his mind now.
He would have to get Brand to economize.

50

The *Grunden Tief* made a noise no louder than a man
breathing as it moved with a steady graceful rhythm
through the calm dark blue sea. Philippe lay on his
back, his hands clasped behind his neck, looking at the
sky. The sky looked ashen at that stilly time. There'd be
a thunder shower before breakfast, he thought.

He felt at peace with the world at that hour. It was
still only a little after six o'clock. Even the thought of
the U-boats—as everybody now called the press
launches that tagged them day and night—couldn't disturb him. It was remarkable what a couple of days at
sea could do. . . . I am not the person I was, he
thought calmly. Yesterday's Prince is not this morning's
Prince. Georgina was right. A man must be his own
phoenix. Thoughts of Georgina now filled his mind a
lot of the time. But . . . did he love her? *Whatever we
love for its uses, we love for itself*. That was one of his
grandfather's favorite sayings. It was perfectly true that
Philippe was using Georgina—but was it something
more than that now? he wondered. The other evening at
dinner, watching her, listening to her laugh, the things
she said and the way she said them in that famous voice
of hers . . . he felt a new closeness to her, an intimacy
that he had felt only once before . . . Love was not a
primary passion in his life. He saw it as a pleasant occupation, the game of love, the alphabet of love, not a
religion. The stakes of love had always been a lot less
than happiness for him. Perhaps that was why he was so
good at it, he thought. He smiled at the sky. What was

it Count de Bussy-Rabutin once said? When we don't
have what we love, we must love what we have. . . .

"Why is this fellow smiling? I ask myself."

Georgina was looking down at him from behind.

He got to his feet and kissed her chastely on the
cheek. They were so careful now in public, even at that
hour they knew there was probably a night watchman's
lens trained on the schooner.

"Good morning," he said.

"I thought only film stars ever got up at this ungodly
hour," she said.

"And insomniac princes," he told her. "Sleep is not
an obedient subject, I'm afraid."

"My father sent me an old Highland saying which
he'd framed for me. I keep it in my dressing room. I
used to complain all the time about having to get up so
early. It says: 'When thou risest unwillingly, think this: I
am rising to the work of a human being. I am going to
do the things for which I exist and for which I was
brought into this world.' It's not much help in the mornings, but it's amusing to read after a pleasant lunch and
a glass of wine."

He touched her arm and they walked to the side of
the boat and stood against the rail, their backs to the
watching cameras.

"Enjoying the trip?"

"Oh yes," she said. "The . . . casting is a little ec-
centric, though."

"Blame Count Cheroffini."

"No man for Liz."

"I think the Count fancied his own chances there. He
used to be quite a ladies' man."

"I can believe it."

"How is Liz?"

"I went in last night. She was still feeling dreadful."

"What does the doctor say?"

"Food poisoning, or gastroenteritis."

"Nobody else has food poisoning."

"There may be just a tiny touch of hypochondria there.
She wants a little attention, perhaps."

"I knew a fellow at school who was just about as hypochondriac as you can be. One day he suddenly announced that he was dead."

"You're mad."

"He was dead and he wanted me to toll the college bell for him."

"I don't believe you."

"Perfectly true. So I went and solemnly tolled the bell, but he felt I wasn't putting my heart into it and he got out of bed to do it himself. He seemed to get better after that. A good toll can obviously work wonders."

"You are such a liar."

"Anyway, I'm sure Liz isn't as bad as that. I've had the plane sent to meet us in Sardinia. Casenave'll fly her back to St. Saladin. She can stay at the palace. My doctor will look after her."

"You are a sweet man, Philippe. Thank you for looking after my friend—whether she's a hypochondriac or not."

They were silent for a moment.

"I like Fon."

"Portago? He is very *simpatico*, isn't he?"

"Very."

"You find him handsome?"

"Not exactly handsome—but there is something there."

"He has a . . . dashing quality. Do you know he flew an aeroplane under one of your London bridges when he was nineteen?"

"No."

"For a bet."

"He looks exactly like a man who'd do that sort of thing."

"He has ridden in your Grand National, too. I lost a small fortune on that little escapade. He assured me he couldn't lose. A hundred-to-one nag called . . . *En Marchant*, I think it was. It should have been called *En Passant*, or *Ennui*. It collapsed at the second fence."

"He . . ."

"Yes . . . he what?"

"I was going to say he has an aura of . . . fate about him."

"You noticed, too? Yes. Poor Fon. I fancy his mother will read that letter he's written soon enough."

"He is a good friend of yours, Philippe?"

"I've known him a long time."

"You are funny."

"Why?" There was surprise in Philippe's voice that lifted it above the quiet tones they had been speaking in.

"You will never commit yourself, that's all. I say, 'Is he your friend?' and you say, 'I've known him a long time.'"

"He is my friend," Philippe said after a long pause. "Fon is my friend."

"There—that wasn't so hard to say, was it?"

"You tease me."

"Yes, I tease you. It isn't fair. Before breakfast."

"I always think of my friends as . . . temporary attachments. It isn't so painful that way . . . when something happens."

"That's a coward's way out."

"It's a coward's philosophy. I'm not sure that it's a way out. What do you make of Onassis?"

"I adore him. I think he's divine. He has these little pat things he says . . . these little Greek homilies . . ."

"Like the thing you have on your dressing-room wall?"

"Yes."

"That's very funny. Tell me. Tell me one. What has he said to you?"

"Well, such as . . . he says I need a small scandal in my life now to bring me—what he calls . . . *alive.*"

"Hasn't he noticed the U-boats?"

"That's nothing, he says. He reckons I still have too many boring virtues—"

"He told Talitha—what was it? Modesty was the citadel of virtue?"

"When you've got his money I suppose you can afford to be a little . . . inconsistent. I think he is quite fantastic. They are very good together, too."

"Ari and Callas?"

"The chemistry is perfect."

"Gottfried and Barbara?"

"Won't last," she said firmly.

"And what do you make of old Brand?"

"I don't know. He seems to have been put together with old pieces of Hollywood's stock Englishmen—a little of Basil Rathbone, a bit of Rex Harrison, a soupçon of Karloff. Liz keeps saying she feels she's met him somewhere before—I bet that's why. He's a complete composite. Even I have this feeling I've heard his name somewhere. . . ."

At the stern end of the long black ship, sailors were washing down the decks. Others were erecting pale-blue canvas sheets around the spar deck between the stern and aftermast. This was the deck used for sunbathing and lunch; the canvas was to foil the photographers.

"We'll get a thunder shower before breakfast," Philippe said. "They're wasting their time washing down the decks now."

"How do you know we'll get a thunder shower?"

"No wind. Wind keeps the atmosphere all stirred up. It prevents parochial overheating, which is the principal condition . . . You see, the thundercloud is really just a . . . a sort of leisurely explosion of moist air . . ."

"You know an awful lot for a prince."

"I've impressed you at last! Well, well."

"Oh you've impressed me before now. Don't worry your little heart about that. I'd like to kiss you now, seriously, right there—" She put her finger to his lips and pushed it inside his mouth, quickly in and out, before the shutters could snap. "But I can't. So there!"

"I admire a woman with restraint," he said.

"I was surprised that you didn't come to my stateroom last night, talking of restraint."

"I'm sorry. I needed a little time to myself last night. There were certain things—"

"Don't explain. Never complain, never explain."

There was a sudden awkward politeness between them. They walked to the other side of the boat and back again. Georgina wore jeans and a tank top. She was barefoot and without shoes she looked much smaller than usual alongside Philippe.

"Things which seemed so simple in the solitude . . .

before you came . . . they're not so easy for me now," he said to her.

"I'm sorry," she said. "I really didn't mean to disturb your—"

"Georgina, sometimes being a prince, sometimes when a man is in the kind of position I now find myself in . . . You see, I want more than anything else in the world to be . . ."

"To be?"

"Or not to be," he said, smiling. Georgina felt he had walked back from the edge of something. A confession, perhaps. A confidence maybe. She was curious.

"What do you want, Philippe?"

"It's never easy."

"I don't know what it is you want. But people who beat about the bush—they're usually after a lot more than they care to admit!" Georgina said in the solemn, teasing tone he now recognized.

"Georgina, will you marry me?"

He spoke so quietly that had the mast creaked or a seagull cried out at that moment the proposal would have been lost.

Georgina said nothing for such a long moment that he wondered whether she had heard him.

"Georgina, I've asked you to be my wife."

"I know." He now saw the tears like tiny crystals in her eyes. "Only . . . sometimes silence is the safest response," she said. "Don't you think?"

"There are a preponderance of reasons in its favor," he started to say.

"Oh Christ, Philippe. You're a strange man." The tears broke free and ran down her cheeks, but she was smiling.

"I'm sorry. I don't mean to be. A strange man."

"Do you love me?"

"I don't know. But I think so."

"You think so!" She wiped the tears from her cheeks with the back of her fingers.

"I know I cannot get away with lying to you."

"That's a start, at least."

"I like you. We are good together."

"Yes, we are that," she said. She smiled at him, but

the smile didn't quite work. She said, "Look, my face is so wet, the smile keeps sliding off. Next time, I want you to watch carefully and tell me . . . what kind of smile it is."

"It's an all-right smile," he said.

"Not a happy smile?"

"Sort of."

"Sort of. A sort of happy smile."

"Don't tease me, Georgina."

"I'm not teasing you, my love. I'm just so . . . scared."

"Good."

"Good?"

"I'm a little bit scared too, you know."

Not touching—the lack of physical contact at such a moment, the knowledge that a kiss, an embrace would start up a forest of cricket sounds from the waiting cameras—was strange: it gave a sharp clarity to the scene in Georgina's eye that might have been spoiled had Philippe taken her in his arms.

"I want to seize you," he said. "I want to hold you."

"Don't," she said.

"No."

"There is something I have to say to you, Philippe. You know that I . . . loved somebody very much and we were going to be married—"

"Yes. I know that."

"He is dead and until you came along I was half dead, too. You are the first man since . . . You have given me so much . . . it is quite beautiful. You have been honest with me. The least I can do is be the same way with you."

"Please."

"I don't love you, Philippe—not yet. But also if I were to lose you . . . I don't know what I'd do."

"I want you."

"I don't understand it—but I guess something is holding us together . . . like something holds together the sun and the stars . . ."

"Georgina?"

"I will marry you, Philippe."

And still they didn't touch.

51

"Darling heart, I'm so happy for you," Liz said.

"Am I doing the right thing?"

"I think so—what am I saying! Of course, you're doing the right thing, stupe."

Despite her obvious weakness, Liz sat up and smiled. She looked so pale, but the pallor on her naked face made her seem like a child. A child waking too early on Christmas morning, Georgina thought, excited and full of the pallor of too little sleep. Her face had wasted slightly, emphasizing her large lovely eyes.

"I just want to hug you and hug you," Liz said.

Georgina silently embraced her and felt Liz press herself to her. A small tremor seemed to shake her body like a last sob.

"You stay just where you are. How're you feeling this morning?"

"A little better." She sank back, obviously exhausted, on the bed. "It's just this pain in my belly. Like a very bad curse pain. And I feel so bloody nauseous all the time. I think it was the bouillabaisse."

"Philippe's sent for his plane and—"

"Yes, Your Highness." Liz grinned.

"Don't—"

"Why not? That's what you're going to be—Princess Georgina of St. Saladin. Wow!" Liz closed her eyes. She was smiling a smile of real childlike happiness.

"I'm not sure that I believe it myself."

"A fairy-tale princess," Liz said, still with closed eyes. "Imagine how I'll be able to swank about my best friend . . . the Princess."

Georgina stroked her forehead. It felt quite cold.

"Do you remember that night in Paris?" Liz said.

"When we heard you'd got *Danger East*—and all that money?"

"Yes."

"It's better than that."

"I thought nothing could be better than that."

"Princess Georgina," Liz said again. "It'll take a little getting used to. . . . You will still be my best friend, won't you?"

"How would you like a poke in the eye with a big stick?"

"Not much right now, thank you."

"As long as . . . as long as I can continue to talk to you . . . open my heart to you," Georgina said.

"Have a good old gossip."

"Promise?"

"Promise."

There was a silence, a long silence, while Liz and Georgina each meditated on her own thoughts.

"It means the end of your career," Liz said eventually.

"I suppose so. We haven't discussed it, but that won't matter a damn—"

"Not acting any more? You won't mind?"

"I might miss the acting, but all the other bullshit, the rest of the business, Hollywood—I've had it up to here."

"You've had a basinful lately."

"All those horrible little people sitting out there now waiting in their little boats for us to pop our heads up—like snipers . . ."

"You'll still have loads of that. But in another way."

"It can never be as bad as it is now."

"What about your contract—?"

Georgina grinned. "So sue me, Sydney!"

"You'll probably get a royal pardon," Liz said. A thin smile parted her pale lips.

"Ha ha," Georgina said. "Very funny."

"They won't sue," Liz said. "Bobby wouldn't sue. He might shout and scream a lot—"

"I told my father a long time ago that I wouldn't stop until I'd made a go of acting—"

"Well, you've done that, my darling. An Oscar to

show your grandchildren, to prove who you once were, can't be bad."

"I'm getting out at the top."

"Undefeated."

"I remember one evening at the very beginning with Richard. We were having dinner—I can't remember where, it may have been at Alexander's, but I can recall his words exactly. I was feeling pretty pleased with myself over something. Some role I'd just got, I suppose. Anyway, he told me that I was young and very beautiful but that I must never forget . . . one day, he said, a woman would come through some door and she would be younger and prettier and maybe more talented than me, and she'd start taking roles away from me. If you are ready for that moment, whenever it comes, then you'll be all right, he said."

"Alexander's," Liz said. "I haven't been there for yonks."

"It was the time when I started to fall in love with Richard . . . he had so much more inside him than people realized." Then, in another, tougher tone, she said: "Oh shut up, Georgina!"

"Remember who you're talking to!" Liz said. "You can't say 'shut up' to royalty!"

"Anyway, you think it's not a bad move."

"It's a great move. How can you top it?"

"Well . . . you're the first to know."

"When will they announce it?"

"As soon as I've told my father. They're trying to get a call through to him now."

"A royal announcement from the boat. How romantic!"

A small sweat had now broken out on Liz's forehead.

"Darling, I'm so worried about you. Is there anything I can do—"

"No. I just hate being sick . . . it means being alone, and that means I have too much time to think about me!"

"Oh, darling."

"Joking!"

"No you weren't. I know you."

"When do you think, then? The wedding?"

"Fairly soon, I think."

"They don't hang about, these princes!"

"I've a little dubbing to do on the picture, but that's all. It's perfect timing. I've got no more commitments." Georgina spoke in a rush, like somebody having to make a point fast. "Hitchcock wants me for his next one with Jimmy Stewart but they still have some work to do on the script and I . . ." Her voice trailed away, like a radio being turned down. Her face clouded.

"Darling? Sweetheart—what's the matter?" Liz asked in an anxious voice. She forced herself up onto an elbow.

"He is a good man. He's a strong man and he makes me feel strong when I'm with him. He's the best thing that's happened to me since . . . Perhaps if he'd come along first . . ."

Georgina moved her hand across her head with a gesture of helplessness. "I don't ever expect to find the kind of love that moves the sun and the other stars. . . . I'm not sure that I love him enough, Liz." Georgina's voice had suddenly broken into small pieces.

"You like him a lot, right? I mean, you really *like* him?" Liz said. With an effort she had made her own voice strong again.

"Yes."

"He's a good lover. He's kind. He makes you laugh."

"He doesn't always know why," Georgina said, smiling a little now.

"Doesn't matter. That's not a bad basis. Marriages have known flimsier beginnings. You can't afford to have too much sensibility in these matters—"

"I cried when he proposed. It was so beautiful. In the early morning, in the middle of the ocean. It was so romantic . . . but do you know why I cried? I suddenly remembered crying when Richard asked me to marry him . . . and I just started to blub again . . ."

"Dry eyes would have been pretty self-deceiving," Liz said.

"What would I do without you, Liz?"

"You know me . . . I'd give you my last Kleenex at the end of *Camille*."

"She has accepted me."

"Congratulations," Cornelius said, shaking Philippe's hand warmly. "God made Eve to save Adam from egotism . . . I was just beginning to think that He'd overlooked you."

"It's a little early in the morning," Philippe said, looking at his watch. "But . . ."

"I'll drink to that, Your Highness."

Philippe smiled and rang for the steward and ordered champagne.

With his tanned weather-beaten face and white hair, in blue jersey and denims, Cornelius looked far from priestly. He reminded Philippe of the old Cuban in *Old Man and the Sea*. A little heavier maybe, better fed certainly, but the face was about right. The lines, the eyes . . .

The steward brought a bottle of Louis Roederer Cristal and two heavy tumblers. Philippe hated drinking champagne from champagne glasses at sea. The steward poured the drinks and offered them to the two men on a silver tray.

Cornelius raised his glass. "God bless you both."

"Well, David," Philippe said. He rarely used the priest's first name. "It's been an interesting . . . contest till now."

"With Stosch?"

"He's got in a few good licks but I feel the tables are beginning to turn in our favor."

"She is a strong woman," Cornelius said.

"Georgina?"

"You do know, don't you, that . . . she appeared on a list Stosch—" Cornelius began in a careful voice.

"She is *my* choice," Philippe said. "*My* woman."

"She will be good for you, Philippe," the priest said.

"I know it."

The two men sat in heavy black leather swivel armchairs, adapted from the seats used in Meteor jetfighters, screwed to the floor of Cornelius' stateroom.

"My land has had a fascinating history—that long ascending line from old barbaric Henri Carigbresci to me," Philippe said in a reflective voice.

"The present isn't exactly without interest."

"But it's the future we must think about now," Philippe said quickly. "The idea of the future fuses itself with every thought I have, with every idea and notion and passion in my body. . . ."

"I guess I've been dealing in futures, in my own small way, for a long time." Cornelius grinned.

They sipped their wine, listening to the gentle straining of the ship as she sped through the sudden thunderstorm.

"Duclos is dying," Philippe said after a while.

"Yes," the priest said. "He was too sick to make the cruise."

"How long?" Philippe asked. There was a cold absence of any note of charity or pity or regret in the question.

"Before he dies?" Cornelius thought about it with an expression closer to the judiciary than the church. "I would guess a matter of weeks, rather than months."

"That means a place to be filled on the Council of State. It is a new Prince's prerogative to make one appointment to the Council when a vacancy occurs—yes?"

"It's in the Prince's gift," said Cornelius.

"So," Philippe said slowly. "So."

"The right guy would certainly help redress the balance there since—"

"But who? Who, Cornelius?" The question was eager and peremptory and Philippe didn't wait for an answer. "You," he said.

"No."

"Why not? Constitutionally there is nothing to stop us. There is a precedent—Florio appointed a bishop—"

"No, Philippe."

"Why not?"

"Apart from the fact that Florio was a well-known atheist who finally bumped off the good bishop . . ." Cornelius grinned. "It'd annoy too many of my people in Rome. As it is, they complain all the time that I'm too close to—"

"Okay. Who then?" Philippe said impatiently but with real concern in his voice.

"Brand?" Cornelius swirled the champagne slowly in

his glass. He watched the tiny bubbles rise to the surface and explode.

"Alwyn Brand?" Philippe said.

"He would be an interesting choice, I think."

"Brand?" Philippe said quietly. "Alwyn Brand."

"He gets on well with Cheroffini," Cornelius said.

"Without Duclos . . . the Count might be more inclined to move back toward the Palace . . ." Philippe said.

"Brand and Cheroffini together . . . it would give us the Council," Cornelius said. "In our pocket."

"Brand is a strange bird. I've never understood him. He was my father's man, but . . ."

"He's full of ambiguities, full of odd paradoxes. But he's worth making an effort with. . . . You've never bothered to use him properly. He is available—"

"He has a sharp mind—beneath that . . . manner?"

"I think he is just about one of the cleverest men I've ever met."

"But *worldly*, Cornelius? Is he *worldly?*"

"Effete . . . but I don't think that makes him any the less worldly."

Philippe got out of the armchair and took the champagne bottle from the table. He refilled their glasses thoughtfully.

He walked to the porthole. The thunderstorm had stopped almost as abruptly as it came. He looked out for a long time. The U-boats were circling, much closer and more of them, as they drew toward the coast of Sardinia. He turned and looked at Cornelius with narrowed eyes.

"Could he be the man to . . . replace Stosch?"

"Replace Stosch? As controller?"

"Completely."

"If there was a way of getting rid of Stosch . . . yes, I think Alwyn could handle the job. Not in the same way, perhaps . . ."

"But he could do it?"

"The Bureau pretty well runs itself now. It's a machine—"

"But Dieter Stosch's machine?"

"Stosch designed it—but . . . somebody once designed the first bank, the first telephone company, the first tax system. A lot of other people soon learned how to run them."

"Brand," Philippe said. He puffed up his cheeks and let the air out slowly, with the dangerous sound of escaping gas. When he was finished, he shook his head and grinned.

"That'd catch Stosch asleep at the base, wouldn't it?"

"A real pea-greener."

"Tell about him, David. Tell me all you know about him."

The extraordinary thing, Cornelius explained, was that there was so very little *to* tell. And the beauty of it was that nobody appeared to take him seriously. They thought of him, if they thought of him at all, as a clever trifler. A man who *dabbled* . . . in history, in art, in various esoteric things which were vaguely ecclesiastical. He was indeed a Biblical papyrologist of some renown. Cornelius knew that he went to Balliol College, Oxford, and later to the Royal College of Science in London, but before and after that—nothing was known. His background, said Cornelius, was obscure not to say cryptic. He never talked about his childhood, his family, or where he was or what he did during the war. However, Cornelius was sure he was an upper-cruster from the off: it was wrong, he had once let slip to Cornelius, to criticize God or the Bible in front of one's servants. Was he homosexual? Cornelius thought he was simply asexual with, perhaps, certain . . . aversions—and an occasional weakness for feminine asides. He had carried out his liaison duties between the Palace and the Bureau with quiet efficiency without joining the say-ditto-to-Stosch school. Cornelius was sure he privately loathed the very ambience surrounding Stosch's personality.

"Tell him, David! Tell him!" Philippe said with enthusiasm when Cornelius had finished his summary. "From now on in, Alwyn Brand's our dark horse. My God, David, who would ever suspect him?"

"What if he declines to run? Our dark horse."

"You're a priest. Turn the screw."

The smile came onto Alwyn Brand's face piecemeal: his left cheek twitched first; then his long thin upper lip stretched and lifted first one, then the other corner of his pale mouth. There was a moment of stress on his overbred English nose. And finally his eyes, the color of withered leaves, moved as if they had been softly stirred by a small breeze.

Then, almost at once, it began to recede: like a film run backward.

The breeze dropped.

The leaves settled.

The smile was gone.

He didn't seem surprised or pleased or grateful. He didn't appear anxious or not anxious, satisfied or not satisfied. He didn't even seem curious, Cornelius told Philippe afterward.

He just said, "Very well."

52

Dieter Stosch returned from the gymnasium that evening with an unusually heavy limp. He had worked out for more than an hour, defying the pain that thrust itself, bit by bit, like a venomous wedge, into the innermost muscles of his abdominal wall. Every nerve end in his body was alive to the pain: there was pain in apprehension, too. He had exceeded his usual amount of paracodeine for the day. He never counted the pills he now had made especially for him, but he knew he must have taken at least one hundred and twenty since that morning—almost an extra grain of morphine, he calculated, over his usual three to four grains a day. He was resolved to get through to midnight without another pill. His legs throbbed with stiffening agony. Yet . . . he was grimly smiling.

It had been a long day.

As the sleek black schooner *Grunden Tief II* hove to in the harbor that morning, St. Saladin went wild. A twenty-one gun salute boomed from the old palace ramparts. Klaxons wailed, rockets exploded, sirens screamed. And seven hundred colored balloons were released from the royal gardens—a hundred balloons for every century of St. Saladin's history.

It was not a bad welcome, Stosch reflected as he put on some Dvořák and poured himself a glass of whisky.

As Philippe and Georgina emerged on deck for their first official public appearance since the announcement, Casenave came in low from nowhere, in a beautiful old Gamecock biplane, and blazed the air above the ship with a thousand red and white roses.

Stosch dressed slowly and still the smile, defaced by time and pain and maybe something else, stayed on his face. He put on a black cashmere polo-neck sweater and black wool trousers and his old military boots to help support his aching calf muscles. As he dressed he was occupied with his thoughts, none of them sartorial. The announcement of the engagement had been an undoubted success: the story appeared on front pages all over the world, including *Pravda*. It had been carried and embellished on radio and television broadcasts: it was being played as the fairy-tale romance of the century. Film and television crews, photographers and writers crowded into St. Saladin to greet the lovers. Hotels were sold out. The casino was doing its best business since the war years. And this was just the beginning. The royal wedding would put millions into the St. Saladin economy . . . and St. Saladin into a million headlines.

Even the one small dark cloud on the horizon would soon be dealt with. . . . He sat and concentrated on the meeting ahead of him that evening but still the pain wouldn't go away. He didn't want to give in . . . not to the morphine. It was simply a habit, he told himself: it wasn't an addiction, it would never become an addiction. The pain tore open his stomach. He went to the bathroom. He took an ampule of amyl nitrite from the cabinet and crushed it quickly in a tissue and inhaled deeply. It worked. The pain fell away for a moment, recoiling against the sudden rush of adrenalin that swept through his entire body. It was a temporary relief, but enough to get him going again, get him to his office, to midnight and the start of another day, another ration. . . . It was now almost eleven-thirty.

His appointment with Alwyn Brand was at twelve o'clock.

Alwyn Brand felt no guilt and no misery for his having changed sides: he saw it merely as a Godly permutation of order, as part of an inescapable destiny, a vicissitude of life. There is always a requisite mutability in human relationships, in loyalties and allegiances. There is order and eloquence even in the warp and whirligig of change. He knew that. Order meant discipline and discipline meant obedience. Order was sanity. Order was survival.

He had that passive look of quiet self-possession, a man simply doing his duty, a man following his inexorable destiny.

Alwyn Brand knew what he had to do.

Dieter Stosch had asked for a complete report on the cruise and Brand had spent the afternoon and most of the evening preparing it. He wrote in his small neat epistolic hand. No one was more aware than he was of his own fastidious vagaries . . . yet nobody had more resolution, more determination, when he made up his mind about something. Had either end of fortune been his lot, like Walpole, he felt he would have made a fine prince but a very dishonest slave.

He worked steadily at his small desk, his head down low, his hand moving across the paper with the continuous unhesitating flow of a seismograph needle. He wore a woollen dressing gown over blue striped pajamas. His naked feet were plunged into carpet slippers piped with fake fur.

After a very long time he stopped writing. He read over the last page he'd written, replaced the top on his gold fountain pen, and stood up slowly. His eyes burned a little bit and he dabbed at them with a small handkerchief he took from the pocket of his dressing gown. It was the polite thoughtful kind of dabbing a very old

woman might perform at the graveside of a distant
cousin.

It was ten-thirty. He went to the kitchenette at the
rear of his apartment in the new palace building. He
took a round blue tin from the shelf and removed a
Dundee cake. He carefully measured and cut himself a
slice the size of an obese wafer. He replaced the cake in
the tin, and put the tin back on the shelf. He poured a
glass of milk from a small silver jug in the refrigerator.
He took the milk and the cake back to the study. He sat
and consumed the cake and sipped the milk, staring into
space, like a shy man eating alone in a tea shop. This
was the best meal he'd had since embarking on the
Grunden Tief, he thought. He derived no pleasure from
eating in company. When he had finished he took the
glass and the plate back to the small kitchen and rinsed
them at once. He let the boiling water pour over the
plate for several minutes, as if wishing to sterilize it utterly. He adjusted the hot and cold mix and washed the
glass with the same fussy attentive thoroughness.

He returned to the study and knelt before a large old
chest. He lifted the lid, using both hands, and stared
inside for several seconds, unmoving, reflective, like a
woman who has opened her purse and can't remember
what it is she wanted. The chest smelled of old books
and old age. Brand's lips moved. It was a little while
before he put his hands into the chest and took out a
small silver pillbox. He opened the box and picked out
one of several pills inside. He sniffed it, held it up to the
light, and sniffed it once more. He looked at it thoughtfully, holding it between his thumb and forefinger. He
started to hum softly, something tuneless, but medieval.
He finally put the pill into his pocket and closed the lid
of the chest slowly, like an undertaker closing a coffin
in front of the relatives. He sighed. It was the sigh of a
man at ease with himself, with his conscience.

He had a slightly scented warm bath. He patted himself dry, sprinkled talcum powder over his small
wizened-looking private parts. He put on cream silk underwear and a herringbone tweed suit with horn buttons
and patch pockets.

It was almost ten minutes to midnight.

On his way out he picked up his report and took the white pill from his dressing gown and slipped it into the ticket pocket of his jacket.

"Jesus, Dave, we could put St. Saladin on the back lot—and still have plennya room to remake *Gone With the Wind*. Does she mean it, Dave?" Bobby Rivkin said in California.

Jarrup held the phone between his ear and Esther's.

"Oh she means it, Bob. I had a quick word with her on the telephone this evening and—that's it. She just doesn't wanna make any more movies. *Finito. Fini*."

"What about her contract? We've got a contract with that bitch. Three more pictures. If she thinks she can just skip off and marry some backlot wind-up prince—"

"Bob—what the hell kind of advice can I give you, Bob? But, you know, this is gonna add a lotta clout to *The Princess and the Cowboy*. Put it into Radio City the week of the wedding—"

"When's the wedding? *Soon* they say! Soon! How can we get a print into the Music Hall—"

"The week of the fucking christening then—" Jarrup said. He sat down behind his cluttered desk at the Hôtel du Cap. Esther sat on the sofa and watched him, smiling. The coffee table, chairs, the floor were littered with newspapers carrying the story. The suite had the fatigued atmosphere of a political campaign headquarters waiting for the last clinching results in a close hard fight.

"She's pregnant? Is she—"

"I don't know, Bob. I'm just pointing out . . . if we miss the wedding boat—"

"Yeah," said Bobby Rivkin in a new thoughtful voice.

"Georgina Game's *last* movie—it has to be worth twice what Georgina Game's *latest* movie would have been worth. Right?"

"I hope so."

"Two for the price of one, Bob. Think about it that way. The stockholders ain't gonna squeal about that."

"They squeal about everything. Even if they buy

that, some bright bastard's gonna stand up and point out she still owes us two more pictures!"

"Has Liz talked to you yet?"

"She called earlier. But she doesn't know too much. She left the fucking boat in Sardinia with a bellyache! Would you believe it! Just when she could really do us all a big favor—"

Jarrup grinned at Esther.

"Anyway, Dave. I want you to stay glued to that bitch. Squeeze everything we can out of it, right?"

"Sure."

"Milk it dry."

"The way it's looking now—"

"Meanwhile, I've got work to do here—getting this horse into the moviehouses. Start collecting a few pesos."

"I'd like to keep Esther on the team here for a while longer, Bob. There's an awful lotta—"

"Just see that you do a job. If there's as much as a peasant in Tibet this time next week who doesn't know that Georgina Game's last movie is *The Princess and the Cowboy*—you're both canned."

"Sounds reasonable," said Jarrup.

"I wanna goose the market before that stockholders' meeting in New York. Kite the stock with this one, we all eat for another year."

"We'll be—"

"And Dave. You'd better make damn sure the studio gets invited to the wedding. *In force.* There are an awful lotta guys in New York already brushing off their top hats—know what I mean?"

"How many, Bob?"

"I'd say we'd need at least a coupla dozen tickets— and good seats! Ringside!"

"Ringside," Jarrup said. "Sure."

"We don't wanna be up in the gods when she's playing to the six front rows. Right?"

"Front-row seats," Jarrup said in a straight voice. "Two dozen."

"Right."

"On the bride's side, I presume," he said.

53

Dieter Stosch was reaching for a tablet when Brand walked through the door.

It was midnight exactly.

"Good evening, Alwyn," Stosch said. His tone conveyed relief, but it wasn't the sight of the tall thin Englishman that did it.

He put the pill into his mouth. He didn't bother to put the bowl, in which he kept them like sweets, away. He was like a heavy smoker, a man who likes to be sure that there's always another smoke in reach.

Brand sat in his usual chair against the wall, opposite Stosch's desk. The lighting in the room, focused on the Bustelli collection, left that wall softly shadowed. Brand draped one bony knee loosely over the other.

"You don't look like a man who has just returned from the most celebrated cruise of the season," Stosch said in a dry voice.

"I'm not immensely fond of boats," Brand said.

He sat perfectly upright, resting the report on his right thigh. Veins wired the back of his pale thin hands.

Stosch leaned half forward and searched Brand's face with a long unhurried look of unusual thoughtfulness. At last he seemed to discover whatever it was he was searching for and leaned back in his chair.

"I apologize," he said. "For sending you. It was necessary."

Brand inclined his head, accepting the apology as a beautiful woman might accept a compliment.

"I cannot, you understand, entirely trust Cheroffini's reports in these matters—"

"His attachment to the Bureau—" Brand began.

"My most devoted servants would become my enemies if it were to their smallest advantage."

Brand seemed slightly amused by the remark.

"Reversinos cannot make a habit of inconstancy," he
said.

"A turncoat is a turncoat," Stosch said. "Once,
twice—"

"Perhaps," said Brand.

"It is not his loyalty I distrust now, but his mind. He
is an old man. He misses things . . ."

It was a careful constrained conversation, as any conversation between two men so deliberate in words, in
thought, would be. Stosch got up slowly and went to the
black lacquer cabinet and poured himself a whisky.

"A mineral water?" He turned to Brand. "A glass of
wine?"

"No thank you," Brand said.

Stosch returned to his desk and sat down. He was in
no hurry, it seemed, to get to the point of Brand's visit.

"Tell me about the cruise," he said.

Brand tapped the report on his lap. "I've prepared a
full report," he said.

Stosch ignored the querulous tone.

"The girl—?"

"Huntington?"

"The other one. Talitha Helme."

"She has exuberant breasts," Brand said without enthusiasm. "They did rather tend to overflow, I thought.
Like Camembert in heat."

Stosch gave him his gun-barrel smile.

"She appears to have some passion for travel. The
only literature she could discuss with any degree of authority was airline schedules." An impenetrable smile
moved across his face with the shriveling speed of a
hearse.

"And the men?" Stosch went on.

"Interesting," Brand said with more enthusiasm, but
not much more. "Broglie and Onassis seem ready to
discuss some kind of venture with the Prince—"

"In St. Saladin?"

"Property development was mentioned—"

"But Onassis is already in the other camp."

"It's over. They're simply playing injury time," Brand said. "He will be out of Monte Carlo within six months."

Stosch had a strange look. It may have been puzzlement. It may have been presentiment. Brand couldn't make up his mind. Whatever it was, it was there and it wouldn't go away.

"Are you sure about this?" he asked after a few moments.

Brand described significant asides and overheard conversations in some detail, detail that was only of interest to specialists and those men who understood the subtleties and intrigues and innuendos of big business. Stosch had an intellectual leaning toward such things. Onassis' Paris lawyers met the *Grunden Tief* in Sardinia and Philippe, Broglie, and the Greek spent a whole day closeted in the Prince's stateroom. They went in at ten o'clock in the morning and did not reappear until dinner. At dinner, Brand continued, Philippe seemed to be a man celebrating *something*—if only a handshake.

Stosch considered all this for a long moment. He shaded his eyes with his hand, resting his elbow on the desk.

"Onassis has a gypsy opportunism," he said. A look of anxious suspicion was now firmly fixed in his hidden eyes. Only two months before, the Greek had turned down his offer to negotiate a St. Saladin development project, including a new marina, a heliport, and a hotel.

"The little Prince is moving into deep waters," he said.

"So it would seem," Brand said. He could feel Stosch's brain working it all out. It was like watching a chess master at work—the sheer beauty of the magnificent unerring machine. It was such a pity, he thought, it wasn't possible to let him live to settle the game, one way or another. It was becoming an interesting contest.

Alwyn Brand felt no guilt, no sense of conscience, or shame. On the contrary, a glow of quiet contentment continued to fill him.

"What did you think of the welcome this morning?" Stosch asked suddenly.

"Terribly noisy," Brand said. He showed no surprise

at the unexpected change of subject, and mood. It was one of Dieter Stosch's tricks. When a problem was gnawing at him, he dropped it and moved on.

"A spontaneous outburst from His Royal Highness's happy subjects," Stosch said.

"As spontaneous as Beethoven's Fifth," Brand said. Now Stosch inclined his head, accepting the compliment.

"The best protection that a prince can have is not to be hated by his subjects—isn't that what they say?" Stosch said quietly. In the worm-soft darkness of the room it sounded somehow threatening, and patient.

"We do have a problem," he said after a long pause.

Brand knew they had finally reached the point of the meeting.

"Elizabeth Huntington."

"Ah. The lady with a heart of gold fillings—"

"So?"

"According to Broglie. But I think she'd declined to accept an invitation of some sort . . ."

"And what do you think?"

"One must be wary . . . she is pretty and not without intelligence."

"She has been working for the Bureau," Stosch said.

"Oh really?" Brand said, but there was no surprise in his voice.

"Last week in the launches . . . we think she recognized Genevieve Lacroix."

"And Mlle. Lacroix has been . . . controlling her?"

"Precisely."

"Ah."

"You do see the difficulty?"

"Oh yes. You'd like me to . . ."

"I think it best. In view of her close associations . . ."

"Yes."

"And quickly, I think."

"It usually is," Brand said. He was perfectly at ease. Nobody could have guessed by as much as a blink that while discussing one murder, he was actively contemplating the killing of his very abettor. He felt safe. And he was safe. He was always safe. That was the beauty of it.

"And how was Cornelius?" Stosch asked in another abrupt change of subject. He never cared to dwell on the details of Alwyn Brand's assignments.

"He got on terribly well with the women."

"He is good at preaching to petticoats," Stosch said.

Brand took a handkerchief from his pocket and touched his nose.

"Well," he said, returning the handkerchief to his pocket. "I think it really is time for bye-byes." He stood up and crossed the room. "I'll leave this with you. I think you will find it of some interest."

As he handed over the report he sent Stosch's bowl of pills spilling across the darkened desk.

"Oh dear," he said in a genuinely distressed voice. "I'm *so* clumsy sometimes."

"An accident," Stosch assured him calmly, amused by his old-womanish anxieties over something so trivial. "An accident."

"What men call accident," Brand said in a complaining tone, picking up the spilled pills and returning them to the bowl, "is often God's will."

He was such a strange man, Dieter Stosch thought. A strange, strange man.

Alwyn Brand walked very slowly back to his *petit appartement*. He undressed and put on his pajamas and, despite the sultry warmth of the evening, a woollen dressing gown. He went into the kitchenette and made himself a glass of warm milk. He wandered through to his study, holding the glass of milk like a night-light before him. He scratched his falcon-like nose and put the milk on the mantel shelf and took a key from behind a framed photograph of a very old woman dressed in riding habit and opened a bureau. From the bureau he took a small package wrapped in a napkin; and a sewing kit. He collected his milk from the mantelshelf and sat in a chintz-covered armchair. He put the sewing kit on the arm of the chair and kept the package in his lap.

He sipped his milk.

Thinking.

He calculated that there had been one hundred and

fifty pills in Stosch's bowl: one hundred and fifty-one, say . . .

"If he may have his jest he never cares, at whose expense . . . nor friend, nor patron spares," he recited aloud as the grim humor of the accountancy struck him.

Dieter Stosch would be dead within seventy-two hours. At the most. There are few things over which time has no sway, no jurisdiction, he thought . . . but it can never change a man's destiny.

He put down his milk and unwrapped the package in his lap. He took out a .22 rimfire Beretta.

From the sewing kit he removed one bullet.

He carefully loaded the bullet into the chamber of the gun.

He was thinking about Liz Huntington all the time.

She had such a . . . masculine mind, he thought.

She had a singular, a *dangerous* faculty for unraveling and defining the thoughts and feelings of others.

Dieter Stosch was quite right.

She had to be done away with.

He finished his milk.

It was two-thirty in the morning.

He picked up the telephone and dialed the palace kitchens and ordered a picnic hamper for two for eleven o'clock. He gave an exact order: roast chicken stuffed with wild garlic and herbs, strawberries, and be sure to leave their hulls on, and cream, and . . .

He telephoned the garage and ordered a car.

He rinsed his glass, cleaned his teeth.

In bed, he wound up his large red clock and set the alarm for seven-thirty.

But he was worried.

Something was preying on his mind.

If he may have his jest he never cares, at whose expense . . .

Where did that line come from?

Sheridan, was it?

Rabelais?

Then he was asleep.

Deeply, dreamlessly asleep.

54

"What an extraordinary man you are, Alwyn," Liz Huntington said in her amused voice. "But an original, I'll say that for you."

She had woken up just before Brand's call at eight o'clock. She was feeling refreshed and much, much better. The bug had completely gone. She sat up. Bright sunlight was already streaming through the tiny gap in the heavy crimson curtains of the palace boudoir.

"Well, it looks like another boringly beautiful day," she said. "Why not? A picnic. *Why* not?" she said.

Brand said how delighted he was and would she be good enough to meet him in the main Marie-Thérèse Square at eleven-thirty? His driving, he apologized, wasn't up to the narrow walled-in streets of St. Saladin—especially with all the extra traffic about.

"This may sound a little unusual, my dear, but . . . will you also not tell a soul about our little rendezvous?"

Liz lifted the telephone away from her ear and smiled quizzically.

"Curiouser and curiouser, Alwyn," she said.

"You see . . . there is a little surprise involved and if the somebody discovers that we're joining forces . . . that somebody might twig . . . and that would spoil the fun."

"Okay, Alwyn. Mum's the word," Liz said. "But I'm burning with curiosity."

"All will be revealed in due course," he said.

"The Marie-Thérèse at eleven-thirty then," Liz said.

She replaced the ornate Victorian telephone by her bed and smiled up at the high frescoed ceiling. She got up at once.

She had a lot to do.

Just after eleven o'clock that morning, Edouard Casenave walked into Giorgio's bar and ordered a black coffee.

"Go away," growled Giorgio. He had not shaved. He'd had a very late night and was not at his best. "We're not open yet."

"You so rich you don't need my custom?" Casenave said amiably. "I'll just take it across the square."

"They don't give credit," Giorgio said.

He poured a coffee and pushed it across the zinc counter.

"How's business, my sour-bellied friend?" Casenave grinned.

"You joke?"

"I saw!"

"Three o'clock this place . . . still it boom-booms. Those bimbos from the newspapers . . ."

"It's amazing what a little romance in your life can do."

"Yeah." Giorgio grinned now.

"It's exactly like a war economy," Casenave said.

"How you mean—war economy?" Giorgio looked guardedly at Casenave.

"War is always good for local trade. Look at Indochina . . . Saigon . . . the taxi business, the bar business, hotels, hookers, pimps . . . War and romance—a game barkeepers always win, Giorgio."

Giorgio poured himself a brandy and said, "A royal toast, my friend—to a long and happy . . . war."

Casenave lifted his coffee: "War . . . and a piece of the action," he said.

"Last night . . . a German pastor, an English vicar, an American preacher—at that very table. Where they come from? The casino—to see the evil they fight. That's what they always say!"

It was one of Giorgio's stories. Casenave had heard it many times before. He still smiled.

He took his black coffee and sat at the corner table by the bar at the back of the café.

Giorgio began putting out the sidewalk tables.

"Another day, another dollar," he said. "That what they say, Captain?"

"You'll have dollars coming out of your ears," Casenave said. "You look like a born money-getter to me."

"You trying scorch me? Huh?"

"I'm happy for you, Giorgio. You're going to be a rich man."

"How can I be rich with you for customer?"

Casenave grinned. He got Giorgio's *Nice-Matin* from behind the bar and opened it to the sports pages.

"Hey! Captain! Come here! Quick!"

There was an odd excitement in the big man's voice. Casenave looked up.

Giorgio was standing just inside the doorway, looking across the square. Casenave got up slowly and went over and stood behind the Italian.

"See. Over there. The Citroen."

Casenave saw the black car standing in the patch of cool shadow on the far side of the square.

"That's exactly where the car was—the morning . . . you remember?"

Casenave said nothing. His mouth felt suddenly dry.

"I think it's the same one," Giorgio said. "Wait here."

He collected an empty wine crate and sauntered across the square.

Casenave watched him from inside the bar. Giorgio went into the grocery store and emerged a few minutes later without the crate, but carrying a carrier bag in his arms. He continued to walk slowly, he stopped and talked to a delivery man outside the butcher's shop. He continued his stroll, passed the waiting Citroen, back to the bar.

"Same car," he said briefly.

"Did you get a good look at the driver?"

"Thin. White hair, but not that old. He look like he might be tall sonofabitch."

Casenave nodded.

"What you do?"

"Wait," Casenave said.

"Just wait?"

"Is your car here, Giorgio?"

"Out back."

"Give me the keys. I might need it."

Without a word, Giorgio gave him the keys. "Green Lancia," he said.

Casenave collected his coffee and sat at a table by the window and watched the car.

Alwyn Brand examined his cuticles, his hands resting on the teakwood steering wheel.

Waiting.

Thinking.

He felt utterly at ease. He had had five hours' sleep, which was all he ever had, or needed. He always slept well. It was, he felt, God's simplest miracle of munificence, that pure nightly oblivion.

He never dreamed.

He felt no sense of immorality now as he waited to keep his appointment with Liz Huntington.

That one man achieves ascendancy over others, regardless of the suffering or misery it may cause those who are vanquished, is the basis of law and order. The very animus of civilization itself. A man's will to possess such power, to render others subservient, is simply a fundamental principle of human nature, he reflected.

He didn't feel bad about it. He didn't feel evil.

Perhaps, he thought, he would keep on Genevieve Lacroix. What had Cornelius once called her? The best pair of pants in the Bureau. Brand just caught his own fleeting smile in the rear-view mirror.

It was true that she knew a great deal about his activities—the special economies he had made—enough not to be surprised by his sudden elevation . . . and certainly enough not to want to question his appointment. It was, after all, preferment as much by merit as favor. No, he thought, Mlle. Lacroix could be of great help, properly handled.

And little Leon Kun? Well, he would have to think about Leon Kun.

She came into the square a few minutes after eleven thirty-five.

"This is the one he's waiting for," Casenave said at once. "Her name is . . . Elizabeth Huntington."

"You know her?"

"I flew her back from Sardinia last week. She was sick."

"English?"

"Yes."

"She's a pretty girl," Giorgio said.

"She looks a damn sight better now than when I last saw her."

She wore a simple unfitted white chemise dress and carried a dark blue blazer jacket. Like most women who wear clothes for a living, she avoided couture fitting rooms whenever possible in her private life. She walked in that special way that consciously beautiful women have, her head held high, a sort of knowing subliminal smile on her lips, a woman being watched, a woman being sized up by other women, fancied by men.

Alwyn Brand had already got out of the car to greet her.

Casenave stood up, jiggling the Lancia keys in his hand. He watched Liz get into the car. Brand walked back to the driver's side and climbed in. Casenave heard the door close on the still summer air. But the engine stayed silent.

"They don't seem in no hurry," Giorgio said after a long silence, his back to the window, listening.

Liz had removed the starter key.

"Is there something wrong?" Brand asked in a mild voice that contained no surprise at all.

"I want to talk to you first," she said. She stared at him demurely, almost meekly, but mockingly so. "Isn't that what whores always say? *Let's talk first?*"

"I really have no idea," Brand said with a small urbane smile.

There was a silence that wasn't awkward or strained, it just wasn't anything. Liz opened her purse and took out a pack of English cigarettes.

"Do you mind?" she said.

"Please." Brand nodded and opened his window.

She lit the cigarette and dropped the dead match out of her window.

She inhaled very deeply and blew the smoke up to the roof where it flattened out and spread around the car like a sea mist.

"Do you remember one evening at dinner on the boat—the race driver . . ." -

"Portago."

"Portago. He told us how he had written to his mother . . . a letter that was only to be delivered if and when he died?"

"I remember," Brand said. "A somewhat melodramatic intrusion, I thought."

"Perhaps."

He looked at her in a puzzled way.

"This morning, after you called and suggested the picnic, I wrote several notes . . . not dissimilar in some ways, perhaps."

Brand cleared his throat but said nothing.

"My notes say things to certain people . . . things that I have no desire for them to know as long as I'm alive and kicking."

"You think you might die?" Brand asked.

"The possibility is always there."

"Fate exists."

"But there are some things one doesn't have to leave to chance," Liz said.

There was a silence then. Longer than the first silence, and more strained.

"You see," Liz said finally. "I wouldn't want Georgina to know, for example, that I have worked for the St. Saladin Statistical Bureau—for your friend Dieter Stosch and . . . Mlle. Genevieve Lacroix. Is that what you call her, Alwyn?"

"I know Mlle. Lacroix," he said. He sounded almost irascible, almost perturbed.

"Do you also know Mlle. Chaire?"

Brand said nothing. His face gave nothing away. He continued to stare straight ahead, his hands resting lightly on the wooden steering wheel.

"And the Principal Consumer? Are you familiar with him, Alwyn?"

"As a Palace aide . . . naturally I have some dealings with the Bureau, Elizabeth," he said calmly. "I know these people . . . and these pseudonyms, these *noms de guerre*, are not unknown to me, of course. But, my dear child, I have very little—"

"Alwyn, you went to California last year. You had a meeting with Richard Antrobus. I don't know what you told him or how you threatened him . . . but whatever it was . . . you literally scared him to death."

"That really is the most preposterous idea—"

"No, Alwyn."

Liz looked at the end of her half-finished cigarette. She turned and dropped it out of the window.

"You had a meeting with him in the Polo Lounge of the Beverly Hills Hotel. You didn't want money, but it was some kind of shakedown, wasn't it, Alwyn?"

"This is a silly and rather tiresome conversation—"

Liz smiled.

"You sound just like Richard," she said.

"You are being quite absurd—"

"You see, Richard had an amazing talent for mimicry . . . for impersonation. It amounted to genius in a small way, I suppose. He could take off on a turtle, if he put his mind to it."

Brand's face was immobile, but now his hands began to slide very slowly down the steering wheel, leaving a faintly damp wake of sweat.

"The night you put the frighteners on him, Alwyn, he came to see me at the beach. He described you, Alwyn, in great detail. It wasn't intentional . . . it was something he always did. He'd got your voice, your mannerisms, the way you hold your head to one side sometimes, like a parrot . . ."

"It is an interesting theory," Brand said. "Albeit a somewhat offensive one."

"Albeit a somewhat offensive one," Liz said, smiling. "Richard had you to a tee, Alwyn. The moment I met you . . . you were so familiar to me. It was uncanny . . . but it was always there. I think we even discussed it . . ."

Brand smiled easily, thinking hard. This was a new

turn of events. He had used his own name at the Château Marmont. He had been convinced that Antrobus would comply with his suggestion . . . and, indeed, he had not been wrong in that assumption. The motor accident was most unfortunate. However, the fact remained that he had not used an alias. He had not covered his tracks. His presence in California at that precise time could be verified and corroborated with one telephone call.

"If what you say is true, Elizabeth . . . what do you have in mind now?" His smile congealed into labored atonement.

"As I say, the last thing in the world I want to happen is for Georgina to find out . . . about me."

"That is perfectly reasonable."

"It just seems to me that Principal Consumer or somebody might be embarrassed by my . . . *proximity*, shall we say?"

"Ah."

"So . . . if anything unfortunate should happen to me . . . Georgina is going to know exactly who was responsible for Richard's death. And you do see the horrid complications that could cause—"

"Oh indeed I do," Brand said.

"Indeed you do."

Brand took out a handkerchief and wiped the palms of his hand. Then he wiped the steering wheel.

"Very well," he said slowly.

"So now you know all about me. And I know all about you. That seems a pretty . . . *safe* arrangement, don't you agree."

"A most stabilizing division of information," he said with just the smallest hint of self-parody.

"They're getting out again," Casenave said in an incredulous voice. "They're coming over here."

Brand and Liz walked slowly across the hot square to Giorgio's. She linked her arm through his.

They came into the café and sat at a table on the side about halfway between the door and the bar. Liz ordered a long Campari and soda, Brand wanted Perrier water, but not iced. It wasn't until Giorgio had brought the drinks, and their eyes had grown used to the cool gloom after the bright sunshine, that Liz noticed Casenave.

"Captain!" she said in a voice that was much huskier and sexier than he remembered. "Come and join us!"

Casenave went over. He took a chair from the next table and sat down.

"You two must know each other," she said.

"Of course," Brand said.

"Captain Casenave saved my life," she said.

"You certainly look a lot better than when I last saw you," he said.

"I feel much better, thank you."

Casenave ordered a glass of white wine.

They talked for maybe five minutes, saying nothing of importance, nothing that Casenave was able later to remember. Then, almost inevitably, their small talk dried up, and there was one of those silences that come between acquaintances at cocktail parties when one feels something ought to be said but nobody quite knows what. One has gone beyond weather and not yet reached sex. There was a sense of restiveness and reticence about Brand that became more marked as the silence lasted. He reminded Casenave of a parent nervous about what a precocious and unpredictable child might say next.

"Where have you two been?"

Casenave was surprised to hear himself asking the question.

"Where have we been?" Brand repeated with a curious sense of wan harassment.

"I thought I saw you going off in a car a while ago," Casenave said lamely.

"We were going on a secret picnic," Liz said. "But we had to change our plans."

Brand gave her a sharp look. In the cool twilight of Giorgio's, he looked paler than ever.

"Now we've been seen together," Liz hurried on in a teasing dramatic tone. "Do you mind very much, Alwyn?"

Brand stood up with a sudden movement.

"I'm sorry," he said in a polite voice that didn't quite

disguise his bleak censuring smile. "But I really do have to be on my way. Elizabeth, my dear, if you wish to stay . . ."

"I'll finish my drink," she said pleasantly, "and chat with the captain."

She lifted her cheek to be kissed. Brand stooped down and pecked at it almost disdainfully.

Casenave watched him walk away across the bright sunny square . . . and he *knew*. It came to him suddenly, unexpectedly, but he *knew*.

"A strange man," Liz said. "I suppose he's just one of those naturally secretive birds. . . ."

"Birds betray their own nests," Casenave said quietly. "The more they try to hide them."

He felt such a coldness, such a terrible coldness. It was strange finding out like that, finding out and being so calm about it, so . . . patient.

A lot of silence must have passed because Liz said: "What are you thinking about?"

Casenave smiled.

"Oh nothing . . . just something I have to do later." He sipped his wine.

"What are you doing for lunch?" he asked.

"I'm open to suggestions," Liz said.

55

On the great cliff of Carigbresci stood the remains of the Column of Augustus, looking toward Italy and Rome. The column had been one of three built by the Romans to celebrate a victory over the Ligurians.

Dieter Stosch, at the west window in the room with no clocks, a timeless room in a palace that René Chalot tried to stop a hundred years ago, smiled at old Chalot's presumption as he thought about the remains of that great Roman edifice two thousand feet above the sea.

Stosch turned from the view and went to his desk, his smile slowly fading. He took a pill from the bowl as he sat at his desk and opened the file on Talitha Helme. Very soon, he knew, he would need an operative to replace Liz Huntington. The beautiful pleasure-loving heiress might very well be the woman the SS Memorandum needed.

Mlle. Lacriox had prepared a complete dossier. He felt profoundly relieved at that moment to be surrounded by experts . . . and whatever else, both Brand and Lacroix were experts of the highest order.

The first stab was no more than a pinprick in the left ventricle chamber of his heart. It came again after a few minutes and was more noticeable. His hand went involuntarily to his chest as he continued to read the report on the heiress.

The third time the pain came it was bad and it lasted and he broke out into a cold sweat. He stood up very slowly and walked to the lacquer cabinet that once contained the underthings of Marie Antoinette at Versailles. He poured himself a large whisky and took another pill.

The pain seemed to pass. His face was the color of aged calico.

He was holding Harlequin when it came for the fourth and last time.

He concentrated very hard on the beautiful Bustelli masterpiece he held so tenderly. . . .

Harlequin, he thought, forcing himself to ignore the pain that now flooded his pulmonary artery like a dam bursting. . . .

Harlequin in the British pantomime, a mischievous fellow supposed to be invisible to all eyes but those of his faithful Colombine . . .

He knew then, but it was too late.

Colombine, he thought as his body crashed down on the priceless collection, who was Colombine . . .

"It really *really* is like a fairy-tale palace," Georgina said as Philippe led her through the endlessly beautiful corridors of a part of the old palace she hadn't visited before.

"Palaces are never quite what they seem." He smiled. "Five princes of St. Saladin have been murdered in their beds."

"Makes the whole place seem more . . . *cosier,* somehow," said Cornelius, who followed a few feet behind.

"Father Cornelius," Georgina said, laughing. "Why can't *you* marry us? Why does it have to be—"

"Because you must be married by an archbishop, if not by a cardinal. In fact, I might arrange for the whole College of Cardinals to marry you. Show Hollywood how to put on a real show."

They passed the priceless oriental tapestries, the chairs and sofas in Kyoto silk in soft shades of gray and rose, the ormolu clocks and Hamons and Monets.

"Where *are* we going?" Georgina asked after a while.

"Wait and see," Philippe told her mysteriously. "You won't miss all the excitement of the movie business?" he asked her suddenly as they paused to admire a Degas dancer on the wide winding marble staircase.

"*No,*" Georgina said firmly. "You don't know me. Once my mind is made up . . ."

"You may never make another film but I promise you this: you will be painted and sculpted, you will be carved on intaglios, enameled on precious boxes, you will be *immortalized*—"

"I love you, Prince Philippe. Do you know that?" Georgina said.

They were in the galleried heart of the old palace building now, above the casino. They had come to the end of a long hallway and stood before a huge double white and gold door.

Philippe paused.

"Dieter Stosch's office," he said, smiling at Georgina and the priest.

"Stosch? *The* Dieter Stosch?" Georgina said with genuine amazement in her voice. "I was beginning to think he really didn't exist."

"This is going to be some confrontation," Cornelius said softly.

"I want you both to be there, to see his face, when I tell him about *my* Onassis deal," the Prince said.

And he opened the door and went in.

Bestsellers
from
BALLANTINE

No one who buys it,
survives it.

THE HOUSE NEXT DOOR

A terrifying novel
by
Anne Rivers Siddons

28172 $2.25

Coming in November

 BALLANTINE BOOKS